Adrian Mathews was born in 1957. His mother is Czech and his father English. He was brought up in South London and read English at Cambridge University. For several years he divided his time between England and France but since 1988 he has been based in Paris and lives near the city's Latin Quarter. *The Hat of Victor Noir* is his first novel.

The Hat of Victor Noir

Adrian Mathews

FOURTH ESTATE • *London*

This edition published in 1997

First published in Great Britain in 1996 by
Fourth Estate Limited
6 Salem Road
London, W2 4BU

1 3 5 7 9 10 8 6 4 2

A catalogue record for this book is available from the British Library.

ISBN 1-85702-569-5

Typeset by Rowland Phototypesetting Limited,
Bury St Edmunds, Suffolk
Printed in Great Britain by Clays Limited, St Ives plc

To Mum, Dad & Marie

At the time that the renowned horse Bucephalus was presented to the young Alexander, no horseman was able to ride that formidable animal. A common man would have commented: 'There goes a spiteful horse.' Alexander, however, sought the pin that was goading the beast, and he was quick to find it, noticing that Bucephalus was frightened of his own shadow; and since the horse's fear made the shadow jump too, there was no end to it. But Alexander turned Bucephalus' nose towards the sun and, holding him in this direction, he was able to reassure and weary him. Thus it was that the student of Aristotle was already aware that we have no power over our passions so long as we do not know what causes them.

Alain, *Propos sur le bonheur* (1928)
[trans. Adrian Mathews]

1

BLACK.

Philip Kovacs pushed through the glass Metro doors and climbed the steps to road-level under the glowering barracks of the Garde Républicaine. He glanced up, caught his breath and shivered. It was what he had wanted.

Black skies.

On the place de la République the huge verdigris statue with a cap like an acorn had her back to him. It was Marianne, figurehead of the Revolution. With one hand she held an olive-branch aloft. With the other she clutched the drapery of her skirts as if she were about to curtsey.

Black skies, black street, black air.

The horizon behind the statue was a glaring strip of oyster-silver light above which feathered streamers of darkness trailed to earth from a dense mass of sooty cloud.

It was the unnatural heat of that late May day that had done it. By the time evening came around something had to give and an impromptu spring storm was in the offing. Brisk but brutal – that sort of thing.

This was exactly what Kovacs had wanted to happen.

The city was tense. People were on edge. He could feel it even now as the traffic stop-started forwards down the rue du Faubourg du Temple, jumpy red tail-lights in the livid darkness. On the pavement a woman elbowed past him with an oddly defensive gesture. A flash storm would douse that hot irritability in her eyes. Catharsis.

But it hadn't started yet. Give it time.

Home was close. Too close, maybe, for he never felt like going there directly after a day at work. He had a number of delaying tactics, a repertoire of circuitous routes. He walked past a fortune-teller's caravan and a nougatine stall parked on the pavement and into the narrow commercial road.

It was a street of restaurants, food-shops, bars, each with its lurid sign shining harshly in the storm-light. The word BOUCH-ERIE stood out in a column of huge rear-lit letters above the meat shop. Then came the wink of defective neon spectacles over the optician's where he bought his disposable contact lenses. He crossed the road to the red carrot of the Tabac and registered his Loto ticket for the next day's draw before weaving back through the traffic to the Temple d'Or – a bar he frequented opposite the Cinémathèque Française. The name of this hallowed watering hole always made him think of Dante Gabriel Rossetti's poem 'The Blessed Damozel':

The blessed damozel leaned out
From the gold bar of heaven

It was, of course, not the done thing to turn fabled Pre-Raphaelite lovers into bar-flies.

There were no blessed damozels in sight on this particular occasion, but there was Ahmed, the barman at the Temple d'Or. He was a man who hardly ever spoke. He just leaned on the metal counter with a towel flung over his shoulder and watched the two-way flow of humanity through the window abstractedly. He was constitutionally immune to the racket of the pinball machine. When Kovacs entered he nodded, poured a glass of Leffe beer and brought it across.

Seven.

Kovacs checked his watch against the clock that hung on the wall among the cinema stills. There was a shot of the actor Patrick McGoohan taken at Clough Williams-Ellis's Italianate town of Portmeirion in Wales. There was a striking photo of Dirk Bogarde in *Death in Venice*, his face powdered and made-up, the hair dyed, to attract the youthful Pole, Tadzio. Then there was another still from Venice – the name of the movie escaped him.

He was trying to remember whether Céline worked late on Fridays. She was a free spirit, of course: perhaps she'd made other arrangements. Then he recalled the Spiegel Club. They'd be meeting in the 6th arrondissement at around nine. There was just time to grab a bite to eat beforehand if he meant to join them. Time to unwind.

A flicker of white caught his eye. Lightning? No, not yet. It was a neon strip outlining the sign of a huge black top hat above a private rock club called the Gibus directly opposite the bar. It was a vaudeville top hat, really, tipped out over the street with a debonair flourish – or a collapsible opera hat, to define that 'Gibus' correctly. But he disliked it intensely. It made him think of funerals and undertakers with their sinister cortèges.

A PVC mini-skirt retained his attention for a second through the plate-glass window. As it passed out of view his eye latched onto a poster on the café window for a Brazilian band, Aquarela, who were playing in Paris. The poster depicted an extraordinary god-like figure, dressed in carnival camp, with thunderclouds and lightning streaming from his outstretched fingers. The word XANGÔ was printed across his chest and he was flanked by stampeding horses. A ghostlike female divinity stood behind him. Kovacs drained his glass, placed a few coins on the table and left.

The road opened out onto a little square where the canal Saint-Martin surfaces to arch north across the 10th arrondissement towards the place de Stalingrad and the bassin de la Villette. He stopped there beside the bust of a dead actor to tie a stray shoelace. As he did so he peered habitually at the clock on the corner of the boulevard Jules Ferry. Its lunar face was supported by two pale cherubs under a fake red-tiled gable-end. He knew the hands were stuck at twelve-twenty but he looked anyway. His instinct annoyed him. It was like a muscular tic. *Stands the Church clock at ten to three? And is there honey still for tea?* The answer was 'No': to both questions. It was almost a relief when a fat wet raindrop hit him square on the back of the head and trickled down his neck and under the collar of his T-shirt. He ran the flat of his hand over the dampened hair. Soon, he thought. The lamp-black underbellies of the clouds seemed to be straining towards him.

He followed the cobbled, tree-lined path beside the wide canal on the quai de Valmy, taking care not to trip over the big iron mooring-rings that were set into the concrete. They were treacherous things: one only had to catch a toe on them and Splash! – into the canal! To his satisfaction, one by one the large splattering drops were coming down now. Splat, split, splat! Plop, plip, plop! They were in no hurry. And there, at last – a muted hollow kettle-drum of thunder over the rooftops to the east.

Locks. Bridges. The bassin du Marais. And a small garden under towering chestnut trees, the lower step of a two-tiered area that bordered the three descending lock-gates of the Ecluses des Récollets. The whole hydrodynamic system was straddled at both ends by metallic green Venetian-style footbridges and, at the southern extremity, by the Pont Tournant Grange aux Belles, a rotating road-bridge.

Kovacs entered the garden and leaned on the railing beside the lock. The floodgate was being opened to bring a barge down to the lower level and the white roar of water lashing against the mossy banks drowned out the traffic behind him. The quayside lamps came on with the drama of theatre-lighting, receding necklaces of soft yellow flames mirrored in the murky green ribbon of the canal. He shut his eyes and exhaled. Paperwork, VDU, College, meetings – the whole day seemed to be blowing up and out of his lungs there and then. Then another cold raindrop caught him on the side of the head and he looked round.

He looked round to the grey zinc roof and sooty chimneypots of the third and fourth floors of 91 quai de Valmy above Carré Revêtements Céramiques, a bathroom tile showroom. It was where he lived. The building was unusually low for Paris and seemed to belong to an older, more parochial world, with its faded orange roller-blinds at the casement windows and pots of red geraniums on the balcony. The Paris of Marcel Carné, perhaps, and the Hôtel du Nord of Carné's film was, indeed, visible on the opposite bank of the canal, the quai de Jemmapes. In fact, only the façade remained: the hotel itself had recently been demolished and replaced with a modern construction. He could see the frontage from the living room of his duplex flat, a little way down from the quayside workshops with names like Décolletage-Savoyard and Protection Industrielle. But something else had just caught his eye and it worried him.

The windows of his neighbour's flat were agleam with light and at one of them a solitary figure stood looking out, utterly motionless.

The ghost of Monsieur Martin!

Martin, a retired CRS *flic*, had died three months before, but the flat had clearly been re-let. Strange that the concierge had said nothing. Anyway – new neighbours . . . that would make a change.

The thought of Monsieur Martin, however, was unexpectedly disconcerting. What *was* it exactly? His lack of sang-froid or reticence or something – the self-betrayal of his excesses. Martin had gone to pot when his wife died. In the evenings, the sound of sobbing and broken conversation had filtered through the walls into Kovacs' flat.

'Darling – have you done the washing up?'

'I told you, I didn't have time.'

Martin would do both voices, as if she were alive. Once Kovacs had opened his front door to find him on all fours on the landing. The ex-policeman had broken down in tears in his arms and insisted on showing him round that grey mausoleum of an apartment. All his wife's possessions had been exhibited in their habitual places – nightdress, slippers, a collection of flea-bitten German teddy bears – but eerily wrapped in sleeves of polythene against the dust. It was obscene. How could a man go so completely to pieces like that? All that, over a *woman*! To the point of *dying*! Such a big man too. They broke three banisters trying to get his coffin down the narrow, twisting stairs.

But no – what was he thinking? Of course not. That was not Monsieur Martin's flat at all!

He tried to swallow but a ball of saliva plugged his throat. The entrance to the building was through a big central archway which led into the courtyard of the ceramic tile workshop. And the lit windows were to the left of this archway, not to the right – as they would have been if they belonged to Monsieur Martin's flat. The lit windows were those of his own apartment.

He was invaded by an unpleasant sense of unease.

Was that Céline – standing at the window, stock-still, looking down at him? Impossible. She didn't have a key. For a disturbing split-second he felt as if he were looking at himself in another remote dimension, silhouetted against the square of soft electric light. Himself looking at himself looking at . . . a queasiness struck him in the pit of the stomach.

But how stupid! How stupid of him! What he had taken for a figure was nothing more than a damp shirt which he had put out to air that morning, draped over a hanger on the window handle. He smiled grimly at his mistake. One thing was certain, though: he had left the lights burning all day. That was not like him.

A low crackle of lightning danced lustrously on the wet metallic roof and with a mighty bang overhead the rain pelted down. He ran across the road and home.

The telephone was ringing when he got in. It was Céline.

'I thought you were never going to answer.'

'I've just got in.'

'You could have branched the answering machine.'

'Plugged in.'

'What?'

'You could have *plugged in* the answering machine.'

'Oh. Anyway, I called the College switchboard and they said you'd left.'

'What are you doing tonight, Céline?'

'I haven't given it much thought. And you?'

'Well there's a Spiegel Club do at nine. Au Chai de l'Abbaye. Not a proper club meeting, just the committee.'

'I thought you'd had enough of that crowd. You're always complaining about them.'

'You know me – I complain about everything. I don't much fancy it, to tell you the truth, but I ought to show my face for an hour or two. It's still a worthy cause and you never know, it might be entertaining. Will you come?'

'OK. If it's just for an hour or two.'

'Eat first, though. They may have snacks but it's not a dinner.'

'OK. And you – have you –?'

'Eaten? I'm just about to. Don't worry about me.'

'Have you seen the weather?'

'Of course, but it'll be over soon. It's just one of those pre-summer things.'

'See you later, then.'

'Yes. See you later.'

He placed the receiver back on its cradle in a slow, ruminant manner. There was something about Céline's voice – the tone of sanity, of pragmatism – that did him good. After the ruction of his divorce from Anne three years previously, there had been a period when he had broken off most human contacts for his own peace of mind. Luckily there were no children to complicate the matter. He had become a Simon Stylites, perched on top of the pole of his own abstraction, observing the rest of humanity with mild indifference. An Ivory Tower Intellectual. It occurred to him that, these days, even Ivory Towers might come in for some stick from the pro-elephant lobby.

Now, at 44, he had begun to value certain people again, albeit in measured doses, and Céline was one of those. She was divorced too, a couple of years younger than Kovacs, and their friendship was straightforward and uncomplicated, by unspoken mutual consent. There was no admixture of melodrama or neurosis, nor was it a physical thing. That was how he liked it, and so did she – or so he imagined. It was a relationship built on abreaction, a curious equilibrium between liberty and commitment that was somehow cleaner than the thing it had grown out of – the reciprocal parasitism and perfidy of most couples. So for them there was the odd evening out. A film. The opera. Or lunch, if she was not travelling for her fashion company. They were like-minded, professional people who had found a *modus vivendi*. And neither he nor she was the interfering type.

His nose tickled and he rubbed it. There was an invisible pressure on his nerves, a tightening tourniquet of anxiety. A large moth dithering around the shade of a standard lamp cast a strange, palpitant shadow around the room. The lights. Of course! He had left them on.

He was experiencing one of those little moments of amnesia, when he forgot what he had meant to do next. His hand was still on the telephone receiver as he sighed and looked around the flat where he had lived for eight years. His books were stacked higgledy-piggledy on the shelves. Their authors – Dennett, Crick, Moravec, Penrose, Eccles – were in the same field of research as him, though he was a mere amateur. There was a framed black-and-white PET scan image of the human brain – Rorschach blots of neural activity – and, next to this, a drawing of a woman in a toga brandishing a knife. The latter was by Janmot, a pupil of Ingres, and he had picked it up from an art dealer in the rue de Tournon. His portable computer sat on a Directoire mahogany desk against a wall. In the corner by the window, a Conran armchair and settee, draped with rugs from Pier Import. And, in the centre of the room, a fair-sized oval dining table. Then the Carrara marble fireplace, where the ashes of the previous evening's fire lay undisturbed. On the mantelpiece above the fireplace there was a bottle of Evian and a half-empty bottle of Ricard. He observed that the word 'evian' on the label of the mineral-water bottle became 'naive' in the large gilt-framed rococo mirror above the fireplace, betraying a general tendency towards inversion amongst the French, especially in the realm of acronyms: UNO, NATO and EEC, for example, transmuting into ONU, OTAN and CEE respectively. Then his gaze slipped to one side of the bottle, refocused, and, with a little jolt of surprise, he glimpsed his own reflection, motionless behind the redoubled bottles.

He could never quite make the connection between the Kovacs who lurked in the turret of his skull, peering out dispassionately upon the world, and that alternative Kovacs out there, the one other people took – or mistook – for him. There it was, five-foot-eleven of it, compact in frame but a little ample in girth. Greying, curly hair, thinning at the temples. The eyes grey-green and a gentle, fleshy face that was a little ruddy, suggesting either over-indulgence or coyness. So that was what they saw. A genetic hybrid, but then who *wasn't*? His mother was 'English', itself a euphemism for elaborate miscegenations, and his father was of Mitteleuropa stock which had migrated to London when a Serbian seaman (complete with Serbian semen) had jumped ship and Kovacs' great-great-grandmother in Victorian days. Sometimes he fancied he could feel the brooding Slav haemoglobin coursing through his veins, and it was true that the sound of a mazurka and the taste of slivovitz were wont to awaken dark atavistic longings in his logico-positivist genes. He was dressed, now, in white T-shirt and blue linen suit, dark in patches from the rain. Not unattractive, he flattered himself

– but it was as if the 'self' he knew through introspection should by all rights have taken a different form. Less congenial, perhaps.

Still, mirrors always make things look unfamiliar, he reflected, and Paris was full of mirrors and their swung-round worlds. He remembered one of Derek's mild witticisms: '"They do it with people," as one mirror said to another.' They were optical palindromes – mirrors – faithful to fact according to their own inverse logic. But why did they reverse things only left-to-right and not top-to-bottom? He could never work that one out. A mathematician had tried to explain it to him once.

Something was irritating him.

He rubbed his nose again.

From nowhere, a childhood memory inserted itself vigorously into the loose flux of his thoughts. It was West London, his family home, and a chill winter night. A Price's Sentinel Night-light flickering at his bedside and a hot-water bottle clamped between his scabby knees. He was down with the flu, wrapped in an eiderdown, and his mother was there with a plastic chemist's spoon, administering thick, syrupy linctus. And slowly, with dreamy slowness, her hands rubbed ointment across his chest. Menthol, eucalyptus . . .

Eucalyptus! His nostrils flared and he shut his eyes in concentration. There it was – that smell . . . Or something like it. It was not the vaseliney smell of Vick but a harsher, more volatile variety, the French equivalent. Not Tiger Balm. What did they call it now? The brand name had escaped him for the moment. There it was, however – a distinct trace, detectable on the air.

He crossed the room and opened the door of the flat. The smell was not there, it was not coming from the landing. No, it was definitely *within* the flat, lingering, an intrusion. It was a smell he loved, a comforting smell, but right now it was troubling, the molecular tincture of another presence. Feliciana, the *femme de ménage*, could not be responsible. She came on Tuesdays. Today was Friday. Perhaps – he crossed to the fireplace, poured himself a neat pastis and glanced at the window – perhaps it came from outside, from the canal, or from the neighbours below. Green vapours, seeping through the hairline fissures of plaster and parquet. He raised the glass, swallowed hard and dismissed the matter.

Quarter to eight.

The storm had played itself out and only plump drops of rainwater, falling from the eaves into the iron guttering, could be heard. That and the traffic – the distinctive shooshing sound of car-tyres on wet roads.

He went to the kitchen and fixed himself an omelette while listening to the news on the radio.

At eight-thirty he went out again, taking the Metro to Odéon.

The Spiegel Club was an informal literary society that held its group discussions in the upstairs room of an American bookshop in the Latin Quarter. The room was dominated by a large German mirror, a relic of the Occupation – hence the club's Teutonic sobriquet. The top moulding of the mirror incorporated an imperial eagle of the Third Reich. A high proportion of the club members were academics so they followed the university year, winding up the monthly meetings in May and recommencing in September. The steering committee was convening its last meeting before the summer recess at a corner brasserie in the rue de Buci. Au Chai de l'Abbaye was brassy and classy, popular for its wine-list and, when Kovacs arrived, the others – seven in number – were already there, with dewy bottles of 1987 Hermitage Blanc in free-standing silver ice-buckets and plates of Poilâne bread and *saucisse de montagne* on the table. Ideas for readings and events in the next session had been jotted down along with a letter drafted for renewal of subscriptions and the occasion was now mostly social.

The place was nearly full but they had managed to hog a long, convivial table at the back under a mirror and one of the brasserie's bright suspended lamps which terminated in a bunch of glowing grapes made from pink glass marbles. The waiters were skittering back and forth in their immaculate white *tabliers* and black ties, tickets clipped between their lips. Céline had beaten him to it and was talking earnestly to Michel Jonas, a dentist and part-time translator, at the far end of the table. At the near end there was a ginger-haired Californian woman – he always forgot her name – who carried a bag full of her own vanity-press poetry wherever she went, and, opposite her, Orriss, a fastidious, thirty-ish Oxford graduate with a gravity-defying coiffure who eyed everyone with alarmed distaste through pebbly glasses. Kovacs could never look at him without thinking of the Van de Graaff generator in the London Science Museum – a device that made the hair stick up on a puppet's head when you switched it on.

He steered tactfully round to the further end of the table and pushed into a place next to Céline, giving her one of his 'good dog' pats on the back as he sat down. He felt like actually saying 'good dog' as he did so, and recalled that these two nonsensical words were the very last spoken by the senile Vladimir Ilyich Lenin as he lay dying: spoken in Russian, of course. The works of Lenin and books based on Walt Disney films were the top-selling literary productions in the world: Kovacs wondered if there was a hidden connection but the presence of Céline soon nipped this idle speculation in the bud.

She was well turned out, in that austere Rive Gauche way: a simple charcoal-grey bodice and her straw-blonde hair tied back with a red velvet ribbon. A tiny black jewelled brooch above her right breast caught Kovacs' attention. It was shaped like a spider.

The middle of the group was a relaxed huddle of bemused concentration. Derek Fairgreave, a colleague of Kovacs' from the College, was holding forth. He was in his early fifties but already years of windracked hill-walking in the Vosges, full-blown addictions to Gauloises and Armagnac and an extremely mobile and expressive physiognomy had transformed his face into a ravaged asteroid, pocked with craters and scored with ravines. The resemblance to the late Auden was striking and as a result he was the envy of many of the more impressionable club members who secretly worked hard on their own facial patinas, following his time-proven methods. Kovacs wondered whether he was alone in perceiving another analogy: to the apeneck, broadbottomed Sweeney of T. S. Eliot's poems. There was something markedly ape-like about Fairgreave.

Fairgreave had ordered a Château Nénin 1989 Pomerol all for himself and was gulping the stuff down in Bacchic mouthfuls and tapping a discoloured forefinger on a Gallimard paperback entitled *La Défense de l'infini* which was on the table in front of him.

'Anyway, to get to the point,' he said briskly, impatient with himself, 'these succubi are female demons that visit men in their sleep. That's what he says here, you see.'

'Who? That's what *who* says *where*?' The question was posed with some petulance by a pale woman with pouting crimson lips and raven hair in a Twenties' bob.

'Aragon. Louis Aragon. In this book. Why don't you listen, Hannah?'

'You didn't say. You always do that, Dewek,' she lisped. 'You think you've said something when you haven't. It's weally iwitating!'

There was a pained silence.

'May I continue?'

She tossed her head back, gave a pettish grimace and fiddled nervously with an agate ring, sliding it from finger to finger.

'As I was saying, no-one seems to be sure how to get rid of them. The succubi, I mean,' – he glared pre-emptively at Hannah. 'Holy relics, prayers, psychoanalysis, petrol bombs . . . none of the usual things work. Once a succubus has got you, she'll keep coming back. Except you can't always tell that it's the same one, because they adopt different disguises.'

'Mine always looks like Isabella Rossellini,' chipped in Orriss.

'Then it's almost certainly not a succubus. What you're experiencing is the wet dream – a projection of your own erotomania or satyriasis. Do you have ads for Lancôme beauty products on your bedroom walls?'

Orriss sniffed and turned back to the Californian, asking if he could read some of her recondite poetry. She was only too happy to oblige.

'This is a rather male-oriented discussion, isn't it?' interrupted Céline aloofly.

'Succubi,' Fairgreave riposted, 'are male-oriented demons. If you want a demon who services the female of the species then the animal you want is the "incubus" – plural, "incubi". There's nothing to stop you forming a separate discussion group, you know. Ladies Only.'

Céline raised her hands in mock apology and Fairgreave picked up where he had left off.

'It sometimes happens that your personal succubus takes a real fancy to you and instead of appearing like a demon, she tarts herself up. She's out to get you and every night your dreams are invaded by a creature of irresistible beauty. What do you do?'

'Give in?' Céline suggested in her innocent *gamine* voice.

'They always give in in the end, anyway,' confided Hannah *entre femmes*. 'Men are *so* pwedictable . . .'

'Well yes, you can of course give in. But what you don't seem to realise,' he insisted, 'is that however much these things appear to be human they are *not* – they are sexual vampires, hotfoot from Hell. What's more, they are virtually insatiable, and they have no conception of the limits of human energy. They don't know how much or how little the human frame can stand. Only a man of inexhaustible stamina can give in to them with any confidence of surviving the ordeal, and there are two kinds of man they go for. One is the virtuous type – but staying virtuous is a struggle for him, so he's terribly vulnerable. Temptation of Saint Anthony scenario, if you know what I mean. That's the first type that attracts them – the virtuous man. Someone like you, Michel.'

The dentist, a freckled middle-aged man with watery blue eyes, smiled wanly and gave a Gallic shrug. 'What do you suggest? Strings of garlic?'

'Just present her with a bill for – how do you say?' Céline pointed to her front teeth, searching for the word. 'Bridgework – and a couple of gold crowns. That should get rid of her. *Bon débarras!*'

Fairgreave gulped back a half glass of Pomerol greedily and wiped his mouth. 'No, the thing to do is go on a debauch. Aragon recommends a seventy-day debauch. Even if it kills you. Even if it breaks the bank. If you're dead to the world for seventy nights, the succubus will give up on you. Sex is like a fuel to them, you see.'

A one-armed man called Cavanagh was tapping a knife rhythmically against the neck of a bottle to attract attention. He was an Irishman in his seventies, a mellow Hibernian version of Gorbachev with his thin white hair and darting blue eyes in a kindly face.

'All of this talk about succubi, Derek – you wouldn't be wanting to tell us something, would you now?'

'What did you have in mind?' asked Fairgreave.

'I mean, you wouldn't be hanging around with one of these termagants yourself, would you? Sounds to me like there's a spot of woman-trouble behind all of this fancy theorising.'

There was a pause. Fairgreave glanced at Céline then flashed a look of irritated amusement at Cavanagh, bit his thumbnail and laughed disagreeably.

'Well done, Sean. *Confiteor Deo omnipotenti* . . .'

'It's true then?'

'*Was*. You want the cards on the table? Well, some time ago, I was – I admit – the object of a succubus's amorous attentions. I shan't deny it. So, you see, what I've been telling you – it's not just Aragon, though I can vouch for every word he says about them. I'm speaking from personal experience.'

'You say *was*,' Cavanagh persisted in the cool tones of a constable who is finally homing in on the truth. 'You obviously got rid of the harpy. Would you be inclined to tell us how you managed the feat? Was it by means of the method you've just described – seventy days of debauchery with the ladies of the night?'

'No, it was not. As I told you earlier, there are two kinds of favourite victim for these phantoms. The first is the virtuous man. He is the fellow for whom the fleshpot debauch is the only way out. However, as all of you here are aware, there is not a scintilla of virtue in my entire person. I make no bones about it. Being a moral anarchist, civic rectitude has no place in my scheme of things. I am a sensualist, an epicurean, a voluptuary. And, as Aragon says, there is a certain class of succubi who go for men such as myself.'

'In that case,' said Cavanagh, 'I would assume that abstinence was not foremost in your mind when you first encountered the demon.'

'You would assume correctly.'

'I would go further, in fact, in assuming that you saw no reason whatsoever for resisting her improbable demands.'

'Again, I take my hat off to you.'

There was a high-pitched squeal from across the table.

'Dewek!' moaned Hannah, curling her upper lip in a look of disgust. 'You didn't *wape* her, did you? I can't believe I am hearing this!'

'You can hardly "rape" a creature whose supernatural vocation is male seduction, can you? Don't be ridiculous, Hannah. I simply – how shall we say? – *acceded* to her wishes.'

'But you're –' Hannah was almost choking on her words. 'But you're all old and *winkly*, Dewek. You're like some kind of wough animal. You have winkles all over your face and goodness knows where else. I'm sowy to have to say it, but it's twue!'

'I grant you that not every female goes for the – the *rugged* type, the man of character,' he conceded. 'Anyway, I've never claimed to be an Adonis. But then again did I ever say the succubus herself was a raving beauty? Well, did I?'

'You said that she could take on any disguise,' said Céline.

'I did. But my one was by nature an ugly harridan, and she didn't hide it. In fact most succubi are reputed to be, at best, *jolie laide*. What is more, succubi can be old or young – there's no telling. Which explains why many men who have been with a succubus won't admit it. It's something they'd prefer you not to know about, see? So, to cut a long story short, I did not, like the virtuous man, resist my nocturnal visitor. On the contrary, I responded with great enthusiasm over many successive nights. In fact, such was my enthusiasm that I outdid the supernatural being in libidinal energy. She became weaker and weaker until she was barely visible and, after two weeks, she simply faded away. Or never came back – it amounts to the same thing.'

'Well, well, well . . . ,' said Céline appreciatively.

'How long ago was this?' asked Jonas.

'Two years.'

'And you've never seen her since?'

'On a couple of occasions I've glimpsed her in the street, or thought I have. But when I push through the crowd to get to her she's gone, or it turns out to be a complete stranger.'

Orriss gave a short dry laugh and pushed his spectacles up onto the bridge of his nose. 'If you glimpsed her in the street,' he sneered, 'I imagine it's because there was more flesh and blood to your succubus than you'd care to say. She was probably on her lunch-break from the bra department in the Bon Marché.'

'As I've already told you a dozen times,' said Fairgreave wearily, 'a succubus is a *demon* – she may look like a person, often a very ordinary person, but she is not.'

Orriss was undeterred. 'Have it your way, but if she wasn't human then she was obviously just a bit of sexual fantasy. I don't know why you have to dress her up as a she-devil, unless it's to make yourself interesting. Personally I'd rather stick to Isabella Rossellini.'

The other man scowled and lit one Gauloise from its predecessor. 'This is exactly why I wanted to get you all onto Aragon. He points out two fundamental errors that people make. The first one is that the dreamer thinks that he or she is the author of desire, but that is quite wrong. The second is that you can do what you want with your own body: wrong again. Most people these days seem to be incapable of getting that into their fat heads. Phil!'

Kovacs jumped slightly. He hadn't expected to be addressed.

'You're too quiet, as usual. What do you think?'

'Of your succubi?'

Fairgreave nodded.

'It's – it's poetic. Not empirically verifiable. Unless you're into pataphysics, I suppose.'

'What? Oh don't answer that! Have you ever come across one yourself?'

'I don't know. Does my ex-wife count?'

Fairgreave chortled and Hannah, sensing misogyny, blew a streamer of cigarette smoke accidentally on purpose into his face.

'I suppose there's something in it,' Kovacs continued. 'Breton had that theory of the Vertiginous Descent, didn't he? The idea was to plunge down into the secret realms of the self to crack the codes of all the apparently contradictory things in our conscious lives. That's where your succubi come in, I imagine.'

'You don't believe in their objective existence?'

'No, I don't. But I do believe in the objective reality of subjective experience. I believe in neuroscience. I should hazard the guess,' he added, smiling faintly at Fairgreave, 'that your succubus was generated by certain neurons in your cerebral cortex oscillating at approximately 40 hertz per second.'

'Christ!' groaned Fairgreave. 'Has the man a heart?'

'The circulation couldn't be carried on without one.'

Fairgreave slapped a hand dramatically to his forehead. 'Now the shit's quoting Dickens at me! Don't call *us*, ducky . . .'

Céline ruffled Kovacs' hair. He pushed her away and laughed sardonically. 'I missed the beginning of the mass debate.'

'I *beg* your pardon?' said Fairgreave, deliberately mishearing.

'Sorry – the *great* debate, I should say. What got you onto the subject in the first place?'

'I was down on the programme to give a talk on Aragon next October and I just seemed to jump the gun,' sighed Fairgreave. 'Can we change the billing, Michel? Make that the influence of the French surrealists on the English – Mary Low, David Gascoyne, Leonora Carrington, and I'll come up with some others. We're supposed to be English-language anyway, aren't we?'

Michel Jonas noted the amendment and looked up at Kovacs. 'There's a free slot in November. Can you suggest anyone, Phil? Unless you want to go for it yourself.'

'Oh yes, *do*! Go on, Philip!' Hannah inveigled. 'I like it when you talk! Aren't you doing some tewibly clever book, or something?'

'Well yes, but it's not *literature*, Hannah. It's philosophy of science. To do with consciousness. Biotechnology, cognitive science, robotics and linguistics – that sort of thing.'

'A bit above our heads, then,' said Céline.

'Inside, actually, rather than above. But I'd rather not, frankly. If you want an extra speaker, I've got a friend in London who writes films. Did you see *Swiss Movement*? That was one of his. He co-scripted it, at least. He'd be very good value. I'll see if I can tempt him over in November. Marty Stein. You may have heard of him.'

Jonas scribbled the name into the draft programme.

'Otherwise,' Kovacs went on, 'who was the lipogram chap who wrote a whole novel without using the letter "E"?'

'Perec,' said Jonas, 'Georges Perec. The book's called *La Disparition*.'

'Well it's been translated into English. Under the title *A Void*. Perhaps we could get the translator over and invite the OuLiPo poets to meet him. You know one or two of them, don't you Derek? And Harry Wotsit should be knocking around somewhere.'

The company fragmented, gradually, into separate corners of conversation. Fairgreave, rocking back on his chair, grabbed the passing *sommelier* by the elbow and ordered a double Armagnac, insisting on a saucer of sugar-lumps – *canards*, as he called them – to dip into the liqueur. Then he rocked back towards Kovacs, landing with a hard bang as his elbows struck the table.

'Going anywhere this vacation?'

'Dunno. I've got a few things to finish off at the College. Meetings with external examiners, that sort of thing. One last class with the Advanced Literature group. The English for Scientists seminars to timetable for next year. Then I can maybe get down to the book, in a week or so if all goes well.'

'Relax a bit, man! You never seem to let up.'

Kovacs coughed into a handkerchief and glanced down at it. A few threads of blood striated the sputum. Bleeding gums again.

'Céline and I may go down to her parents in Perpignan. Either that or a week in Sicily in July. I mean, she's snowed under too, so we don't really plan ahead all that much. How about you?'

'Well there's the London course next week. We've got forty people signed up for that,' said Fairgreave.

'And that lasts – what? Ten days?'

'Uh-huh. Then I'm thinking of going on a painting holiday in Tuscany.' He dropped his voice and edged closer. 'Trying to persuade Hannah to accompany me!'

'I thought she was –'

'Married? Well, yes. Sort of. You know the kind of thing. She's *sort* of married. The man's a jackass.'

'I didn't know she painted, either.'

'Neither did she. That's why I invited her. I thought I could bring out hidden qualities in her. Anyway – it'll probably all come to nothing, old boy, which is better than ending in tears. That's one of the perils in being a notorious rake: nobody takes me seriously any more.'

'You're lucky. People never *stop* taking me seriously.'

Hannah was staring across at them brazenly, vaguely aware that her name had been taken in vain. Fairgreave gave one of his gormless chimpanzee smiles and burped involuntarily.

'Listen, I'll be around in Paris most of the summer. Give me a bell sometime if you like. We could –'

'Go for a drink?'

'Exactly.'

'I will, Derek – promise.'

Céline took Kovacs by the arm as they left the brasserie. The cool, ionised air entered them like an elixir. Canvas shop-awnings above their heads were still dripping but the last squall had now blown over, leaving a ragged strip of cosmic darkness between the listing roofs and squat chimneypots of the rue de Buci. It was one of those streets that seemed oddly askew, the cambered walls and shop-fronts and lop-sided windows leering over the narrow antiquated thoroughfare at impossible angles, like a German expressionist stage-set. A thin but swift stream of rainwater eddied and gargled along the gutters before disappearing through cavernous slits beneath the kerbstones into dank invisible galleries beneath their feet.

Through the luminous frontage of one of the lower dives they saw a girlish figure in a sailor suit dancing jerkily on a table while playing the squeezebox and singing to a full house. They paused to watch and the sprite turned her face towards them. It was a wizened crone with the tiny hopping body of a sparrow and a pierrot's head, her features white as a death-mask. She was piping a Leo Ferré song in pure, penetrating notes – the top octave of a piccolo. The stirring sentimental air seemed to be torn quivering from her throat, sapping every last ounce of force in her infantile body. When she caught sight of them in the outer darkness she raised her sailor's cap and beckoned them to come in, baring her black teeth in a hideous grin. The audience turned to follow her gaze and squinted out at the two obscure figures on the pavement through beer-glazed eyes and a fog of smoke. Céline tightened her hold on Kovacs' arm and they hurried on.

'I've parked the car by the Institut,' she said. 'Can I give you a lift?'

'Yes, but let's stop somewhere by the river. On the place Dauphine, if you like. I need a breath of air.'

They crossed the Pont Neuf in her Peugeot and parked by the place Dauphine, wandering down to the square du Vert-Galant which had been named, it seemed, either in ignorance or xenophobic defiance of English geometric terms, since the 'square' was incontestably triangular. If the Ile de la Cité was a ship, this was its prow, angled north-west, mid-stream: a prow with a back-to-front figurehead, for the green statue of a man on a horse above and behind them, on a raised stone embankment, was facing inwards towards the Cathedral as if royally snubbing the romantics and solitary hash-smokers who frequented the little tree-lined garden below. To André Breton, on the other hand – as Kovacs recalled – the garden had another significance. To him, Paris was a woman and this little delta of turf was her sex, squeezed between the liquid thighs of the Seine. That last memory-flash was Fairgreave's influence. He'd got surrealists on the brain.

They leaned silently against some railings beneath the trees and looked out across the black perspective of water towards the Louvre and the elegant succession of bridges: the Pont des Arts, the Pont du Carrousel, the Pont Royal, then the Musée d'Orsay's distinctive roof to the left. All was silent but for a regular background hum of traffic when behind them, from the back of the jetty for the small Vedettes du Pont Neuf riverboats, the sound of approaching engine noise slowly impinged on their senses. Above it a shrill crackly tannoy repeated a sentence in several languages, each delivery punctuated with a trill of electronic notes. They could make out the words 'Conciergerie' and 'Marie-Antoinette': the rest was a raucous blur of phonemes and static.

It was a vast bateau-mouche with a full cargo of tourists encased within its low oblong bubble of Plexiglas. To starboard and port, long banks of halogen lamps emerged into view, napalming the quaysides with a flamboyant explosion of light. The couple were instantly blinded. The hard shadows of trees, lamp-posts, a wooden bench rotated violently round their axes as the boat soared by, twisting the familiar garden with the torque-like grip of a strangler. For a few breathless seconds Céline and Kovacs were trapped in the voyeuristic light. It was chilling, somehow. They could sense hundreds of gawking eyes and pointing fingers singling them out from the geodesic structure, dim behind the battery of lamps. They were being taken for two lovers, of course, their privacy momentarily and dazzlingly invaded. A random pattern of camera-flashes fired from the dim zone above the floodlamps and a furtive whisper seemed to run beneath the low murmur of the vessel's motor, knowing smiles exchanged, insinuations murmured in a dozen alien tongues, coursing like lit fuse-wires across the broad grandstand of the deck. Then just as suddenly it was over, all but the bright tinny voice – free of static, now – piercing the nocturnal silence: 'The Pont Neuf, the city's oldest bridge, was gift-wrapped several years ago in 44,000 square metres of nylon sheeting by the Bulgarian artist Christo . . .'

They could relax, anonymous again in the fragrant shadows beneath the trees. He heard Céline catch her breath as the bateau-mouche diminished upstream like a gorgeous spaceship, floating brilliantly away on the dark river of the night.

The wake of the vessel lapped softly against the cobblestone embankment below and a warm breeze sighed in from the south. A stray wisp of Céline's hair levitated eerily above her forehead. Kovacs followed the clean lines of her face in silhouette with his gaze: the small nose, the pear-shaped dip in the upper lip, the chin, the slender neck. Her very features were reticent and restrained, but *sexy* – there was no getting away from that. And perhaps he wanted to get away from that. The last light of the riverboat cast a pearly sheen on her dilating pupils and twinkled wickedly from the black spider brooch. The thought crossed his mind that she was a wild animal, slim-limbed and farouche – a doe, possibly, a roe deer in the covert, peering out at the world with perpetual wariness from her dim inaccessible sanctuary. But perhaps that was the wrong animal, he corrected himself – too Bambi-ish, altogether.

He liked her silence, all the same, her unassuming ways. It was a relief after the squabbling, querulous English voices of Fairgreave and his motley crew. They were amusing in rationed doses but ultimately wearied him. They belonged to the past – Little Englanders, uprooted and 'unhomed' – a past he forswore and yet continually returned to, as if he hoped for some form of higher communion with them which he never received.

And wasn't the world full of Fairgreaves and Hannahs and Orrisses and their like? And Kovacses, come to that. It was a rueful thought. After all, by what right did he dissociate himself from them? He too was a *metoikos*, and suddenly he could picture them all, the 'resident aliens': exclusive little clubs of Englishness peppered throughout the world, little outposts of progress, with that mean post-colonial arrogance, that instinct to subdue and control, that hubbub of plummy County voices. The chattering classes. He thought of them infesting every corner of the globe, jaw-jawing their way into the silence of the night in golf clubs, estaminets, British Councils, desert shacks or island cocktail bars from Alice Springs to New Delhi, Bahrain to the Bahamas, the reeking fumes of gin and beer ascending like incense towards the opal moon. Little Churchills, he thought, Little Hitlers, Little Napoleons – where was the difference?

And then there was silence, there was Céline. Her presence was, curiously, almost an absence. He liked her because she was only half there. Anne, his wife, had been a chirpy and exigent personality from whom he could not retreat. She trespassed into the walled garden of his solitude and turned it into a car-park. But Céline, like him, was a loner and they supported each other in their shared sense of solitude and clean singularity. It was because they were not a 'couple' as such, because they were not lumped crudely together, that he could bear being with her. He looked at her again. But for the floating strand of hair she was motionless, statuesque. Then as if she could hear his thoughts she shivered and bit her lower lip. He took off his jacket and draped it obligingly over her shoulders.

'It must look so different to the person behind the light,' she said.

'I'm sorry?'

'The people on the bateau-mouche. It must all look so different to them. No shadows. Just those searchlights poking into the darkness.'

'Yes.'

He had been at ease a moment ago but now her harmless observation irritated him, made him aware again of that different perspective. Paris by Night. A man and a woman on the quai.

What were they doing there? To any casual observer the situation was tritely romantic, straight from one of those grainy Fifties' postcards. All at once the two of them standing there did seem an absurd cliché. For a horrible moment it was as if he had changed places with one of the ogling tourists on the boat. He could see them both *sub specie aeternitatis* – marooned sweethearts on an obscure spit of land, dwindling into darkness after the sudden flares, contracting to a dim pinpoint in space beneath the mute silhouette of Notre-Dame. It was a gross misrepresentation. They were not 'sweethearts' at all. He wanted to jump back into his own skin and explain this, to set the record straight. He wanted to chase those hints of intimacy away.

'How – how is the collection going? It's autumn/winter, isn't it? You fashion people are always living in the future.'

She looked away and didn't answer for a few moments, then: 'You're nervy tonight. What is it?'

His voice lost its vivacity and lowered a tone. He was grateful, in a way, to drop the pretence.

'Nothing. Well, no – not nothing. Fairgreave perhaps. There's something about his manner.'

She tutted and gave him a nervous, sidelong glance. 'You *were* rather quiet. But he's perfectly harmless, really. All bark, you know – no bite.'

'Of course. Don't forget, I *know* Derek, Céline. I work with the sod. But he's so – he's such an ape, you know. Or a bull – so curmudgeonly.'

She furrowed her brow, not knowing the word – a rare event for her.

'A bull in a china shop,' he added by way of explanation, making two horns on his head with his forefingers.

'If he's a bull in a china shop, Philip,' she commented significantly, 'then you are a piece of china in a bull shop.'

Kovacs smiled quickly, then flapped a hand dismissively in the air. 'It's not just Fairgreave. It's the whole crowd. I'm no good in company. I can't take other people seriously. Like Kafka, I suppose. Everyone said he was frightened of solitude but the truth was he hated company. *L'Enfer, c'est les autres*. Hell is other people. Who was it said that? Not Kafka.'

She ignored his question. 'You're a teacher. You should be used to other people.'

'Yes, but that's different. I can't explain why. It just *is*. Teaching is – it's like being an actor with a script or an autocue or something. You don't have to be yourself. It's stupid. I can be myself *by* myself, but not with other people. Does that make any sense?'

'No. Aren't you being yourself now?'

'Of course, Céline. I'm sorry. But you – you're not other people.'

'Well, I'm not *you*, Philip, so I must be "other people".'

'You're – you're *you*. I'm just more used to you, that's all.'

There was a dark, reproving note in her voice when she spoke next. 'You know what your problem is, don't you?'

'Tell me.'

'You cut yourself off from people. It isn't good. You'll become –'

'Yes? What will I become?'

'An endangered species.' Then, after a moment's pause: 'If you aren't one already . . .'

They were silent again, at a loss, and looked away across the sombre flux of the river bearing down on them, diverging to left and to right at their feet. There were moments – and now was one of them – when he felt he was holding her back selfishly, preventing her from meeting another man and re-marrying, though she would have vigorously denied that such was her wish. There was something pathetic in her willingness to tag along with him, loosely, intermittently, like a stray dog. But she was not a stray dog. She was an adult, free to do as she pleased, as indeed was he. Free bloody birds. It was not, after all, as if they thrived on each other's company – day in, day out. Then why should he feel so guilty about things? Why should the most casual human relationship seem like a *crime*?

A tiny pipistrelle bat dropped out of the sky and shot across the top of their heads, a hot black ball of fur and leathery wings perceived instantaneously against the glimmering façade of the Louvre. Kovacs cowered.

'*Merde!* I could feel it! It nearly touched my hair.' His voice quavered, fear souring to disgust. She observed his reaction with more than usual interest.

They returned to the car and drove in silence over to the right bank of the Seine and up towards the 10th.

On the boulevard de Sébastopol Céline braked hard as a scrawny wreck of a man with wide narcotised eyes jaywalked across the street twirling a broken toilet chain.

'Reefer madness,' murmured Kovacs. He instinctively hit the buttons to wind up the electric windows but after turning manically on them for a moment the haunted moon-face moved on.

The jolt burst open the glove compartment, tipping the contents at Kovacs' feet: a card of fabric samples; a book of matches from a bar called Le Toubib; a Tampax in its paper sheath; liquorice breath-fresheners; no end of screwed up tissues and used Q-tips, a plastic box of neatly folded blank letter-cards that had split open on impact, and other things. Kovacs stuffed the chattels back into the hinged drawer and banged it shut.

When they got to the quai de Valmy she parked up on the kerb beside the canal. He looked up from the car window and recalled his return home earlier in the evening.

'Come up for a few minutes,' he said.

She glanced doubtfully at the LED clock on the dashboard. It was just past eleven.

'A coffee,' he insisted, 'and I've got that book I promised you. The Althusser autobiography.'

After eight o'clock every evening the main door to the courtyard was closed. He tapped four numbers into the digicode to unlock it and, once inside, they took the left-hand staircase to his flat. Céline walked ahead of him. As she came to the second landing, she let out a cry – '*Aïe!*' – and stopped dead.

'What is it?'

'I trod on something. A piece of wire. It twisted round, sort of, and scratched my foot.'

She grasped the offending object and held it up in the dim light before raising her right foot to inspect the damage, leaning on the iron banister.

'Bleeding?'

'No. My stockings. I've – *comment vous dîtes? – une échelle* –'

'Laddered them?'

'Yes. Laddered them.'

They reached the flat and he opened the door. The staircase always smelt of dust and stale dinners but immediately he crossed the threshold it hit him again – eucalyptus. It was fainter now, just the slightest vestige, but discernible, enough to revive that unpleasant sense of apprehension. He paused and turned to Céline.

'Can you smell anything?' he asked.

She raised her head quizzically, scenting the air like a hunted, or hunting, animal.

'Yes I can. *Essence Algérienne*, isn't it?'

'That's what it's called! I was trying to find the name earlier on.'

'Have you had a cold?'

'No, it's not me,' he explained. 'When I came home from work the lights were on and there was this smell. I thought it might be the cleaning lady, but it's not her day. Do you think it could be coming from downstairs?'

'It's possible,' she said, staring dubiously at the parquet. 'They might be taking it in a *bain de vapeur* – an inhalation, you know. But I can't imagine it penetrating walls and ceilings.'

Kovacs stood with his hands on his hips, turning his head slowly to scan the apartment once again. It was as if the four walls held the answer to an unspoken question and they were not going to talk. His gaze passed in swift saccades across the familiar paraphernalia, the unique baggage of belongings that he had accrued over the years. The bronze statuette of a seated Mercury which had come down from his maternal grandmother. The glass fishbowl full of perfectly egg-shaped stones that he had gathered on the beach at Looe Bar in Cornwall. He called them his 'ova' and it amused him that this little clutch of letters could be found nestling in his name, like nest-eggs themselves. 'What's in a name?' as Juliet said. Quite a lot, in his case, or so he reckoned.

Each trifling object in the flat had its place in the random itinerary of his life, a meaning to him alone – a satellite of himself, an odd concretion of past experience. His eyes wandered to the spiral staircase that led to his bedroom and bathroom on the upper floor. It was an insoluble Spot the Difference puzzle – insoluble because there were no differences to spot. But why should he think something had changed? Why should he *expect* something to have changed? Céline was watching him in his absorption and when their eyes met he snapped out of it, smiled apologetically and went over to her, removing his jacket from her shoulders.

'Sorry,' he said. 'I was lost in space. Here – here's the book. Have a seat and I'll make that coffee. I won't be long.'

He went into the kitchen, put the water to boil and shook the black grounds into the paper filter. As the boiling water sank through the damp silt of the grounds, the aroma was heartening. It filled the flat, repossessing the place, making it home again.

At first, when he returned with the coffee things on a tray, he couldn't see where Céline had got to. She was on her knees beside the main door.

He placed the tray on the carpet beside the settee.

'What are you doing down there?'

She didn't answer but signalled for him to come over, then rubbed her forefinger over the tuft of the carpet by the door.

'What is it?' he asked.

'Sawdust. Look.' A fine powder of minute woodchips flicked up into the air.

'Odd. Where did that come from?'

'From here,' she said, pointing to a tiny hole that had been drilled through the door beside the lock. She opened the door and fed the wire she had found on the landing through the hole from the outside. The hooked end of the wire caught on the latch and when she pulled it back the latch opened. She repeated the action four times while Kovacs watched. Click, click, click, click.

'That's how they did it,' she said.

'Did what?'

'You've been burgled.' There was a matter-of-fact tone to her voice as she looked up at him, watching for his reaction. 'You knew, didn't you? You've known all along.'

2

A MAN WAS dancing down the street.

He was of medium stature, obese and black: African, at first sight. His round bloodshot eyes were just visible behind Ray-Bans. His hair fell in long tousled locks and his thick lips stretched into an impossibly wide, happy-go-lucky grin. As he danced, his plump pectorals bounced contrapuntally under an orange T-shirt with the words 'The Best of Olodum' printed diagonally in white across it. The rim of the T-shirt rode up and down over the impressive mound of his belly. A Walkman was clipped to his belt with tiny earphones plugged neatly in place. He was shuffling and skipping blithely to a Gilberto Gil samba. From time to time he sang along in snatches. The Portuguese words tripped from his tongue, he clapped his hands and snapped his fingers rhythmically above his head.

It was morning and the raw lateral sun had turned the boulevard de Ménilmontant into a ravine of light. Nobody paid much attention to Babalu dos Santos. A pop-eyed chihuahua strained at its leash and yapped neurotically at his passing sandalled feet. A few eyebrows were raised at café tables. But most passers-by were blasé, only tacitly acknowledging his existence by giving him a wide berth. Paris is full of oddballs, so better to be on the safe side. Babalu, however, was not in Paris. Babalu was in Salvador, Brazil. He was dancing down the steep streets of his home town, past pink and blue and green façades of houses and baroque churches. He was breathing in the rich aromas of Bahian cuisine from open doorways. He was skipping beneath wind-rocked palms on the hot gold sands on Itapuã beach.

It was only when he came to the entrance to Père Lachaise

cemetery that his demeanour changed and he woke up to his true surroundings. He plucked out the earphones and switched off the Walkman, then removed the Ray-Bans – they hung, now, round his neck by a black cord – and pulled down his rucked T-shirt with a fussy, self-conscious gesture. Babalu had great respect for the dead.

As he entered the burial ground the pleasantly familiar spectacle of arthritic necropolitan avenues and the chaotic muddle of antiquated monuments, obelisks and sepulchres zigzagged around him, climbing the forty-four hectares of the hill of Charonne in tier after funerary tier. '*Um dia lindo!*' he murmured, blinking slowly – a beautiful day! Something unspeakably wonderful was happening.

It was snowing.

He extended his fat spatulate hands, palms upwards, and gazed into the bright spring sky. Snow everywhere. Pink snow! An untimely winter had come to pass. The full pink snow-blossoms of the horse chestnut trees tumbled soundlessly out of the sky, tossed into the air by invisible seraphim, settling as delicately as confetti on the avenues, the tombs, the stone-feathered fan of a weeping angel's wing. It was as if the clouds themselves – had there been any – were gently disintegrating, scattering crumbs of cloud-stuff over the sleeping scene.

'*Lindo!*' he repeated. His melting, brown-cow eyes welled up with tears, piteous as an El Greco saint. His smile, too, mellowed to a beatific glow, transfiguring the softly upholstered features of his face. Even his chubby bottom, extruding between the sagging top of his trousers and the edge of the orange T-shirt, had a certain childish sanctity about it as he waddled off down the avenue du Puits, hands still uplifted in voiceless exaltation.

Babalu was a typical Bahian. The Brazilian province, with its capital Salvador, was home to the black descendants of Nigerian and Angolan slaves. There were three small cuts in the centre of his forehead, the sign of the Nago tribe from Africa. He was not, however, pure African: there was an unusual angularity to the bone-structure of his forehead and the pigmentation of his skin was uneven, particularly on his neck and the back of his hands. 'In Brazil,' he would say, 'fucking is the national pastime. Everybody fucks everybody else. Except the English!' – and here he would raise a finger, holding the attention of his interlocutor on a thread. 'The English *shoot* everybody else. The English come to Brazil and shoot the Indians. Then the Portuguese come to Brazil and fuck the Indians. Then the African women come to Brazil, and the Portuguese fuck them. And the African men fuck the Portuguese women and the Indians fuck the Africans and the Africans fuck the Indians . . .' Here he would run out of breath and throw his hands up despairingly in the air. 'See what I mean? That, brother, is the history of my country. *Mamelucos*, *cafusos*, *mulattos* – cross-breeds everywhere you look. If you had a history like that, my friend, you'd look the way I do.'

In Paris, Babalu was nothing. In Salvador, he was a somebody, though in a footloose, freelance way. He was a somebody because he was a *despachante* – a fixer, or middleman – who had been around the block a few times. The *despachante* is a lifesaver in Brazil, for in a country entangled with bureaucracy he slices his way like a billhook through the undergrowth of red tape. He is a past-master of *jeitos*, or 'solutions', the magical back-stage antidotes to a filibustering administration. Whatever the law insists upon – be it birth certificate or demolition permit, chest X-ray or bill of lading – the *despachante* delivers, for a fee. Babalu made sure he was paid twice, by his client and by the bureaucrats: for they were all as lost as each other in the same farrago of officialdom and were equally glad of his services. As a sideline he would top up his coffers with a little friendly marriage-brokerage.

He had been born in the *favelas*, the shanty town, and married young, but his native wit and charm had buoyed him up, not to mention his literacy. And his reading was not restricted to tax returns and civil code. He was an autodidact with a gift for languages who had found in his extensive and precocious delvings into world literature another world of human fellowship in which he wanted to share. Above all, Babalu wanted to share. In his dreams he would invite the poor and needy of Salvador to his magnificent homestead and hold them for hours in conversation, serving them great dishes of *feijoada*, steaming black beans with pig snout, beef tongue, sausage, bacon, garlic and bay leaves. And when they had supped, he would show them to rooms where huge feather beds awaited them. He liked to picture the expressions on their faces as they thanked him, while he would raise his hands in seigneurial self-deprecation and quietly retire.

He was no Croesus yet but by Salvadorian standards he was doing well, with a modest townhouse and six fat, well-nourished children.

Babalu was a hard worker with an eye for business: where there was a demand, he was in supply. He had begun as a rubber tapper in Amazonia working alongside Chico Mendes, the tapper who had tried to form a union to stop the devastation of the rain forest. When Mendes was shot in 1988, Babalu got scared. He suspected that he was on a hit-list too. The cause was just but he had a family to think of. He hesitated a week after Mendes' death, drinking himself stupid with his co-workers and weeping over the photograph of his wife, Raimunda Maria, and the kids. In his mind's eye, he could see them following his coffin – a hero's funeral, of course – as it was carried down the street towards the church of Nosso Senhor do Bonfim, Our Lord of Good Ending. 'How could I do that to them?' he said to his comrades. 'You can't,' they agreed, also in their cups. 'I am not a unionist, my friends,' he pleaded in his defence, 'I knot drops of water,' a local saying which meant that, in life, he would do anything to get by. It was virtually the motto of the *despachante*.

Then he struck gold: for once, the phrase was entirely appropriate. Babalu had a distant cousin who had married an American in California and he wangled a visitor's visa, valid for two months. He stayed two years, working vast, laborious shifts in a goldmine. He made money: a good sum by Californian standards, a little fortune to a Bahian.

This profitable adventure changed Babalu's life. His family were delighted to see him and he could now spoil them materially.

But his life had changed in other ways too. He had learnt English in California: an ungrammatical, offshore English, true, botched together from crude attempts to communicate with Chinese, Puerto Ricans and a Czech-American former abattoir worker from Chicago whom he had befriended in the mine. Makeshift though it was, Babalu was proud of his English. It was the great universal lingua franca – his unofficial passport, his intangible ticket to ride. He was restless and his wanderlust revived. It was not enough to be sitting proudly on the wrought iron balcony of his new townhouse, smoking the pipe of the complacent patriarch. He was still relatively young – in his late thirties – and he wanted to use that passport again. 'Brazil,' he would say, shaking his head philosophically, 'is the land of the future – and unfortunately it always will be.'

The experience of America, moreover, had sharpened the sense of injustice and outrage he had felt when Chico Mendes had been killed. He knew the reality of poverty, exploitation and oppression.

Back in Salvador he joined Bloco Olodum, an organisation that fought racism. His commitment to the fight was tempered by realism. Brazil, he knew, was a land where the twentieth century, the nineteenth century, the Middle Ages and the Stone Age co-existed. A Golden Age of social justice was not going to be won overnight. He could understand the millenarian hopes of many of his people: the Valley of the Dawn movement near Brasilia, for example, waiting for the final rain of stars and the transition of themselves, the chosen few, into the never-never land of the after-death. He could understand them, but as an adult understands a child.

One of Babalu's sisters was a college girl, bright and good-looking. With her French ethnographer husband, she had moved to Paris. Why shouldn't he visit them? In Salvador a rich elderly woman whom he had successfully married off gave him a book called *The Best of Kisses*. It was an album of Paris photographs, all of lovers kissing. There were pictures by Robert Doisneau, Jeanloup Sieff, Frank Horvat, Sabine Weiss, Brassaï and André Kertész, and the book obsessed him, fired his imagination. It was not that he wanted to escape his wife and find a lover himself. Far from it! It was the place itself – Paris – that drew him, a city that lived for love. Surely here, of all places, his soul would find a guiding light in the darkness? He could slip through the net as he had done before, overstaying the term of his visa and moonlighting – that was not a problem. But his reasons went deeper than this. For Babalu, a trip to Paris would be a pilgrimage.

Many Bahians were racial hybrids, and their religion was a

hybrid too. Babalu practised Umbanda, the mystic fusion of Christianity with Brazilian and, above all, African cults. He worshipped Christ but he worshipped Oxala too, Christ's African alter ego: to him there was no contradiction. The Umbandan Pantheon was generous and accommodating: no end of passportless deities and semi-deities found their way into it. Umbanda drew part of its inspiration from the mystical spiritism of the Frenchman Allan Kardec, who was buried at Père Lachaise. As for many Bahians, it was his dream to visit Kardec's grave. The idea grew and grew in Babalu's mind. He read in translation whatever works of French literature he could get his hands on. He pored over books on Paris and yearned to be there. The City of Light! He suspected that, like California, it would be a beautiful monument to vanity and frippery, but so what if it was? He, Babalu, carried the torch of love in his heart. In the words of the Bahian musician Carlinhos Brown, he would bring to Paris the 'religion of the smile'.

He had been in Paris a year now and that smile had not got him as far as he might have wished. There were no goldmines to swallow him up and regurgitate him later, his pockets replenished with lucre. Even his English had limited use and he had to start picking up French. He acquired an evening job – cash in hand – just off the place de la Bastille, in the rue de la Roquette, making crêpes and galettes. He could legitimately wire a percentage of that money home through his sister and her husband. For the first few weeks he stayed with them but he could hardly move in indefinitely, so they helped him find a bare room, with broken floorboards, a couple of old mattresses and a washstand, in a dilapidated tenement by the place de Stalingrad. By day, he had time on his hands, and so it was that he discovered Père Lachaise. By the end of six months he had studied the cemetery like a scholar, he had learnt the geography of its avenues and lanes, his heart had gone out to its illustrious, silent denizens.

When he entered Père Lachaise, he crossed the threshold that divides the covetous agitation of the living from the celestial equanimity of the dead. It was a final haven of peace and love. A hundred thousand sepulchres, a million dead, a million plots. Each plot had a beginning, most plots had a middle, but all shared the common end. There were tragical plots, farcical plots, pastoral-comical, historical-pastoral, tragical-historical plots. There were one-act plots, three-act plots, five-act plots. But here – in this city of extinguished spirits, of crammed graves and empty dreams – here was the twist in the plot, the plot to beat all plots. Here was the burial plot – the final, insoluble *sub*-plot.

At Père Lachaise, in the green heart of the living city, life and love lay slain. Or did they? Babalu had serious doubts. Death may be a subject that leaves most people cold, but not Babalu. He loved the cemetery. For him it was *alive* and plotting. Beneath its trees love lay sleeping, merely sleeping in the shade. Beneath their shade, a million dreamers lay entombed in a million dreams. Beneath his feet . . . he would often stop in his tracks and stare down at the mute earth. They had spread their dreams under his feet. And what dreams! Dreams no mortal ever dared to dream. Dreams of dangerous supernatural love, blind and unholy; dreams of illicit spirit sports in bosky groves.

This soft bright morning, he was passing the sepulchre of Rachel, the actress who had loved both Alfred de Musset and Napoleon III. He had read all about them in the course of his eclectic necropolitan researches and now there she was, Rachel, asleep beneath his feet. Was she dreaming of her lovers still? Not far away, in the 4th division, de Musset was probably dreaming of George Sand. Poor Rachel, thought Babalu, with her unrequited dreams. But she had not been short of suitors. Didn't a prince once send her the message 'When? Where? How much?' to which she replied 'Tomorrow. My place. Nothing'? Now here it was – Tomorrow. Her place. Nothing. Yet threaded through the iron fretwork of the mausoleum door was a single fresh red rose.

A crow flapped lazily overhead and Babalu looked up. The sun was climbing high. He screwed up his eyes and tiny rainbows appeared where his eyelashes meshed. He put his Ray-Bans back on and, hands in pockets, continued his promenade.

A little further down the avenue, turning left beyond Rothschild and Pissarro, he came upon the ogival dais of a Gothic chapel which sheltered two recumbent statues and the mortal remains of Abelard and Héloïse. Here was the oldest love of them all, smouldering after eight and a half centuries. He lingered sadly at the railing and read the inscription. He knew their story backwards: the little volume of their letters had been in the library at Salvador, and he had read it in his teens. Why did you do it, Peter? A man of the cloth and tutor in Canon Fulbert's house: how could you have seduced his niece! You spoke of love, not books, and when the words ran out the kisses didn't. As for your hands, you used them for more than turning pages. And where did it get you? Héloïse got pregnant and her family cut off 'those parts of my body whereby I had done that which was the cause of their sorrow.' Babalu had a good memory for certain turns of phrase.

Lovers everywhere – dead lovers, the loving dead. Babalu knew them all. Here were Proust and Oscar Wilde – the love that dared not speak its name. 'I can't stand this wallpaper. One of us will have to go.' Those were Wilde's last words, as he lay dying in the Hôtel d'Alsace, rue des Beaux-Arts. The wallpaper remained. And here he lay, some corner of a foreign field, beneath a stone sphinx that, like poor Abelard, had been castrated by prudes. Where were the testicles? A guard had told him that they were used by the cemetery director as a paperweight.

Here were ill-starred, doomed affairs too. Poor Gérard de Nerval was driven mad by Jenny Colan. She was all the Sylvies and Aurélias of his novels rolled into one – or *they* were rolled out of one. She haunted his thoughts in the clinic at Passy, tortured his soul as he walked his pet lobster on a leash of blue ribbon in the Jardin du Luxembourg. Finally he had put a slipknot leash of another sort around his own neck. He loved a woman but claimed to prefer lobsters. 'Because they are calm, serious, and know the secrets of the sea.'

Babalu was a walking encyclopaedia of romance. Whatever secrets the grave had to yield it had yielded them up unto him.

He knew where Daudet lay, dreaming of Anne Rieu and their wild first meeting, high on absinthe, at the brasserie in the rue des Martyrs. He knew where Molière dreamt of Armande Béjart, his nubile actress wife, while his friend – La Fontaine – revelled in the fabulous bestiaries of his mind. He knew where Apollinaire was, or where he should have been, for the poet was a bird who built his nest in the air. They said he was the son of the Pope. They said he was not one man but many. They said that he took on the characteristics of those he spoke to, a human chameleon, and that he had invented the art of capnomancy – how to judge people by the smell of their cooking.

And the women! Who was he dreaming of, Guillaume Apollinaire? Annie Playden, his English governess, who had rejected him? Madeleine Pages? Or Jacqueline Kolb, the beautiful Russian? He was dreaming – Babalu thought – of Anne Laurençin, as she was dreaming of him, two blocks away in the 88th division. Picasso had spotted her, a fellow painter, in a gallery and sent Apollinaire to meet her. He knew they were made for each other, two halves of a tango. But Picasso had not always been a minister of love. When Apollinaire was in prison, accused of stealing the *Mona Lisa* from the Louvre, the Spaniard had denied all knowledge of him – the swine! But bygones were bygones. Pablo was dead, in another city. And Apollinaire and Anne were dead too, the chestnut blossom, falling slowly, feathering their silent tombs.

And what, wondered Babalu, did Chopin dream of, his body here, his heart in a pillar in the Church of the Holy Cross in Warsaw? Perhaps (like de Musset) of George Sand, or a fugitive amorous smile he once intercepted from the front row of a concert-hall. Clésinger, who sculpted the bust on Chopin's tomb, lay buried with his model, Berthe Courrière. A lover of black Masses, she was also the lover of Huysmans, Villiers de l'Isle-Adam and Rémy de Gourmont. And so she lies, between Clésinger and de Gourmont – two ex-lovers – in a posthumous *ménage à trois*.

All of Napoleon's mistresses were here – Mlle Duchesnois, Mme Saqui, Mlle Mars, Mlle George, Eléanore de la Plaigne, Pauline Bellisle, Anne Walewska. Mme Saqui, the daughter of a circus acrobat, had danced for Napoleon on a high wire strung between the two towers of Notre-Dame. And poor Mlle George, the actress – despite her imperial flings (Tsar Alexander too!) – where did she end up? A lavatory attendant, a *Dame Pipi*. How are the mighty fallen . . .

The mighty! Here Félix Faure, President of the Republic, lay in bronze effigy, draped triumphally in the French flag. Babalu smiled. He knew the truth from his books. Félix had died in the arms of his mistress. Oh Death, where is thy sting?

And all the others: the painters, writers, dancers, singers, composers, actresses, film directors. Max Ernst, Delacroix, Paul

Eluard, Isadora Duncan, Modigliani, Rossini, Piaf, Ophuls, Bizet, Colette, Balzac – Balzac, whose *Père Goriot* ended in Père Lachaise, as he did too – what hidden telegraphies of dreams united them now, beneath the impacted soil?

In a year Babalu had learnt their stories and at least once a week he would pay his social calls. He talked to the illustrious and gifted dead and they answered him; he knew their *chagrins d'amour*. A winged Cupid, he bore their messages from tomb to tomb.

It was scandalous, really, what went on behind the decorous walls of marble. Was there no dignity in death? Père Lachaise, who gave the cemetery its name, had been Jesuit confessor to Louis XIV and a known libertine himself. He would 'try out' the ladies of the court for the king: Mme de Vantadour, Mme Scarron, Mme d'Olonne, Mme de Chatillon. All had yielded to his unecclesiastical charms.

During the Commune the site had been transformed into a brothel. The *fédérés*, cornered and knowing they would die, struck camp here, turned the vaults into munitions dumps and wine cellars and brought women in to console them, making love on the marble slabs, under the shady branches of the thujas. It was summer and the women gathered the fruit of the laden cherry-trees. The next day the combatants met their death dead drunk and with crimson cherries bunched behind their ears.

So it was right and fitting that the one landmark in the cemetery visible from both the Eiffel Tower and the heights of Sacré-Coeur should be a 16-metre column known as *la grande bitte*, the giant prick, beneath which, in the sepulchre of the diplomat Baron Félix de Beaujour, black Masses and saturnalian debauches were said to take place at the dead of night.

Desperate with desire, the dead of Père Lachaise even stowed away on public transport. In 1874, when the tunnel of the *chemin de fer de ceinture* started collapsing, coffins dropped through and hitched a ride on trains.

Suddenly there were chevrons everywhere.

Babalu was sweating profusely, his T-shirt sticking damply to him. He was climbing the hill towards the 6th division. Volleys of aerosolled arrows drew him on.

The route to Jim Morrison's grave was littered with empty

beer bottles and the air buzzed with multicoloured spraycan epitaphs. *SEASONED SLEEPER SLEEP WELL; NO ETERNAL REWARD WILL FORGIVE US NOW FOR WASTING THE DAWN.* A Babel of pilgrim voices could be heard from the tomb and a whiff of fragrant smoke crossed his path.

He circled the huge carrefour du Grand-Rond and walked up past the colossal duplex tomb of the Princess Demidov-Strogonov, adorned with wolves' heads and miners' hammers. The family wealth had come from goldmines in central Asia, but the poor little rich girl was lonely. Her will left a pack of roubles to whoever would come and live in the tomb, to keep her company. Enquire within.

Babalu was nearing the first of his two destinations. He followed the avenue Transversale No. 1, straight as a die, and turned right into the avenue des Combattants-Etrangers. Hard on the corner of the 33rd division, he joined a small group of silent people, some holding hands, heads bowed in meditation. Watched by the stone owls of the megalithic domed sepulchre of the Marquis de Casariera, the group circled a druidic roofed dolmen of rough-hewn slabs of stone. Inside, surrounded by massed nosegays and posies of flowers and illuminated by a dozen guttering candles, was the bronze bust of a man: Allan Kardec.

Another worshipper touched his arm and addressed him in Portuguese with a thick Brazilian accent.

'Babalu! *Como está?*'

'*Mui bem, obrigado*. And you, Antonio?'

The men smiled and they both rubbed the coarse stone of the dolmen in veneration. Babalu read again the familiar inscriptions on the roof and the plinth beneath the bust.

TO BE BORN, TO DIE, TO BE REBORN AGAIN

AND TO CEASELESSLY PROGRESS

SUCH IS THE LAW

ALLAN KARDEC

FOUNDER

OF THE

SPIRITIST PHILOSOPHY

EACH RESULT HAS A CAUSE

EACH INTELLIGENT RESULT

HAS AN INTELLIGENT CAUSE

THE POWER OF THE

CAUSE IS IN PROPORTION

TO THE MAGNITUDE

OF THE RESULT

3 OCTOBER 1804

31 MARCH 1869

The man named Antonio tugged at Babalu's T-shirt and guided him round to the back of the dolmen.

'Have you seen the notice they've put up?' he said, pointing out one paragraph on a small glass-paned text.

Babalu read the words slowly, asking Antonio for help with the French:

Advice to the Public

The criticism has been made that the tomb of Allan Kardec is being used for demonstrations of idolatry, such as: *the placing of hands on the stone of the monument or on the bust of the master, and the depositing of objects or candles, as if on an altar*. Informed people and the spirits forbid these acts as belonging to another age. Our enemies find in this an opportunity to rise up against spiritism *and to liken it to magic and sorcery*.

'What do you think?'

'I don't agree, Antonio. They're thinking of Quimbanda voodoo magic. Umbanda is white magic. We don't do no harm.'

'You know what it is!' whispered the other Brazilian. 'They're frightened of another bombing, like they had a few years ago. The roof was blown off the dolmen.'

'Maybe, Antonio.'

'It doesn't change anything, does it?'

'No, it doesn't change anything.'

They stared at the profusion of flowers in silence.

'Babalu, did you go back to Salvador in February? For Our Lady of Conception – Iemanjá?'

'I didn't, no. Did you?'

Antonio nodded, smiling.

'Did you see Raimunda Maria?'

Antonio laughed. 'Yes, my friend, she is very well. Oh it was just as usual, Babalu! Such fun! All the girls in white, throwing flowers and perfume and lipstick and stuff into the sea! Then dancing, dancing, dancing . . . I didn't sleep for three days!'

'Are you going to Rio for the New Year?'

'Of course! We're trying to book a group flight. Come with us! We will all be there, on the beach at Copacabana.'

'Maybe, Antonio, but –' Babalu made the money sign. 'I've just sent Raimunda the cash to come and see me soon. She's never been to Paris, my friend.'

They shook hands and Babalu headed off along the chemin du Quinconce. The golden sunlight quivered through the drifting chestnut blossom, stippling an eight-pillared round pavilion, an angel dropping stone roses onto the victims of the Liberation, smashed gaping graves and a solitary column supporting a cracked and mossgrown urn. Babalu jumped aside as he glanced into a vault and a macabre female bust glared back, bathed in a chilling blue light from a stained-glass cross-shaped window behind, a withered pink wreath suspended eerily above her head. He had forgotten that she was there.

The flurry of blossom was now abetted by a whirring mist of greenfly and midges. They tickled his sweaty face, stuck to his lips and slipped behind the lenses of his Ray-Bans. He waved them away impatiently and pressed on.

Scrub-a-Dub-Dub! Scrub-a-Dub-Dub! Materialising from behind a tent-shaped monument, the dome of the Columbarium beyond, a workman in blue overalls was scrubbing away at the letters on a headstone. Babalu could only see two letters of the name on the headstone because the man was blocking his view: first a 'J', then an 'O'. Scrub-a-Dub-Dub! Beside him was a man with a head like an old potato who – though he was in plain clothes – looked like a gendarme. He peered down into the crepuscular pit of an open grave, squared off with planks and wooden struts, and jotted something hurriedly in a notebook before moving away. The workman set about feeding ropes into the pit. 'Someone going in? Or someone coming out?' thought Babalu, but there was no time to hang around to satisfy his mild curiosity.

A grey cat shot across Babalu's path from right to left. He veered aside to follow it. There were cats everywhere in Père Lachaise, though they rarely trespassed outside their own division. There were the musicians' cats, the writers' cats, the cats of the Marshals of the Empire, and so on. And they were kept well-fed by the crazy old women who wandered the necropolis with plastic bags full of scraps – the *mamans chatomanes*, the cat-crazy mums, as they were known. The grey cat leaped under the catafalque of Sarah Bernhardt's tomb and stared with electrical green eyes from the concrete coffin below: Bernhardt who, when alive, slept in a rosewood coffin in her home.

Babalu emerged onto the intersection with the chemin des Anglais, where chivalric crests and pyramidal follies cluttered around the statue of the Good Shepherd. He was getting warmer.

Turning left where a green roadsign announced in white lettering 'Avenue Greffülhe, 42^{e} Division', a cobbled street bordered with yew trees, he slackened his pace as he came to the brilliant white mausoleum and green water-pump on the corner of the avenue Transversale No. 2. He approached the corner gingerly, almost on tiptoe, and peeped round.

No-one about. Business was not brisk today! But he had time, all the time in the world. He could wait. Unless, of course, person or persons unknown had already been.

He reconnoitred again – the coast was clear – and scurried along the avenue.

1-2-3-4 – the horizontal figure of Victor Noir was fifteen along on the right, the green boots of his recumbent bronze protruding surreally, as if the grave-diggers had forgotten to inter him, between the dull mausoleum of the Familles Boudot et Thierry and the white De Ycaza folly which sprouted winged cherubs with eagles' bodies on all four corners.

Victor Noir. This was the tomb to which Babalu always returned. He gazed admiringly at the effigy of the youthful journalist, shot in a duel on the 10th of January 1870 by Prince Pierre Bonaparte after being caught with his wife. He was sculpted by Dalor as he had fallen, his top hat lying next to him on its side, a bullet-hole in his chest and his clothing extravagantly *déboutonné*. Everything about him was unbuttoned – his frock coat, his jacket, his shirt, even his trousers. And everything about him was verdigris, that mouldy aeruginous green that afflicts alloys of copper and tin. Everything, that is, except for one conspicuous spot – a prominent swelling, a tumescence, at the groin. Victor, *in articulo mortis*, was rampant; Victor was erect. This was at once an indecorous effect of rigor mortis and Exhibit A, his instrument of crime. There it was, for all to see – sculpted with Parisian gallows' humour.

It had been a *cause célèbre* and the bronze had been financed by national subscription. And so, since 1870, the tomb had become a place of pilgrimage for the women of Paris. Those who were unrequited in love; those who wished to become pregnant; daughters on behalf of their widowed mothers; mothers on behalf of their virginal daughters; even those who wished their lovers to be shot dead – all paid a visit to Victor Noir. He was the secret fertility symbol of Paris, a deity of erotic love, and his tomb had become a wishing tomb, for every day flowers and messages accumulated in his discarded hat. It was this that drew Babalu and enthralled him. This was the spot in Paris where the Religion of Love was alive, the 'omphalos' of the city. Here Babalu could help the living, not just the dead. Doubting perhaps Victor's posthumous ability to fulfil the lofty commissions entrusted to him, Babalu would – whenever he could – empty the hat and where possible act on behalf of the forlorn or hopeful ladies, more often than not by informing a man that he was sought after. He was their messenger too, their fixer. A *despachante*. Here he could make himself useful. He would watch them deliver their billets-doux then follow them home to establish who they were: the notes did not always run to supplying names and addresses.

And there had certainly been enough to keep him busy. Little Inès, for example, who had fallen in love with her dentist. The latter had pulled two molars because of her bad gingivitis and she'd sent a dozen red roses – anonymously – that very day. But all was to no avail. It took a note to Victor to set things right. Babalu visited the dentist and explained the situation, man to man. Now Inès had the finest crowns and dentures in Belleville and no-one had to tell her to say 'Ahhhh!' Or what about Sophie and Pierre? He could hardly forget them! Pierre was an estate agent and Sophie visited flats with him as often as three times a week. She had turned down so many for the most trifling reasons that Pierre had put her down as a pest. But a call from Babalu did the trick and solved the flat problem virtually overnight. Of course there were failures too, and screwballs. Those salacious fantasies of a male domestic servant for an unattainable policeman, for instance, knocked off in a spidery hand on the back of postcards. He couldn't make head or tail of them, nor did he want to. He simply threw them in a bin. But on the whole there was good work to be done, and Babalu was there to do it.

He scratched himself in the small of the back, then bent down and peered into the sombre cavity of Victor's topper. So far, nothing today! Only a bedraggled carnation. He would have to wait.

He crossed the avenue and took up his usual look-out post, seated on a well-concealed tomb. He checked his watch. It was eleven. It might be a long wait, there was no telling. But he doubted it. He rarely had to wait long. Nevertheless, he listened to his Walkman with one earphone while he waited. Only one, mind you. The other ear had work to do too.

At eleven-thirty precisely he heard the distinctive crunch of stilettos on gravel. He crouched down as far as his ballooning belly would allow. Whoever she was, at this moment her eyes were certain to be swivelling anxiously in their sockets ensuring that her own coast was clear. He could imagine every movement of her body, every nervous twitch of her head. He held his breath and waited.

After a few seconds he peered round slowly, ever so slowly. She had her back to him. It was a woman in a tight arsenic green skirt, a bolero jacket of the same material, and a black peaked cap – a baseball cap, worn backwards, after the Holden Caulfield fashion. With a sudden movement she hitched up her dress and straddled the recumbent Victor Noir. Babalu raised his Ray-Bans and a knowing smile plumped out his cheeks. How many times had he seen this before? Not all of them went the whole hog. The timid ones simply teetered for a few moments on the toe-tip of one of his boots, or prudishly patted the tumescence. This one was sitting square on Victor's crotch, polishing the family metalware. Her backside slid like an oarsman's in a rowing-eight.

Despite appearances, this was a purely symbolic act. It lasted no more than a few seconds. It ended with a familiar French curse. She seemed to have pulled a muscle.

Babalu retreated cautiously as she dismounted the bronze and picked up her handbag, a black leather affair with gold chain and buckle. This was the moment he had been waiting for. Was she going to open the bag? As she looked about her for a second time he was so paralysed with muscular tension that he could have been mistaken by a myopic passer-by for another caprice of the monumental mason. He would not have been the only oddity in the cemetery. There was a pelican, a Montgolfier hot-air balloon, and a lifelike girl with bobbed Twenties' hairstyle reading a book. Why not an overweight black Brazilian with El Greco eyes and a pair of Ray-Bans perched on his forehead?

The gold buckle of her handbag clicked open, a hand flitted in and out of Victor's topper and in a trice she was off, slightly unsteady on her high heels.

Babalu waited until she was just out of earshot, then streaked across the avenue. Despite his bulk there was an almost balletic lightness about his movement. He retrieved the small sealed envelope from the bronze hat where she had deposited it and made after her, dodging in and out between the monuments like a seasoned – though still balletic – commando.

Damn!

Two catwomen emerged from behind a mawkish statue of a dead mother mourned by a tearful child. They stared in surprise, then suspicion, at Babalu as he bobbed and weaved. He slowed down and began flexing his arms, chopping the air and huffing and puffing in an attempt to pass himself off as an eccentric ju-jitsu fanatic, doing battle with invisible regiments of oriental combatants. The old birds linked arms and scuttled hastily away.

By now the arsenic green two-piece was disappearing round the corner past the gold-domed Columbarium with its sinister black-stacked chimneys. Babalu put everything he'd got into it and raced up to the corner, his mammiform pectorals and belly wobbling madly. But his mass and momentum were no match for a long stride.

When he got to the corner she was already leaving the cemetery by the Porte de la Dhuys. He raced past the big memorials to the war-dead and came to the white and green pillar of a poorbox – *Tronc pour les Pauvres de Paris.* He was dreadfully unfit, his body douched with sweat, and stopped momentarily to regain his breath, pulling a brown bandanna out of his pocket to swab the moisture from his eyes.

She was well on her way towards the place Gambetta, hips swinging and handbag bouncing against her side. He groaned and propelled himself after her. In the place Gambetta she paused to look in a shop window and he gained a little ground, but by the time he'd reached the square she was already disappearing into the mouth of the Metro.

Now he'd got her! She would have to wait at least two minutes for a train. He bounced down the steps after her, plunging his hand into his back trouser pocket. No! He was out of Metro tickets. Could he jump over the barrier? It was like asking an elephant to pole-vault – and besides, what if he were caught? His visa out of date. No working papers. It was too risky. He felt quickly in his trouser pocket and found a ten-franc piece. One man ahead of him at the ticket window, a woman at his side. There was no reason to worry.

'*Nein, nein! Zwei Fahrkarten. Warum verstehen sie nicht?*'

The RATP employee was staring at the German tourist with the insolent assurance of one who watches the world through bullet-proof glass.

'*Zwei! Bitte schön!*'

The ticket-seller answered in obstinate French. '*Désolé, je ne comprends rien. Revenez quand vous parlerez le français.*'

The German, wracked with frustration, held up two fingers in a manner that might have been misunderstood by an English official.

'*Bon d'accord! Il fallait le dire. Deux tickets, c'est ça?*'

'*Ja ja! Wieviel kostet das?*'

'*Comment?*'

'*Wieviel?*'

'*Je ne comprends rien . . .*'

Babalu was performing a little variation on the Saint Vitus dance. His blood was bubbling with impatience. When he finally got his ticket he charged through the turnstile but immediately realised that he didn't know which way to turn. There were three possibilities: the lines to Porte des Lilas, Gallieni and Pont de Lavallois Becon. It would have to be a gamble. He chose Gallieni. He hurtled down the steps and, as he arrived on the platform, he saw her distantly on the opposite side, boarding the Pont de Lavallois train.

He crashed down onto a red plastic chair and mopped his brow. It was too bad. He didn't normally lose them like this. Didn't they realise that he was doing this for them? He had the depressing feeling that he was losing his touch. Now he would never know who she was or where she lived, that was the important thing. Unless she paid a return visit. And even if she did, how was he to ensure that he was there at the same time? He couldn't *live* in the cemetery, could he? Let's face it, he thought, he did his best for the lovelorn ladies – *and* for Victor Noir – but this one had got away.

He sat there despondently for a minute, waiting for his breathing to return to normal. Then he remembered the letter. Pulling the crumpled envelope from his pocket, he turned it round in his hand. A name was typewritten with an odd incompleteness on each side. On the front of the envelope it was addressed to `Vctor Nor` while the back flap bore the name `Phlp Kovacs`, surrounded by a sketchy lipstick heart.

Babalu sighed and popped in his earphones. Soon he was tapping his foot to a cool bossa nova beat. A train drew up at his platform and he watched as it disgorged and devoured passengers then accelerated away into the coal-black hole of the tunnel. After a while he caught the side of his plump little finger under the corner of the gummed flap and – whistling along to Gilberto Gil – flicked it upwards, tearing open the neat white envelope.

3

'A TYPEWRITER!' EXCLAIMED the police officer, raising the white tufts of his eyebrows.

'Yes,' said Kovacs. He shifted uneasily in his seat and tried to avoid the official's eager gaze, fixing his attention instead on a huge wall-chart of the Paris arrondissements which was stippled with blue, red, yellow and green map pins arranged in a pattern similar to those used by opticians to check for colour-blindness. Beneath it was an attractive old brown leather armchair. There was an exaggerated alacrity in his questioner's manner as if he expected a hilarious punchline to materialise at any moment. He was the most unhealthy person Kovacs could ever remember seeing. Damp patches of pungent sweat bled into his shirt at the armpits and his skin was the colour and texture of an indeterminate putrefying vegetable. Wet strings of hair had been raked pathetically across the large balding pate. He seemed inordinately pleased to have company. Perhaps, thought Kovacs, he never left that grey, institutional office in the Commissariat, tigered with shadows from the broken jalousie that hung in limp defiance of the day across the sun-blanched window.

'Nothing else?' said the policeman, disappointed. 'Just a typewriter?' He smiled desperately. He wanted, it seemed, to delve into every crevice of conversational possibility.

'That's right. That's all they took. It was a day before I noticed that it had been taken.'

'You have other things of value, I presume.'

'Yes. A television. CD player. Pictures. Even a portable computer. None of that was touched.'

The policeman was filing a report on the terminal on the desk before him. The keys rattled as he typed with his index fingers. He was hunched close to the screen and his face phosphoresced with its green, submarine light.

'Can you describe this – this *typewriter* to me?'

'It was a Remington. I kept it in my bedroom. A 1960s' portable model, in burgundy-coloured metal. It had sentimental value. My ex-wife gave it to me on the day that we were married. I'd had it for ages. I hardly ever used it, except for the odd letter. In fact, it was broken.'

'Broken?' The question was fired, again, with an avid hunger in his voice, as if a new and appetising piece of evidence had been unearthed.

'Yes. There was no letter "I". The metal hammer on the end of the key had broken off. I can't even remember when it happened. I must have hit it too hard on some occasion, or used that key too often.'

'Broken,' the policeman repeated under his breath, mulling it over. 'And why – why, Mr Kovacs, have you waited *one week* – one week *to the day* – before coming to see me?'

Kovacs winced. The question seemed to imply a calculated breach of good manners on his part.

'I, I didn't think there was anything to be done. I wasn't going to make an insurance claim because I didn't want to lose the no-claims bonus. Anyway, the typewriter was valueless. I couldn't see how reporting it to the police could help.'

'And yet,' said the policeman, resting his chin on his fists like a chess player, 'here you are now!' There was a note of demented triumph in his voice as he exposed the paradox.

'Yes. It must seem odd, I admit. You see, originally I didn't want to make an official report because nothing much had been taken. But now I *do* want to make an official report for the same reason. The thing is, it was not an ordinary burglary. And – well, other things have been happening. Since the burglary I mean.'

'Other things?'

'Phone calls. Anonymous. The person doesn't speak, they just hang up. Or hang *on*. The same on the answerphone.'

The policeman stretched back importantly, locking his omoplates over the top of his chair. It occurred to Kovacs that what his head looked like was a grey potato in a sunless cellar, soft, puffy and ready to sprout: the eyebrows and the strings of flaxen hair suggested radicles, pallid shoots of growth.

When the man spoke it was with great deliberation and seriousness, weighing his words. A fugitive fear of ridicule swept through Kovacs' mind.

'Who, Mr Kovacs? Do you have any idea *who*?'

'None whatsoever. I am a relatively private person. There are no scores to settle in my life, no enemies.'

'Are any of your friends enemies?' asked the Inspector.

'No,' said Kovacs, unthinkingly, 'I realise – '

'Yes?'

'I realise there's nothing you can do, of course. You're not going to come round and take fingerprints!'

'Why not?' the other man asked brusquely.

'I – I don't know. Because it's trivial, I suppose. It's not exactly a bank robbery.'

'Mr Kovacs, this matter is clearly distressing you. I wouldn't call that "trivial". Some things are more important than money, don't you think? Your health, your feeling of well-being for example. My own health is not what I would wish it to be, so I can put myself in your shoes. We all want to live in a safe society, not one where our sense of security and happiness is constantly undermined by – by fears and anxieties. If, by taking fingerprints, I can set your mind at rest, then that is what I shall do.'

Kovacs was silenced for a moment by the policeman's prodigal code of honour.

'We had one astonishing case,' mused the Inspector, relaxing into anecdotage, 'a cat-burglar by the name of Deray. He never left fingerprints because he didn't have any. You see, he had worked for years as a lathe-operator in a joiner's workshop in Saint-Denis and the machine had obliterated his fingerprints. The fingers were worn smooth.'

'Then how did you catch him?'

'We didn't, unfortunately,' sighed the Inspector.

Kovacs wrinkled his brow. There was obviously more to the story than met his eye. He bypassed a couple of burning questions, however, and returned to his own predicament.

'I was wondering, really, what you would suggest. Are there any measures I should take?'

'Get a *porte blindée.* A reinforced door. It's expensive but worth it. You know what they look like – a steel plate behind the main door and it locks in three directions.'

'Yes, I was thinking of doing that.'

'And have a safe fitted. *Un coffre fort.* For your valuables – the irreplaceable things.'

'Anything else?'

'You could go ex-directory.'

'I'm already on the *liste rouge.* That's partly what has aroused my suspicions.'

'You suspect that you were burgled by someone you know?'

'If the burglar and the anonymous caller are one and the same. Yes.'

'Well, you can always change your number on the *liste rouge.* But then you'd have to go to the bother of informing your friends . . . if you have any.'

The last remark was cast in as an aside, almost an afterthought. Kovacs knitted his brow and looked questioningly at the policeman but he had already moved on to other matters.

The man snapped his fingers in self-reproach. '*Zut!* Did I offer you a coffee when you came in? Did I?'

'A coffee? No, I don't think so. Why?'

'It's so impolite of me. I'm sorry. I am not a great coffee drinker myself – it's a dreadful carcinogen. Perhaps you would like one now?' He made to get up from his chair.

'No, really, it's not necessary. I should be getting along soon. I just wanted to ask you – about the phone. Is there any way of finding out who is calling?'

'There is a system called Caller ID. It reveals the caller's number even before you pick up the handset. And there's another system, where you dial a number after having been called and you're told the number of your last caller. But neither is on the French market yet. We *could* put a tracer on your phone . . . it's an expensive business . . .'

'Well I wouldn't want to put you –'

'No, of course not. This is not Watergate, or Clintongate, or Squidgygate, is it Mr Kovacs? Not yet, anyway. Perhaps we should just wait and see. If you have any more trouble, come and see me straight away.' He withdrew a card from the top drawer of the desk and scribbled something on the back.

'I'll give you my home and cellphone numbers, as well,' he said and passed it across. The name on the card was 'Laroche'.

'Monsieur Laroche,' said Kovacs, picking it up.

'*Inspector* Laroche,' the man corrected him.

'Of course. I'm sorry.'

'You were not to know.'

Something appeared to be niggling Laroche. He had slipped his hand between two of his shirt buttons and was rubbing his chest. The pose was inadvertently Napoleonic and Kovacs resisted an inclination to smile.

'You are not French, are you Mr Kovacs?'

'No. English. I've lived and worked here for fifteen years.'

'Married?'

'I *was* married. I was married for eight years to a French woman. We divorced three years ago.'

'You never considered changing your nationality?'

'No,' said Kovacs, somewhat nonplussed. 'There was no need.'

'Of course not. We are all Europeans now, aren't we? Good Europeans, and bad Europeans – we're all Europeans.' He sighed quietly to himself. 'I suppose it's all for the best. And now the Channel Tunnel! Any day now.' He looked up, smiling vaguely at Kovacs, as if he expected an opinion.

'Yes.'

'The *Channel Tunnel*!' he repeated for emphasis. 'Back and forth, back and forth. Trains going under the sea. Everybody moving, moving about all the time. The Englishman has his holiday home in the Dordogne. There is even a company that transports Normandy barns, lock, stock and barrel, over to England – stealing our heritage. Meanwhile, the Frenchman goes to London to see the Queen – very proud on her big horse! You English! You think we are going to give you rabies!'

Kovacs tweaked back the sleeve of his jacket and glanced at his watch. 'I really must be going,' he apologised.

Laroche frowned slightly and leaned over to his right, pressing a key on the computer.

'Before you go, I must see your *carte de séjour*. I need the number for the report.'

Kovacs fumbled for his wallet and drew out his resident's permit. Outside, the sun had advanced perceptibly; a diagonal strip of light crossed the policeman's tuberous face. His tired bureaucratic eyes scanned the card and he entered the number on the terminal. Somewhere in hyperspace a databank had been accessed and a new window with an exclamation mark in the middle of it flashed open on the screen. Laroche curled his upper lip and muttered something inaudible before checking the validity date on the card and turning again to Kovacs.

'It's very strange,' he said.

'What is?'

'This. This *carte de séjour*. We have no record of you. There is no record corresponding to this number.'

Again Kovacs shifted in his chair and his gaze wandered, alighting on a Missing Person poster on the far wall in the centre of which was a colour photo of a woman about his age. She had long, dark hair and her cast of features suggested Mediterranean origins – Sicilian perhaps – he wasn't sure what. Her eyes were an intense Arctic blue – they were intelligent, tense and anguished and there was a beseeching light in them that sent a physical pang of sadness through him. He felt he had known her, somewhere in the past, and he found himself questioning the purport of the poster: wasn't this person *seeking* rather than being sought?

'According to our archives,' Laroche continued, 'you don't exist!'

The man was beginning to annoy Kovacs. His every remark ended on a rising tone of astonishment, as if to say 'And what do you think of that?'

'My papers are in order,' Kovacs said flatly. 'It must be a computer error.'

'You wouldn't, by any chance, have your passport on you, would you? These damn machines are constantly letting us down. It would help me set the record straight.'

'As it happens, I've just sent my passport in to the British Embassy for renewal. I have –,' he dipped again into the wallet, 'an English driving licence.'

Laroche took the licence and his yellow eye rotated down in the white ribbon of sunlight.

'There's no photograph,' he said.

'No. There isn't on English driving licences. But there *is* a photograph on the *carte de séjour*.'

The policeman picked up the resident's permit again and flipped it over. 'Ah yes, of course!' he said. There was just a trace, a flicker of amusement as he looked at the photograph.

'You've changed!'

'I have, yes,' said Kovacs, barely concealing his irritation. 'That was taken five years ago. I had a moustache.'

Laroche held the permit at arm's length, smiling and cocking his head to one side. He looked from the photograph to Kovacs and back again.

'I think,' he said slowly, 'it was a mistake.'

'I beg your pardon?'

'It was a mistake to shave it off. You are the kind of man that a moustache *suits*. It looks so – ' He searched for the word. '– So *British*, I suppose!' He pronounced the adjective in the characteristic French manner, with equal stress on both syllables and the slightest hint of mockery.

Kovacs was silent.

Laroche sighed again and tapped the edge of the plasticated card against the top of the desk. 'May I hang on to this?'

'Sorry?'

'If I'm going to get to the bottom of the computer error,' he explained, 'I'll need to retain it for the time being. Just a few days. I'll post it back to you once we've reinstated your file.'

'If you must, you must, I suppose.'

Laroche scribbled out what looked like a receipt, folded it in four and pushed it over.

'Keep this. And Mr Kovacs – don't worry about all of these trials and tribulations. If anything new crops up, just give me a ring. I am very keen to help you. We have our own – how shall we say? – *entente cordiale* now, haven't we?' He shook Kovacs clammily by the hand, then added with a rather theatrical flourish, 'France and England! Once joined, but torn apart by continental drift. Two halves, as someone once said, of a perfect civilisation.'

Laroche saw Kovacs to the door with a great show of cordiality and stood watching him as he retreated down the institutional corridor. From a distant office the sweet sound of the 'In Paradisum' section of Fauré's Requiem could be heard. The second he disappeared from view the smile on the policeman's face abruptly slackened and dropped, as if a tiny spring somewhere in the concealed mechanism of his emotions had been stretched just a millimetre too far and had snapped.

'England!' he muttered, as the door swung shut behind him, '*la perfide Albion* . . .'

Friday was one of Kovacs' free days, though he sometimes decided to go in to the College on administrative matters. May was soon to crossfade into June. There were loose ends to tie up before the end of term but he had time on his hands and the long summer vacation spread before him like a serene blue lake on which he was soon to launch his little one-man boat. The S. S. *Arsoleia*, as he liked to call that imaginary vessel. His thoughts were turning to the book he had begun to write and to the misanthropic pleasures of solitude and self-sufficiency. Céline was only a marginal presence, hovering on the periphery of his preoccupations. She would not be free from the fashion industry until August.

The first scent of summer and its windborne allergens was already in the air. He put his hands in his pockets and walked home from the Commissariat de Police in the rue Louis Blanc by an unhurried, roundabout route, idling beside the canal to watch the freshly painted pleasurecraft, the fishermen with their boxes of tackle and the aerobatic courtship rituals of the city birds. He had a sudden whim for a *panaché*, a drink that he invariably associated with the approach of summer. He slaked his thirst at a café near the Hôtel du Nord before crossing the canal back and mounting the stairs to his flat.

On the mat, outside his door, he found a PTT form notifying him that the postman had called in his absence with a registered package: he could pick it up from the post office after four in the afternoon. To one side of the mat, there was a potted chrysanthemum and a bottle of Calvados. He picked up the gifts and carried them in to the living-room table. Though he looked hard, no note accompanied them. There was no sign of their provenance.

The table was cluttered with boxes of stuff that he had been sorting through, a consequence of the burglary. In a variation on Pelmanism, he had searched the flat not for things but for *absences* – the lacunae of stolen goods. Finding none, apart from the typewriter, he discovered instead caches of memorabilia, letters and photo albums, which creaked open like old doors onto the unique random blend of his past. They too were 'absences', glimpses of non-existence. Now in the middle of all this stood a potted chrysanthemum and a bottle of Calvados. He fetched a glass from the kitchen and poured out a tot, downing it in one, *coup sec.* It was autumn in spring, a rich windfall of apples across the palate – obliterating the aftertaste of cheap lemonade shandy. The spirit immediately went to his head. He relaxed and helped himself to another, pondering, as he did so, the potted plant.

A chrysanthemum.

It had large, composite blooms, the petals tinted with mauve. He had never liked chrysanthemums, and it slowly dawned on him why. The reason was perfectly simple. In England potted chrysanthemums were quite acceptable gifts. In France, on the other hand, they were flowers of death, as were carnations, bought on All Souls' Day to adorn the graves of the dear departed. In France it was a classic blunder on the part of the English dinner guest to present a potted chrysanthemum or a bunch of carnations to the horrified host and hostess. In England the converse gaffe would be to offer lilies. So *why* – he was beginning to wonder – should someone offer him a chrysanthemum? Anonymously, too. This was no social *faux pas*. The burglary, the phone calls . . . was the same 'well-wisher' behind it all? He sniffed the Calvados suspiciously and pushed the glass aside, placing the bottle and the plant behind him on the mantelpiece where he would not have to look at them.

Kovacs was rigorously methodical. He hated sloppiness and half-measures. The boxes and albums of photographs before him were carefully ordered, each bearing a sticker with the precise dates in his copperplate hand and signed off with his name and a conclusive paraph, the ceremonious flourish with which he finished the signature. In this manner each recorded phase of his existence had been underwritten.

It was all there, to be quickened at the turn of a page. The schooldays at Portland Upper that now evoked only the sweaty smell of plimsolls and an image of ink-stained hands. The school motto, stitched on the left tit of his blazer, had also lodged in his memory: *Per ardua ad astra*. Then there were the summer holidays at the bungalow in Cromer, beachcombing on the tide-ribbed shore (being an only child, this world had been his alone – his and his parents'). The successive transitions were acted out like the Signs of the Cross, a veritable Via Dolorosa reaching Gethsemane at last. University, a degree in linguistics. The girlfriends, grinning in ballgowns or screaming from rollercoasters and Vienna Waltzers. The first job, as a *lecteur* at the University of Toulouse. The return to England and back – back again to France, to Paris, the College, the marriage, the divorce. Yes, there was even a last photograph of him and Anne together, taken less than a week after the divorce, attending – of all things – a friend's wedding. Only the last three years were sparsely documented. All of the photographs belonging to this period could be found in one slim album and they were mostly of a neutral character, free of life's obscure objects of desire, for the events of his second bachelorhood were largely mental events, invisible to the conventional lens. Marriage, on the other hand, had meant holidays, and holidays meant snapshots. So, sure enough, here they were – in their hundreds, he realised with a gasp. They were relics of expired emotion, bearing silent witness to the look of love. They invaded him with sadness and quantified his loss. But if blame were to be attributed he need look no further than himself. He and Anne had divorced on grounds of adultery, *his* adultery – and yet he had never been unfaithful in eight years of marriage. He had 'confessed' to his wife that he had been having an affair. It was a lie. No mistress was produced – there was none – but the spurious confession was accepted; she was hurt, deeply hurt; and divorce proceedings began. Why had he done it? He flipped open an album dated 1984 and there she was, in her Courrèges bathing suit, riding a beach donkey on the Ile de Ré.

There was no denying her looks. The grey, mangy donkey

and the tendency of Kodachrome to favour the warm end of the spectrum conspired to breathe preternatural life into the vivid image of the departed woman. She was holding the reins and laughing coquettishly at the camera, her dark hair tucked up under a sunhat – unusual, for Anne had never been a lover of hats. Her eyes were a glacial blue, her chest was fuller, her hips wider, than he remembered them. She had often been mistaken for a Sicilian, and there was indeed Sicilian blood somewhere along the line. He could almost smell her, the orangey smell of the brand of suntan lotion she used. He could almost hear the brassy timbre of her voice with its playful, taunting edge. What was she saying to him, as he took the photograph? Her voice contending with the crash of the Atlantic, the laughter of children, the skirl of seagulls and the tick-tock of the couple behind her, batting a rubber ball to and fro. What was she saying? Her words were on the edge of his consciousness, just out of reach.

Naturally enough, she took her leave. He had heard nothing from her in three years, though he knew she was still in Paris. It was a city she thrived upon and from which her work as a theatre director drew its sustenance. From time to time she was panned or praised in the *Nouvel Obs* or *Libération* and he followed her career vicariously, sharing her joys and frustrations. But some stubborn English reticence or pride held him back from physically attending the shows. There was still love there, he acknowledged, but it should be left to perish. That's what he had decided, and there was no going back.

So why had he done it? Why had he lied? It had not been a disastrous marriage. Sexually and personally they had been compatible enough in the ordinary run of things. She had that way of creating a world of events that turned merrily round herself at its axis. It was quite unconscious on her part. It was a way that many women have. But was it through lassitude that he had allowed himself at first to fall easily into place, to lapse into her orbit? Was it indulgence that, for a time at least, had made him so tractable – so *laissez faire*? It was as if her identity, her indivisible 'self', had natural ascendancy, a magnetic field of being that his own identity, his own indivisible 'self', could neither counteract nor counterbalance in its weakness because . . . but that was where his reasoning, such as it was, ran out of steam. She took the high road, and he took the low road and nobody got anywhere first.

And so he had lied. He had lied and she had believed him, and that was that. Why *do* people get divorced anyway? – in droves, it sometimes seemed to him. For his part, maybe he had simply had enough. In his head he tried to urge the matter into words again, though words alone never ceased to shortchange him on this issue. Anne, the directorial Anne, had pushed him onto the tellurian stage and into the workaday limelight. Marriage had been play-acting, but there was nothing wrong with that. He was, ironically, quite prepared for the theatricality of matrimony, but he was not prepared to be miscast. He wanted breadth, barn-storming, burlesque. He wanted scope. Not the petty fixity of the cameo role. And in that, Anne had failed him. She had failed to free his 'soul' – 'soul', he thought, tonguing the unwelcome syllable on the roof of his mouth, for want of a better word! But hadn't they all failed, both before and since? Céline fell dismally into the same pattern. Hadn't they all failed? The women? Some lines from George Herbert crossed his mind: *Dare to be true: nothing can need a lie; / A fault, which needs it most, grows two thereby.*

He snapped the album shut and held it upright, biting hard on his lower lip, and from between its pages another photograph, much older, fell between his fingers. What was that doing there? It was Philip. Not himself, but the other Philip. His uncle, his father's brother, who had been killed in the D-day landings. He was photographed in battle fatigues on an armoured car. Kovacs turned the picture over. It was dated 'May 1944' – just before the landings. A curious *frisson* passed through him. He looked quickly at his Filofax which lay open to one side of the boxes of snapshots. It was, indeed, exactly half a century since the photo had been taken, and hadn't he only been reading that morning in the paper that preparations were well under way in Normandy to commemorate the event in June? But it was not this that had struck Kovacs as strange, or not *only* this. It was the fact that it was May 27th, his wedding anniversary, eleven years to the day. Overcoming his previous apprehensions, he retrieved the bottle of Calvados from the mantelpiece and helped himself to another – and then another. He began to lose count.

He woke sharply, still seated at the table, his head resting on his folded arms.

A ferocious banging resounded through the room. He sat up, startled. It was coming from behind the mirror, behind the wall – from Monsieur Martin's vacated flat. A tiny headache, a reef-knot of nerves behind the forehead, reminded him of the Calvados. His vision and thoughts were a touch swimmy, though this could just as well be attributable to his rude awakening. The banging ceased then resumed with increased vigour, travelling now up, now down the wall, now left, now right. Exasperated, he took off his shoe and, holding it by the toe, hit the hard heel repeatedly against the wall. The banging promptly stopped and Kovacs sat down relieved.

In the hollow silence that ensued, he recalled his dream of a few seconds before with veridic clarity. He was walking in the Jardin Marco Polo, near the Jardin du Luxembourg, and came to a halt beside the fountain designed by Carpeaux across the road from the Closerie des Lilas. Eight turtles spat water inwards towards four pairs of rearing fish-tailed horses. Above this curious bestiary was a group of four naked human figures, representing the continents, holding the globe of the Earth aloft. As he approached, one of the figures, a woman, turned and smiled. At first, the face was unmistakably that of the woman he had seen on the Missing Person poster in Laroche's office but under his gaze it cunningly transmuted into that of his ex-wife. The angle was such that the faces of the other three emblematic figures were concealed, though one of them was wearing a Red Indian head-dress.

Kovacs was in the habit of noting down his dreams while they were still fresh in his memory. In his experience whatever the stuff of dreams was made on it was invariably a slippery substance, sharply objectified in the mind one moment and gone the next, absconding through invisible portals into subliminal anti-matter. These data, of questionable utility though potentially relevant to his researches, he would enter into his portable computer. He was on the point of doing just this when the hammering began again, or rather three raps, sharp and peremptory. But the acoustics were different.

There was someone at the door.

A young couple stood in the hallway smiling gawkishly. They were dressed in dungarees and covered in flecks of white paint. Both were Germanic in appearance, blonde and fresh-faced with freckled complexions and limpid blue eyes that suggested mountains and hiking.

'I'm afraid our hammering annoyed you,' the man said. His French was perfect but inflected. He was not from Germany, but Alsace, Kovacs rapidly deduced.

'Oh, was it you?' said Kovacs. He was trying to get a grasp on things. 'I thought it came from next door, from Monsieur Martin's flat.'

A private look of incomprehension passed between the couple and the man took one step back. To his embarrassment, Kovacs realised that he was stinking of alcohol.

'We don't know any "Monsieur Martin",' the woman said, also with an Alsatian accent.

'No,' the man chipped in, 'but we *are* next door. We just arrived today. Perhaps Madame da Silva, the concierge, forgot to tell you. We're your new neighbours.'

'Oh!' It seemed appropriate to offer his hand.

'Better not,' said the man cheerfully, 'we're covered in paint! We're decorating the place, putting up shelves – that sort of thing. We can't move in properly here until all of that has been done.'

'Of course not.' Kovacs brushed aside his confusion, pulled his thoughts together. 'Oh, I'm so sorry. I banged on the wall with my shoe. I must explain. I was fast asleep and you woke me up – it was a kind of reflex action. I shouldn't have done that. You have every right to be putting up shelves in your own apartment!'

'Well, yes,' said the man, 'legally speaking I suppose we are not disturbing the peace, not before eleven anyway. But we really didn't mean to disturb you. We assumed that any neighbours would be out at work.'

'No, not always on a Friday. I don't always work on Fridays.'

'Perhaps we could come to some arrangement. If you told us when you were going out, we could –'

'No, no! Please! It was stupid of me. I wasn't fully awake. As I said, you have every right to decorate your flat. Please carry on. What *is* the time?' He looked at his watch. 'See – it's past four. I have to be going out anyway. Please carry on with your decorating. I can always wear those wax things for the ears – *Boules Quiès*, you know – or go upstairs. I have a duplex, you see, and the upstairs bedroom is very well insulated against noise.'

'Well, if you're sure . . .' said the man.

The woman, meanwhile, had been looking past Kovacs into the flat and now caught her husband by the shoulder-strap of his dungarees.

'Look,' she said, astonished, 'there's my chrysanthemum!'

All three of them turned round and stared at the potted plant on the mantelpiece.

'*Bon Dieu!*' said Kovacs. 'Is it *yours*?'

'Yes. We left it outside our front door while we were fetching our tools and painting gear in from the car,' she said.

'I – I must apologise. It was just here, wasn't it? I thought it was outside *my* front door. I thought it was a present.'

Again a look passed between the couple. He knew what they were thinking: who, in France, would give a chrysanthemum as a present? And he was immediately proved to be right.

'No. One of my wife's ancestors is buried at Père Lachaise. Since we were coming into Paris from the suburbs we decided to bring a plant for his tomb. We were wondering where it had got to!'

'As you can see,' said Kovacs, 'our front doors are very close together. Standing here, it didn't occur to me that it was outside your door as well as mine. Anyway, I didn't know you were here. I thought the flat was empty.'

'Of course,' he said, 'it was a perfectly natural mistake to make.'

The woman was still craning her neck to look into the room. 'There wasn't –?' she began.

'What?'

'– anything else? There wasn't anything *else*, was there?'

The truth suddenly dawned on Kovacs.

'Oh my God – the bottle of Calvados! That was yours too!'

The couple smiled affably and nodded.

'I'm afraid . . . I'm so sorry, but I'm afraid I've drunk some of it. I thought it was a present too. This is *so* – I really don't know how I can apologise to you enough . . .'

He fetched the plant and bottle, handing one to the woman and the other to the man. Two-thirds of the bottle had been drunk. He had drunk two-thirds of a bottle in three and a half hours – in the middle of the afternoon too. The couple were silent and he realised that they were making the same ineluctable computation.

'I – I must get you another one right now. Tell me, where did you buy it?'

'It comes directly from my uncle,' the woman said, her voice slightly strained. 'He's a producer in Normandy and it was a numbered bottle, from his cellar. They can't be bought over the counter.'

Kovacs expressed his regret with a pained expression.

'Look,' said the man, 'it really doesn't matter. Please – keep the bottle.' He handed it back to Kovacs. 'A gesture of friendship, now that we're neighbours. To apologise for the noise too.'

'Really, I can't . . .'

'You must. We insist, don't we Corinne?'

The woman nodded half-heartedly.

'What can I say? Thank you. Thank you very much indeed.'

'By the way,' the man recollected, 'we haven't introduced ourselves. I'm Gilles and this is my wife, Corinne.'

All three made a Pavlovian move to shake hands then, remembering the paint, aborted the gesture and laughed shyly.

'Kovacs. *Philip* Kovacs.' He noticed their ears prick up at the pronunciation of his first name. 'English,' he explained, 'if you hadn't guessed from the accent.'

'Actually, I think we *had*,' Corinne confessed, smiling.

'Listen, if there's anything I can do for you – anything you need – just knock. When you're settled in you must come round for dinner sometime.'

'We'd like that,' said Gilles, putting his hand on his wife's shoulder and moving towards their door.

'And thank you again!' added Kovacs, holding the bottle of Calvados in the air with a stupid blush on his face.

Kovacs shut the door on them and cursed himself repeatedly. He leaned against the wall and slid down until he was squatting on his haunches. Why hadn't he insisted on them taking the bottle of Calvados back? They had probably been looking forward to a tipple in the evening, once their exertions were over. But it was too late now – the public gesture had been made. He cupped a hand over his mouth and nose and breathed into it. There was no getting away from the smell of Calvados. They must have taken him for a dipsomaniac. A fine way to get to know your new neighbours.

There was something else. What was it? Something he had forgotten. He dug the heels of his shoes into his backside and tapped his head gently against the wall. It was past four, and he had to go out. Where? Of course! The post office. A registered package. Unless that was theirs too? He checked the name on the PTT form. At least that was his. He hadn't slipped up there.

He brushed his teeth and splashed on the most aromatic liquid in his arsenal of after-shaves and went out to the post office.

When he entered this or any urban French post office, he was immediately faced with a dilemma – or trilemma, or quadrilemma, or polylemma, to be more precise. The French had not adopted the judicious English system of having one queue at the head of which the customer looks for the flashing arrow indicating the next available window for service. Something in the French resisted the blinding good sense of the Anglo-Saxon system. Perhaps it bled life of contingency and unpredictability, mainstays of the Latin mind. Instead there were some seven or eight short queues and it was always a lottery as to which one would advance rapidly and which would not. It was a lottery Kovacs habitually lost – as, indeed, he lost the state lottery. Each week, he faithfully registered a haphazard combination of digits, though with ever-decreasing optimism. The same defeatism marked his attitude to the post office queues.

In the post office, it was possible to simply count the number of people and head directly for the shortest queue, but more often than not this purely mathematical calculation proved sophistical. It failed, in short, to account for the human factor. The human factor itself, however, lay beyond the bounds of calculation. One would have imagined that children, the elderly and tourists were obvious candidates for dithering incomprehension and time-wasting. But, at least in Kovacs' case, it was always the well-dressed, snappy-looking woman in her twenties, with an intelligent face and alert eyes, carrying an envelope for which she evidently required only *one* stamp, it was always this person who turned out to be impressively dilatory, for whatever reason – a crippling speech impediment, an impossibly complex procedural problem, an incorrectly completed form. However, were Kovacs – recognising and acting on this paradox – to revert to the queue of nonagenarians, infants and Lithuanian backpackers, his initial *prima facie* expectations would instantly be confirmed and a half-hour wait would ensue. It was a jinx, a hex. Thus it was always with a sagging spirit that he made his choice. Once made, he inspected the backs of the heads in front of him for phrenological omens of mental inertia. It filled him with malefic intolerance towards the unknown citizens before him and for this, in his more lucid moments, he would sometimes quietly chastise himself.

Today, the portents were positively apocalyptic. There were three geriatrics ahead of him and a hollow-eyed man with a tic who was obviously on day-release from a psychiatric institution. Had they been carrying black cats and open umbrellas, shuffling forwards over spilt salt and under ladders, their persons draped in inverted horseshoes and owls' gizzards whilst outside the sky rained comets, the auspices could not have been more depressing. It was to his complete surprise, then, that he reached the head of the queue in less than three minutes. His humour took a bullish upturn.

'Yes?'

The woman behind the counter had had a long afternoon and the signs of repetitive strain injury invested her musculature. She performed her functions, even down to that 'Yes?', with the usual robotic movements and utterances that afflict the bureaucrat. Kovacs remembered the insinuating friendliness of Laroche that morning and knew which approach he preferred: hers. He handed her the PTT form giving details of the package. She disappeared to a back room and reappeared with the official-looking envelope.

'Registered letter. I need your *carte d'identité*.'

There is a psychological phenomenon known as *jamais vu*,

meaning the illusion of having never experienced a situation when in fact it is quite familiar. This was Kovacs' initial condition, but in a matter of milliseconds it was mutating into its more celebrated opposite: *déjà vu.*

'I'm not French. I don't have a *carte d'identité*,' he stated calmly.

'A passport, then. Any identification papers.'

For the second time that day, Kovacs ransacked his wallet.

'I have a driving licence.'

'That'll do.'

He extracted the document and handed it over. There was an aura of optimism about the act but in his palpitating heart a more accurate prognosis had already been made.

'There is no photograph,' she said, looking up at him.

'No, it's an English driving licence. They don't have photographs.'

'Then I can't accept it. Haven't you got a passport?'

Kovacs laughed nervously, looking at the British embassy stamp on the back of the registered letter. 'The problem is,' he said, as if letting her in on a joke, 'my passport is in *there*.' He pointed to the envelope. 'I sent in my old passport for renewal and that is the new one, by return of post.'

The woman's face was impassive. 'I still need to see some identification. It's the rules.'

Kovacs glanced over his shoulder. A lengthy queue was building up behind him and a number of its members were showing signs of stress.

'Couldn't *you* open it?' he pleaded. 'Here and now, in front of me?'

'I can't do that, Monsieur. It's against post office regulations. This letter can only be opened by the person to whom it is addressed. That is why the sender paid an additional sum in order to register it.'

'But *I* am the person to whom it is addressed.'

'So you say, but I have no proof of that.'

'Supposing,' Kovacs speculated, looking up at the ceiling in a pensive and accommodating mood, 'supposing I were to open it here in front of you. You would then be able to inspect the passport that is inside this envelope, check the photograph and details and you would have definitive proof that it was indeed my passport. What do you think?'

'Impossible,' she said. 'If there were no passport inside, and the packet was not for you, I would be unable to re-seal it and I would then be in breach of the regulations governing registered mail. I could lose my job.'

Kovacs gave up. 'Then what do *you* suggest I do? I've explained the situation to you.'

'If you're not French, you must have a *carte de séjour*. That would do for purposes of identification.'

Kovacs' morale had sunk to that of a laboratory rat. It was not the first time he had felt like this and, he knew, it would not be the last. He recalled a cartoon he had seen in a newspaper. Two rats have met in a maze. One asks for directions, and the other says: 'Sorry mate, I'm a stranger here myself.' Now what had the woman asked for? Oh yes! His *carte de séjour*.

'By one of life's unfortunate coincidences,' he began, labouring to keep his voice under control, 'I had to hand my *carte de séjour* in to the police this morning. They had had a computer error which wiped out my details and they needed the document to set things straight.'

'Didn't they give you a receipt?'

There was a luminous pause. 'As a matter of fact they *did*,' he remembered, brightening.

'Well that would do. An official receipt, on Commissariat paper with a signature. I suppose I could accept that.'

'Marvellous!' said Kovacs. 'I knew we'd find a way out of this little *impasse*!'

From his jacket pocket he retrieved the paper Laroche had passed him and handed it over to the lady behind the counter. She unfolded it, read it and stared at him blankly. At the same time one of her hands slipped under the counter and pressed a concealed button.

'Why are you showing me this?' she asked coldly. There was incipient panic in her face.

Kovacs grabbed the paper from her hand and read it. On the little sheet of otherwise pristine A5 paper Laroche had written *N'oubliez pas le coffre fort* – 'Don't forget the safe.'

They retired to a back office for nearly an hour. When the

whole situation had been explained to the post officer manager, who had been alerted by the concealed bell (and after a lengthy phone call to Laroche), it was agreed that Kovacs could have his envelope only once the original *carte de séjour* had been returned by the police. No immediately satisfactory solution could be found and, though Kovacs was not to know it, this was partly because the mixed fumes of Egoïste aftershave and vintage Calvados did little to inspire confidence in his arbitrator. Kovacs' probity was seriously in doubt. The lady behind the counter, meanwhile, was trembling, had tears in her eyes: the manager put his arm around her shoulders. Kovacs apologised clumsily to the two officials as he left the establishment, shying clear of the ravening eyes of a new set of customers.

'*Tout me nuit, et conspire à me nuire*,' he thought with Phèdre. It had been a hell of a day. It could hardly get any worse.

He walked home along the canal as the evening traffic was beginning to thicken. Car-horns added their clamour to the multifarious jungly sounds of late afternoon. He resolved to go to bed. A dose of sweet oblivion was called for, and tomorrow was another healing day.

As he entered his building, he was obliged to pass in front of the net-curtained windows of his concierge's *loge*, where an overweight grey Persian cat acted as sedentary sentinel. His concierge, Madame da Silva, was Portuguese, as many Paris concierges are. She was normally quiet as a mouse but this afternoon he could hear her screaming with laughter, a confused babble of high-pitched Portuguese words filling the courtyard outside. Counterpointing her voice, a tuba to her piccolo, was a man's voice – also discoursing gaily in Portuguese. Kovacs was reflecting that it was unusual for Madame da Silva to have visitors, let alone male visitors, given her age and semi-deafness, not to mention her partiality for fortified wines (which rendered her insensible to most means of communication), when the curtain flicked back smartly and the concierge's raddled face appeared. She knocked sharply on the glass with her knuckles, then came to the door.

'Good evening, Madame da Silva. What can I do for you?'

A powerful smell of the dry Sercial Madeira that she favoured preceded her, so it was with some self-assurance that Kovacs could approach, knowing that under such circumstances the vestigial traces of Calvados probably clinging to his person were unlikely to betray their presence, especially if the after-shave was doing its job. Madame da Silva, moreover, seemed utterly overcome. She was wiping tears of laughter from her eyes and chortling irrepressibly. He had never seen her in such a state.

'You wanted to see me?' he asked.

'Yes, Monsieur Kovacs. I mean – no! Not me. Monsieur dos Santos is here. You have marvellous friends, Monsieur Kovacs – *marvellous* friends!' She gripped him by the elbow for emphasis and her voice rattled with emotion. 'I never would have guessed!'

'Monsieur *who* is here to see me?'

From behind the diminutive concierge the bulky black figure of Babalu dos Santos appeared, his T-shirt straining at his teats under a dapper white linen jacket. There was a fine, cream-coloured Panama perched nonchalantly atop his rat-tailed mop of hair and a brown spotted bandanna tied loosely round his neck which added a raffish air: the gentleman *banditto*. He was grinning broadly from ear to ear.

'Babalu dos Santos,' he said, '*à votre service*.' He placed his left hand on his prominent navel and bowed deeply.

It was the first time that Kovacs had been bowed to.

'I don't think I've had the pleasure,' he managed to reply.

4

THE MINUTE KOVACS saw the envelope he knew instinctively that this was not a matter to be put off. The black man had come with a purpose and, however whacked Kovacs was feeling, it was only just that he should give the stranger a hearing.

Phlp Kovacs

There was little doubt about it in the back-rooms of his mind. The missing 'i's; Courier 12 point; the partial fill-in on the dirty '**o**', a key he had been meaning to clean for some time. All the man had said was 'I brought this for you, Mister'. His part in the affair was unclear. But Kovacs knew that they had to talk.

Babalu had addressed him in English and continued to do so, breezily confident of his linguistic prowess. It was passable, all-purpose English, slightly Americanised and with see-saw Latin articulations: the odd gap in vocabulary was plugged with a Portuguese word and left at that. His voice was slow and rich, a vibrant bass; it made the other man think of coffee or molten chocolate. It was less a voice than an *aroma* or a dark warm liquid that poured over the mind.

'Shall we talk outside?' said Kovacs. 'I don't want to sound inhospitable but I have new neighbours and they're decorating. It's very noisy in the flat. There's a lot of hammering.'

They left Madame da Silva and crossed the street to the small garden beside the lock, the Ecluse des Récollets, where they sat on one of the four benches in the shifting reticulated shade from the chestnuts and their thick meshed canopy of broad serrated leaves. A vagrant slept fitfully on a bench opposite them. Kovacs opened the envelope and read the typewritten message on the folded letter-card inside.

> Dear V.N., Mr dead man, take my message to ears and heart of P. Kovacs for you are a ghost and you know who me talk about.
> So Mr K: the person who bothered you was me. Me burgle flat and steal broken type apparatus, me on the telephone not know what to say. Why do you do that to me you want to know.
> Because you done me bad and now every joy has gone and me sad but small hope stays and saves me from deep sorrow. Me love you ever but you must treat me good and not curse me. You know me but you want to forget, bad man. Why you wrecked my small chance, my small heaven on earth why? That's not over, you shall hear me to the end.

Babalu watched him closely as he read. 'Is English – but she no write so great!' he said with a grin when Kovacs had finished.

'That's hardly surprising,' Kovacs replied, 'the author of this message is respecting a tight formal constraint. It's what we call a lipogram.' He handed the letter back to Babalu. 'Read it again. The whole thing is written without using the letter "I" for the simple reason that there isn't one. Whoever typed this used a broken typewriter that was stolen a week ago from my flat up there. The typewriter was perfect except for the letter "I". The key had broken off.'

Babalu said nothing, but Kovacs backtracked.

'You said *her* English?'

'Yes – is no letter from a man, I think!' said Babalu, grinning obscurely.

'No, of course not. At least I hope not. But you said *her* as if –'

'As if Babalu know? As if he see her?' Babalu's left arm was resting on the top of the bench and in a quick placatory movement he raised the hand and patted Kovacs limply on the bony extremity of his shoulder. 'Yeah! It was a woman! Don't worry about that, my friend. I saw her!'

'Where?'

'At Père Lachaise, *naturalmente. O cemitério.*'

Kovacs was hopeless at those Tetris computer games where descending blocks have to be manoeuvred into position before they slot into the wrong place of their own malevolent accord. Any attempt to play them resulted in headache and confusion and those same symptoms were beginning to issue from this conversation.

'I'm afraid you haven't even begun to explain to me how you acquired this letter – or how you found me.'

'The *lista telefónica*, my friend,' said Babalu. He smiled again but with a trace of irritation in his eyes. Though it was not the first time he had been in such a situation he was finding the grilling discomfiting.

'I'm ex-directory,' Kovacs responded flatly.

Babalu crossed his muscular arms and frowned.

'I *removed* my name from the directory,' Kovacs said.

'And when you do that, Mister?'

'Three years ago.'

'Ah! That explains! I find you in old *lista* – from 1989. The number no good – I try it and get, you know, tape recorder – but address was good, so here I am. Many Kovacs in *lista* but only two Philips. *Philippe* Kovacs and *Philip* Kovacs. I do this.' He scratched his head and rolled his eyeballs up in the Stan Laurel manner. 'I think: letter in English – *Philip* is English – my boy is English! I get you right first time!'

He laughed and there was a loose, almost hysterical, edge to his laugh – a nasal laugh, like sawing or braying – which was amusingly at odds with the regular somniferous growl of the voice. Kovacs smiled despite himself, though this was partly the nervous reaction of a mystified man. The laughter created a hiatus during which they both became aware of the spangle of late sunlight, the ambient noise of children playing in the nearby recreation area, the traffic and the heat. Babalu picked the Panama off the top of his head and fanned himself with the rim, still smiling.

Kovacs looked over the envelope again.

'Who is Vctor Nor?' he said, stumbling over the pronunciation. 'I presume that by adding an "i" we get *Victor* –'

'*Noir*,' added Babalu. 'Victor Noir. You don't know 'bout Victor Noir?' He slapped his thigh, feigning astonishment. 'I am only here one year but he's like old *amigo*, you know!' Again the hysterical laugh held up the proceedings and the vagrant opposite muttered and coughed in his sleep. Babalu laid the Panama on his lap, unknotted the brown spotted bandanna at his neck and wiped his forehead which was lustrous with sweat. He replaced his hat, cleared his throat and explained.

He explained how Victor Noir had at the age of twenty-two been killed in a duel by Prince Pierre Bonaparte for seducing his wife. He described in detail the unorthodox tomb, its postbox hat and his own unofficial role as courier or emissary. Kovacs listened with rapt attention. He had never heard of Victor Noir in all his years in Paris.

'Is not many men know this. Not even French,' said Babalu, reassuring Kovacs. 'Is the *senhoras* – the ladies, you know. Their little *segredo*!' He made the 'hush hush' sign, a forefinger raised to his lips.

'But how many people have you brought together like this?' asked Kovacs.

'Ahhh!' Babalu dallied, counting slowly on his big fingers. 'Dauphine – very nice! – she like very much Paul. Inès and her dentist. Sophie and Pierre. Madame Daniel who work in laundry – she like very much her boss – *a viúva* – a widow you say. Lady from TV – Khaled at the Mosque . . . Oh, I dunno!' he abandoned the count. 'Lots and lots, my friend! Eleven, twelve, thirteen. Of course, is not always success for couple but is nothing Babalu can do after – you know – after introduction! *Não sou o responsável*.'

A fleeting image of Babalu dominating Piccadilly Circus crossed Kovacs' mind – an overweight black Eros with bow, arrow and Panama hat, grinning down on the metropolitan theatre-goers and commuters. 'So,' he said, 'you are a sort of self-appointed postman? A Cupid. Smoothing the path to true love.'

'Yes! Babalu is *despachante*, my friend. *Excepto* – excuse me say this – I have big doubt about you. This is different situation, you see.'

'What do you mean?'

'Because she say,' he glanced at the letter again, 'she say "you done me bad". Is someone you know maybe? She say this in letter. Is – 'ow you say? – is *more to these than meet the eye*!' He was visibly pleased with himself at alighting on an idiom.

'You're right, there is,' said Kovacs after a moment's hesitation. 'As I said, the person who sent this burgled my flat a week ago. You understand *burgle*?'

'Yes, yes.'

'She stole the typewriter it was written on. And I honestly have no idea who it could be. You said you saw her?'

Babalu nodded. 'I see her, yes. I see her post letter. But she is very far. Babalu must hide, my friend – you understand? I see her from behind. I no see face. She –' he outlined the form of her clothes with his hands, '– little jacket, like this, *entende*? *Verde* – green. And short skirt, also green. Black cap – like for baseball, you know – round like this, back to front. And bag.' He sketched a handbag shape with his fat hands. 'Leather, gold chains – all that stuff. Now *normalmente*, I see lady post letter and I follow. I find out where she live, see? Is not always address on letter. But this one – *rápida*! Too quick for me, my friend!'

'I see. I can't think of anyone I know who dresses like that.'

A shadow passed over Babalu's face. He clucked his tongue reprovingly and raised a finger. 'You have wife, Mr Kovacs?'

'No. Divorced.'

'Is not your old wife, perhaps?'

'My ex-wife? No. Anne would never carry on like that. And besides, the clothes you described – she'd never dress like that. Certainly not a baseball cap. She hates everything American. And she never wears hats.' Kovacs' curiosity was getting the better of him. 'How did *you* find out about Victor Noir? What drew you to the cemetery in the first place?'

'You know Allan Kardec?'

Kovacs shook his head.

'You know Umbanda?'

He shook it again.

'Oh well!' grinned Babalu. 'Is long story! But you tell me, where you think – where you think I come from?'

'Brazil – obviously. You're not Portuguese, so only a Brazilian would be able to chat with Madame da Silva as you were doing.'

'*É isso!* You are right. *Sou brasileiro.* I come from Bahia in Brazil.'

Babalu picked up a stick and sketched the outline of South America in the dusty gravel of the garden then pushed the stick into one north-easterly point.

'Bahia. *Ali!*'

And suddenly he was lost for words, utterly self-absorbed. There was something immensely touching in the sight of the bulky man with the Panama on his head hovering over the geographical contour of his remote home continent. He was like an ancient god perusing the world from the eighth Ptolemaic sphere, a world from which he was exiled and estranged. An invisible wave of emotion had passed over Babalu and Kovacs was surprised at his own sensitivity to this change. For the first time he was dimly aware that a link, a sympathetic force, had been established between himself and Babalu. From the outset he had felt little of his habitual reserve towards strangers and after a day-long catalogue of absurd misunderstandings Babalu had appeared in the concierge's *loge* like a genie or *deus ex machina* who would set the world to rights. It went against the grain for Kovacs to admit such a thing to himself, but there it was nonetheless: the man inspired confidence, he radiated an attractive inner strength. And now he was talking again, almost to himself, relating the life of Bahia, his other life. Kovacs brushed aside his ambling thoughts and attended.

He was telling Kovacs, in his broken English, about the candomblés, the African fetish cults that, in the religious hybrid known as Umbanda in Bahia, were syncretised with Catholicism. For every Catholic divinity or saint there was an African opposite number, drawn from the ancient spirit religions. Our Lady of Conception was Iemanjá and every year flowers and trinkets were thrown into the sea in her honour. Saint Barbara was Iansã, Saint George Xangô – and so on. The religious rites were like those of Haitian voodoo, with animal blood being smeared on foreheads and frenetic chanting and dancing to the sound of the African atabaque drums. Umbanda was white sympathetic magic, Babalu insisted, unlike Quimbanda which was sinister black magic where destructive hexes were used. Through

Umbanda, worshippers gained direct access to the spirit world, and the mystical theology which underpinned the movement came from the Frenchman Allan Kardec, buried at Père Lachaise. Kovacs registered the connection while Babalu continued. Spiritists, he said, did not fear death. For them there was no original sin and hence no eternal punishment. They believed, above all, in the reality of the spirit-world and in the acquisition of wisdom and benevolence as the sole conditions for happiness in the hereafter. In Umbanda, all adepts believed that animals had special spiritual powers, and many had their own totemic animal. They also had their orixá – a favourite deity from which they derived their axé or power. Babalu's was Exu, the messenger of the gods, the other orixás. Exu, he explained, made him feel strong, replenishing his soul with thaumaturgic energy.

'Her orixá,' said Babalu, pointing to the mystery letter, 'is Iansã.'

'And who is that?' asked Kovacs.

'She is warrior goddess of winds and tempests. Wife of Xangô. She like very much to be in control. She fight hard and use fire and – how you say? –' He drew in the air with his finger.

'Lightning,' said Kovacs.

'Yes, lightning. She know what she want and she's a powerful one, my friend,' he added with a dark smile.

'It could be *any* woman, then, in my experience,' said Kovacs.

'Not *any*, no. This one is hurt – very bad hurt! Read the letter, *compadre*. She say you do something. I no know what this thing can be but you must go into past if you want to find this thing. She want to love you but she want to hurt you too. I know Iansã, my friend, and I feel this danger to you. Is a big danger. You see,' he added, resting his hand on Kovacs' shoulder again, 'love is for us very big and important thing! It make sad person happy. It make shy person laugh out loud. Ha! Ha! Ha! I am lucky. *Sou casado*. My love is in my family and children. But sometime love go bad, very bad, and then – *Perigo*! Big danger, you see.'

Kovacs felt uncomfortable. He got up and walked over to lean on the railing overlooking the lock-gates, turning his back on

Babalu. A sudden gust of wind tugged at his grey forelocks which were pasted to his brow with perspiration. It struck him as ironic that he, whose private researches and introspection were devoted to undoing the trenchant mind–brain dualism, should now find himself listening tongue-tied to talk of spirits and magic and supernatural powers. He was deeply opposed to the notion that the 'mind' was an immaterial spectator in the Cartesian theatre of consciousness, observing the phenomenology of the brain. It followed that he was opposed to other ether-like abstracts – ectoplasm, spirits, souls. Babalu's talk was sad to him in a way, the relic of a primitive mode of consciousness. His own scientific rationalism, his materialism, was of course unshaken. He believed none of the man's spirit talk, but he was not going to enter into arguments. There was no fight left in it all. Science and blind faith had not been on speaking terms for quite some time. All the same, Babalu's beliefs captivated the anthropologist in him. The two men had, after all, been brought together by a random pattern of events, the human equivalent of Brownian Motion in physics, the arbitrary swim and collision of molecules. But no sooner had this thought occurred to him than the metaphor failed dismally. This was *not* random or arbitrary, he corrected himself. Something or someone was behind it.

A green bolero jacket, a green skirt, a black baseball cap.

Someone was making this happen.

When he turned again Babalu was sitting with his right arm fully extended. Along it ran a tiny white mouse. Babalu inclined his head and the mouse climbed the side of his neck and face, sitting finally above his ear where it set about cleaning its front paws.

'Where did he come from?' laughed Kovacs.

'*She*,' Babalu corrected him. 'This is Cotinho. She is my trained mouse.'

'Trained? Trained to do what?'

'Watch. Cotinho! *Algibeira!* That is Portuguese for "pocket".'

The mouse pricked up her ears and scuttled down the side of the face, over the shoulder and directly into the breast pocket, only the pink nose and red eyes showing over the lip.

'Amazing!' said Kovacs. 'Did you bring her from Brazil?'

'No, no. In Salvador I have trained monkey – marmoset, you know. "Lucia! Lucia!" I say. She love to sit on my head and hunt for small deer.'

'Small deer?'

'Yeah – fleas, you know. In hair.'

'Oh.'

'But Cotinho, I find her here, in my room, and I train her. She's good girl. She like to live in my pocket, don't you *bébé*?' He stroked the mouse on the head with the pad of his fingertip.

The conversation between the two men had reached a natural term: a point at which it could either be curtailed politely or, by mutual consent, extended. Kovacs looked at his watch. It was already eight, though the late May evening was still flushed with light. His previous desire to sleep, however, had passed and – curiously – he had no wish to detach himself from the fat black man with three notches on his forehead and a white mouse in his pocket. He was in a mood to talk on.

'Monsieur dos – ?'

'Dos Santos.'

'*Senhor* dos Santos, I should say – '

'Please – Babalu.'

'Are you – are you hungry? We could eat something, some oysters perhaps. There is a place around the corner. You have put yourself to the trouble of bringing this letter to me and I would – I'd like to invite you, to thank you. Unless, of course, you have other plans for the evening.'

'No, no plan,' said Babalu. 'Is very kind of you – but "oyster" – what is "oyster"?'

Kovacs described them.

'Ah! *Ostras!* Yes, yes, I like. In Bahia, this grow on the trees.'

Kovacs stared at him in disbelief.

'Impossible. It's a shellfish. It grows in the sea.'

'Yes, of course, my friend. *Claro.* But in Bahia is much, much water by sea. Many many trees grow in water. How you say? How you say?'

'Mangrove trees, perhaps?'

'Yes! Mangrove tree! Sea come up!' He raised his hands like a conductor when the orchestra is about to strike up. 'And cover tree. Sea go down!' – the hands swept down – 'And tree full of *ostras* – oysters, yes. They stick to branch. Is very strange.'

They walked through the side-streets to the place de la République then crossed to Chez Jenny on the boulevard du Temple where they sat on the terrace in the open air under a huge red parasol. A broad silver platter was served on a raised metal frame with twelve large Britanny oysters on a bed of crushed ice. There were thin slices of brown bread and butter, quarters of lemon, and a wet bottle of Chardonnay, wrapped round with a pristine white napkin. The light repast, the impudence of the wine, were tokens of an incipient and improbable friendship and in acknowledgement of this the talk ran freely, unchecked by niggling mutual suspicions.

At Babalu's behest, Kovacs spoke dismissively, with embarrassment almost, of himself: his London childhood, his days at university, his work as a language and literature teacher at the College, even his marriage. Babalu listened sympathetically to the unassuming factual account.

'A man with no family – he is nothing – *nothing*!' he declared, but Kovacs begged to differ. He had his work, his integrity, his research. These were defensible advantages. He was engaged in self-culture, a private process of intellectual evolution, and there was rigour and value in this quest which lay outside most people's capacities. Babalu was not convinced.

'Is sad have no wife, no religion, no children – what you got, my friend, in your life? Is nothing there!'

'I have my *self*,' said Kovacs.

'But your *self* is *sozinho* my friend – all alone. This is sad thing. Man who is alone have big delusion, big delusion in head. He talk and he talk, but is always to himself. You understand? Nobody answer him except himself, and himself always say same thing. Big delusion,' he repeated, shaking his head. 'Man who is alone suffer much. People is needing many other people: family, friends, community, country. Is only when man *belong*, you understand, that he find peace in heart.' He waved a hand in a grand inclusive gesture. 'All this – the big city. Is very easy for man like you be alone and nobody notice. Slowly time go by, you no realise, and one day you are old. Very bad. Is big delusion, as I say.' He concluded by shaking his head once again, a mournful cast to his thick dark lips.

Eventually Kovacs managed to turn the conversation onto Babalu. As the daylight was quenched behind the great canyon of rooftops, chimneys and television aerials, the black man talked of Bahia with easy vitality, throwing his whole body into the animated dramaturgy of description and anecdote. He described his home town of Salvador, its beautiful baroque churches and cobbled lanes, winding down to the palm-fringed bay and the great sweep of ocean pricked, at twilight, with the orange lamps of fishing smacks. He talked of Bahia nights, nights of stars and songs, of thunderous African drumming and samba rhythms, of fluid laughter, *caxaça* rum and slack, carefree talk. He described the humming birds, the butterflies, the hammocks, the niches in the walls for idols and the miracle room in one of the churches, filled with coloured drawings showing how people were preserved from disasters. The ceiling was hung with wax models of the arms, legs and breasts of those who had recovered from malignant diseases and, in the corner, there was a pile of crutches from the lame who now miraculously walked. He talked of the black women with their turbans and silk parasols, the poverty of the shanty towns and the role of Olodum in fighting racism. The names of musicians, artists, religious leaders and political activists reeled off his tongue. He described the feather flowers that were made at the Solidade convent and the splendid drums, calabash gourds ornamented with beads, shards of mirrors and ribbon, that were the pulse of night in carnival time, and the wax balls in the shape of fruit that were filled with water and thrown at passers-by – again during the frenzied anarchy of carnival. He talked of the capoeira martial kick-fighting, of hard labour in the sugar refineries and beach waifs who made a living selling cigarettes, reefers and knives. He talked of the legendary Gafieira do Barão dance-hall where he had met his wife, of his brother who was in prison for petty theft and of his own association with Chico Mendes and the rubber tappers and his time in California. He paused only to detach the slippery, silver oysters from their nacreous shells with a fork and then, raising the shell to his lips, swallow the bivalve whole.

'I tell you,' he said, his mouth full as he swallowed a particularly fat specimen, 'I tell you about Saint Anthony. Girls who are *solteiras* – single, you know – they pray to him for husband. In Salvador, statues of Santo Antonio – they carry Christ child in they arms. The *raparigas* – the girls – they take child away. Santo Antonio, he get really mad! Will do anything to get Jesus back, see? So he have to find husband for these girls. And then, when they get husband, they take Jesus back and Santo Antonio is happy again!'

'A Brazilian Victor Noir,' said Kovacs.

'Yes!' laughed Babalu. 'I never think this, but you are right! A difference though,' he added, with sudden reverence. 'Santo Antonio is saint, right? Victor Noir – well, not such a good man I think!'

By now they were half-way through their second platter of oysters and Kovacs topped up Babalu's glass.

'Tell me,' he said, 'what am I going to do about this?' He tapped the letter, which he had folded into his breast pocket, with a forefinger. 'What am I going to do about the woman in green?'

Babalu shrugged. 'You know, I want to help you, *compadre*, but I work. As I tell you, most evening I make crêpes. In day my sister and landlord get me job – "Fix this!", "Paint that!" You see? Every Tuesday Babalu go to Père Lachaise. Maybe this *rapariga* she come back, maybe no. Maybe she leave more letters. I dunno. If I see her, I follow, right? But no big chance of that. Is a problem.'

'Yes, it is.'

'Anyway, is English philosophy, no – *wait and see*?'

'You could say that.'

'You must wait and see, my friend. Is no possible otherwise.'

'No, I suppose not.'

They had just finished the last of the oysters and wine when a tall pedestrian, who had apparently been bending down to tie a shoelace, approached their table. He was an elegant Frenchman in his forties with a distinguished goatee beard and an immaculate grey silk suit and tie. Without a word he smiled politely, placed a fifty-franc note on the table in front of Kovacs and walked off. Kovacs picked up the note and turned it round as if looking for clues. There were none. It was one of the new notes, depicting on one side the aviator-author Antoine de Saint-Exupéry and his literary invention *Le Petit Prince*, while a biplane graced the verso. On one corner of the note the letter 'J' had been scribbled in ballpoint. He suddenly became aware that the other diners had observed this mysterious offering and were discreetly watching him. His first overwhelming thought was that he had been mistaken for a tramp or a beggar. He looked down aghast at his clothing. It was true that he was not in his best subfusc: just a pair of jeans, sandals, open-neck shirt and his rucked and crumpled linen jacket. But a beggar! Surely it was clear that he was a *customer*. He was sitting on the terrace of a reputable brasserie, the remains of a modest feast before him: not on the steps of the Metro with a plastic beaker! Unless the note was intended for Babalu. That was another possibility. He glanced speculatively at his companion who was dropping breadcrumbs into his breast pocket for the benefit of the mouse. As he was mulling over this conundrum, the money still between his fingers, another pedestrian approached and snatched the note from his grasp. It was a woman with filthy orange hair, a loose serendipity of charity clothes and a long, slender face like an old nag fit for the knacker's yard. Her complexion and eyes were inflamed with alcohol or worse. There were foul hypodermic contusions on her inner arms, following the blue routes of her veins.

'*Alors!*' she yelled. '*C'est comme ça qu'on fait les affaires?*'

'*De quoi parlez-vous, Madame?*' said Kovacs. There was a violent tremor in his voice which he struggled to control. His peripheral vision informed him that the scene had instantly drawn the attention of the entire terrace and as he glanced edgily around he perceived a vaguely familiar figure, though no sooner had he spotted it than it dodged behind a potted conifer. He turned back nervously to the ranting woman.

'I clean your shirts!' she screamed in her hectoring voice. 'I boil your pants! I polish your shoes! And what do I get? *Rien!*' The exclamation sent a fine spray of spit across Kovacs' face. 'This,' she said, brandishing the note, 'is mine! And don't tell me I haven't earned it! I've earned every *sou*! *C'est ça, hein? Les hommes! Ils sont tous pareils!*' By now she was addressing everyone present. 'And if you think I'm going to be waiting in bed for you when you come reeling home – forget it! *Je t'emmerde!'* She gave the familiar Gallic *bras d'honneur* gesture of insult and staggered off. An unearthly silence filled the void she had left. After a while a waiter came over and placed the bill coldly on the table.

'I've never seen her before in my life!' Kovacs appealed, half to Babalu, half to those who were within earshot at adjoining tables. 'And as for the fifty francs – where did that come from? The man just walked up and put it on the table!'

'I think he found it on the ground,' a neighbouring diner explained, leaning over, in an understanding tone. 'He must have thought it had dropped down from your table. A gust of wind, perhaps.'

'Oh! And the woman?'

The diner shrugged and protruded his lower lip dumbly. Kovacs turned to Babalu for elucidation, but the Brazilian was a closed book. He pulled his Panama down over his forehead and stared thoughtfully at Kovacs from under the rim.

'You have big trouble with women, my friend,' he murmured. 'I think this when I meet you and I think it now. Big delusion!'

'But she – ,' he pointed desperately in the direction the crazy woman had taken. 'I've never seen her before!' The other woman, though – Kovacs was now thinking – the one who had dodged behind the potted conifer, *she* was someone he half-recognised. He turned confusedly to Babalu. 'I've never seen her before,' he repeated. 'Surely *you* believe me? You saw what happened!'

'I believe you, *amigo*. But why she choose you? Why not some other fella?'

'Because I was holding the money, I suppose.'

'And why you? Why *you* holding money?'

'Because,' Kovacs faltered, 'because someone mistakenly gave it to me! Why else?'

'No mistake, my friend. Time – space – is like spider web. All lines lead to centre. Oxala know that nothing happen without explain.'

'"Explanation", you mean – but what is the explanation?'

'I will help you, but you are only one who hold the answer.

When fly struggle in web, spider – she feel struggle and up she come – very fast!'

'I am not a fly, Monsieur dos Santos.'

'No. Is true,' said Babalu, smiling philosophically. 'Fly, he see everything, even when he no can do nothing. You – many, many thing you no see. Is a problem.'

Kovacs filled in the cheque with brusque, aggressive pen-strokes. There was nothing like gnomic wisdom to rattle a scientific rationalist. Yet though the warmth of fellow-feeling towards Babalu may have cooled imperceptibly an invisible agent had unwittingly yoked them together, an invisible agent pursuing invisible purposes. He peered up sternly at Babalu. The white mouse had hooked its pink paws over the breast pocket of his companion's jacket and was staring back at Kovacs, its body palpitating, its red eyes glinting like miniature glâcé cherries.

'Cotinho! *Ombro!*' snapped Babalu, and the mouse shimmied up onto his shoulder, turned and looked again at Kovacs expectantly, her perfect pink nose twitching with mischief above two white needle-thin incisors.

Back home, he met his new neighbours on the landing. The couple were packing their tools and decorating gear together in preparation for departure. From his own flat came the sound of the telephone ringing.

'It's been going all evening,' said the man. 'I hope it's nothing urgent.'

'Shouldn't think so,' said Kovacs. He let himself in quickly and picked up the receiver. Nothing. Or rather – yes, something. A thin asthmatic breathing, an occasional gasp.

'Who is this?' he demanded.

No reply. He slammed the phone down and pulled the lead out of its socket. He had not put on the lights and the suffused yellow-green glow from the lamps by the canal was barely enough to see by. He went to the kitchen to fetch himself a cool glass of Evian water and, finding the stub of a candle in a drawer, lit the wick and stood it beside the hotplate. The box-shaped room, barely larger than a telephone kiosk, flickered with shadows from the dancing tongue of flame.

The kitchen window gave onto the rear court and a bank of

windows, some empty darknesses, others bright with forbidden glimpses into the lives of strangers. A couple making a bed. A girl taking a shower, the blurred pink of her body visible through frosted glass. Another room was alight with the blue shudder of television. Directly opposite his kitchen window an elegant society party was under way behind a row of three windows. Well-bred women in flouncy gowns floated back and forth. Men in evening dress formed a small, mobile group around a gilt-framed oil painting. At one of the open windows, a couple leaned dreamily on the balustrade, sipping whisky and romancing the night.

The strains of Johann Strauss and the sociable prattle of refined French voices carried across to Kovacs' ears. He half-closed his eyes like a painter judging tonal contrast and immediately the scene factorised into its essential components and, in doing so, was startlingly dehumanised. What had been people were now coloured protozoan blobs edging randomly around each other, touching, recoiling, engulfing, advancing. The scene was positively Darwinian. Kovacs had the growing conviction that this was *it* – society was no more than this. A vast amoebic waltz, dancing to the music of time, prey avoiding predator, predator seeking prey. The inchoate dance from which consciousness had been born, way back in the primaeval soup, was still going on before his very eyes. Essentially nothing had changed. Amoebas in evening dress, protoplasm with pearls. There was little comfort or warmth in the thought. He rejected whatever biological dictate it was that defined him as part of *that.* He was a secular schismatic, yes, a Raskolnikov but without murderous intentions. He remembered the typed letter-card, retrieved it from his breast pocket and read it again in the wavering flamelight. 'You shall hear me to the end,' it concluded. Perhaps, after all, he had got this badly wrong. He was not Raskolnikov after all – not predator, but *prey*.

A green bolero jacket, a green skirt, a black baseball cap.

However much he objected to the thought, he was being led a pretty dance himself. But who was she? He could picture her from Babalu's description but the face was a broken pattern of pixels like the blanked-out faces on police videos seen on TV. Who could she be? He would find out – and soon.

The couple at the window opposite nuzzled closer.

'Look,' said the woman. 'Over there. Do you see that face? He's staring at us. You don't suppose it's a Peeping Tom, do you?' She giggled nervously.

'No,' replied the man, adjusting his bow-tie with his beautifully manicured fingers. 'It's just a lonely old guy watching the fun. He probably wishes he could change places with us.'

'*Qu'est-ce que c'est triste!*' she whispered.

'Let's give him his money's worth,' said the man, a capricious smile on his face. He fished an ice-cube out of the whisky glass and dropped it straight down his partner's cleavage.

The woman's scream tore like murder through the night.

5

It was ten to twelve on Saturday the fourth of June. Kovacs was standing by the whiteboard in the classroom and looking out of the tall nineteenth-century windows on the third floor. Above the rooftops of the rue de Grenelle he could see the upper half of the Eiffel Tower – the 'Awful Tower', as Fairgreave whimsically called it – and the little orange lifts busing slowly up and down between the second and third stages. A few puff-balls of cumulus dawdled by.

He was turning over that morning's bewildering occurrence in his thoughts. The post had been delivered at eight o'clock sharp to a table outside the concierge's *loge*. Madame da Silva was late getting up and had not as yet had time to distribute the letters to the various flats in the building. On the top of the pile of letters was one addressed to 'Madame Turckheim'. Turckheim was his wife's maiden name and it struck him as extremely unusual that she should receive mail now, three years after their separation. It was all the more unusual that the letter should be addressed thus, combining the title for a married woman with her *nom de jeune fille* – her maiden name. Nevertheless, he opened the letter. The contents made no sense at all. It was a scrawled, chatty missive from someone called 'Fabienne', beginning '*Chère amie*', in the course of which his wife was congratulated on her recent wedding. So Anne had remarried! The news made him jump and pitched his thoughts into jittery confusion.

As he was reading the letter, Madame da Silva emerged, yawning, into the hallway and he pointed out the oddity to her. She looked at the envelope and at Kovacs, noticing his perturbation. 'Oh no, Monsieur Kovacs, that is not for you! That is for your new neighbours. Their name is "Turckheim".' The coincidence was extraordinary. Turckheim was not a common patronymic, though perhaps it was in Alsace where there was a village and a celebrated wine of that name. His wife, indeed, had Alsatian ancestry on her father's side, while her mother had southern roots. The new neighbours were also Alsatian. While he was engaged in this feat of gymnastic lateral thinking the neighbours appeared, armed for another day's decorating. Inevitably the scene that followed was a modified second-take of their first embarrassing encounter.

'I am afraid I have opened your letter in error,' he began before going on to point out the unusual coincidence.

The husband, Gilles, seemed relatively unfazed. 'Anne is my second cousin,' he explained.

Unknown to Kovacs, Anne had remained on friendly terms with Madame da Silva after the divorce so when Monsieur Martin died she was one of the first to hear about it and she spread the news of the available flat through the extensive family grapevine. Gilles and his new wife Corinne had leapt at the opportunity.

'I scarcely know Anne,' Gilles said, 'I met her once at a family gathering some three or four years ago.'

'And you didn't know that she had lived here with me – that we had been married?' Kovacs asked.

'No, we didn't. Your name was never mentioned.'

The young couple took the letter and, with a now familiar awkwardness, excused themselves. So there it was. All perfectly logical. Nothing to get into a sweat about. Nevertheless, it was an odd coincidence that the couple had moved in on the anniversary of his wedding.

'Monsieur Kovacs?'

Had the man been telling the truth? Perhaps he was on closer terms with Anne than he had made out. Alternatively, now that he had made the family connection – or now that the connection had been offered him on a plate, free, gratis and for nothing – perhaps he would get in touch with second cousin Anne. What sort of glowing account of his new neighbour would Gilles Turckheim have to narrate then? Hammerer upon walls; stealer of funereal flowers; desperate alcoholic; interceptor of private correspondence. Not that he, Philip Kovacs, cared. There was no reason why Anne's opinion should matter to him any more. Well there wasn't, was there?

'*Philip*!'

He blinked and looked around him. He was not accustomed to being addressed by his first name. Seven or eight students, all in their early twenties and all female, were sitting around him, waiting. The speaker was a girl with black plaited hair and a large mole on her left cheek.

'Elodie,' he said, 'I'm sorry. I was miles away. What were we talking about?'

'Anne Boleyn,' the girl prompted.

He glanced at the photocopy in his hand and read the opening line of the poem again:

'*Whoso list to hunt I know where is an hinde*.'

'Yes, of course,' Kovacs said, gathering his thoughts. 'It is believed that Anne Boleyn was admired by Thomas Wyatt. When Henry the Eighth began to show an interest in Anne, Wyatt had a choice. He could either bid farewell to Anne or his head.'

He smiled at this spontaneous little zeugma and a ripple of girlish laughter greeted the pleasantry.

'In the sonnet, he is announcing that he is no longer going to take part in the hunt – the sexual pursuit.'

'So the inscription on the collar around the hind's neck –' began Elodie, keenly.

'Yes – *Noli me tangere*. Christ's words after the resurrection. "Do not touch me." She – Anne Boleyn – is now a hind in the royal park and therefore untouchable. That is the conceit. But there is also an echo here of "Render therefore unto Caesar the things which are Caesar's; and unto God the things which are God's". The Gospel According to Saint Matthew. It's a beautiful little poem. Petrarchan, of course. And terribly melancholy, don't you think?'

He looked around him with a wistful smile.

'What time is it?' he asked, sensing that the two-hour period had come to a close.

'It's twelve,' one of the girls answered. 'This is our last class of the year. You said you'd booked a table for lunch.'

'So I did. I booked a table for all of us at Thoumieux in the rue Saint-Dominique. Can everyone come?'

As a matter of courtesy, the teachers at the College went out with their students at the end of the year. It was his fourth such lunch that week but this was scarcely burdensome. It was a fact of life that most Parisian existences were frittered away contemplating the *menu du jour*. For Kovacs' students, these convivial occasions were a way of breaking down the barriers, dispensing with the formal conventions of the classroom. They could converse and joke with him on the same footing, tell him about their favourite rap idols, their career ambitions, and indulge in magnanimous and largely mendacious panegyrics on all things English. And one or two of them, he knew, had a sneaking *faiblesse*, a shy little unspoken crush. This was one of the things he had learnt to perceive and silently admonish – never, of course, to act on. There was something utterly sexless about teaching, of that he was convinced. It was strictly contractual, the exercise of an abstract power, and even if on occasions he found an acolyte pretty beyond the ordinary bounds of prettiness – even if this were the case, he could appreciate those looks on a purely aesthetic level, with no hint of sexuality. He was no January, he told himself, thinking of Chaucer's *Merchant's Tale*. The thought of dating someone half his age never survived serious consideration.

Kovacs too was enjoying himself today, but not for the same reasons as the students. For him, these lunches were conducted in a spirit of 'nunc dimittis', to quote the Song of Simeon. It was an atrocious thing to admit, even to himself, but he was filled with immoderate joy at getting shot – one by one – of his interminable seminars, the source of his daily bread. What was it Shaw said about teaching? 'Those who can, do; those who can't, teach.' Something like that. But what, thought Kovacs, about those who *can't teach*? Or those, like himself, who could teach yet would rather not, bearing the yoke only to stay in funds. As the meal drew to a close he found himself whistling, under his breath, the melody to the song from *Paint Your Wagon* and thinking through the words:

Do you know where Hell is?
Hell is in 'Hello'.
Heaven is in 'Goodbye forever,
It's time for me to go.'

The bill arrived, the girls pooled their money and he pocketed it, producing his *Carte Bleue* to pay the global sum. It was not long, however, before the waiter brought the card back.

'I'm sorry, sir, but our machine says your card is invalid.'

'Impossible,' said Kovacs, 'look.' He pointed out the expiry date on the card.

'Nevertheless,' said the waiter, and wagged his arms in the conventional gesture of individual fatalism before the massed forces of a bludgeoning bureaucracy. The gesticulation left plenty of room for deductions to be drawn – for example, that Kovacs was plumbing Jules-Vernean depths, overdraft-wise.

In the end, one of the girls paid with her card and the kitty of money was passed over with Kovacs' own cash addition. However trivial, the incident had taken the wind out of Kovacs' sails. As the girls said goodbye and left him outside the restaurant they seemed to be sniggering together, obviously – he reckoned – assuming that he was uncreditworthy. *Un prof fauché, hein?* He might well never see them again but his professional pride, not to mention his *amour propre*, had singed its cat's whiskers and grazed its bee's knees. It happened that his branch of the Crédit Lyonnais was opposite the restaurant. Resolving to get to the bottom of the matter there and then, he crossed the narrow street.

'Your wife rang in and closed the account,' the clerk said. 'It was five days ago. I took the call personally. We entered the closure on the computer, which is why your *Carte Bleue* no longer works on the computer network. She told us you would be in to withdraw the remaining balance in cash.'

'First of all,' said Kovacs slowly, 'I *have* no wife.'

The clerk blushed and fiddled with a rubber thimble-grip.

'What did she sound like?' Kovacs asked with genuine curiosity.

'French,' said the clerk inadequately. He could remember no more.

'Secondly,' Kovacs continued, 'since when do you accept instructions over the phone? It is *my* account, and *I* decide if and when it is going to be closed. Surely according to your procedures you require a written instruction from me to close the account?'

'Normally, yes,' the young man admitted, 'but I was so sure. She had your account number and the number of your credit card. She knew exactly what the balance was. I had no reason to believe that it was a – a hoax.'

Kovacs drummed his fingers in irritation on the counter. 'What is your name?' he asked.

'G-Gaillard,' the clerk replied stammering, and pointed to the nameplate on his desk. 'I shall, of course, open the account again immediately. Unfortunately, you will have to apply for a new credit card. The closure procedure is irreversible.'

'*Merde!*' blurted Kovacs. 'And how long will I have to wait for that?'

'I am so sorry. This is all my fault. I shall ensure that this gets top priority.'

'I should think so too.'

'You won't –?'

'I won't what?'

'You won't be *reporting* this, will you?'

Kovacs tutted and shook his head. The official smiled anxiously and thanked him.

'In the meantime,' the young man said, 'you can go ahead and use your cheque-book. All the cheques you make out will be honoured. And I shall ensure that you get a new card within a fortnight.'

'OK,' said Kovacs, resigned to this stroke of fate.

The clerk plucked up courage to go on. 'Don't you – don't you think you should go to the police? I mean, whoever it was who rang up knew everything about your account.' There was an extraordinary element of doubt in his enquiry, as if he was laying life and limb on the line.

'You're right,' said Kovacs, 'I should.' No sooner had he said this than a mental image of a sprouting cellared potato greeted his inner eye – Inspector Laroche, at the Commissariat – and he baulked at the idea. Besides, he reasoned, it was Saturday and Laroche would almost certainly be off work and – what was more – he had an appointment, hadn't he? He was due to meet Céline in the Parc des Buttes-Chaumont at three. It was their way of rusticating, one of their little pseudo-country walks: a rendezvous that had been formally scheduled for some weeks. He looked at the bank clock. It was two, on the dot. He just had time to get there if he hurried. After a final placatory exchange of promises with the despondent clerk he made his way to the RER station at Invalides.

The Parc des Buttes-Chaumont, in the 19th arrondissement of Paris, is a hilly patch of green in the form of an eagle's beak, planted, like an arboretum, with an eclectic variety of trees. In the centre of the park is a lake dominated by a craggy promontory of rock, nearly a hundred feet high, on the summit of which is a classical stone rotunda known as the Temple de Sybille. Below, beside the lake, is a bandstand, a children's sandpit and a green wooden hut called the Chalet de Gauffres where one can buy waffles and other fare. That Saturday, a few tables and chairs had been put out in front of the chalet for customers and over each table was a red and white parasol advertising Coca-Cola.

Céline was late. He sat down on a bench beside the hut and waited. This was their regular meeting place.

The park had a chequered history. For five centuries it had been a place of execution, the site of the notorious Montfaucon gibbet, the subject of a Villon poem, and thereafter it was nothing more than a rubbish dump until Napoleon III ordered its transformation in the 1860s. Despite the skeletons in its cupboard it was now a restful place to flee the turmoil of the city, a place where the only sounds were the suspirations of leaves from the breezes that eddied round the promontory, the plaintive quack of ducks, the cries of children and the regular whishing tick of the water-sprays on the flowerbeds as their nozzles flicked to and fro. Already June had brought a minor heatwave and the yellow plastic pipes for the irrigation system trailed brightly across the park's meandering switchback of avenues.

Kovacs held his breath for a moment then let it out, puckering his lips to make a long, low whistle. He looked around. A dozen children were playing in the sandpit and within the bandstand a group of adults were doing Tai Chi movements, the slow-motion Chinese dance of the Yin and the Yang. Next to the lake, several fishermen sat on their canvas stools chatting in Italian while they stared dead ahead at the motionless fluorescent floats denting the meniscus on the otherwise flat sheen of the lake's surface. One fisherman – slightly apart and silent – looked dimly familiar from behind.

Kovacs meshed his fingers round the back of his neck, gently massaging the crick that had developed there during the morning's class. A single magpie, evidently a widow or widower, landed on a branch of the Japanese Sophara tree in front of him and fanned its wings out lazily. Beyond the lake, the brown-black, beetling pike of rock reared up impressively. A path zigzagged up its kinked and ridged western face, twisting inwards at two points towards dark Romantic grottoes hewn into the rock. Atop it was the rotunda with its eight Corinthian columns and the dome which budded upwards into a shape that reminded him of the form of a clove. *Clou de girofle*, as the French called that spice: he had nearly said *clou de giraffe*, 'giraffe's nail', he thought to himself half-amused. Yes, *clou de girofle*: this was one of those French names which, come hell or high water, had remained chiselled on the headstone of his memory where thousands of other more practical terms had vanished from his mental lexicon. Now why, do you think, was that? This was the sort of question he used to be fond of posing in his academic papers on language acquisition and the role of memory. In this particular case it was almost certainly due to what pedants called 'depth processing'. When he first came to France, during his year off before university, he had worked on a dairy farm in the Ardèche. He woke one morning with agonising toothache. The farmer told him to go to the village pharmacy and ask for *huile de clou de girofle*, clove oil, which was an effective analgesic. It was a three-mile walk to the pharmacy and, along the way, he had repeated the words incessantly to himself – *huile de clou de girofle*, *huile de clou de girofle* – in order not to forget. The clue to the *clou*, so to speak, the key to this particular lock-mechanism of effective memorisation, was the existence of pain: the sensation of intense pain had interlocked in his psyche with the cure, or at least the means to relief, and the route from suffering to solace was printed across with those three little words – *clou de girofle*.

He could never forget them, even if he tried.

The children had left the sandpit and it was now profoundly quiet. He narrowed his eyes against the sun's white blaze. A shadow, a tiny human speck, had entered the rotunda and was sitting side-saddle on the stone balustrade that girded the architectural folly. The figure was motionless but something in the posture, the angling of the spine and neck, told him that it was looking down, perhaps at him – at least containing him within its field of vision. But why 'it'? He formed a visor with his hand and shaded his eyes. He could see now that 'it' was a woman from the slope of the shoulders and the contours of the breast, but there was no more information than that. She was just a silhouette, and a minuscule silhouette at that. The whack-whack-whack of rotor blades sounded overhead as a police helicopter tacked north-north-west across the sky and when he looked back the figure under the rotunda had gone.

A few minutes later Céline appeared walking briskly along the right-hand path. She was out of breath and plonked her Dior handbag, black with gilt trimmings, on the bench between them. Her black brooch twinkled archly: it was not the same as the one she had worn before. This one was not in the form of a spider but a bat. Kovacs noticed that her lipstick was smeared. It was brighter, more garish, than her regular brand.

'Sorry I'm late,' she gasped. 'I've been feeding faxes to New York all day. We had a big order for garments from Barneys in Madison Avenue and no-one in the office can ever understand their arrangements for letters of credit.'

'But it's Saturday!'

'I'm afraid the cut-throat world of fashion doesn't stop for little things like weekends. Here,' she said, opening her bag and handing him back the book he had lent her.

'What did you think?'

'I don't know how you can lend me such stuff,' she said, furrowing her forehead. '*C'était un fou, non?* The man was absolutely mad.'

'Althusser was a great philosopher.'

'I don't care if he was – he murdered his wife, then he sat down calmly in the psychiatric hospital and wrote this, explaining why he had done it. It's – it's sick.'

'He wrote it because he was considered *non compos mentis*. He was put into psychiatric care, under French law, without a trial. He felt he should have had a trial so that he could justify his action.'

'I gathered that much. But he *was* mad, wasn't he?'

'In a way, yes. But there's something incredibly sane about the book. He wrote it very quickly, in a short period of lucidity. Then as soon as he'd finished it he slipped back into insanity and died. It's very curious – as a human document, I mean. It is a faultless piece of self-analysis. Totally rational – and nothing escapes his attention.'

'I don't like it,' she said adamantly.

'You must learn to distinguish between what a book *tells* and what a book *shows*.'

Céline was looking at him distrustfully. 'You're a bit like him.'

'What do you mean?' asked Kovacs, surprised.

'I don't know – what do you say in English? – "a cold fish", "a wet blanket".'

'Thank you! But I don't see how I can be a cold fish *and* a wet blanket. Unless the fish is wrapped in the blanket, which I suppose would explain why the blanket is wet. And probably why the fish was cold as well, come to think of it, since a fish in a blanket would almost certainly be dead. Though, on the other hand, I've never had the good fortune to come across a warm fish. Except on a plate, naturally. Which reminds me: I think it was Dr Spooner who said "Which of us has not felt in his heart a half-warmed fish?"'

Céline failed to respond.

'If you hadn't noticed, I'm trying to be a shining wit – which is another Spoonerism, come to think of it.'

Céline's wayward thoughts, meantime, had been playing on the comparison with Althusser. 'What happened to your wife? You never speak about her. It's as if she had never existed.'

Kovacs made a clicking sound with his tongue and raised his eyes lethargically. 'Anne *did* exist and no doubt continues to exist somewhere in this City of Light. We divorced. We were incompatible – or *I* was incompatible, if you prefer. I have nothing against her but thoughts of Anne do not fill my every waking hour. Do you think I poisoned her with ground glass and pushed her into the Seine during a lunar eclipse?'

'The people we know who were friends with Anne tell me you were not *that* incompatible,' Céline persisted. 'They say you had things in common.'

'Sure we had things in common. For example, we were married on the same day.'

Céline was silenced for a while but her irascible mood was simply refuelling.

'I don't really *know* you, do I, Philip? Nobody knows you. Perhaps you don't know anybody either.'

'I don't pretend to be the sociable type,' he defended himself.

'No, but it's more than that, isn't it? I know what I would call you. I would call you *self-effacing* – you efface yourself out of existence. And don't tell me that all the English are like that, because they're not. I know many English people and they're not at all like you. No, it's just you. There's something not quite right about you. You're too detached, detached from everything.' She was searching around for words to define him and eventually flipped a French idiom into English. 'You are constantly pedalling in the sauerkraut of your own preoccupations, though goodness knows what they are! Your book, or whatever you call it.'

'I've explained my book to you before. It's about how the brain processes linguistic information. I compare it to serial processing in computerised data systems. You're welcome to read bits of it if you like.'

His offer fell on deaf ears.

'I'm not really complaining,' she continued, 'but what does our friendship amount to? We have a meal from time to time. We go to the movies. Don't get me wrong. I know that's how we agreed things. I'm not looking for romance and wedding bells. I have no more illusions than you do on that score. But it would be nice, just – to get to know you better, I suppose. To break through this *skin* you have grown around yourself. I'm not the only one who thinks that.'

'Who else have you been speaking to?'

'Nobody. Don't worry. But they all think the same as me:

Derek, Michel, Orriss, Hannah. I know they do. I can tell.'

Kovacs recognised that the diagnosis was correct but he rather liked his impregnability. It was something he cultivated. It irked him to talk about himself. He felt it was gushy and womanly. Why should anyone want to know about him anyway? It was presumptuous. Nevertheless, he was in a complaisant mood and decided to yield marginally.

'As a matter of fact,' he said, somewhat importantly, 'I do have a new friend who knows quite a lot about me.'

'And who is that?'

'His name is Babalu. He is a fat black Brazilian. He wears a Panama hat and he carries a trained mouse in his pocket.'

Céline eyed him incredulously. 'And what does he do?'

'He makes crêpes near the place de la Bastille and is a matchmaker in his spare time. A very resourceful fellow.'

'Well this is a turn-up for the books! Where did you come across him?'

Kovacs recounted the whole story since the burglary: the meeting with Laroche; the appearance of Babalu and the hat of Victor Noir; and everything which had happened that day. She listened quizzically, making stubborn humphing noises whenever anything far-fetched emerged in the telling.

'Did you know about Victor Noir?' Kovacs asked, when he had finished. 'Apparently it's something men don't know about but women do.'

'I have heard about the tomb, vaguely. I went on a tour of Père Lachaise once and bought a postcard. I think Victor Noir's tomb was on it along with Oscar Wilde's – a sphinx sculpted by Epstein if I remember rightly. So. It seems you have a new woman in your life. Not to mention a new man.'

'I wish I could get her out of my life, I can tell you. Especially since the problem with the bank.'

'Serious,' she murmured.

'Yes. Babalu – the Brazilian – may be able to help me, but I'm thinking of taking a look at the tomb myself. I can't concentrate, you see. I can't get down to my work. I constantly feel as if I'm being watched and done things to.'

'You poor soul,' said Céline in spoof sympathy. 'You are obviously a pawn in the great international conspiracy of womankind.

A plaything of the goddesses. You know, there is something Byronic about you. I've often thought that.'

Kovacs laughed. 'You of all people, Céline, should know that I'm not a womaniser. I don't even know what the word means. To *womanise.* It sounds like something you do with a Moulinex food blender.'

'I was not suggesting that you are a womaniser. I'm saying that sex is all in the mind.'

'Sure. But only if you've got a fertile imagination.'

'Ha – bloody – ha!'

'OK,' he said, 'what exactly do you mean?'

'Well, people naïvely consider Byron, like his Don Juan, to have been a lady-killer. You're obviously no exception. But the truth is that he was a victim of women. He couldn't get them out of his head or out of his life. It was not just a sex thing but more of a mental obsession. Probably something to do with the ego. Think of Augusta. Think of Lady Caroline Lamb and the little Italian countess. They were not his victims. He was *theirs.* His wife too – what was her name?'

'Annabella Milbanke.'

'Yes – the Princess of Parallelograms, as Lord Byron called her. All *femmes fatales* in their different ways. You've got the same syndrome in that film, *L'Homme qui aimait les femmes*. Truffaut, isn't it? The hero of the movie is a sick man. He is not happy, he is not fulfilled. It's an intellectual sickness, really.'

'Stop it,' said Kovacs, 'you're reminding me of Derek Fairgreave and his blasted succubi!'

'Well at least Derek is honest about his passions. At least he *has* passions.' She looked at him again with the same brutal, interrogatory regard. He was shocked by the vigour of her defence of Fairgreave. 'I suppose it's always the *mother* to blame in these cases, isn't it? Didn't you tell me something about your mother and your uncle once? You had an uncle who had the same name as you.'

'I was named after him. I've told you before, Céline. My mother was engaged to the other Philip Kovacs but he was killed during the D-day landings. She was heartbroken and Philip's brother, my father, offered his hand in marriage. She accepted but she never got over the death of her fiancé. His photograph was always beside her and I was named after him. It was strange –'

'Yes?'

'When she looked at me, it was as if she were looking *through* me – as if she could see the other Philip behind me, in the distance somewhere. I never felt I could win her love because she had expended it all on the dead man. I suppose I had to be like him, to become like him, to get any response out of her. I was a born method actor,' he added wryly.

'He was dead. I presume that to become like him you would have to die.'

'That is a stupid thing to say, Céline.'

'I was speaking metaphorically. At any rate, your mother was an obsessed woman. And unhappy, no?'

'That's right. My parents' marriage was badly damaged by that obsession. If I am *detached*, as you say, I have no doubt that it has got something to do with being brought up like that. At least I am aware of it. As an adult, I can do what I can to overcome it. Self-knowledge is half the battle.'

'Are they still alive?'

'My father, no. My mother, yes. She's very elderly and frail. She's in a nursing home in Bournemouth. I visit her whenever I go over.'

'Well, well, well . . . ,' said Céline meditatively. It was her habitual way of avoiding comment. Whenever it popped out Kovacs added 'Ding-Dong-Bell!' in his mind.

'Does that answer your request?' he asked haughtily. 'Have you pierced my thick hide now?'

'A little,' she smiled.

'Well stay tuned. There may be more where that came from.'

'Good,' she said with a little note of satisfaction. 'We've made a start, anyway.'

A thought occurred to Kovacs. 'I haven't seen you for ages, have I?'

'No. A fortnight, in fact.'

'How are things?'

'Work,' she said unhelpfully.

'Is it rough?'

'No more than usual.'

'Have you given any thought to July? Remember we were talking of going to Sicily. I wanted to rent that house in Taormina where D. H. Lawrence and Truman Capote had lived – not simultaneously, naturally.'

Céline was in cryptic mood. 'I don't know about that,' she said. 'I'm not sure I like the idea of living next to a volcano.'

'You don't mean *me*, do you?'

'No!' she laughed. 'Etna, of course!'

'One has to live dangerously, doesn't one?' he urged in an access of Nietzschean intrepidity.

'No, one doesn't. I want to live safely.'

'Well perhaps it is possible to live *over* the volcano rather than under it.'

'To be perfectly honest,' said Céline seriously, 'I think I need time on my own, a holiday on my own. I'm thinking of going to Tuscany.'

'On your own?'

'Yes. I just want to sunbathe, visit the Uffizi, read a few books, maybe do some sketching. It's supposed to be very beautiful there, with umbrella pines and little villas and things like that.'

'Isn't Derek Fairgreave going on a painting holiday somewhere in Tuscany?'

She looked at him askance. 'Ye-es, I think so. He was trying to rope Hannah into a trip, wasn't he? I don't know how his plans lie. I suppose we *could* all meet up . . .'

'And what about me?' said Kovacs, mildly out of sorts.

'Well you've got your book, haven't you *chéri*? I thought you wanted to finish it this summer. This way you'll have plenty of time to lavish on it.'

There was a long sullen silence, then she tapped her watch.

'Got to go. The fax machine will be exploding by now.' An expression of sympathy flickered across her face as she pecked him on the cheek. 'Don't worry about things so much, Philip. I'll give you a ring, all right?'

She gathered her bag and walked off. A feeling of inertia and inconclusiveness permeated Kovacs' body like fog. After a couple of minutes he stretched, yawned and stood up, then set off down the same avenue that Céline had taken, the avenue de la Grotte.

He rounded a bend and the path bifurcated. The left-hand fork climbed up among the rocks and bushes, past a greyish stream gurgling gently as it trickled through a sham concrete rockery. This was the route he took. It was heavy going on the legs, as the path mounted higher and higher. Coming down, a couple of young policemen were discussing something with an air of uncertainty. The green band on their caps indicated, in fact, that they were greenhorns, recruited by the police as an alternative to military service.

'We should warn them not to, shouldn't we?' one of them was saying.

'Forget it!' said the other who looked older. 'They're just having fun.'

Kovacs was curious to know what they were talking about and his curiosity was soon satisfied when he turned the bend that led to a huge man-made waterfall. Three bathing beauties in 1940s-style swimsuits were posing for a photographer friend. They were dripping wet and had clearly just been for a swim in the rockpool beneath the cascade. This was no doubt what the policemen had been discussing. Bathing was in all probability against park regulations. The three girls, all brunettes, linked arms and shouted '*Un! Deux! Trois!*', giving a high kick on the count of three which was when the camera shutter clicked. These were Busby Berkeley antics on a small scale and low budget. Kovacs smiled self-consciously as he edged past the three pin-up Fates and, as soon as he was out of shot, they did it again. '*Un! Deux! Trois!*' – and Click! Kovacs almost felt like ordering a copy of the picture: he was fond of bathing beauties (though it was some time since he'd bathed one).

He came at length to the high upper bridge that spanned across to the peak of the spur of rock. It was called Le Pont des Suicidés. Louis Aragon had mentioned it in *Le Paysan de Paris*. He had written that before the metal grilles on each side of the bridge were erected it claimed victims from passers-by who had no intention whatsoever of killing themselves but were suddenly tempted by the abyss. It was an awesome thought – that a place, its *genius loci*, or a sudden seductive vertigo, could provoke unpremeditated suicide. A *mise en abîme*, indeed. Knowing Aragon's theory (and this was a testament to human perversity) he could not resist lingering for a few seconds and looking down, taunting the tutelary spirit that governed the place into a silent battle of wills.

The bridge arched loftily over a path and a strip of water that curled round the back of the rock. It provided a view of a lower bridge over the lake. Immediately below, there was a sheer, overgrown precipice on the surface of which were little ledges, just a few inches in width. On one of these ledges Kovacs spotted two cats – one black and one white – facing each other. They had clearly been walking the ledge from opposite directions and had suddenly encountered each other. Kovacs was considering Breton's remark upon the extraordinary fact that cats have two holes cut in their skin at exactly the points at which their eyes are to be found when he noticed their predicament. They could not pass each other, nor could they turn round: the ledge was too narrow for that manoeuvre. It was like two lorries on a narrow country lane, except that reversing – or walking backwards – did not, as far as he could recollect, form part of the feline repertoire. From time to time one of the cats would slowly raise a paw and slap the other, apparently trying to destabilise it. Clearly if one of the cats fell the other would be able to advance and reach safety. If they fought, however, they would risk falling to perdition together. It was an appalling situation. As he followed his chain of reasoning he had the distinct telepathic impression that the same thoughts were passing through the brains of the cats. Their caution, the occasional tentative pat, the fixity with which they regarded each other – all seemed to confirm this. After two or three minutes, Kovacs could stand no more. He felt macabre, morbid, just watching them. He turned sharply and crossed the bridge to the summit of the rock and half-ran up a further flight of wood-grained concrete steps to the rotunda.

The view from the top was prodigious. Paris stepped away into the blue haze of the late afternoon. Trees, nineteenth-century buildings with red and orange sunblinds, a cluster of high-rises and the jumbled urban skyline with its roof-gardens, satellite dishes, domes and flashing windows. The basilica of Sacré-Coeur and the hill of Montmartre. And at his back the tall pencil of a TV transmission tower that looked like the minaret of a mosque.

He was by the balustrade which encircled the rotunda now, exactly where the tiny silhouette had been about an hour earlier. Down below, like part of a model village, was the lake, the bandstand, the sandpit and the chalet. He pinpointed the bench where he and Céline had been chatting only minutes before. 'I was *there*, and now I am *here*,' he thought dumbly. He seemed to be taking part in an experiment to test Einstein's Theory of Relativity, a leap into non-Euclidean space. Even from that height the symphony of whispering water-sprays rose to meet his ears.

He turned and entered the rotunda, the Temple de Sybille. Polyglot graffiti and anatomical diagrams had been liberally added with felt-tip marker to the Corinthian columns: '*les heures sont longues sans toi*' read one of the more poetic legends. In the centre of the edifice was a circular stone bench. The bench turned round a truncated column, resembling a capstan in appearance, which served as a back-rest. On the top of the capstan was a round, discoloured bronze disc on which one expected to see an official dedication – a name, perhaps, or a year – but in fact there was nothing of the sort. Instead, someone had drawn a large heart with Tippex correction fluid onto the disk. The heart was divided by an angular slash of white, like lightning and – on each side of this slash – there was an initial: 'K' on one side, 'J' on the other. Kovacs touched the Tippex and looked at his finger. It was still wet.

On an impulse, he ran back to the Bridge of Suicides and looked down into the abyss. Below, he could see part of the lower bridge, the suspension bridge, and someone – evidently in a hurry – walking quickly across it towards the park exit. He saw the figure only for a split second – almost a subliminal movement across the retina, no more. There was no time for any detail to be taken in. Who was it? Céline? Or someone else? Someone whose initial was 'J'? They were close, her initial and his: 'J' and 'K', neighbours in the alphabet. And if – just supposing – *if* it was 'her' – his mystery persecutor – whoever she was and assuming she was not Anne or even Céline herself, how had she known that he would be here now, at this hour, at this spot? How?

'J'. Jeanette? Janine? Julie? Unless the initial represented a surname. *Cherchez la femme!* The answer was somewhere, spelt from Sibyl's leaves.

He left the park by the same route that the mystery woman must have taken, so absorbed in speculation that he even forgot to check on the cats. Had he remembered, it might have interested him for at the exact moment that he was crossing back over the bridge they got out of their predicament by an ingenious ruse.

He had missed something there, which was a pity.

It might have taught him a lesson.

6

When Kovacs visited the tomb of Victor Noir the hat was empty. He was almost disappointed. He lingered, all the same, to observe the extraordinary supine bronze of the one man to whom the women of Paris entrusted their deepest secrets and opened their heart of hearts. As Babalu had told him, the green figure's anatomical state and sartorial disarray in death were flagrant: overcoat, jacket and trousers were all unbuttoned, as was the shirt, down to the waist. Oscar Wilde's dictum that 'A really well-made buttonhole is the only link between art and nature' tickertaped through his mind. Yet the face of the reckless libertine was that of a live man in repose, merely cat-napping. It was a handsome face, crowned with thick curlicues of hair. The eyelids were shut, the nose was small and upturned and the jaw had dropped a fraction as if he were lightly snoring. A dashing moustache graced his upper lip. He looked, in fact, much as Kovacs himself had looked at twenty-two, even down to the moustache. Only the nose was perhaps a little too feminine in a disdainful, drawing-room kind of way: in fact, it reminded him of the nose of Corinne, his new next-door neighbour. His own was longer and more plebeian, a nose for the great outdoors betraying proboscis genes of Serbian peasant origin.

It was Babalu who found the next letter, a fortnight after his first contact with Kovacs. The envelope was simply marked 'K' and it was stuffed behind a limp and rotting potted chrysanthemum in the sculpted topper. Babalu had walked to the cemetery from his modest quarters on the quai de la Loire, the room his sister had found him for money down, no questions asked, and was now doubling back to the Gare du Nord to take a train to the airport north of Paris: Roissy-Charles de Gaulle. Today was a special day and he was in fine fettle. In just over an hour his wife's flight from Rio would touch down and they had not seen each other for nearly a year. She was only staying for two weeks but they would be two marvellous weeks, two weeks of tenderness and joy: they would have so much to tell each other, so much to see and do and so much happiness to share.

For Babalu, things were looking up. He had left the crêpe stall for a job as a barman six nights a week (he had Tuesdays off) at a bar called Le Toubib in the rue de Lappe. The pay was not to be sneezed at and he got on well with the other bartender, a dour Scottish sculptor who, like him, was a bird of passage, a knight of the cosmopolitan road: the Scot's accent was so unfamiliar that Babalu could understand virtually nothing that he said but by one of life's little ironies this fact alone, and the endless misconstructions and improvised sign-systems it led to, had proved a winning formula. The bizarre Brazilo-Caledonian double-act was an instant magnet for the marginal world of ethnic night-clubbers who frequented that twilit zone of the city. The two of them made a little fortune in tips and soon learned how to play to the gallery.

The flap of the envelope was not stuck down so once he was settled in the train Babalu opened the folded white letter-card inside.

Help me, V.N.
Mr K, hours, days and weeks pass but me not forget you: never. Sorry about bank. Me phoned bank when depressed and sad. My anger was too much, wanted to hurt you as you hurt me, hurt me always when the dark comes and thoughts of you come too to my small room. Cannot control my anger. Too strong. Days go by, all OK, then suddenly hate comes back, me know that's bad and wrong. Pardon me and me shall pardon you. The woman you met at the park not for you, not your type. Jealousy wounds me. Whatever happens, pardon me for all. Love and fury struggle to control my heart. Soon the day when you were born shall

come. Me shall not forget. Not wallet, not vase, but another present shall be for you from your J.

When he got to the airport Babalu sealed the envelope, addressed it to Kovacs, attached a stamp and posted it after adding a little note on the back to say that he was the sender.

Raimunda Maria dos Santos arrived in clouds of glory through customs at Terminal 2, all sixteen stone of her, shunting a trolley laden with cases and bursting carrier bags. She wore a long white dress like a caftan and a dazzling turban of gold and blue set off with a single toucan feather. Discs of gold were suspended from her large ears and a gold charm-necklace circled the trunk of her neck and reposed on the slopes of her ample matriarchal bosom. The whiteness of the dress deepened, by contrast, the matt darkness of her skin, and her face – that of a true Bahian Magna Mater, stoically accustomed to hard graft and the tribulations of child-rearing – lit up spectacularly when she saw her husband.

'Babalu! *Querido!*' she screamed, and grabbed him to her, attempting a kiss across the wide buffer-zone of their conjoined bellies.

They returned to his room in a rundown tenement block overlooking the aerial Metro and the bassin de la Villette. Bags split open, suitcases dehisced – and the contents of her luggage outnumbered fourfold the meagre handful of belongings that had ensured Babalu's subsistence over the past year. Much of it was food: sacks of manioc flour, *malagueta* chilis, dried shrimp and cashew nuts, flagons of coconut milk and *dendê* oil, bananas, salted codfish and a bag of the little stuffed *salgadinhos* pastries that she had made herself, just before leaving Salvador. She had bought a handful of Chinese oil-paints in tubes to replenish Babalu's paintbox, photographs of the children – Gilberto, José, Cleide, Tadeu, Joselito and Flávio – and a massive kitsch picture of Jesus with a bleeding heart and supplicating eyes to nail above his bedstead. There were cassettes of Caetano Veloso and Carlinhos Brown, local musicians, for his Walkman, and much, much more.

The commotion of unpacking was accompanied by bulletins

of family news: Sem, Babalu's brother, had been released from prison but he had turned into a real *malandro*, a good-for-nothing who wasted his time strumming a guitar and drinking rum; Horácio had bought a house on Whipping Post Hill; Dana was now old enough to become one of the *filhas de santo*, the female ceremonial dancers in the candomblé who whirl around the initiates until they are possessed by their orixá; and Joachim worked the sailing vessels that traded between the ports of the Recôncavo or along the Paraguaça sea.

It was Raimunda's first visit to Europe but she was so full of news that she was oblivious to everything else. Once the cargo of family chronicles was unloaded, however, she could observe her surroundings and take stock. The room was dreadful. But Paris – she loved it instantly! She looked out of his grimy window as a green and white train rumbled along the iron track overhead. She gazed down at the broad swathe of water that was the bassin de la Villette. It was so different from Bahia: the noise, the shops, the endless stream of cars! Even the smell of the city was different: what was it, the smell of Paris?

'It is a mixture of French cigarettes, urine and hot rubber,' explained Babalu. 'The men piss in the streets, you see.'

'Not the women?'

'No, only the men. And the Metro trains have rubber wheels.'

It was another world. She knew she was going to love it.

Babalu had finished painting the walls and ceiling of a studio flat for the crooked landlord who in return wrote off two weeks' rent on the room. He was free in the daytime to take Raimunda around town, while in the evenings – when he worked – she was put into the custody of her sister-in-law whose flat was a short walk away.

A week passed, and every day they were out. They saw the tourist sights and travelled down the Seine; they went to the Science Park nearby; they viewed the exotic animals in the Jardin des Plantes and paraded their Sunday best in the Parc de Bagatelle which, in mid-June, was resplendent with flowers. In an act of summer folly, the Mayor's office had issued a decree to the effect that the entire Pont Neuf, the oldest bridge across the Seine, be covered in thousands of begonias of every colour they could find and the sight drew Parisians in their masses.

Red, yellow, blue, pink – the begonias spilled over the parapet of the bridge and cascaded down concealed frames on the sides. Raimunda was agog. But most of all she loved the elegant shops in the swanky areas of town, full of frocks, jewellery, leatherware and irresistible hats. It was just like the magazines! She couldn't keep away from them, and Babalu was secretly embarrassed that everything in these emporia of *bon chic* was beyond his improved but still limited means. Rather sheepishly, he steered her instead towards the local cut-price Tati store and the clothes shops around Montmartre where at least he could exercise a little munificence.

Kovacs, meanwhile, had received the second missive from 'J': apart from the tone and the confirmation that it had indeed been her in the park, what had surprised him most was her inside knowledge of his life. She knew, sure enough, that his birthday was fast approaching, but the allusions to a wallet and a vase had stopped him in his tracks. Anne's last birthday present to him before they separated had been a wallet; Céline's last birthday present to him the previous year had been a vase. How could she possibly have known all of that? It seemed unlikely that even Anne and Céline would know what the other woman, in each case, had given him. He wrote back to Babalu, thanking him for forwarding the letter and suggesting they meet.

'*Inglês!*' said Raimunda in surprise. 'Who is he?'

Babalu had already shown her Victor Noir's grave when they visited the cromlech of Allan Kardec and now he recounted what he knew of Kovacs.

'He is all right, I think,' he said. 'A kind man but with many many worries.'

'Does he have a wife?'

'He *had* a wife. They separated – divorced. He is very alone and very worried.'

'And the woman who writes to him – perhaps she is a good woman for him?'

'No, I do not think so. She is not good news. I told him her orixá is Iansã, but Iansã in a bad mood with a very domineering temperament. She is warlike and she is not happy with him. There is something in the past. He does not know what.'

'You must pray for him, *marido*.'

'Yes, I must. I do not know why, but I want to help this man. He has a good soul but he does not know it is there.'

'You must introduce him to me, Babalu.'

'He does not speak our language.'

'This does not matter. Good souls speak the same language.'

Babalu got up and walked over to his wall calendar. 'Look!' he said. 'Next Tuesday, the 21st, is my night off, and it is also the Fête de la Musique.'

'What is that, Babalu?'

'It is a great day, like carnival in Salvador. Many hundreds of musicians and singers come to play in the streets and in the concert halls all day and all night all over France. It is like a holiday in Paris, once a year. Aquarela will be playing in one place and there is a bigger carnival somewhere else.'

'Why did you not tell me about this before?'

'I forgot, Raimunda. We have been so busy. Perhaps, in the evening, we could invite Senhor Kovacs to dinner and go with him to hear the music? He is a very intellectual man, Raimunda – *inteligente*. I think it would do him good to get out of himself, you know.'

'This is a kind idea, husband. You must phone him tonight.'

On the evening of the 21st, Kovacs arrived in his best suit, a fine-spun silk the shimmery colour of fish-skin, and sporting his old Cambridge college tie, maroon with pink stripes. His curly grey hair had been carefully backcombed off the high, florid forehead, though to one side it had been flicked forward an inch to hide a patch of squamous skin – latent psoriasis, a disorder of nervous origin to which he was prone. He was a picture of Englishness, straight out of the shop window of Simpsons in Piccadilly. Raimunda took to him immediately, particularly his slight awkwardness in company: he was like someone out of an old film she had seen on her brother's television. He brought peach-coloured roses and a box of Belgian chocolates for her.

Babalu only had the one room but all he needed was a bed, a table to eat off and a shelf for his collection of French literature in translation and a few novels by Jorge Amado, another native Bahian. There was an adjoining cooking area no bigger than a toilet (the toilet itself being communal, on the landing) but since her arrival Raimunda had done her best to make it a fit place to receive guests: she had nailed cheap printed calico sheets from India to the walls to cover the wet rot and improvised a lampshade for the single lightbulb out of a wire coathanger and a couple of red bandannas.

The meal was extravagant. They began with cocktails, *batida de maracujá* and *caipirinha*, then stuffed crab followed by fish in coconut milk and topped off with lime sorbet. Babalu, meanwhile, dispensed little noggins of rum, insisting that Kovacs compare the brand made from molasses with the superior brand made from cane juice. For the first time in weeks Kovacs felt quite jolly. These simple people had put themselves out to make him feel important. His every remark was instantly translated into Portuguese for Raimunda's benefit and she listened eagerly when she wasn't commuting with dishes between the table and the kitchenette, over the entrance of which she had carefully hung a bead curtain so that their guest would not see that she had prepared the entire meal on a single butane camping cooker.

Kovacs was unexpectedly outgoing. He surprised even himself. He plied them with questions about Bahian life and Umbanda and complimented Raimunda profusely on her cuisine. They laughed out loud when he told them about the pigeon he had seen at Passy which waited at a zebra crossing for the traffic lights to change before walking across the road with the human pedestrians. He put forward his theory that Paris had developed superior genetic mutant pigeons that, unlike their woodland cousins, had mastered the art of vertical take-off, something like helicopters or Harrier Jump-Jets. This was a survival necessity, given the speed and indiscipline of the traffic. He tried to explain the unwritten lore of French highway comportment: why, Raimunda asked, when the green walking man lit up and you tried to cross the road, did the cars suddenly come hurtling down upon you, expecting you to get out of the way? Babalu remarked that it was as if, from the inside, French car windscreens had the property of making pedestrians and cyclists invisible. 'The method you have to use is called *le forcing*,' said Kovacs. 'God knows why they give it an English name. You just have to look straight ahead, march forwards without hesitation and do not show any fear. In Paris, there are two kinds of pedestrian – the quick and the dead.'

'Ha! This is right – *é verdade!*' said Babalu. 'Is what I always tell Raimunda: hedgehog know one big thing, but fox know many little thing. You, Philip, are a fox!'

For some reason Raimunda commented that it was virtually impossible to go through life without a bunch of keys somewhere on one's person. The moral and spiritual implications of this observation were vigorously debated.

Even Kovacs' linguistic researches were touched on and Raimunda, who had never wholly approved of her husband's bookishness, demurred.

'Words have nothing to do with real life,' she declared, and Babalu translated reluctantly. 'What does a Jaburu bird or an alligator or a monkey know of words? Words are dead things that are buried in the tombs of books.'

'I quite agree,' answered Kovacs. 'But the written word is a Lazarus, you see. It is waiting in its tomb to rise from the dead. So the reader is like Christ, a redeemer – your Oxala, I should say. Merely by opening the book and reading he can bring the dead to life.'

Babalu was delighted with this response and translated it enthusiastically for his wife, then leapt up and fetched a notepad from his bookshelf above the bed to jot down his guest's aphoristic wisdom before he forgot it. As for Kovacs, he was slightly taken aback: his comments were catchpenny stuff, really, but they were buying him cheap triumphs.

The conversation reached emotional boiling-point when Brazil's chances of success in the World Cup came under scrutiny: sure, Germany had won it more often, but Babalu was convinced that the firepower of Branco and the playmaking skills of Rai would put them back at the top of the world. Kovacs would have put his money on Italy. A framed photograph of the legendary Pelé stood, he noticed, on a chair beside the bed and there were two candles in front of it – an extemporised votive shrine.

At ten past nine the master of ceremonies clapped his hands magisterially and said 'Well, my friend, shall we go?'

'I don't know. Shall we?'

'Come! We will have another rum!' He poured two shots and they chinked glasses. 'The people from Persia – how you say?'

'Persians?'

'Yes! The ancient Persians, they say that when man have decision to make, he must decide these thing twice: one time drunk, other time sober!'

'In which order?' asked Kovacs.

'I don't know. Does it matter, my friend?'

'I do not think that is a proverb which the modern Persians would agree with.'

First they were to go to the small Brazilian carnival in the 14th arrondissement on the other side of Paris; Kovacs insisted on paying for a taxi. The centre of town would be filling up with crowds but if the cab took the Périphérique ring-road it could avoid all the jams. Raimunda had never been in a taxi before and she felt like a queen.

They were dropped at the rank on the place Denfert Rochereau, across the street from the huge statue of a seated lion and the entrance to the catacombs: there a bandstand had been set up for another musical event which had not yet commenced, and the logo of 'Ricard S.A.', one of the sponsors, had been splashed around everywhere, on flags, bunting and stickers. It was a hot evening and the chirruping of police whistles sounded like jungle calls in the humid air: the police had erected barriers and only a trickle of official traffic was being allowed through.

Kovacs' heart skipped a beat. There was an undercurrent of abandon, of misrule, in the crowd that had gathered at the neck of the rue Daguerre; it threw him woozily off balance. The cafés were packed, high-speed roller-skaters with helmets and knee-pads wove adroitly through the outer margins of the crowd, and people were bunched up together, peering over each other's heads, parents carrying toddlers on their shoulders. A fast and breathtaking drumbeat thundered out from the middle of the crowd.

Babalu put his thumb and forefinger into his mouth and whistled. 'That is Aquarela!' he laughed. 'Come on! Let us go to front!'

Despite the density of the crowd and the corpulence of Senhor and Senhora dos Santos, they advanced with little trouble, as if a concealed Moses had parted the Red Sea of the rabble. The truth was that Babalu in white shirt and Panama and Raimunda in a gawdy poplin dress festooned with printed birds and butterflies, her height considerably increased by a hat resembling a decorated Amazonian gourd, cut an impressive figure as a couple. They were part of the show – or so everyone assumed – and they had to be made way for, while Kovacs followed invisibly in their wake.

As they got closer to the thunder of drums Kovacs craned to see. Above the crowd's heads, banners and flags and miniature multicoloured parasols were waved in time to the rhythm. The band's name was emblazoned on one such banner; the flags were those of Brazil: green, yellow and blue, with the image of a globe and the motto 'Ordem E Progresso'. And a number of revellers bore huge photographs of Ayrton Senna, the daring racing driver who had died in an accident two months previously, while others carried pictures of the Brazilian football team, their future hope. The carnival represented the towns of Salvador, Olinda and Rio. Some fifteen percussionists ranged in a circle and dressed in blue tunics with gold, green and red patterns, beat out their wild, blood-racing rhythm on bright chromium drums, accompanied by rattles, guitars, swaying saxophones and grotesque carnival dancers – a man painted entirely in red, his body stuck with glitter, a half-caste woman in a white bikini hung with swinging gold tassels, people with yellow and blue faces, a little hunchback with a gun-holster and a Stetson who hammered his fist against a tambourine, grinning savagely. Babalu was shaking hands with the musicians and kissing the dancers, clapping and bouncing about, happy as a sandboy. Kovacs was standing behind a man with the words 'PLAY DEAD' printed in red on the back of his T-shirt, and when Babalu noticed that he had been left behind somewhat he grabbed his hand and dragged him into the circle, thrusting a pair of borrowed maracas into his hands.

'Shake them, my friend! Dance!' he yelled.

Kovacs had not been expecting this. He smiled awkwardly and waved the shakers up and down with half-hearted Anglo-Saxon ineptitude. Such flamboyant behaviour was hardly his thing. It was like asking Prince Charles to join in a Maori tribal dance.

'Not like that, my friend!' Babalu shouted. 'With rhythm! *Energia!*' Coming behind Kovacs he put his arms round the Englishman's sides and grabbed his wrists, forcing them up and down like pistons in vigorous time to the music. Kovacs could feel Babalu's belly pressing into the small of his back and – gripped in this position – he was obliged to hop up and down, from foot to foot, looking like a puppet or a toddler on a baby-bouncer. He was not sure that he was enjoying this. Those in the inner circle of the crowd were smirking, enjoying the spectacle, and Raimunda was weeping with laughter. Then Babalu left him to it and suddenly a change came over him – he was enjoying himself, incredible but true, or possibly enjoying someone *else*, for he felt like another person, scarcely recognising himself. The little moment of puerile embarrassment had given way to another power: he was one with it all, he belonged. The mind-searing tachycardic pulse of the drums, the frantic strumming on the metal-string guitars, the urgent blasts on an Acme Thunderer referee's whistle just to his left – all seemed to enter his limbs, even his internal organs, and drive out the dark shadows of habit and taboo.

'Yeah!' Babalu shouted, as he danced with swinging carefree ease, snapping his fingers above his head.

But Kovacs' fun was short-lived. As the drums built up to a stirring crescendo, the energy of his dancing increased. He was jumping and stamping in rhythm when suddenly a sharp pain bit into his left eyeball and eyelid. Damn! That could only be one thing.

One of his contact lenses had dislodged.

When the first dance had finished, he took Babalu aside.

'I've got to go to the toilet,' he said, 'in that bar. Shall I meet you and Raimunda over there in a few minutes?'

'Sure, *amigo*. Is exciting, no?'

He went directly to the washbasin outside the underground lavatory of the bar and turned on the tap. He wore soft, disposable contact lenses and one of them had flipped up, folding back on itself to create two sharp points at the edge of the crease. It was this that was causing him so much pain. He pulled back the eyelid close to the mirror and felt around for the maverick lens. One moment he had it and the next it was gone. It had come off on the tip of his forefinger, a little taco of transparent plastic, and dropped straight into the sink, disappearing immediately down the plughole. He cursed again. It was not the money: he changed them every two weeks anyway and had replacement pairs at home. It was the inconvenience. What was he to do now? Either he removed the other lens from the right eye for the rest of the evening, in which case he would be well and truly blind, or he left it in and made do. He decided to leave it in and, standing there in front of the mirror, practised looking at things near and far. He found that if he half-closed the left eye and depended on the right he saw better, but this contrivance had the unfortunate side-effect of making him look like someone peering through an invisible telescope, a mad old sea-dog scanning the horizon for U-boats and destroyers. It couldn't be helped. He met Babalu and Raimunda as arranged, on the terrace of the bar, not mentioning the little incident.

'My friend Antonio, he tell me we must go to other carnival,' said Babalu. 'Is much bigger. Here is just one band, but there are many. Is more Caribbean.'

'OK,' said Kovacs. 'Where is it?'

'Ah! Problem. It is moving, but now, ten-thirty, maybe place Saint-Michel.'

'Shall we go on foot? It's only twenty minutes' walk.'

As they walked, the dissonant cross-currents of music thrummed in the background, a cat's concert of rock, jazz, classical and ethnic rhythms. They passed leisurely through the Marco Polo garden and entered the Jardin du Luxembourg, skirting the large boating pond and the bristling palms in their green wooden tubs, pausing for a while beneath some trees to listen to the baroque a cappella singing that was under way.

On the boulevard Saint-Michel, teenage heavy metal ensembles vied for attention at each corner. The Caribbean carnival was indeed on the place Saint-Michel, a great train of floats and colour and costume amid a massive crowd. The ringing rhythms of a steel band led the music, and the dancing was orchestrated by a dark woman in red Turkish trousers on enormous stilts with a little red waistcoat, long hair and a rubber Dracula mask. She staggered around with bared fangs and pulled faces at children on their parents' shoulders.

To Kovacs, squinting through the telescope of his one eye, it was like observing a coral reef through one goggle, a shifting two-dimensional kaleidoscope of marine exotica. Screaming ambulances flashed helplessly in gridlocked traffic, phantasmagoric dresses swung in and out of view, a woman with spiralling violet cones over her breasts, a small black grandmotherly figure painted entirely in gold. They followed each other through and Raimunda held on to Kovacs' hand so they wouldn't lose him. And over it all the bright, bell-like drumming rebounded from all sides of the *place*, the waters of the fountain glittered in flashes of light and the smell of hot sugared peanuts drifted across from the stalls of the street-vendors.

At a sign from the stilt-legged vampire the tractors that pulled the floats circled round, preparing for the last leg of their journey to the place de l'Odéon. A garish reveller loomed out of the darkness towards Kovacs. The man was almost stark naked, but for a loin cloth and hobnailed boots, and his whole body had been painted black with pink patches, with a baboonish splurge of blue and red on the buttocks. He was wearing a head-dress of multicoloured feathers and beads and a gold cardboard mask over his eyes. Not even the greasepaint could disguise that cratered complexion, however, and the ape-like hang of the shoulders.

'Derek!'

Derek Fairgreave stopped dead and stared at Kovacs, then pulled his gold mask down off his bleary eyes to make sure.

'Philip! Good Lord!' he replied and greeted the other man by clapping his hands in his, smearing them with stains of body-paint. 'Well, well! Fancy seeing *you* joining in the fun!' He scrutinised Kovacs' face. 'Something wrong with your eye?' Then his gaze slipped round him to Babalu and Raimunda and a *risus sardonicus* crept across his lips.

'Lost a contact lens, that's all,' explained Kovacs. He looked Fairgreave up and down with his one good eye, at a temporary loss for words. 'Er, how did the London course go?' he asked eventually.

'Oh it churned on, you know. Like gorgonzola under a microscope. I say, be a good chap and don't mention this – my get-up, I mean – at the College, will you? I'd never live it down. Look,' he said, feeling around his body as if he had lost something, 'no pockets. Nowhere to keep my bloody fags. Wish I'd thought of that! I'm pissed as a fart,' he confided merrily.

He blew on a plastic whistle round his neck, winked and rejoined the throng, dancing disjointedly and swinging his arms like an enraged, grinning primate.

The tractors honked to clear the crowd and some of the floats clipped the kerb and rode up onto the pavement. The threesome were forced back somewhat against a shop-front. Towards the middle of the cortège two black plumed horses were pulling a gold Roman chariot with a shapely bare-breasted carnival queen waving to the crowd from inside. Turning into the boulevard the horses panicked and reared, halting that section of the carnival, though the queen – a little unnerved – continued waving and smiling. A quivering cataplexy seemed to pass over the sweat-hot flanks of the horses, they snorted and stared wildly, and their combined gaze was directed at them – or at Babalu, as Kovacs thought, whose mouse was emerging tentatively from his shirt pocket.

'They're looking at you,' said Kovacs in surprise.

Babalu smiled, took off his Panama and placed it on Kovacs' head. 'No they are not, my friend. They are looking at *you*!'

'Ridiculous! Why should they look at me? You're the one who can communicate with animals,' he added, pointing to the red-eyed Cotinho.

'Yes. It is because I understand with animals that I know they look at you.'

Kovacs went silent. He remembered his dream of the Jardin Marco Polo, the rearing horses in the fountain and the live female figure above them – he had been reminded of it only a few minutes before when they passed the fountain on their way here. And he remembered too the etymology of his own name: *philo* and *hippos*, lover of horses. This was the sort of thing he hated: he hated it when codified connections signalled blandly to him out of the blue. What was he supposed to do? Were they supposed to *mean* something? Well?

Babalu had placed a hand in front of him, as if to bar his progress or warn him. Kovacs squinted at him to search the cause of this action but Babalu was stock-still, his broad nostrils quivering attentively and his bloodshot eyes trained alertly on the middle-distance. The man's tension passed like a crackling magnetic current into Kovacs and his nerves trembled. He felt a swift crispation, a spasmodic contraction of the skin muscles.

'What is it?'

'Is her,' he whispered.

'Who, Babalu?'

'Look. Is her!'

'Who?'

'The girl! The girl who send you letters! The one I see in *cemitério*!'

He pointed towards the place Saint-André-des-Arts. A group of young people were jumping up, one by one, onto some pavement bollards and pushing each other off, playing catch with an empty Schweppes can.

Kovacs caught his breath. 'Are you sure? Are you absolutely sure?'

'I am sure, yes.'

'Which one? Who is she?'

He moved closer to Kovacs and pointed again, inviting the other man to follow the alignment of his arm. 'There – to left. No skirt, jeans this time. But she have same green jacket. And cap – baseball cap.'

'What shall I do?' Kovacs was rooted to the spot.

'Follow her! Find out where she live. Perhaps you will recognise her.'

'And you?'

'I must stay with Raimunda, my friend. Is no good to be alone. Paris is strange city.'

'Of course.'

'But tell me – tell me who you find!'

'I will.'

Babalu pushed him so hard in the back that he nearly fell over but, regaining his equilibrium, he made for the girl. He had to squint hard to find her. Night had fallen like a sledgehammer and the rue Saint-André-des-Arts was a dense swarm of commingling humanity.

There – there she was! She was waving goodbye to her friends and heading into the crowded road. He would have to get closer. Under no circumstances must he lose her now.

The narrow passage, however, was choked. In addition to the beggars and drunks who sprawled across the opening of the street a number of bands were playing further up and the throng got denser and denser. He was helped a little in his progress by the fact that those who saw him coming veered out of his way. With his left eye screwed completely closed, the right eye glaring desperately and the oversized Panama engulfing most of the rest of his head, he looked less like the Ancient Mariner than a dyspeptic Cyclops-turned-cotton-planter. He was doing his level best to keep the bobbing back-to-front black baseball cap in view but she was moving fast.

There was one chance – a gamble. The crowd was limited to the rue Saint-André-des-Arts. To his left, the rue Suger – relatively unpopulated – turned off and looped round in darkness to rejoin the main road beside the Lycée Fénelon. There was just a chance that, if he ran round, he could either get ahead of her or at least closer. If the odds were against him she might turn right, down one of the roads which led to the Seine. Then he would not see her doing so and that would be that: he would have lost her. But this way . . . in a split-second he had made up his mind and lurched urgently into the rue Suger.

He was not on top form. When he emerged again onto the main thoroughfare he was blowing and panting. He looked back down the road. No sign. His heart was sinking when he spotted her no more than twenty yards ahead of him. Baseball cap, green jacket – yes, it was her! – and she was still moving fast, skipping on and off the kerb, turning sidelong to slip through knots of people. On one turn he saw her in profile. She was young, very young. In her early twenties. The hair was clearly in a chignon, bundled up into the hat. But he had glimpsed her profile sharply against the bright brasserie lights of the Carrefour de Buci. A neat, girlish face, with small nose, strong chin and a pouting lower lip. What was more, her body, the deliberately jaywalking lilt of her stride, the way the hands flopped loosely at her side – this was familiar. He knew her. He had seen her before.

She hesitated and turned back for a moment and, like a stalker in a gangster movie, he stopped dead and turned to look in a shop window. It must have looked damned suspicious. The window lights were all off and there was nothing to see behind the security grille. Nobody was looking in the shop windows anyway. They were all there for the music and the bars. Had she noticed him? He couldn't be sure. He decided to pull back.

But not too far, he mustn't pull back too far. She was going like greased lightning. The rue de Buci – the rue de l'Abbaye – the rue Guillaume-Apollinaire – all disappeared in a trice behind her. Then suddenly she had turned right into the rue Saint-Benoît and when he rounded the corner she had gone. Vanished. But this was impossible! She didn't even have time to get to the end of the road! He stared madly down the street which terminated in the glowing frontage of a bar called Aux Assassins. To the right was a little restaurant named La Brocherie under a painted sign of a penny-farthing which, for the merest moment, rang a little bell in the hinterland of his consciousness.

He ran halfway down the street, zigzagging to right and to left and attracting the attention of some diners at the street tables of one of the little restaurants who paused – their forks en route to their mouths – to watch him race past.

And to his relief there she was. An insane wave of triumph shot through him like adrenaline. He had just caught her in time.

To the left was a cul-de-sac.

The Impasse des Deux Anges.

At the bottom end of the cul-de-sac, under a wall-mounted streetlamp, he could see her. She was letting herself in with a key. She was home. One second later and he would have been too late. As the door banged shut he ran up to the illuminated façade of the building.

No. 8, Impasse des Deux Anges.

It was a bland, unexceptional construction in a secluded corner of the *quartier*, opposite a carpet salesroom. He looked up and the lights went on at the fourth floor, below a little roof terrace of flower-boxes and trelliswork.

Fourth floor, No. 8, Impasse des Deux Anges.

Beside the door were the bells to the various apartments,

arranged in ascending order with the surnames of the occupants beside them.

One, two, three, *four.*

And there it was: Jones. Her name. And an English name, at that.

He had found his 'J'.

The profile, the sulky lower lip, the lilting walk – and most of all, the name. Suddenly it all came back to him. Tomorrow he would check, but it was hardly necessary: he knew exactly who she was.

7

THE FOLLOWING MORNING, Wednesday June the 22nd, he was at the reception desk of the College at 9.30, the moment it opened. As Madame Duluc, the receptionist, looked on, he keyed the name 'Jones' into the search facility on the College records. A recent development in the registration process had involved scanning in photographs of the students for their pass-cards and, at the press of a button there she was: Delphine Jones, 8, Impasse des Deux Anges, 75006 Paris. He saw from her year of birth that she was twenty-two: the same age, he thought, as Victor Noir. The phone number and other coded data were dropped into an info-box beneath the image of her face. It was a handsome, rather than pretty, face. The hair was raven black and dishevelled, the eyebrows bold inky strokes – unusually strong. There was a sulky, adolescent remoteness about her, especially in the pouty lower lip and the vague elsewheres of the large eyes which looked indifferently to one side. The effect was no doubt due to a refusal to smile for the camera, a resistance to any impulse to coquetry. At his request, Madame Duluc made a print-out of the image.

'Can I tell from these codes which classes she has followed?'

The receptionist cross-checked on a pop-up menu and the details appeared.

'She took the advanced language course with you, until December,' said Madame Duluc, 'and before that a term of laboratory work with Derek Fairgreave.' A note of concern appeared in the receptionist's voice. 'It says here she failed the CPE. Wasn't this the girl who cheated?'

'Yes, it was.'

It was indeed. The minute he had seen the nameplate by the bell-push it had come back to him.

She was one of many he had helped prepare an advanced international exam in English and it was he who had invigilated the exam in the Maison des Examens, a huge purpose-built examination centre to the south of Paris which was appropriately cruciform in groundplan.

He remembered it well now, her Calvary. It was a cold December day and the heating had broken down. Some two hundred and fifty candidates in the room he was responsible for hugged their overcoats around them as they scribbled off their answers to the four examination papers, working from nine in the morning until nearly five in the afternoon. The cold was atrocious and the caretaker of the building had assured him that an engineer was working on the problem in the boiler-room though no palpable improvement was ever made.

It was a long, drawn-out day with certain clearly defined duties to perform: a team of helpers to patrol the room, checking on identity papers, answering questions, escorting the sick and incontinent to the lavatories. Then there was a plan of the room to make, in order to tick off absentees, and after each paper further lists had to be drafted and checked. The whole thing was a bore, but bearable because mindless and mechanical. There were pauses for coffee breaks and long gaps in time during which he looked across the rows and rows of bowed heads, each at a little square desk, or out of the window at the grey, mist-logged suburb: the Hôtel La Place, *Chambres à partir de 140F*, and the RER station where trains pulled in all day long with a groan of brakes then eased heavily out, heading for Paris or out of town. Every now and then – more to stretch his legs than anything else – he walked up and down the aisles himself, ensuring that candidates were using pens rather than pencils, handing out more rough paper, showing his watch to confirm the time on request.

He was walking in soft shoes back up the exam room when he caught her. She had obviously not heard him approaching. It was during a paper which tested English grammar and syntax and, as he came up behind her desk, he was met by a curious sight. He had heard of elaborate and far-fetched methods of cheating but this one was new to him. The girl was in a knee-length pleated skirt and, with one hand, had pulled the skirt up to the top of her thigh. Covering the thigh were elaborate columns of English verbs, copied out on her skin in fine black ink and grouped, it was later ascertained, according to whether they were followed by the gerund, the infinitive, or both. Suddenly she was aware of his presence behind her and she pulled the skirt down to the knee and glanced back. She instantly realised that it was too late, blushing deeply and looking directly into his eyes. Now, with the photographic print-out to help him, he remembered that moment distinctly. It was a look that was almost beseeching, as if she could have doubted the official consequences of her discovery. It was true that none of the other adjoining candidates had noticed what was happening. Was she, with her eyes, pleading with him to simply walk on?

He did not walk on. For her, perhaps, there was a moment when it could have gone one of two ways, but for him there was only a single course of action. He beckoned to her to follow him and, putting down her pen, she did so. As they passed down the aisle he asked a middle-aged woman who was invigilating to come with him too. Outside the closed doors of the exam hall the female helper, at his request, inspected the unusual crib-sheet as a second confirmatory witness. She would later countersign his official report.

'There's obviously no point in you staying to the end of the exam,' he said to the girl. 'You might as well go back in, fetch your bag and coat, and leave.'

She nodded silently. He recalled that there were hot tears of frustration in her eyes.

'It was a stupid thing to do, wasn't it?' That, if he remembered correctly, was what he had said.

It had not been an easy moment for him, given the fact that Delphine Jones had been his student, though hardly someone he had had much personal contact with. For a year she had sat at the back of a large-ish group of twenty and had not been one to join in discussions. 'Jones' – yes, she had an English father and French mother, that was it. Consequently her command of the language was good. She had produced above-average essays and there had really been no need to cheat. Perhaps lack of self-confidence was behind it all, a bout of pre-exam nerves. The incident had spoilt his appetite at lunch a little that cold

December day – he had left his potatoes and skipped the profiterole dessert in the canteen – and then he had thought no more about it.

Until now.

For now, adding the whole concatenation of circumstances together, a much more complicated picture was taking shape: the burglary, the letters, the bank problems, the phone calls. 'You done me bad,' she had said in the first typed letter. 'Why you wrecked my small chance?' It was now clear that success in that exam had been of great importance to her, and this was not surprising: it was a diploma required in a number of professional fields and the competition was stiff. But the letters were also distinctly *love* letters – a love contaminated by injury and virulent resentment verging on malice. The picture was beginning to make sense. The student crush was a common enough phenomenon, but to then be betrayed by the object of that crush – to be denounced by the very person in whom that unspoken admiration had been invested, the very person who for one year had prepared you for that day, that exam, and then exposed you to a moment of unspeakable humiliation – however much it was your own fault, the consequence of your own calculated risk-taking – that was the nub of the matter, the rub. Viewed like that, she was trapped in a ferocious double-bind, a vipers' nest of conflicting emotions which, at her age, she could probably barely cope with. If, on top of that, she had been put to shame in front of family and friends – her little plans for a career or further education nipped in the bud by this invisible worm (him!) or at the very least retarded for a good year – was it really surprising? Was it really surprising that, in the frozen moment when she had looked at him in the exam hall, every nerve in her body had wanted it to go the other way, had wanted him to cough, to look out of the window, to amble silently on? The Nelson Touch: it was almost a British tradition under nobler, more justifiable, circumstances. He hadn't of course obliged, and he still wouldn't if he were to find himself in that situation again: it was a question of professional conscience.

In the half-year that had intervened since that misty December day, the whole tumultuous ferment of emotions that boiled behind those remote eyes had gone over the top, had transmuted into bitter, vindictive and at the same time hurt and apologetic words and actions, a terrible self-divisive energy – with him, Kovacs, as its moving target. 'Moving,' he thought, in the passionate sense of the word.

This, in the couple of minutes it took for him to climb three flights of stairs to his office, was what went through his mind as it had been doing throughout the tail-end of the previous day. Logically, his conclusion was irrefutable. Everything married up.

He placed the photo-scan square on the table in front of him. Delphine Jones. The young woman looked up and round him, the eyes refusing to meet his. He cocked his head to one side to catch her but it was no use. No amount of manoeuvring would align her gaze with his. The focal point was elsewhere, a few inches off-centre.

There was no doubt in his mind as to what he should do and, picking up the telephone receiver, he tapped out the number that appeared just below the girl's photograph.

He spread out his hand and inspected his fingernails abstractedly as the phone rang – once, twice, three times.

'*Allô, oui?*'

'Delphine? Delphine Jones?'

'*Oui?*'

'This is Mr Kovacs, Philip Kovacs.' He addressed her, unthinking, in English.

There was a long, muffled silence. He was vaguely aware of a hand being placed over the receiver and a distant, panicky mumble of words filtering through the gag of flesh and blood.

'*Oui?*' she said again.

He resolved to get straight to the point.

'I think you know why I am calling. It is you, isn't it? You have been to my flat. You have been leaving me letters in the cemetery. You phoned my bank. All you have to do is say "Yes".'

Again there was an extended pause, then: 'No. I don't understand.'

'Let me spell it out then. I believe that you have burgled my flat and stolen my typewriter. I believe that with this typewriter you have been sending me letters which you place in the hat on the tomb of Victor Noir in the Père Lachaise cemetery. You have also been keeping me under observation and making anonymous and phoney phone calls.' He winced slightly to himself at the head-rhyme. '*Hoax* phone calls, I mean. Are you going to admit that this is true?'

Silence.

'Very well, I'm going to give you a chance. I am here at the College for a couple of hours or so. I shall be working in the library. When you feel ready to speak to me, phone reception and they will call me to my office. All right?'

'*Oui*.' The voice was terribly small, barely a whisper. There was a quaver of fear in it and this confirmed to him beyond any shadow of a doubt that he had been right in his assessment of the matter.

'I'm giving you a chance to explain yourself. If you behave sensibly there's no reason why we can't sort this out between ourselves.'

He could hear that she was still on the line – she sniffed a couple of times and he sensed that she was on the verge of tears – but once more there was no reply and after a few seconds he put down the receiver before ringing through to reception to tell them where he would be and that he was expecting a call.

The library on the first floor was a large, oak-panelled room in the English manor house style, with pseudo-Gothic nooks and alcoves. He settled down at a table, switched on the brass reading lamp, and ran his eye down a list of journal articles he had ordered some weeks back. The ticked titles were those that the librarian had managed to acquire in photocopy and these he had in a thick stack beside him. He read just the titles, glossing over the names of the authors and the details of publication.

[1] The Brain as a Darwin Machine ✔
[2] Why We Think What We Do about Why We Think What We Do
[3] Is Seeing Believing?: Notes on Clinical Recovery ✔
[4] Congenital Insensitivity to Pain in an Imbecile Boy ✔
[5] Eye Movement Guidance in Reading: The Role of Parafoveal and Space Information
[6] What is it Like to Be a Bat? ✔
[7] Do Mental Events Have Durations?

[8] Why Are Verbally Expressed Thoughts Conscious?
[9] Mental Rotation of Three-Dimensional Objects ✔
[10] Non-Conscious Face Recognition in Patients with Face Agnosia ✔
[11] Outlooks for Blindsight: Explicit Methodologies for Implicit Processes ✔

On a whim, he chose the sixth title, rifled through the stack to find it and settled down to read, a pad at his side to take the odd note. He had had time to read this and the fourth article – perhaps an hour – when a low-tone phone rang at the librarian's desk and he was summoned over.

'For me?' he said. 'Can you tell them I'll take the call in my office?'

'No, it's not from outside,' said the librarian. 'It's an internal line. The principal would like to see you in his office.'

'Oh damn! Listen, I'm expecting a call. Could you do me a favour, Harry, and ask reception to divert it to Allwright's office when it arrives? It's rather important.'

What could Allwright want? It wasn't even term-time. He bundled his papers under his arm and took the lift to the principal's office on the 5th floor.

'He'll be across in a second,' said the secretary. 'If you'd just like to go in and wait.'

He entered the principal's office. There were two glass-fronted bookcases then a wall taken up from floor to ceiling with yellowing East-Light lockspring box files, the pre-computer filing system. Behind the principal's desk a portrait of the College's lexicographer founding father hung at a slight angle, making it look as if he was about to slide off his chair and only preventing this by clawing at the armrests. Kovacs noted a bottle of R. White's lemonade, the seal freshly broken, and a box of Liquorice All-Sorts, both items probably flown over in a diplomatic bag, for Allwright was hand in glove with someone at the Embassy. It took him back to the headmaster's study at school. He half expected to see a cane hanging prominently on the wall. He wandered over to the window and looked down on the road below.

On the opposite pavement he could see Fairgreave with

Céline. They were talking with animation, even intimacy, he thought. Céline laughed and did the *bises* – four kisses, from one cheek back to the other. It was the standard Parisian tariff between friends. But there was something in the way that she gripped his sleeve as she did so, the way she held his upper arm tightly as she kissed, that for one exquisite crystalline moment said just a little more. Even from five storeys up he could see that. Céline left in the direction of the Metro and Fairgreave turned on his heels, disappearing from view into the main entrance of the College below.

Dr Allwright was whistling to himself when he arrived in the outer office. It was a jaunty little melody and sounded familiar to Kovacs.

'What's that tune?' he asked when the principal came in. It was just to make small talk.

Allwright stalled and reflected blankly on the matter.

'Don't know, I'm afraid. Something I must have picked up. I think it's one of those Rodgers and Hart songs.'

'Ah!'

'Sit down, Philip,' he said, gesturing to an armchair. His voice was weak and neutral in tone, lacking in force like that of a patient, etherised, recovering from an operation, but this was nothing out of the ordinary. Allwright reminded Kovacs of the present Minister of Culture, Jacques Toubon, to look at. The latter was currently attempting to pass a law banning all English words from the French language, and Kovacs recalled that the French press had wittily dubbed him 'Mister Allgood'. Allgood – Allwright – Allgood. The man in front of him would not have sanctioned such a campaign, but he was a creature of unfathomable manners and motives. In the middle of summer he wore heavy worsted suits and a yellow Tootal scarf with heraldic crests on it and his black Derby shoes were always polished to a high military shine. He was so short that when he sat down and tried to cross his legs it never quite worked: the leg that was on top slipped off and he ended up sitting with knees clamped together, ankles apart and the shiny toe-caps of the shoes touching each other. The frailty of his voice was matched only by the valetudinarian pallor of his face, but the old man's alert grey eyes never missed a trick and his tight-lipped mouth had a reputation for never opening in vain. The air of sickly enervation was sheer pose, more Waugh than Toubon: there was no infirmity of purpose. He was a Pooh-Bah with fingers in numerous pies. He ran the College with a quiet and unfalteringly diplomatic touch.

'You wanted to see me?' said Kovacs.

'Yes I did, Philip.' He coughed lightly into a neatly ironed silk handkerchief. 'I must do something about the dust in here. I wanted to see you, yes. How are things, generally speaking?'

'Fine.'

'A good year?'

'I think so. Madame Duluc said that enrolments are already beginning to take off for next September.'

'Yes, I've just been speaking to her. You haven't had any particular . . . worries, any *problems*, have you?'

'How do you mean?'

'Anything you'd like to discuss with me, I mean. You know that that's what I'm here for, don't you?'

'Yes, of course. But no – everything at the College has gone very well indeed.' Kovacs ran his tongue along the tartared backs of his teeth.

'So you're all right, then?'

Kovacs sniggered involuntarily – he was tempted to say 'No, *you're* Allwright!' but thought better of it. The principal raised his eyebrows effetely.

'Something amusing you?'

'No, nothing really.'

'Well let me get to the point. It's just that we've had a phone call, a rather worrying phone call. I don't know what to make of it. Perhaps you can help me.'

'I'll do my best if you tell me what it's about.'

'A Madame Jones rang up half an hour ago. She says that you have been harassing her daughter. It seems you phoned the girl, who was a former student here, only this morning and accused her of burglary, anonymous phone calls and goodness knows what else. Then Madame Duluc said you were asking for information about the girl this morning when she opened the office. Is all of this correct?'

Kovacs could feel the principal's grey gaze alighting on him gently like a moth.

'Yes, it is correct.'

'Would you like to tell me what is going on?'

He took a deep breath. There was nothing for it but to embark on the whole story and this he did, sparing little detail. Allwright tried unsuccessfully to cross his legs again and settled for crossing his arms, nestling his chin thoughtfully on the knot at his neck where the yellow scarf was tied. There was not a flicker of response in his politic demeanour. Kovacs knew from experience that this was not a good sign. When he had neared the end the principal began interrupting.

'I'm sorry, you were saying that these letters were delivered to you from the tomb somehow?'

'Yes, by Babalu – the man I mentioned.'

'Who is . . . ?'

'An Afro-Brazilian – well, a half-caste really. He's a spiritist, which is why he goes to the cemetery. To see Allan Kardec's grave. He makes crêpes for a living. Or he used to, I should say. He works in a cocktail bar now.'

'And you were dancing with this Booby –'

'Babalu.'

'You were dancing with him at a Brazilian carnival when you saw the girl?'

'When *he* saw the girl, yes. Or not exactly: it was a Caribbean carnival. The Brazilian carnival was earlier. And we were dancing in the Brazilian carnival but not at the Caribbean carnival. We were just watching, there. With Raimunda.'

'Raimunda?'

'Babalu's wife.'

'I see.'

Kovacs' account petered to a close, spent itself like a dying soda syphon, and a minute of silence intervened during which the erratic one-finger typing of the secretary could be heard from next door.

'I know it's hard to believe,' Kovacs confessed lamely.

After due deliberation Allwright spoke. 'Naturally I take your word for all this, Philip. You are a respected member of staff and we've known each other a long time. The problem for me is that this could reflect very badly on the College.'

'I understand that.'

'Do you? Then why – if you have these serious accusations to make – why don't you go through the proper channels? Why don't you contact the police?'

'I *did* contact the police, as I told you.'

'Yes, you did. But when this matter came to a head, when you identified your alleged persecutor, why didn't you go back to the police?'

'That was only last night. I thought that under the circumstances it would be more tactful to resolve the matter without resorting to the police.'

Allwright looked foxed. 'Forgive me, but if that is what you thought why did you contact the police in the first place?'

'That was before I knew who was responsible. When I found out that it was the girl I thought that the matter could be cleared up out of court, so to speak.'

'I see. Your attitude to all of this does not seem very consistent, if you don't mind me saying so.'

'Perhaps not. But circumstances change. One's judgement is not necessarily the same at any given moment.'

'No, quite,' murmured Allwright.

'You said you wanted to help. May I ask what you would suggest I do?'

'Go back to the police. Given that the family are turning this back against you – denying your accusations, effectively, and accusing you of harassment – I do think you should now make this a police matter. If, that is, you feel as sure of your position as you say you do.'

'I do. And you're right. Thank you. That is what I shall do.'

Allwright tightened the knot of the scarf at his neck like a noose and got up to show Kovacs to the door.

'You know, it doesn't take much,' he added, as a last word of warning. 'It doesn't take much to sully the good name of an institution like this. A tawdry little trial. An article in a newspaper. We have a good professional reputation and I'm sure you'll understand when I say that I wouldn't want to see it dragged through the dirt, all because of some ambiguous little affair like this.'

Kovacs, in parting, felt emboldened. 'I do understand that, yes, but when you say "ambiguous" I should tell you that for me there is no ambiguity at all. Things are exactly as I have told you.'

'I'm not doubting you, Philip,' said Allwright, smiling infirmly for the first time. 'But sometimes one doesn't grasp all of the elements as fully as one would like to. It takes time before the whole truth is known. Maybe even you are capable of jumping to wrong or half-baked conclusions.'

'Maybe, but I think this situation is perfectly clear-cut.'

As he was about to leave the principal called after him.

'Oh Philip! Just one thing. When does your contract come up for renewal?'

Kovacs could feel himself tensing.

'Next December. Why?'

'Nothing! I just wanted to be sure. It's simply that we're in the process of revising the conditions of service and discussing these things with Accounts. Bye! And keep me informed, won't you?'

On the way down the corridor he passed Fairgreave sitting in the corner of a shared teachers' office. The craggy features looked up from a test-paper.

'Philip!' he called cheerily. 'Come in for a moment! What's up? You look like a Greek tragedy.'

'Nothing's up,' Kovacs responded coolly. 'What are you doing here?'

'I've just finished marking these fucking placement tests. Here, listen to this one. A gap-fill. You know when it says "Vanessa had not been feeling her usual *something* that evening"? You're supposed to find the missing word. This stupid Ada has put in "guests": "Vanessa had not been feeling her usual *guests* that evening". You have to laugh, don't you? Anyway, I've just seen the bottom of my in-tray for the first time this year.'

'Really. I didn't know they had bottoms.'

Kovacs sat on the desk beside Fairgreave and put down his pile of photocopies with the bibliography and the print-out of the girl on top. Fairgreave smelt strongly: it was not just the *tabac noir*. Kovacs was not sure what a goat's testicles smelt like but he felt that it must be something like this. Fairgreave inspected the photo-scan of Delphine Jones.

'Hmmm, she was one of mine once, wasn't she? "A face born from the wake left by the tail of a comet in a polar mist", as someone once said.'

'I saw you in the street with Céline just now,' Kovacs interrupted. 'What was she doing here?'

'Oh nothing much,' said Fairgreave, bringing a hand up to scratch himself under the armpit. Kovacs was momentarily reminded of his dancing in the carnival. 'If I'd known you were here, I'd have told her. I'm sure she'd have loved to see you.'

'She seemed to be quite happy enough seeing you.'

Fairgreave pursed his lips and glanced amusedly at his colleague.

'Oh you know Céline – she's a free bird. Does what she wants. Goes where she pleases,' said Fairgreave cryptically.

'Is there something between you?' asked Kovacs directly. 'I don't mind, but it would be interesting to know.'

Fairgreave cleared his throat. 'There *is* a possibility that we might be going on a painting holiday together in July. Not at my insistence, mind you. She asked me if she could tag along.'

'And Hannah? I thought you were going with Hannah?'

'She backed out. Or I did, I'm not sure. One or both of us backed out. Anyway,' he added cheerfully, 'I hear you've got yourself a succubus!'

Kovacs felt embittered, a confidence betrayed. 'I see Céline tells you everything. But no, I haven't got a "succubus". I'm just having a few problems with an ex-student.'

Fairgreave glanced at the photo-scan, adding two plus two.

'Perhaps,' he said, 'you *should* get yourself a succubus. You're turning into a professional Leibnizian monad, if you don't mind my saying so. You know you can always advertise on the Minitel? "Tartless wreck seeks reckless tart".'

Kovacs didn't answer and Fairgreave, humming to himself, looked over the other man's bibliography.

'What's all this, then? Holiday reading? "The Brain as a Darwin Machine". Blimey!'

'Well I wouldn't expect you to take an interest in that, Derek,' he replied sarcastically.

'Oh but I do! I love all that Darwin stuff – the social Darwinism. So do the ladies, you know. They're all looking for the Missing Link!'

'How do you mean?'

'Well take the case of Otzi . . .'

'Who?'

'He's the 5,000-year-old man they found perfectly preserved in ice in the Tyrolean Alps two or three years ago. He died in an avalanche when he was about thirty-five. The oldest discovered man, perfectly preserved. You must have read about him?'

'I think I did.'

'They bunged his body into a fridge or something in Innsbruck and bugger me blue if they didn't start getting all these women turning up asking for donations of his frozen sperm. Apparently the phone never stopped ringing too.'

'What are you trying to tell me?'

'Social Darwinism, Philip. I'm telling you that it's always the women who decide. If men look the way they do today it's purely and simply because women want them to. In genetic selection it is the women who are the decision-makers, when they choose a mate. Now *your* problem . . .'

'I have a problem, do I?' Kovacs interrupted irritably.

'Yes, frankly, you do. Your problem is you *are* a social Darwinist but you see it all from the outside – like a scientist. Very cool, very distant, very aloof. And what you see, you don't like. The mating game puts you off. Because you're watching it as if it's all going on on a slide: sperms and eggs and genes all squiggling around. Yuk! See what I mean? You can't stand it! You want to wash your hands of it.'

'I don't see anything particularly noble in *couples*, if that's what you mean,' he protested.

'Why not?'

'Well, it's like two one-legged people holding hands because, from a distance, they look like one two-legged person. See what I mean? A lean-to ideology. I think it was Robert Louis Stevenson who said that marriage is a sort of friendship recognised by the police.'

'Why did you divorce Anne?' asked Fairgreave suddenly.

Kovacs fumed silently. Fairgreave had never been one to

mince words. He was tossing up as to whether to hit the man or simply storm out, slamming the door petulantly behind him.

'You see! I can tell that I'm right! I'm not getting at you, old boy, I'm simply trying to help. I'm not even blaming you for divorcing. No – your problem is that when you look at a rose you don't see the rose, you see the thorns. Ouch! They hurt. So you don't want the rose. Social Darwinism, looked at as a mechanistic biological process, *does* hurt. It's horrific! Once one knows – properly knows – how it works, the whole lovey-dovey thing goes to pot. I mean, you can't believe in Romantic love when you know that the two candidates are really eyeing each other up through the genetic imperative, can you?'

Kovacs shook his head. Despite himself, Fairgreave's argument was beginning to intrigue him.

'As Shakespeare says,' Fairgreave continued, '"All the world's a stage".'

'Yes?'

'Well, if all the world's a stage, where is the audience? There isn't one! There can't be one, because there's no auditorium – only a stage. Do you see what I'm getting at?'

'No.'

'The scientific type of social Darwinist thinks he's a spectator, uninvolved, sitting in the auditorium. He's making a big mistake, because there isn't an auditorium. There *are* no spectators, only participants, only actors. He doesn't realise that he's right up there on the stage.'

'You're saying that one should *live* social Darwinism, from the inside?'

'Exactly! Subjectively, not with a spurious scientific objectivity. Be a good animal! You're not a disembodied brain hovering above the human race. You're a man. You shouldn't let your brains go to your head. You should get over your distaste and join in – join in the Darwinian circus, get on the merry-go-round. You never know: it might be fun!'

'Well thank you for the advice.' Kovacs' tone was still facetious but he couldn't disguise his interest. 'It's not very Buddhistic, but it's what one would expect from you.'

'Oh bugger Buddha, Philip! You know, that man in America – what's his name? – the one who ran the sperm bank. Dr

Alnsem, I think. I can't help admiring the bastard. Imagine! He secretly used his own sperm to father seventy-five kids – at least seventy-five. Of course the siring record is held by Emperor Moulay Ismail the Bloodthirsty of Morocco. He had 888. But with science to help things along, Alnsem could well have exceeded that if he hadn't been stopped in time. Unfortunately, he's an ugly sod. You can just imagine them all in twenty years, can't you, coming back for the Sperm Bank Annual Reunion: seventy-five fat little lookalikes with glasses!'

'Sometimes,' said Kovacs with conviction, 'the modern world just makes me want to retch.'

'You're out of touch, old boy. This isn't the modern world. This is the *post*-modern world. Hasn't anyone told you? The age of post-modernism.'

'I always thought post-modernism was when your mail gets delivered on time.'

'So did I,' said Fairgreave, 'until I discovered Smirnoff.'

That evening Kovacs determined to follow Allwright's advice, for form's sake and to protect himself against any repercussions. He would have to go back to Inspector Laroche at the Commissariat. Only this time he would recruit Babalu's help, to back him up, to confirm his story. As he cooked his evening meal, he turned on the radio – a music channel, to escape the depressing news bulletins from Rwanda – and to his surprise the first thing he heard was the tune that Allwright had been whistling as he came into his office. The DJ had announced it as a 1937 song from the musical *I'd Rather Be Rich*. He listened, aghast, to the words:

'Have you met Miss Jones?'
Someone said as we shook hands.
She was just Miss Jones to me.
Then I said, 'Miss Jones,
You're a girl who understands
I'm a man who must be free.'
And all at once I lost my breath,
And all at once was scared to death,
And all at once I owned the earth and sky!

Now I've met Miss Jones,
And we'll keep on meeting till we die,
Miss Jones and I.

Allwright had not been mistaken. It was a Rodgers and Hart composition, the DJ announced at the end. 'DJ' – the initials snagged in Kovacs' mind. Holy shit! There was no getting away from her. DJ – Delphine Jones. Delphine Jones – Mademoiselle Jones – Miss Jones: the mother's phone call must have triggered the song off unconsciously in Allwright's head. And now here it was again on the radio, by special supernatural request. It was all of a piece. Kovacs banged his hand down on the radio's off switch, finished his meal and went to bed.

He slept badly. His bedroom on the upper floor abutted a neighbour's toilet and bedroom and the ballcock in the cistern must have been broken because he could hear constant running water. It sounded like a clepsydra, he thought. When he did finally get to sleep he dreamed. In a purely tactile sense it was a vivid and unpleasant dream. He was in a strange house in pitch darkness, climbing the stairs, guiding himself with his fingertips along the walls and banister. At length he raised a foot, feeling around for a stair, but there was nothing there: he must have reached the top. But moving forward, not only was there no top stair – there was no landing. He hurtled forward, spinning through space into a bottomless abyss. In full flight, he was woken by the telephone ringing and he picked up the extension by his bed.

'Who is it? Don't you know it is three in the morning?'

'It's your next-door neighbour, Monsieur Stassopoulos.'

Stassopoulos was a crotchety old Greek who lived in the tiny adjoining flat on the top floor and above the new neighbours. He was in the rag trade, running a sweatshop full of underpaid immigrant seamstresses in some northern slum.

'What do you want?'

'I rang to make you stop snoring. I can't get to sleep.'

'Well you can repair your bloody cistern then! I can't get to sleep with it dribbling water all night.'

'What are you talking about? You *were* sleeping! You were snoring. That's why I rang you in the first place!'

Kovacs slammed down the phone and tried – *forced* – himself to get to sleep once again, but it was well nigh impossible. Not only was the water still running but a bloodthirsty mosquito had got him repeatedly and was still whining persistently like a minuscule dentist's drill. The buildings flanking the canal were infested with them. At one moment he sensed that it was close to his nose and he clapped his hands together. The whining stopped. He had got it and was pleased, and finally he slipped off to sleep.

The mosquito must have been hauling a plump swagbag of his own blood because when he woke up in the morning sizeable bloodstains were imprinted in the centre of each palm. They looked like stigmata. As he got up to dress he noticed the crumpled pillow on which he had been sleeping. In the lateral light from beneath the roller blind the wrinkles and folds formed a perfect face, the face of a perfect stranger sleeping in his bed. Viewed from a certain angle, it could have been Victor Noir.

He wearily recalled his dream of the dark house and the treacherous stair. There were times, he reflected, when the whole universe seemed to be made of the same material as that last, impalpable step.

8

It was imperative that Kovacs see Laroche, but not only to please the principal of the College, to launch an investigation and to defend himself against serious charges of harassment and false accusations: not only to 'go through the proper channels', in Allwright's statesmanlike phrase. The latter expression jarred when he even thought of Laroche. There was something unseemly and, indeed, indefinably *improper* about the police inspector and this, combined with the man's subtly concealed pique at the existence of the newly completed Channel Tunnel – he hadn't forgotten that – made Kovacs want to say: 'to go through the improper Chunnel'. Silly, but that's how it was.

His other reason for needing to see Laroche was that things had reached a pretty pass and, as yet, there was no light at the end of that improper Chunnel – the pun was now engraved somewhere in the speech motor centre of his cerebral cortex. He had heard nothing from Laroche with regard to his confiscated *carte de séjour*. Each time he had phoned the Commissariat he was told that Laroche was off sick and that nobody could help. Without this resident's permit he was still unable to retrieve the registered letter containing his new passport which remained in the possession of the local post office. He had, therefore, no valid means of identification whatsoever. What is more, his bank had failed as yet to supply a new *Carte Bleue* with secret PIN so he could not withdraw money from cash dispensers or make credit card purchases. He was still, it was true, allowed to use his cheque-book, but on the day after his awkward encounter with Allwright he discovered that he had no cheques left. This was a bind, but not insoluble. He could simply go to the bank and pick up a new cheque-book.

He was in a hurry because he had rung through to Babalu's sister (his new friend not having a phone himself and relying on call-boxes for his own communications) and asked her to drop round on Babalu to say that he would be there on an urgent matter in under an hour. He had with him Babalu's Panama which had been in his possession since the night of the carnivals. There was not much time to lose as he entered his branch of the Crédit Lyonnais in the rue Saint-Dominique. He went to the counter and asked for a new cheque-book.

'Do you have any identification?' the girl asked, inevitably.

'I'm afraid not, but I do have my name and account number.' He had written these down on a slip of paper which he handed to her. She looked disgruntled, as if this was not strictly speaking correct procedure, but went to a drawer all the same to seek out a new book.

'No, sorry,' she said, 'they haven't been printed up yet. Come back in a week's time.'

'Well what am I to do for money in the meantime?'

'Don't you have a credit card?'

'No. One of your clerks, acting on false information, cancelled my card. He was supposed to be getting me a new one but I've heard nothing from him.'

The girl frowned.

'Your account is at this branch of course?'

'Yes.'

'Well it isn't essential to have a cheque-book to withdraw money from your account, in that case. All you have to do is fill in one of these slips of paper.' She pointed to a plastic box of official forms to one side. 'The problem is you need some identification.'

'I told you. I don't have any.'

'No passport? No *carte de séjour*?'

'No.'

It was deadlock. They were facing and staring at each other – Kovacs thought – exactly as he and the woman in the post office had faced and stared at each other and, indeed, as the two cats he had seen on the rock ledge in the Parc des Buttes-Chaumont had faced and stared at each other. If only he had hung around long enough to see the issue of that feline encounter.

'The clerk,' said the girl after a while. 'The clerk who was getting you a new *Carte Bleue.* He would know who you are, wouldn't he?'

'Yes!' Kovacs was relieved. 'I'm sure he would. We had a long talk. He was so embarrassed about the mistake he had made.'

'Do you know his name?'

Kovacs reflected a second. 'Yes, yes – a young man – it was Gaillard. That's right – Gaillard.'

The girl's face dropped.

'Is anything wrong?' said Kovacs.

'He's gone,' she said quietly.

'To lunch?'

'No *gone.*'

'Not *dead*?'

'No! He's left.'

'What? Just walked out?'

She looked around shiftily, not wanting to be overheard.

'He was sacked!' she whispered, approaching her face to his confidingly.

'What for?' asked Kovacs, also whispering.

'Embezzlement. There are charges against him. They took him away!'

The hushed conversation was beginning to attract the attention of other customers and employees who probably assumed that a private family matter was being discussed.

'Christ!' said Kovacs to himself and an additional current of anxiety crossed his mind. 'Did he embezzle from specific accounts?' he asked.

'Nobody knows. They've only just begun to investigate the matter. All we know is that he'd been taking money for some time. Over a period of years.'

Kovacs pushed up his lower lip fatalistically. He was in a grim mood.

'I think we should discuss this with the manager,' said the girl sympathetically.

'Yes. Or rather, no – I mean, I don't have time. I have a rendezvous. I'll have to come back.'

'Let me keep this,' the girl said reassuringly, referring to the piece of paper with his name and account number. 'And I shall get someone to look into the matter and sort things out.'

'It'll have to be quick. I have virtually no cash at all. Just a few francs. There's plenty in the account, but no way of getting at it.'

'I'll make sure it's looked into very quickly. If you could just add your phone number we'll give you a ring as soon as we know how things stand.'

Kovacs scribbled his number on the scrap of paper and left. Outside, on the pavement, he turned out his pockets. Thirty-three francs and fifteen centimes, a few unused Metro tickets and a sugared peanut from the carnival that had stuck to the pocket lining. A Man of Means, he thought, as he popped the Panama onto his head.

He took the train to Babalu's.

When he knocked at the door of Babalu's room there was no answer but the door swung open. The smell of stale cooking hung like smog in the room. The mouse was scrabbling around on the table, eating crumbs of cake and Babalu was lying flat out on his bed in a pair of pink pyjama bottoms. If it were possible for him to look white, then he looked white – pale and poorly. A great white whale, in fact – a Moby Dick – for his huge naked stomach swelled up into the air like the dorsal hump of that singular mammalian species. The Brazilian was staring straight up at a cloud-shaped stain of mildew on the ceiling. Kovacs could not be sure, but there seemed to be tears in his eyes. He placed the Panama on the table and turned to Babalu.

'My dear chap! What *is* the matter?'

Babalu eased himself up onto his elbows. He was a sorry sight.

'Ah! *Amigo* – it is you. Welcome. Babalu is not so happy today. *Triste.*'

'May I ask why?'

'This morning I take Raimunda to *aeroporto*. Many tears, my friend, much sadness. Maybe we no see each other again for long time.'

'Surely not. Surely something can be arranged?'

Babalu put a finger in his ear and wiggled it about for a moment before withdrawing it and inspecting the fingertip.

'No – is nothing to do. Now you see I am like you again –

sozinho, alone. Is OK, you know, but is not marvellous. With my wife and children is *maravilhoso*. Wonderful time.'

'Couldn't you visit her, for a change, or ask her to come back next month?'

'Money, money, money, money, money,' repeated Babalu tediously, rocking his head from side to side. 'Always money. Big money problem. I need *dinheiro*. Is never enough. Never!'

Kovacs hesitated. Now was perhaps not the moment but – he thought – what the hell?

'Actually, I was going to ask you if you could lend me some. Money, I mean. This is a bit of a nuisance, I know, but I'm almost broke.'

'Broke?'

'No money. None at all.'

'No money! My friend, how can this be? You are *inteligente* man – big job, nice flat. How can this be?'

Kovacs laughed. 'Well, I'm not exactly broke you know. I'm just having problems with my bank. I have no credit card or cheque-book so I can't get at the money in my account. I *do* have money in the account, but I can't get to it. It's such a long story that I won't bore you with the details.'

Babalu sat up, stretched and wiped his nose on the back of his hand leaving a snail's trail of mucus on the dark skin.

'This is why you come to see Babalu?' he asked. 'For money?'

'No, not exactly. There is another matter. I'm sorry if I offend you by asking for money.'

'Offend? Oh no, my friend! I am happy, very happy, that you come to me. This show me we are real good – how you say? – *pals*, you know. You do not go to your teacher friends, you do not go to your neighbour – you come to Babalu. I am very happy. I give much money to Raimunda to take back but there is some left. How much I give you?'

'If you could spare four or five hundred francs, that should be quite enough.'

'No problem, my friend.' He pulled a brightly ornamented red leather wallet out from under his pillow and handed over five hundred francs, all in fifty-franc notes. 'My boss, he's crazy – he always pay me in fifties.'

'Thank you,' said Kovacs, sincerely. 'You know Benjamin

Franklin once said "If you want to know the value of money, try borrowing some". You have proved to be the exception to the cynical implications of that remark.'

Babalu scratched his head. 'I not sure I understand you, my friend.'

'It doesn't matter. I was just saying that you are very generous. Thank you very much. I shall naturally pay you back as soon as things are back to normal with the bank.'

'When you like,' said Babalu, dismissing the matter. 'You want some coffee?'

'I'd love some, thank you.'

The pink pyjamas hung low over the rear cleavage of his plump buttocks as he pulled back the curtain and shuffled into the tiny kitchen area to light the gas and prepare the Lavazza grounds. He came back and leaned against the corner of the wall while the water was heating.

'You say you want to discuss other matter, my friend?'

'Yes, to do with the girl.'

'Ah yes!' Babalu's manner quickened. 'I nearly forget! I think so much about Raimunda that I nearly forget. Did you find her? Did you find where she live?'

'I did. Look.'

Kovacs had written Delphine Jones' name and address down on a sheet of paper and he handed it to Babalu.

'This is not a name you have seen before, is it? You have followed other women back from the cemetery, after all.'

Babalu read it carefully. 'No, this is new one. She's no two-timing my friend,' he added, smiling. 'She's just for you!'

He put the sheet of paper away on his shelf, fetched the coffee and the two men sat at the table.

'So many things have happened,' said Kovacs, 'that I don't know where to begin. This may sound stupid, but it is as if – as if Victor Noir were trying to communicate from beyond the grave.'

As he said this, the Panama – which he had placed on the table – began to move. Babalu screamed and leapt up, knocking his chair over backwards. Even Kovacs stared in amazement. The hat travelled the whole breadth of the table and then back again. Suddenly Kovacs realised what had happened. He grabbed the hat and lifted it up, revealing the mouse – Cotinho. She had been trapped under the hat when he had put it down. 'Ah!' sighed Babalu, relaxing with relief, and the two men laughed heartily.

'*Esquisito!* I thought – you know – I thought . . .' began Babalu.

'Yes, I know exactly what you thought! So did I!'

When the laughter had died down, Babalu folded his arms on the table and leaned towards Kovacs.

'Tell me about the girl,' he said. 'You must tell me all that happen to you – *tudo*. Everything!'

Kovacs recounted everything that had occurred in the simplest terms he could find, from the moment they had parted company on the night of the Fête de la Musique. Babalu listened carefully, nodding his head, posing the occasional question, taking it all in.

'So you understand,' Kovacs concluded, 'I have to go back to the police. I am being accused by the person I am accusing. And if things go wrong I could lose my job – maybe worse. Last time I went to the police was before I met you, just after the burglary. In order for me to explain exactly what has happened I need you with me – as a witness. You saw her at Père Lachaise. You brought me the letters. You saw her again at the carnival.'

Babalu's good humour gradually melted away. He shook his head sadly.

'I can't, my friend.'

'How do you mean, you *can't*?'

'I can trust you, of course, to keep secret?'

'But of course! You can trust me absolutely.'

'I can't go to police. I have no working papers. I am illegal immigrant. You know how they say in French – *Je travaille au noir*. I come over a year ago to visit my sister. Tourist visa, you see. One month holiday. But I no go back. Police come to my sister. She say "I no see Babalu. He go – *adeus*!" They no believe but is nothing they can do. Is big problem because now I not so sure how to go back to Brazil. I send money to Raimunda through my sister, so is legitimate. They can't get money back from me. But one day I must buy ticket for Brazil and hope, big hope, that they no arrest me at *aeroporto*.'

'I see,' mused Kovacs. 'But I think it is unlikely that they would arrest you. After all, if they did arrest you it would only be to deport you to Brazil. And what is the point of arresting someone to deport them to Brazil when they are on the point of going back to Brazil anyway?'

Babalu brightened. 'That's true! I no think of that – you see! I said to Raimunda, Mister Kovacs is clever man – *inteligente.* I was right when I say this. Now you make me happy. *But* –' His voice fell on the syllable with a less than jovial note. 'I can no come to police with you because then they find out straight way. No papers. You go back to Brazil now. And I no want to go back now. For Raimunda and the *filhos* I need to send more money. I need to work more time.'

'I understand,' said Kovacs, sighing. 'If it's any consolation, neither do I have any papers – as I told you. No *carte de séjour*, no passport, no credit card, no cheque-book. Just a fucking English driving licence that nobody wants to look at. We are stateless people, you and I, Babalu.'

'I read in *jornal*,' said Babalu, 'there is stateless man in Roissy airport. He arrive by *avião* – no passport, nothing. I forget which country he come from. They phone his country: "We no want here," they say. The French no want him neither. So what happen? For two years he live in arrival lounge at airport. People very kind. They give him hamburger, newspaper, cup of tea. He sleep in sleeping bag on bench. Two years this go on. I don't know, perhaps he is still there.'

'Well, we're lucky not to be in that predicament yet, aren't we?' said Kovacs, as he took his leave. 'And don't worry about the police. I shall think of something. It might be simpler if I lied. I shall tell them that *I* found the letters in Victor Noir's hat. It seems an improbable coincidence, but there are so many of those in this bloody affair that I'm sure nobody will give it a second thought.'

The two men shook hands and parted, agreeing to meet up socially in the near future.

Kovacs went out into the street and looked around. Under the grey girders of the aerial Metro there was a telephone box. He crossed the road. Luckily, it was not a card-operated phone. He only had cash. He counted his coins again, selecting the silver for his call. He was put through directly to Laroche. The familiar voice greeted him on the line.

'Monsieur Kovacs! *Quel plaisir!* I was wondering why I had not heard from you. Tell me, please, what can I do for you?'

'Can we meet? As soon as possible. It's quite an urgent matter.'

'What time is it now?'

'It's one o'clock.'

'Damn! I'm supposed to be seeing the deputy minister for police affairs at two-thirty. We could well be in conversation for several hours.'

'Well when I say *urgent* I mean relatively urgent. Perhaps we could meet tomorrow.'

'No, no!' pleaded Laroche. 'I wouldn't dream of it. You need help, I quite understand. This is an urgent matter. Come *now*, Monsieur Kovacs. I shall be waiting for you. I shall cancel my meeting with the deputy minister.'

Kovacs was embarrassed. 'But you can't do that.'

'Monsieur Kovacs, I can do what I like. Come now. Do as I say.'

The line went dead and Kovacs looked with Actors' Studio astonishment at the receiver as if the handset itself were directly responsible for what had been said.

When he arrived at Laroche's office in the Commissariat he was surprised by the changes. An elegant tubular steel filing system had been installed, along with comfortable black leather bucket chairs that swivelled on their stems. The broken jalousie had been ripped out and replaced with beautiful rose-coloured damask curtains that were tied back with elegant gold sashes terminating in tassels. Everything on the desk was punctiliously arranged – papers, pen-set, blotting pad, computer – and the coloured map-pins on the wall-mounted map of Paris had been reinserted to form what looked like an enormous question-mark, the route of which carefully picked its way through the roads of the city, beginning near the place de la République, circling round the 19th and 20th arrondissements, and terminating with a full-stop, a little bouquet of green-headed pins, near Saint-Germain-des-Prés. The room smelt fabulous, like a flower-shop, and was flooded with golden light. But this was the least of his surprises.

When Laroche emerged from a side-room to greet him the man had utterly changed. Kovacs scarcely recognised him. He wore a beautiful beige Armani suit, a crisp white open-necked shirt with the initials 'YSL' embroidered on the cuffs, mother-of-pearl cufflinks, and a dapper silk kerchief, black with white polka dots, arranged with a little flourish – a semblance of lackadaisical artlessness – in the breast pocket of the jacket. His head was no longer the colour of a rotting potato, exuding tendrils of hair. He was in the full bloom of health. The hair had been washed, trimmed and elegantly groomed, with just a touch of brilliantine; the face was deeply tanned, his eyes twinkling with life; and he sported a splendid moustache which, unlike the sparse hair on his head, had emerged a rich chestnut brown, doubtless the original colouring of his entire *chevelure*. He looked twenty years younger.

'*Mon cher ami!*' he effused, shaking Kovacs' hand energetically, '*Monsieur l'Anglais!* How good of you to come!'

'I phoned many times, Inspector Laroche, but I was told that you were off sick.'

'And so I was, Monsieur Kovacs. I was most abominably ill, and I still have to take the tablets.' He indicated a little bottle of pills on the desktop, marked 'Stelazine® trifluoperazine 5 mg' on the label. 'But a most extraordinary thing happened. A miracle!'

'Might I ask what that was?'

'Of course. Look!' he pointed to an empty flowerbox hanging outside the closed window into which a vase of big gorgeous lilies had been placed. The petals were pink and white, with blood-dark leopard-like spots, and from the centre of the flowers projected pale green shoots terminating in heavy drooping stamens, laden with orange pollen.

'Lilies,' said Kovacs. 'I always imagined that lilies were white.'

'Not these – they're Star Gazer lilies. I was terribly ill. I came in to work from time to time, but nothing seemed to improve. They took advantage of my absences to redecorate the office, as you can see. I think they reckoned I was done for!' he added with a triumphant smirk. 'Inspector Garreau ordered the changes and he's been after this office for quite some time. But he'll just have to cool his heels, won't he? Anyway, when I got back, Jeanette – one of the secretaries here – gave me those flowers. *C'était extraordinaire!* It was over a week ago now and I was just well enough to put in a full day's work. The flowers were in front of me on the desk. When I got home that evening, I undressed to go to bed and I found that my chest was covered in pollen – all yellow and orange! And yet my shirt had been buttoned up all day. How do you explain that? It had passed straight through the shirt.'

'Are you telling me that the – how do you call them?'

'Star Gazer lilies.'

'Are you telling me that the Star Gazer lilies were trying to *pollinate* you?'

Laroche raised his hands incredulously. 'I do not know. All I know is that from that moment on I felt better. I took one more day off. It was a nice sunny day. I went fishing in a local park. And then I was right as rain. I feel like a young man again!'

'I'm very glad to hear it. And what a strange story. But why have you put the flowers outside – in that flowerbox?'

Laroche's expression clouded a mite. 'To tell you the truth, they frighten me. They give me the creeps. I can't get rid of them, and at the same time I don't want to have them in here.'

'But why not?'

'Well, I have had one dose of this pollen, but what would happen if I had *more*? There is no telling, is there?'

'Have you asked the secretary where she got them?'

'Yes. She bought them at a local florist. No mystery there at all.'

Laroche pulled at the side of his moustache as he thought for a moment. 'Would *you* like them?' he asked suddenly. '*Do* let me give them to you! Perhaps – perhaps you too could benefit from them!'

'No, really,' said Kovacs, overcome with embarrassment. 'I couldn't, really.'

It was the first time a man had offered him flowers.

Laroche shrugged and sat down. 'Well, perhaps you will change your mind.'

Kovacs sat down too, in the plush bucket seat, the desk between them as during their last encounter.

'But you,' said Laroche. 'Let us talk about you. Things are bad, are they not?'

'Yes. How did you know?'

'All this business in Brussels. Every single member of the EEC chose the Belgian man – Jean-Luc Dehaene, isn't it? – to succeed Delors. And what do the English do? They veto the candidate! How? How can they do this? Where is the harmony, the unity, the concord? Sovereignty, sovereignty, always sovereignty!' He tutted and shook his head disapprovingly. 'What about *esprit de corps*?'

Kovacs was beginning to expect this kind of digression and this time he took the snub personally.

'I have not been following the matter in the papers,' he said, 'but it is sometimes worth pointing out that if it were not for England this very office would probably be a sub-division of Gestapo headquarters today.'

Laroche glared frigidly at him. His mood had flipped inside out.

'My own uncle died in the D-day landings in Normandy which are being commemorated this month,' Kovacs added, to give the observation a personal flavour.

There was a Gobi desert of silence during which Kovacs fancied he could smell the pungent odour of the lilies penetrating the office window. Laroche shuffled some papers and switched his computer on.

'Now,' he said at length, after clearing his throat with an elaborate ceremony of coughing and gargling, 'the last I heard of you was when the post office phoned up to check on your story, remember? They thought you were trying to hold the place up.'

'It was because I gave them the note you wrote for me. "*N'oubliez pas le coffre fort.*" I hadn't read it and assumed that it was a receipt for my *carte de séjour*. I think all of that was explained to you on the phone.'

'Yes, I remember. Tell me, did you do as I said? Did you fit a safe and a reinforced door?'

'No, I haven't got round to that yet. I have had other preoccupations. Perhaps you could tell me: have you got my *carte de séjour*? It's a dreadful nuisance not having it. Without that or my passport I have no means of identification and this has created further problems at the bank.'

'Ah yes,' said Laroche, 'the *carte de séjour*. That was another funny business. The secretary accessed the databank of resident aliens and reinstated your file. But each time we attempted to call it up again it had disappeared. A blip, I suppose. Added to which, she lost your card. A most unfortunate business. I think there's nothing for it but for you to apply for a new one.'

Kovacs was utterly crestfallen. 'It's an infernal process,' he muttered between his teeth.

'*Je n'y peux rien!*' said Laroche defeatedly. 'But tell me – the last time we met was just after the burglary. Have you made any progress? You thought the person responsible might have been someone you knew. How do things stand now?'

Yet again, Kovacs went through the whole epic saga, leaving no stone unturned, no detail unmentioned. As he had promised Babalu, the only change he made was to state that it was *he*, Kovacs, who had spotted the girl in the cemetery and that it was consequently he, Kovacs, who had recognised her at the carnival. The agency and indeed all mention of Babalu and Raimunda were scrupulously avoided. Nor did he mention the name and address of the girl: he did not want Laroche to take action behind his back, without clearing it with him first. Laroche listened earnestly, jotting down a note from time to time and fiddling contemplatively with the ends of his unhabituated moustache. He had a good Cartesian brain and nothing relevant escaped him.

'How extraordinary, if you will permit me to say so, that you were present in the cemetery at the precise moment that the person you believe to be persecuting you should deposit the letter!' Laroche knitted his brow. 'I find it quite remarkable – an almost supernatural coincidence.'

Kovacs had hoped this would not happen. 'Yes,' he said, clumsily, 'but coincidence seems to have been the order of the day over the last few weeks. Your own experience with the Star Gazer lilies is no less amazing.'

'True,' acknowledged Laroche. 'Do you have the two letters on you?'

'Yes, I brought them to show you.'

He handed the letters to the Inspector, still in their envelopes. Laroche read them carefully, asking for help from time to time with the translation, for he had a modicum of English, and Kovacs explained what a lipogram was and the connection between this artful literary form and the broken typewriter. Laroche nodded seriously then folded the letters and put them back in their envelopes.

'Just one question,' he said. 'You say that you found both of these letters in the hat of Victor Noir?'

'Yes. The first time I saw the girl putting it there. The second time I had missed her but the letter was in the hat nevertheless.'

'If that is so, how do you explain that the second letter bears a postage stamp and your home address, while on the back of the envelope are the words "I find this for you, Babalu"?'

If the last silence had been a Gobi, this one was a Sahara – eight million square kilometres of silence – and there were no oases in sight. How, thought Kovacs, could he have been so stupid! How could he have overlooked such a simple thing! His mind raced – that rodent in the labyrinth again! – desperate to find an exit from the daedalian plot in which he had impounded himself. Were he to now mention Babalu – thereby betraying the Brazilian – it would be an admission that he had lied. He would have to tell the whole story again: he would have, eventually, to admit *why* he had omitted to mention Babalu. It was out of the question. Eventually, he did his best.

'I'm sorry, I was mistaken,' he began, speaking very slowly, trying to keep one step ahead in his thoughts. 'I have left the second letter at home, the letter I took from the hat. That is the third letter, which as you can see was posted from the airport. I have no idea what the writing on the back means.'

Laroche's bronzed face was a visor of incomprehension.

'But you distinctly told me there were only two letters,' he said.

'It was a mistake,' said Kovacs flatly. '*Un trou de mémoire*. I've been under a lot of pressure. It's hard for me to keep all the details of this lamentable adventure in my memory. I occasionally – as you have seen – trip over my own tongue.'

Laroche slowly clicked open the childproof stopper on the

medicine bottle and took one blue pill, washing it down with a glass of water. He was beginning to look queasy and when he spoke again there was a strong flavour of disgust in his voice.

'What do you want me to do?'

'As I said, I am reporting this at the suggestion of my boss, Dr Allwright. You're the policeman, but I suppose there are two possible courses of action.'

'Namely?'

'Either the police intervene and get a search warrant for the girl's flat, where I am sure they will find the missing typewriter. Alternatively, now that you are fully apprised of my version of the story, if there are further consequences – further counter-accusations – at least you will understand how things stand. You never know, now that I've confronted the girl the whole thing may blow over. I won't get my typewriter back, but I'm really not worried about that.'

'As for your first option,' Laroche replied severely, 'it is a serious business getting a search warrant. *Il faut faire les démarches.*' ('The improper Chunnel,' thought Kovacs.) 'We cannot undertake such a move lightly. For one thing, you would need sound evidence on which to make it. Your story – with your *trous de mémoire*, as you call them – is simply not convincing enough.'

Kovacs bit the inside of his lip.

'The first option,' Laroche continued, 'is downright stupid. "When in doubt, stick a spanner in the works," one might say.' (He used the English expression.) 'It is an option that might well appeal to you, as it seems to appeal to your government and fellow countrymen. Spanners – the adjustable variety, at least – are, after all, what we call *les clefs anglaises.*'

Again Kovacs bristled, but said nothing.

'The second option is clearly the wiser one. "When in doubt, do nothing." As before, if there are any developments contact me directly and I shall reassess the situation.'

Kovacs nodded. Given his gaffe, he felt that he had got off lightly. He slipped his hand under his shirt and scratched, as if the mental irritation he felt could be alleviated somatically in this way. Laroche smirked and started to snort, quite forgetting his previous sour temper.

'What is it?' said Kovacs, nonplussed.

'You will think me a foolish old man, but you resemble Napoleon Bonaparte with your hand like that! Imagine – an *English* Napoleon!' He laughed out loud now. 'Don't worry, Monsieur Kovacs! We will get you out of your Waterloo! I shall personally see to it that we find a little island for you somewhere – unless you choose to go back to your own little island, that is – over there, across *La Manche* – how do you call it in English?'

'The English Channel.'

'The *English Channel*,' Laroche parroted derisively. 'Why *English*, I ask you? Does the *whole* of it belong to you? You English are so – so Imperial! *Rule Britannia, Britannia rules the waves!*' He had suddenly begun to sing, thoroughly off-key. Kovacs felt like pointing out that it was not 'Britannia rules the waves' but 'Britannia *rule* the waves': a subjunctive rather than the third person singular in the simple present, a fact which distinctly modified the alleged imperialism. He thought better, however, of this pedantic impulse.

Kovacs and the policeman were standing now, and Laroche patted him affably on the side of the arm. 'Don't mind me, Monsieur Kovacs. I must have my little joke. I'm known for it in the office. I mean no harm. I've been damnably busy with another case,' he said, waving a file in the air, 'and a little humour relieves the stress.'

Kovacs managed a conciliatory smile, then glanced at the file Laroche was holding. The name 'Gaillard' was felt-tipped on the cover-sheet.

'And please – take the lilies.'

'No really, I can't.'

'But you must, and you *will*. I insist. You need them, I can feel that. Look what they have done for me!'

A queue of burly police cadets was waiting outside Laroche's office when Kovacs left, clutching the bunch of Star Gazer lilies which were wrapped, at the stem, with an old piece of computer printout. Rarely in his life had he felt so ridiculous: I am, he thought, a complete and utter fool.

He walked slowly back to his apartment and sat there for what remained of the day, trying – in a desultory fashion – to get on with his reading. He skim-read Freud's *Totem and Taboo* and *Civilisation and its Discontents*, but his mind constantly reverted to the lilies and the total hash he had made of his interview with Laroche. And, he remembered, he still hadn't got his *carte de séjour* back. Nothing further had been said about that. He was in absolute, abject misery, but all of that changed at nine p.m.

The telephone rang. It was Babalu, very probably in the same call-box he himself had used to call Laroche because he could hear the telltale thunder of the overhead Metro.

'Philip! *Amigo!* Is no problem any more for you. Babalu has been very busy – very busy man!'

'What are you talking about, Babalu?'

'I go to see girl!'

'Who? Delphine Jones?'

'Yes. You give me address, remember?'

'Oh no, you *didn't*! Why? What happened? What did she say?'

'She alone. I see her. Very nice girl. I explain her, Mister Kovacs my friend, I want to help him. He no want to hurt nobody. "Yes, yes!" she say, and she understand very well. I was right – her orixá is Iansã, but today very good Iansã – no storm, no trouble.'

'Oh do get on with it, Babalu!'

'We talk a long time. Philip, she admit everything. She say she did it. She want to meet with you to explain.'

'Marvellous! Marvellous, Babalu!'

'You must ring her tomorrow morning after nine o'clock. She want to say sorry. Is no problem. Everything is arrange.'

'God bless you, my friend!'

'You make me laugh, *amigo*. You no believe no God.'

'No, but I believe in you. You've done me a great service.'

'Is no problem, no problem at all.'

Kovacs put down the phone and clasped his hands together in triumph. He was humming something to himself and, sure enough, there it was again – that tune. *'Have you met Miss Jones?' Someone said as we shook hands*. It was a chirpy little tune, all things considered. And pretty soon now he would be able to say 'Yes – Yes, I *have* met Miss Jones', and that would be that. *Basta!* Met her *again*, he should say, since he had known her before. Then he could pack all his troubles in some great metaphysical Old Kit-Bag and it would all be over. 'No problem,' as Babalu was so fond of saying: 'No problem at all!'

9

HIS DREAM THAT night was infernal. It was probably a consequence of reading Freud and then watching a nature programme on TV. The half-hour programme was about African wildlife and in the course of the documentary they showed a remarkable jungle-dwelling tribe of apes: a 'shrewdness' of apes, they had said, for this was the correct collective noun. He could no longer recall the name of this particular sub-species of ape but the fact was that they had developed a unique form of social organisation based on free love. Anyone could copulate with anyone else, and constantly did: they lived only for sex and food. Young coupled with old, old with young, men with men, brothers with sisters, nephews with aunts – and so on, ad nauseam. According to the commentary, sex – for them – was as simple as saying 'Hello': the reason for this was that sex *was* saying 'Hello', an accepted form of greeting. They were also unique among primates in experimenting with a variety of sexual positions, including – and this was unusual in the animal kingdom – the missionary position, face to face. Coupling in this manner they would look lovingly into each other's eyes, suggesting that real affection (romantic love, even) had blossomed in this eccentric community. Moreover – and it was this that had struck Kovacs forcibly, particularly in the light of his reading of Freud – the ape community was utterly non-violent, a unique phenomenon in the simian world. Not even the threat of violence was used between its members or against outsiders. Sex, in short, had replaced aggression. He was thinking this over, and considering the fact that he had read somewhere that humans share 98.7% of their genes with chimpanzees, when he began to fall asleep, a loose diagram of thoughts entangling his mind.

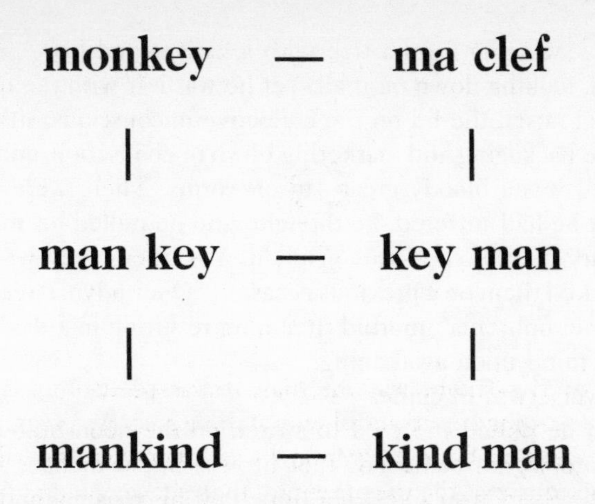

He looked at his mental chart for a while. Who was that 'key man'? Was it him? Was he a 'marked' man too – chosen to help man back to his kind, to put the *man* into *man*kind? And the 'monkey' too? There was a 'monk' in every monkey, and that's what he'd become. No, he was not that 'key man'. Why not? Because he did not have the 'man key'. Because he was not a 'kind man'. Because he had no *kin*. This, he thought – holding that word-chart in his mind's eye again – was doing the thing mirrors couldn't do, reversing left–right *and* top–bottom. And, as he was about to find out to his cost, dreams can go one dimension further.

His dream was more or less a re-enactment of the orgiastic behaviour he had witnessed on the TV screen, but with one significant modification: the heads of the apes were replaced by those of his friends and acquaintances. Céline, Orriss, Hannah, Michel, Anne, Madame da Silva, the Turckheims, Babalu, Raimunda, Allwright, Madame Duluc, Fairgreave – in Fairgreave's case the dream did not have to effect much in the way of cosmetic surgery. Even Laroche had starred in the show – *especially* Laroche, he now recollected with horror, featuring as a rather foppish ape got up like Beau Brummel with a Velcro codpiece. It was a bestial and abandoned wallowing in hedonism, a 'bonanza' of bonking, he thought – searching for one of those collective nouns again – a 'funfair' of fucks. *He* was not there, naturally:

probably swinging from a tree with a banana and his reporter's notepad, looking down on it all. Yet he was left with the feeling of having raised the lid on the collective unconscious, stripping away the packaging and marketing blurb of civilisation, and what he found was a bloody great can of worms. There were words for what he had suffered, he thought, and he pulled his medical dictionary off the shelf to consult it. Yes, there they were: he had marked them on a previous occasion. 'Oneirodynia' resulting in 'Malneirophrenia': morbid dreaming resulting in a distressed state of mind upon awakening.

But worse was to come.

When he pulled the cord to switch on the neon bulb above the bathroom mirror he saw that he was bright orange, almost gold. The Star Gazer lilies! He ripped off his pyjamas and leapt into the shower, spraying himself with scalding water and scrubbing every inch of his anatomy with a hard-bristled nail brush. When he looked in the mirror again there was some improvement. A great deal of the pollen had gone, but there was still a generalised *glow* of orangeness about him, he was not sure what kind – apricot, tangerine, old gold, marmalade, cadmium, ochre, or just plain old orangey orange, the Jaffa kind. It looked like the cheap instant suntan that deskbound secretaries purchase in bottles. He certainly did not feel any better, as Laroche clearly had done: on the contrary, he felt rather seedy (his old problem with bleeding gums had returned) and he reflected that perhaps the Star Gazer lilies did not affect everyone in the same manner. One man's pollen was another man's poison, to put it another way. Perhaps he was simply not made to be pollinated and Laroche was. He would have to monitor his state of health carefully in the course of the day. But first of all, he was going to get rid of those lilies.

He dressed quickly, grabbed the flowers from the vase on the table and trotted downstairs to the cubby-hole where the wheely-bins were kept. Madame da Silva bumped into him on the way.

'Oh, Monsieur Kovacs!' she declared. 'Are those for me?'

'Yes they are, as a matter of fact, Madame da Silva,' he improvised after a moment's hesitation. 'It's such a lovely day, I thought these might cheer you up.'

'Thank you! Thank you so much! You have made me a very happy woman!' She took the flowers carefully from him, cradled them in her arms and toddled back into her *loge* under the fastidious gaze of her fat Persian cat.

'And may the Force be with you,' murmured Kovacs beneath his breath.

'There!' she said, returning with the flowers in a blue earthenware vase. 'Don't they look lovely?'

'Absolutely,' he said. 'Was there any mail?'

'Let me see.' She picked up the letters from a chair by her window. 'Deray, Mémin, Stassopoulos, Lopez, Schwarz. No, nothing for you today, Monsieur Kovacs.'

'Who is Schwarz?' he asked curiously. 'I didn't know there was anyone here of that name?'

'Oh that is Corinne – Corinne Turckheim. Schwarz was her maiden name. Some of her old friends still use it.'

'I see.'

Kovacs went back to his flat. His bout of hypersomnia had been intense and it was now well past ten. It was time to phone Miss Jones. Babalu had said that he should call after nine. He found the College photo-scan amongst his papers and tapped out the number.

'*Allô, oui?*'

'Delphine?'

'Er, yes.'

'Philip Kovacs here. I understand you've met my friend Babalu and wanted to see me.'

'Yes.'

'I was right, when I phoned you, wasn't I? It is you who have been doing all these things.'

'Yes. Monsieur Kovacs, I am *so* sorry. It was childish and stupid of me.'

'Never mind. I think we should meet, don't you?'

'Yes.'

'For one thing you have my typewriter to return.'

'Yes, I do.'

'But more importantly, we should try to clear up any misunderstandings. Make a clean breast of things, so that there are no hard feelings. Do you agree?'

'Yes. You are very kind.'
'Why am I kind?'
'Well, you could have gone to the police.'
'I *did* go to the police.'
There was an awkward silence.
'But don't worry,' Kovacs continued hurriedly, 'they're not going to do anything. They advised me to wait and see. I think, like me, they thought it was best to settle this matter between ourselves.'
'Yes. Shall I come to your flat?' the girl asked.
'It's not terribly convenient. I'd been planning on doing some shopping today. I'll tell you what: one of the shops I want to go to is near you. Why don't I come round to your place? 8, Impasse des Deux Anges, isn't it? I know where it is.'
'Fine, but what time were you thinking of coming?'
'Around twelve-thirty. Does that suit you?'
'Yes.'
'See you later, then.'
'Yes. *A plus tard.*'

He was particularly fond of the shops in and around the boulevard Saint-Germain. At Duriez, an office supply store, he bought an ink cartridge for his computer printer, then wandered around the numerous clothes stores. One of his favourites was Le Mouton à Cinq Pattes, a boutique that sold top designer label clothes but from the previous season: being end-of-line, the prices were low and there was a constant turnover of stock. He often liked to drop in and rummage through their latest acquisitions and had come across a smart Valentino jacket in this manner and a Gaultier shirt. Today he was looking through a mixed bin of small items – T-shirts, headscarves, ties – when he tumbled on the same spotted kerchief Laroche possessed. The police inspector possibly did his shopping here too. The kerchief was black with white spots. Kovacs hated to admit it, but he had taken rather a fancy to this fashion accessory during his last interview with the policeman. However, the thought of having exactly the same kerchief as Laroche did not please him. Suppose they were to meet: like two women wearing the same frock to a party? No, that would never do. Further down in the bin, though, he came across another kerchief from the same manufacturer, but this one was white with black spots. Now *that* he could possibly get away with. There was no real element of mimicry there. On the contrary, it was, as it were, the negative image of Laroche's kerchief, or Laroche's kerchief was the negative image of his – either way, and it didn't really matter. It was made of the most beautiful silk, luxurious to the touch, and – at fifty francs – he could afford to break a little further into the precious five hundred francs that Babalu had lent him. It was pure frippery, of course, but so what? The bank would soon clear up their own bureaucratic mess and he would be writing cheques and blowing money like nobody's business. He bought the kerchief and poked it into the breast pocket of his jacket, attempting to flounce it up with a little swagger and swank as Laroche had successfully done. Then, checking his appearance in the shop mirror, he made his way to Delphine Jones' flat just five minutes away at the Impasse des Deux Anges.

When he got there, he recalled with a *frisson* the chase on the night of the carnival. It was thanks to that hot pursuit that he was here now and the whole saga was about to be wrapped up. By daylight he saw that it was really quite an ordinary little cul-de-sac, lacking the Fritz Langian vibrations it had in the depths of sidereal night. It backed onto the rear of an ugly University of Paris building in the rue des Saints Pères. There were two cars parked outside the house: a green Peugeot 205 and a black Renault 5. He edged forward between their bumpers. Looking up at the fourth-floor window, he puffed out his chest and rang the bell.

The girl answered with a woeful smile and even shook his hand. She greeted him in French and thereon this was the language they used.

'You're looking well,' she observed. 'Tanned.'

He remembered her clearly from class, now, though for a whole year she had not made much of an impression on him. In teaching, he thought, one rarely remembers the silent ones. Some people think they contain hidden depths; he had always been of the opinion that they contained all-too-visible shallows.

She was a willowy little thing, dressed in jeans, Reebok sneakers and a green pullover: something of a *garçonne*, in fact, a tomboy. He remembered how she had been romping around the bollards on the place Saint-Michel. Her face and more specifically her eyes, however, now arrested his attention. The irises were eau-de-Nil in colour. He read in them the vying warm and cool tones of embarrassment and relief at the imminent showdown, but there was also a hard glint of mulish intractability that went with her 'awkward age'. The longish, coal-black hair and eyebrows were strong framing devices that held the expressive gaze in check. He found himself thinking of Falconetti playing Joan of Arc in Dreyer's classic 1928 film.

They climbed the stairs to the fourth floor.

'Sit down, please. Can I get you anything?' she said.

'Perhaps a glass of water.'

'Fizzy or still?'

'Fizzy – *pétillante*.'

For the few seconds that she disappeared into the kitchen he took in what he could of the flat. There were glowing bouquets of roses and it was furnished in a bright, modern manner: a number of the fittings and pieces of furniture, he recognised, came from the stylish new Terence Conran shop in Paris. It was a pleasing environment, conducive to sanity. The only old item was a brown leather armchair, similar to the one he had seen in Laroche's office on his first visit. There was a writing desk with an Apple Macintosh computer and a familiar black and yellow box in the corner: on it was an oval violet picture of a girl holding up a bottle under the words VOILA MON REMEDE. Above the writing desk, on the wall, was a calendar and tourist map of Paris. A series of framed jocular eighteenth-century hunting prints on the opposite wall were clearly English, with ribald English captions, and this fact served to remind Kovacs that Delphine's surname was Jones – that her father was English. He glanced down and at his foot was a single flower petal. He picked it up. It was indisputably a petal from a Star Gazer lily. How strange! It must have stuck to his clothing somehow that morning and dropped off here. This was as much as he had time to observe before she reappeared.

She gave him a glass of water and placed the bottle of Badoit beside it in case he should need any more. Then she sat down carelessly opposite him, her left leg folded and the foot tucked under the right thigh.

He sniffed and rubbed his nose. Something was irking him. Eventually, it was he who started talking. He had decided to be as humane as possible, to conduct this conversation in a simple and understanding manner.

'We have a lot to talk about, don't we?'

One strand of her hair had been plaited into a Björk knot, with red and green beads at the end. This she absent-mindedly coiled and uncoiled round her forefinger, waiting for him to continue.

'Why don't we do it this way? I'm going to ask you some simple questions and you give me direct and honest answers. How does that sound?'

She shrugged and smiled her acceptance.

Kovacs contemplated the petal in his hand, cleared his throat and began.

'Let's start at the beginning. You were, as we both know, in my advanced language class for a whole year, preparing to take the CPE.'

She nodded.

'Would I be right in thinking that in the course of this year you developed a – how shall we say? – an *affection*? An affection for *me* is what I mean.'

Again she nodded. Her gaze was abstract. She bit the beaded end of the Björk knot between her front teeth.

'It's nothing to be embarrassed about,' he said warmly, though even as he spoke he found his words inappropriate. Her demeanour, indeed, suggested juvenile listlessness rather than embarrassment. Having begun thus, however, he was obliged to continue. 'It's the sort of thing that often happens in classroom situations. When I was at school we had a French mistress that I was crazy about. I sometimes think that if I live in France now it was because of her!'

Delphine raised her eyebrows at the revelation, then switched her attention from the hair-knot to a hole in the cuff of her jumper which she prised wider, unravelling the frayed end of wool.

'To continue,' said Kovacs, 'we also both know that when it came to the day of the CPE exam you decided to cheat. As luck would have it, I was the exam invigilator on that day and I was the one who caught you. It was a most ingenious method of cheating.'

'I wondered –' said Delphine hesitantly, raising her head and speaking almost for the first time, though she was uncertain whether to go on.

'Yes?'

'I've always wondered why you were looking at my legs in the first place.'

Kovacs experienced a wave of irritation but curbed it with an affable smile. 'I wasn't, I can assure you!' he remonstrated. 'When an invigilator passes down a row of desks he or she looks at the things that are on or near the desk. Inevitably the candidate's lap is in the same line of vision.'

'Oh,' said Delphine, looking down, apparently accepting his response.

There was a pause during which Kovacs glanced again at the black and yellow box on the writing desk and scratched his nose.

'But tell me, *why* did you cheat?' he said. 'It seemed so unnecessary. Your standard of English was quite good enough for you to have passed the exam with a good grade. You are half-English, aren't you? You have an English father.'

'*Had*,' she said. 'He died last December, shortly before I took the exam. He choked on his food one morning at breakfast and died.'

Kovacs felt his features contort into a standard reflex expression of condolence.

'It was . . . it was a shock,' she went on. 'I almost didn't go through with the exam. I was shaken up. But my mother persuaded me to do it. I'd applied for a post at this very prestigious hotel and tourism school in Lausanne and I had to have the CPE to get the place.'

'So naturally you never got the place,' he deduced. He felt himself relaxing, yielding internally at her slow release of confidences.

'No – you see, the death of my father, the need to get the

place in Lausanne. I think it all added up. It was that which made me cheat. I was at the end of my tether.'

Kovacs observed a few seconds of compassionate silence before speaking again. 'Are things . . . are things better now?'

'Oh yes. It's impossible to get over something like that in six months. But I'm applying to the school again, and I shall have to sit the CPE again. Possibly next December.'

'I'm so sorry to hear this,' said Kovacs. He was running a finger slowly round the rim of his glass as if half-heartedly coaxing its inner harmonics. 'I now have some idea of what you must have been going through. To get back to now, though, this whole thing – me catching you cheating – has held up your career for at least a year?'

'Yes.'

Her frankness touched him. It was so at odds with the twisted epistolary style of the lipograms. And, strangely, her own honesty nurtured his. After some hesitation, he spoke again.

'You know, I shouldn't be telling you this really, but I cheated in an exam once myself. It was an O-level, in England. I believe they don't even exist any more. It was a history exam and I wrote a few dates on the back of my watch-strap. I don't think they did me any good, but that is the fact of the matter. I've never admitted that to anyone before.'

'Then why are you telling me?' asked Delphine candidly. She held her fist to her face and bit at the whites of the knuckle.

'It was just to say that life is unfair. I got away with it, you didn't. And I – the person who got away with it – was also the person who stopped you getting away with it. Do you see what I mean? It's hypocritical.'

A washing machine that had been turning quietly in another room suddenly clicked into a loud spin and she looked round smartly. Kovacs was vaguely disappointed that his spontaneous confession had had so little impact.

'None of us is perfect, you see,' he added with quick bitterness, pushing his digression aside. 'Now, shall I go on with my questions?'

She gave a reflex smile of compliance.

'I am going to do a little mathematical calculation. Love plus Hate equals Frustration. Am I right? The person for whom you felt a genuine affection – even though he was unaware of it – was the person who turned round and hurt you, the person who betrayed you. You felt terrible. You no longer knew what you thought of him. On the other hand, you were sure that he was totally indifferent to you. A sort of mindless official. Right? For months and months these thoughts were going round in your head. You wanted to act – to do something – to make him sit up and pay attention to you. You wanted to overcome his indifference. And that is when you hit on the idea of burgling his flat.'

Délphine stretched and stood up, then wandered over to a window where she looked out onto the grey cul-de-sac below, her arms folded against her chest. 'I thought you were a bastard,' she murmured after a while. 'I thought you were a bastard and I wanted you to know it.'

A harsh tickling sensation at the epiglottis caused Kovacs to cough and he drank quickly from his glass, splashing his shirt-front inadvertently.

'Of course *before* that,' she continued, 'I had a thing about you. I thought you were OK. A "crush"!' She used the English word, pronouncing it with some self-disgust and casting a critical glance his way as if mentally superimposing the man who was sitting in her living-room and the false idol of expired Romantic idealism.

'I hope you don't think I encouraged this feeling,' said Kovacs in a nervous attempt to acquit himself.

'No, you didn't encourage it,' she replied matter-of-factly. She turned to face him and came back to the armchair where she balanced her weight demurely on the arm-rest. 'But you needn't worry, you know. I've grown out of it. Besides, I have a boyfriend now.'

The news surprised him. 'This must be quite a recent development. It wasn't long ago that I received your last Victor Noir letter which was definitely written by someone with a crush.'

'You're right. It *is* very recent. I mean, I've known him a long time but it was only on the evening of the carnival, the Fête de la Musique, that we decided to see more of each other.' She raised her shoulders and brushed a wisp of hair from her eyes. 'He's just a regular kind of guy. He treats me OK.'

'He must have been one of the people you were with at the place Saint-Michel,' said Kovacs, half to himself.

She looked at him questioningly then suddenly cottoned on. 'Oh yes, of course. The carnival. Your friend, the black – he told me that you were there and that you followed me home. He filled me in on all that.'

The washing machine stopped its spin. The abrupt cessation came like a gasp, as if a gossiping crowd had been shocked into silence by the sight of something untoward.

Kovacs looked at her curiously, and she met his gaze.

'I want to ask you about the burglary,' he said quietly. 'I want to ask you about the *means*. *How* you did what you did. You drilled a hole into my door and passed a bit of wire from a coat-hanger through, I think, to release the latch. How did you learn to do that?'

'It's easy. Any schoolkid can show you how. It doesn't always work, though. If the door has been locked you can't do it. But most people just click their front doors to when they're in a hurry. If they do that, it's a cinch.'

'And you got my address – ?'

'From an old telephone directory, before you went ex-directory.'

'Right. I'm going to come back to that matter later. But let's stick with the burglary for the time being. So you broke in, and you stole my typewriter. Now, did you know you were going to steal the typewriter and, if so, *why* that typewriter? Why not something else?'

She bit her fingernail and smiled. 'Don't you remember? You were always going on about your typewriter in class. It was one of your jokes. It got kind of boring after a while. When your computer was in to be serviced you typed out some class notes on it for us and we all had a laugh. We could see where you had to write in all the "I"s by hand. We also knew that it was a present from your ex-wife and that it was a sort of special object for you.'

'Did I tell you all of that?'

'You told us lots of things about yourself in class. I remembered them all.'

Kovacs was taken aback. He had always considered himself

to be an inscrutable pedagogue but now the truth was out: he was, to all appearances, an inveterate self-publicist.

'I suppose the idea of writing your messages to me – or to Victor Noir, rather – in the form of lipograms also came from me?'

'Yeah. You did a class on wordplay, remember? We played Fictionary Dictionary and looked at anagrams, acrostics, acronyms, antigrams, chronograms, palindromes, pangrams, univocalics – and, of course, lipograms.'

He couldn't, in truth, remember precisely, but he was impressed by her recall.

'You gave hand-outs,' she went on. 'I often go over them when I'm bored. I do them with my mother. It makes a change from crosswords.'

'So the idea for the lipograms came from me.'

'You and A. Ross Eckler.'

The name was unfamiliar to Kovacs.

'Don't you know his lipograms?' she asked. 'He wrote two based on "Mary Had a Little Lamb". I made some photocopies for my friends. Would you like one?'

'Yes,' he said, surprised, 'I'd love one.'

She went over to the writing desk and retrieved a sheet from a drawer.

'There's one without the letter "S", and the other leaves out the letter "E",' she explained.

Kovacs took it and read the lipograms carefully, chuckling mildly as he went.

Mary had a little lamb,
With fleece a pale white hue,
And everywhere that Mary went
The lamb kept her in view;
To academe he went with her,
Illegal, and quite rare;
It made the children laugh and play
To view a lamb in there.

Mary had a tiny lamb,
Its wool was pallid as snow,

And any spot that Mary did walk
This lamb would always go;
This lamb did follow Mary to school,
Although against a law;
How girls and boys did laugh and play
That lamb in class all saw.

'And of course I know Perec's book, *La Disparition*,' added the girl when she saw that he had finished. 'Everyone knows that.'

'Thank you, thank you for this,' said Kovacs, folding the photocopy and sliding it into his jacket pocket. A vacant lull intervened during which it occurred to him that they were drifting from the matter in hand and he abruptly reasserted his control. 'Victor Noir,' he said. 'Tell me about Victor Noir. I know that he is regarded as a sort of fertility symbol and lots of women put messages in his hat, but how could you have known that they would be delivered to me? After all, there was no address – just my name, and even that was turned into a sort of lipogram.'

'I didn't know they would be delivered,' said Delphine. 'It didn't really matter, either way, though I did kind of hope that they would get to you. But a friend of mine – Elodie, you may remember her – told me that she had placed messages in the hat and they had disappeared, so we assumed that someone was doing the delivering. I thought maybe it was one of the cemetery guards. But when I met the black yesterday I realised that it was him.'

'Babalu,' said Kovacs.

'I beg your pardon?'

'The black. His name is Babalu.' Kovacs rubbed his nose between thumb and forefinger: he was running through his mental list of enigmas. The sound of a telephone ringing in an adjoining flat prompted his memory. 'The calls,' he said. 'I take it you were responsible for all those anonymous phone calls I received?'

'Yes, I was.'

'Well my number is ex-directory, and I want to know how you got it. But there's more than just that. There are a lot of things you seem to know about my private life that nobody else knows. Let's go through them. You know, as I said, my ex-directory number. You know all the details of my private bank account and were able to convince the clerk at the Crédit Lyonnais that you were my wife and that you wanted to close my account for me. You knew that I would be in the Parc des Buttes-Chaumont at three o'clock on Saturday the fourth of June to meet my friend Céline and you were there to observe me. You also knew that my birthday was coming up – still *is*, in fact – and that in previous years I had received a wallet and a vase for my birthday – from my ex-wife and Céline respectively. I think that is everything. So tell me, please, *how*? *How* could you possibly know all of this? I'm dying to know.'

For the first time, the girl showed signs of embarrassment and reluctance. She bit her lip and fiddled with the latex logo on her sneakers. When she spoke it was almost in a whisper. 'The typewriter was not the only thing I stole,' she confessed. 'When I broke into your apartment, I mean.'

Kovacs was genuinely perplexed. 'I'm sure it *was*,' he said. 'I searched the entire flat methodically looking for missing things.'

'Well you wouldn't have *seen* what I stole.'

He stared rigidly at her, waiting for her explanation.

'I saw your portable computer – your PowerBook – on the desk, right? Well, I switched it on and I saw that you had *things* – information about yourself – on the hard disk. You had a notebook of ideas. You had a programme called *Cal. 3.03* which was your calendar, with dates and notes. That's how I found your birthday and the appointment to meet your friend in the park. You also had a programme called *Tous Comptes Faits* – a personal finance programme – with all of the details about your bank and your *Carte Bleue* on it. That's how I cancelled the card and closed your account. Then you had a file containing all of your personal correspondence. In a lot of the letters you wrote to people you gave them your new ex-directory number, so that was how I confirmed that. You also have your diary and that was where I found out what you got for your birthday in previous years.'

Kovacs whistled thinly between his teeth. Like the principle of communicating vases, where she had gained colour in the cheeks he had been drained very rapidly of his. 'I can't believe it,' he managed. 'How could you have had time – how did you have time to read all of that?'

'I didn't,' she replied. 'Next to your computer there were a couple of open boxes of formatted disks and I simply took a couple and made copies of the interesting things.'

She had explained herself as if it was the simplest thing in the world. Kovacs was beginning to feel distinctly unwell.

'You know *everything* about me? You've read all of my diaries?'

She removed the wet hair-knot from her mouth and nodded.

'The worst thing was the file where you write down all your dreams,' she said. She seemed to Kovacs to have overcome her initial edginess and the confidences were now flying thick and fast.

'You copied *that*? You read that too?'

'Yes. It was – you know, *weird*.' She grimaced involuntarily. 'It gave me nightmares for a long time. But in the end it was good, because I got to know you better. Really *well*, in fact.'

'I'm sure you did!' Kovacs exclaimed, flabbergasted. He took a long draught of water to cool himself off.

'The more I got to know about you, the more I wanted to help you. I could see you had problems.'

'What the devil do you mean?'

'You know,' she said, seeing nothing obscure in the matter, 'you have problems with the way you look at the world. And women too, perhaps. I think that was when my crush started to wear off, when I saw what you were really like. It was good for me, because I could break off with you and start going out with my boyfriend. You really helped, there.'

'Well, thanks!'

'But at the same time,' she went on, 'I kind of wanted to help you. After all, we have things in common.'

'What? What on earth can we have in common?'

'Well, we both have English blood: you more than me. Your father is dead and so is mine. We're loners, I suppose. I don't know. There were things in your diary I really liked too. Some good bits. I thought they were really clever.'

'Thank you very much!' said Kovacs, still in his astounded

tone of voice. 'I'll have to employ you as my literary agent. Your talents would clearly be wasted on the hotel and tourism industry unless, of course, hotels require permanent private detectives on the staff. Tell me, what does your mother know about all of this?'

'Nothing,' said Delphine, shaking her head. 'Nothing at all. That's why, when you phoned, she put on the loudspeaker and heard everything you said. She was furious. She complained to your boss. I tried to stop her, but I couldn't. She said she was sticking up for me. I simply couldn't bring myself to tell her that all your accusations against me were true. It would have broken her heart.'

Kovacs drew his breath in deeply and sighed. All his questions had been answered. He had found out everything he wanted to know. So there it was. Extraordinary! Paradoxically, it was he – and not she – who felt entangled inside, a mess of conflicting emotions. He felt admiration – he admired her ingenuity. Anger – she had violated his personal space. Embarrassment – she knew everything about him, even down to his most sordid dreams. Compassion – there was something touching about her despite it all, a good heart behind all the semblance of malice. Outrage – she had made a fool of him in front of Allwright, Céline, Fairgreave, Laroche and Christ knows who else. Pride – she admired his literary style (but how *dare* she?!). And, finally, disappointment – yes, he was disappointed – with himself, in all probability – that she thought he had problems with the way he looked at the world (she wasn't the first, he knew, to have said it).

He checked his watch. It seemed to have stopped. The hands said twelve-twenty. It was impossible that this entire conversation could have taken *minus* ten minutes! He was sure that he had arrived at around twelve-thirty, as prearranged. He wound it up and listened. Silence – there was definitely something wrong there. The second hand had stopped over the number 6.

'My watch seems to be broken,' he said. 'Do you have the time?'

She pointed to a wall-clock, saying 'It's half past one.'

'That's more like it. I thought we had been here a long time. Delphine, *thank you* – thank you for your honesty.' He stood up, preparing to leave, and brushed flat his trousers and jacket as he did so.

She smiled and her flawed green eyes met his in brief sympathy.

'I wanted to apologise to you, Mr Kovacs,' she said earnestly. 'It was dreadful, really, everything I did. I can see that now. I've pried into your affairs and I've made your life unhappy. There was a time when I really would never have wanted that – when I wanted you to be happy more than anything.'

'Thank you,' said Kovacs. 'I accept your apology and I appreciate above all your frankness. You're young, and you're beginning to realise that life – love, emotions, sexuality, all of that – can be an immensely complicated business. Half the time we don't know what is going on inside ourselves. We think we do, but we don't. We don't always say what we mean and we don't always mean what we say. I hope that our little chat today has helped you understand yourself better and that you will lead a better life. You're not a bad girl, I can see that. And I forgive you for everything. I know this may sound odd, but I'd also like to ask you to forgive me for catching you cheating.'

'What!'

'Yes, I mean it. Well, I mean it and I don't mean it at the same time, if you know what I mean.'

She laughed. 'I *think* I do!'

'Forgive and forget, right?'

'Right!' she said, smiling gratefully. 'You could have really got me into trouble with the police but you didn't. Thank you. You are a kind man, Mr Kovacs. I always knew that. I think that was why I liked you.'

Kovacs felt himself blushing. The mutual compliments were beginning to drag on too long.

'I just have a few things to ask you before I go. First, I want you to write out a simple account of what you did, a sort of confession.'

Delphine looked suddenly out of sorts.

'Now don't worry,' he insisted. 'I'm not going to use it against you. I simply wish to show it to my boss to convince him that I was telling the truth. Maybe one or two other people as well. I shall show it to them, that's all. No copies will be distributed.

The reason for this is that the whole story has been so incredibly convoluted that many people who were indirectly involved began to doubt what I was saying. I want to prove to them that I was telling the truth. In no way would there be any repercussions against you. Is that too much to ask?'

'No, I suppose not,' she said diffidently. 'Can I post it to you?'

'Of course. And secondly, I would like you to return the disks with my files on them and the typewriter.'

'I've got them ready here.' She gave him the box of disks and the little portable typewriter in its case. 'I've had the typewriter repaired,' she said.

'Have you?'

'Yes, I found a man who does up old typewriters and he was able to replace the broken key. So you do have an "I" now. He made a very good job of it.'

'How kind of you! But I'll have nothing more to joke about in class now! No more involuntary lipograms!'

'No, I suppose not!' she said.

He picked up his belongings and she saw him to the door of the flat.

'Don't worry, I'll see myself downstairs,' he said. 'Be good,' he added with a grin as he turned to say goodbye.

She was a sort of damaged angel, he thought as the apartment door closed, occluding her from his vision – an imperfect black-haired angel. Or a stabbed dove . . . He played with the idea, dimly recollecting a poem by Apollinaire – trying, and failing, to define her in one stark mental image.

He made his way slowly downstairs, and on the staircase he sniffed and stopped. Yes, there it was. Eucalyptus! It had been in the flat too, the same smell she had left behind her in his apartment when she had burgled it. And he suddenly remembered the black and yellow box on the writing desk and realised what it was: the packaging for *Essence Algérienne*, the product he had smelt in his burgled apartment. VOILA MON REMEDE.

He was happy now, relieved, that everything had turned out as it had. He stepped into the cul-de-sac, stretched his arms and looked down towards the main street. There was the penny-farthing sign again, hanging over the restaurant, and now he knew what it made him think of: the emblem of The Village in the cult Sixties British TV series *The Prisoner*. Appropriate, he thought. Number 6 (he glanced again at his watch) had finally found out who Number 1 was. Result: freedom! The world was bright and beautiful, de-misted and de-mystified. The 'radiant, rainless, lazily rowdy and skyblue' summer months still stretched ahead, he thought – in the words of Dylan Thomas. He could get on, calmly, undisturbed, with his research. And everything would be OK. For the whole thing now made perfect sense to him – it was bizarre, but perfect. The anguish of not knowing was over, *over* at long last.

That, at least, is what he thought.

10

Kovacs slept like a little lamb. His night was white as snow. Not a white night in the French sense – *une nuit blanche* – not a sleepless night, but a pure night, a silent night, like a night of softly falling snow high up in the mountains, away from the black grime and squalor and noise of the demon metropolis. Up the spiral staircase in the little upper room where he had his bed he felt safe and sound: the linen was fresh and clean, reminding him of his mother's impeccable bedmaking. There was no chimps' sex party to disturb his slumbers. There was no banging from the Turckheims. There were no phone calls from Stassopoulos. And in the morning, when he looked at his pillow, there was no Victor Noir staring back at him: nor, when he looked in the mirror, did he see a glowing floricultural specimen ripe for the Chelsea Show. The pollen had worn clean away.

It was Saturday, and the weekend. Not that this mattered for he was on holiday. He was not a Number. Not any longer.

He was a Free Man.

So free was he, in fact, that he scarcely knew what to do with himself. He bathed and shaved, drawing the process out just that little bit longer to ensure that no rogue corner of stubble missed his attention, and chose a mild and unaggressive after-shave from his collection: not Egoïste but Eternity. Yes, he liked that name. Then he studied the contents of his chest of drawers and wardrobe with the discerning eye of one who frequents the best gentleman's outfitters. He opted, in the end, for white cricket trousers, brown brogues, an open-neck cream-coloured shirt and his best Valentino blazer, grey in colour, prodding the new silk kerchief into the pocket. 'Why should he wear a polka-dot kerchief?' 'Because he wanted to be spotted!' Then he popped a fluid container and spare pair of contact lenses into his pocket – he was not going to be caught out again. So there he was: A Man About Town. Not a man of rags and patches, but a man of songs and snatches, and he sang quietly to himself as he went about his business. *Dressed up like a million-dollar trooper, Trying mighty hard to look like Gary Cooper!* The total effect was rich but modest – pleasing when pondered in the large rococo mirror, but for whom was he going to such lengths of beautification? For himself, he assured himself. He felt good today, there was no denying it, and he was damn well going to look good too.

The sight of the white silk kerchief with its peppering of black polka dots – the sight of the kerchief sprouting discreetly from his top pocket – reminded him not only, vaguely, of Laroche but more specifically of what it had cost and the fact that he was, indeed, down to his last few francs. He searched in the pocket of the pair of trousers he had been wearing the previous day and found all that was left. A fifty-franc note: next to nothing. He inspected its design – the picture of Antoine de Saint-Exupéry, the cartoon of *Le Petit Prince* – as intensely as he had done on a previous occasion and there, on the corner of the note, was the letter 'J' scribbled in ballpoint. Where had he got this note? It was one of the notes that Babalu had given him: the entire five-hundred franc loan had been in fifty-franc notes. It was inconceivable that this could be precisely the same note that he had momentarily held the night that he and Babalu had met. They had been outside Chez Jenny's, on the terrace, and no sooner had the patrician gentleman given it to him (imagining that he had dropped it) than the demented female junkie had whisked it away. The *same* note? Coming from Babalu too, who was with him when it happened? The thought was so preposterous – so colossally cock-eyed – that he brushed it aside like a gnat.

Money, he reminded himself, *that* was the problem. It was in fact virtually the last outstanding problem which stood between him and beatitude, between the niggling minutiae of life and the lofty grandeur of his research. Once he had sorted this problem out he would be free. It being Saturday was not a problem as far as the bank was concerned: branches of Crédit Lyonnais, ever mindful of the convenience of their customers, were open on Saturdays. The problem was that he had heard nothing from the bank and in all likelihood – even if they had got him a new *Carte Bleue*, even if they had printed him a new cheque-book (hopefully with different pictures of Paris on each cheque, those were the ones he liked) – even if those conditions were fulfilled, he was worldly-wise enough now to know that without identification they would still refuse to put the instruments of credit into his hands. He was tired of being illegible. He wanted to be legible and eligible. He was tired of being a con-man. He was not *un homme con*. (‘*T'es un homme ou une omelette?*’ Anne used to ask.) He was tired of the uncreditable, the incredible and the incredulous. He wanted to be credit-worthy, creditable, credible. But to be all of these things one needed, not a creed, but credence – one needed to be trusted and believed. One needed, in a word, *credentials*. He had got back his ‘I’, thanks to Delphine Jones. Her ‘J’, after all, was the only letter of the alphabet that stood between his ‘K’ and his ‘I’. So, yes – he had got back his ‘I’. Now all he had to do was to find a ‘D’ to go with it. ‘ID.’ And today – well, today was his ‘D-day’.

Carte de séjour - passport – credit card – cheques.

It still came down to that.

So now, this happy morning – when he was up with the lark, in the height of fashion (without being merely voguish) and clean in mind and body – would it not be sensible, not to say essential, to tackle this final hurdle with a clear, unhungover mind, a spring in his step and a song in his logico-positivist heart? Well of course it would! And that is what he determined to do. He was out to get his ‘ID’ and, as he considered this resolve, the Freudian implications did not escape him. There was no doubt that he had got his ‘ego’, his conscious ‘self’ – or got it *back*, he should say, with that ‘I’, the ‘I’ on the typewriter, or perhaps he should say ‘Ii’s for there were two of them, UPPER and lower case. If, then, he had recovered his ‘ego’ was he now trying to find his ‘id’? What a singular idea! And even as he expressed his amazement thus it struck him further that the initials ‘ID’, pronounced in French, gave *Idée* – ‘Idea’. There had even been a car marketed on this pun, the Citroën ID 19, precursor of the DS which was another pun: ‘DS’, pronounced in French *Déesse*, Goddess. The delights of this Barthesian intellectual escapade were beginning to pall: what he needed was a bit of intellectual escapology. He was tying himself up in knots again, an amateur and accident-prone Houdini. Even the expression 'D-day' was freighted with the tenebrous ghosts of his past: his dead uncle, specifically, Philip Kovacs, his alter ego whom his mother had loved. So he decided to leave it just at '*Jour-J*' – the equivalent expression to 'D-day' in French. That at least did not trigger off a chain reaction of associations from the past. It summoned no ghosts. *Jour-J* – then – is what it would be.

As things turned out, it was a wholly appropriate choice. But not for the reason he thought.

Step one, then, was to phone Laroche, since step one in the process of resolving his troubles was to retrieve his lost *carte de séjour*. Even if it were irretrievably lost, he would put his foot down this time: after all, it was Laroche's office which had lost it so they could damn well come up with a replacement – and pronto! – even if it meant a temporary card. There was no reason why he should continue to be so severely inconvenienced by this flagrant case of clerical error and gross ineptitude at the Commissariat. He would be polite but firm.

He rang the Commissariat.

'*C'est samedi, Monsieur – le week-en – la fin de semaine, je veux dire.*' The receptionist had nearly said 'weekend' but of course Jacques Toubon, supported by the Académie Française, had been trying to ban English words: '*fin de semaine*' was the official Francophone alternative. Nobody paid any attention to these decrees but the police, Kovacs supposed, must be under instructions, no doubt straight from the top.

This, of course, did not improve his situation. It was indeed Saturday and Laroche would not be back in his office until Monday. The whole thing was a bloody bore.

Then he remembered that Laroche had given him his home phone number. Why not? Why shouldn't he disturb him at home? He'd had enough of being kept waiting and at the very least Laroche could phone through to the weekend staff at the Commissariat and order them to draw up a new *carte de séjour* for him. He searched through his papers and found Laroche's business card with the home number scrawled on the back.

'The Laroche residence?' It was a man's voice, though oddly epicene.

'Hello, Inspector Laroche, I'm sorry to bother you at home, but –'

'I'm sorry, Monsieur, this is not Inspector Laroche. This is his butler. Can I do anything for you?'

Strange, thought Kovacs – a butler!

'Could I speak to the Inspector, please?'

'I'm afraid he is not here. He is away hang-gliding in the Vosges mountains.'

'I see.'

Kovacs raised his eyebrows faintly. He was becoming relatively unshockable.

'I suppose he will be back on Sunday evening.'

'At present, Monsieur, the Inspector's movements are something of a mystery. I myself have not been able to follow them with any degree of accuracy. He has taken to spending a lot of time in a local gymnasium and he may well travel back to Paris overnight on Sunday and go directly there on Monday.'

'How, then, is one supposed to get in touch with him?'

'I have been asking myself the same question, Monsieur. The Inspector has a cellphone and I have tried the number, but there was no reply: one is led to assume that those otherwise practical instruments do not function at high altitude. Perhaps *I* can be of help?'

'Well, you see, the Inspector was helping me deal with a private matter. The Inspector has something that I need desperately.'

'I know, Monsieur. I have been feeling the same way for a long time.'

'I'm sorry? Look – what I am trying to say is that I have a big problem and I would like the Inspector to take it in hand.'

'No problem is too big for the Inspector, Monsieur, but as I say there is little one can do when he is suspended from a glorified kite hundreds of metres above a mountainside somewhere in Alsace.'

'Well could you tell him I rang? Kovacs – Philip Kovacs. Tell him I want my *carte de séjour*. He'll know what it's all about.'

'Kovacs,' said the butler, evidently recognising the name and writing it down. 'So *you* are the gentleman. I have been wondering who you were for some time.'

'I'm sorry? I'm afraid I have no idea what you're talking about.'

'Don't worry, Monsieur, I am not jealous. But if you have any concern for my feelings please do not come to this house and do not ring this number ever again.'

The line went dead.

Kovacs began to go over the implications of this eldritch conversation in his head, then tutted and went to the kitchen for a glass of the lemon-scented Perrier he had bought that morning. He had found, recently, that water was a marvellous thing for drowning one's problems. It simply washed them clean away. Spirits, on the other hand, seemed to amplify them in an alarming manner familiar to the likes of Ray Milland or fictitious British ex-consuls in Mexico: the kind whose livers couldn't spot a glass of water in an identity parade. The 'gin-and-tonic-to-catatonic' kind. He thought of Fairgreave, whose Cartesian motto was: 'I drink, therefore I am.' For Fairgreave, cognition and cognac were cognate terms. Kovacs, in this respect, was rather proud of himself: he had not touched a drop for quite some time. The very thought, however, that he had not touched a drop seemed to whet his thirst, or at least remind him of some of his favourite haunts – the bars and cafés that he had not been into for ages.

Fifty francs, he thought, looking at the crumpled bank-note. Why not nip out for a drink?

After all, there was precious little else he could do with that sum of money. And he could survive the weekend without cash: the fridge was full, he'd have no excuse to go out and he could simply press on with his research. It sounded like a good idea. Certainly Laroche's absence put paid to all hope that he could sort out his credentials there and then. So much for the *Grande Idée* – his 'ID'!

He pulled the door to behind him and made his way downstairs.

As he neared the ground floor a racing drumbeat and a terrific blast of rock 'n' roll music could be heard, getting louder all the time. It was Elvis Presley's 'Blue Suede Shoes'. He couldn't, for the life of him, think where it might be coming from. Apart from the retiring young couple next door most of the other residents of the building were elderly old scarecrows who were more at home with Piaf than Presley. When he came towards the courtyard, however, there was no doubt in his mind that the deafening din was coming from Madame da Silva's *loge.* He approached stealthily, though there was hardly any need for this: nobody would have heard him anyway.

The net curtains were open behind the large inner window of the concierge's *loge* and inside Madame da Silva and Monsieur Stassopoulos were dancing to the Presley hit which emanated from a massive ghetto-blaster next to the Star Gazer lilies in the centre of the table. The performance was really quite impressive. Stassopoulos was a tattered coat upon a stick and one would never have believed the rickety little old Greek capable of such exertions. He picked Madame da Silva up – itself a prodigious feat, given her tonnage – and swung her through the air, then bent down and she leap-frogged over his back. Kovacs approached the window in disbelief until his nose was pressed up against the pane. The grey cat eyed him with patrician disdain. Both Madame da Silva and Monsieur Stassopoulos, he now noticed, were bright orange. When the rock song crashed to a finish, they screamed with laughter, Stassopoulos grabbed the concierge in a passionate carnal embrace and they collapsed together onto the zinging springs of her single bed. Kovacs was speechless. He had also completely forgotten his manners. Stassopoulos happened to look up, saw Kovacs there, then leapt into action, storming over and drawing the curtains shut in fury.

Kovacs wandered out onto the quai de Valmy beside the canal.

It was another lovely day: there seemed to be no end to them this June. The beautiful horse chestnut trees beside the lock were flourishing and the flaw of birds' wings filled the air as fanfaring clouds of pigeons flew up from the pavement at the honk of a car-horn into the branches, onto the zinc roofs and chimneypots or across the canal to the roof of the Hôtel du Nord. He could almost imagine Arletty, the wonderful Parisian actress, looking out of her hotel window, or standing on the

Venetian iron bridge and yelling '*Atmosphère! Atmosphère! Est-ce que j'ai une gueule d'atmosphère?*' – it was the most famous line in the film, known to every man and woman in France.

He strolled nonchalantly down the side of the canal, stepping gingerly – as usual – over the treacherous iron mooring-rings on the bank, and came at length to the square Frédéric Lemaître, named after the actor whose bust could be found there. He glanced at the clock on the corner of the boulevard Jules Ferry but, as ever, its hands were stuck at twelve-twenty. He had, by force of habit, put his watch on that morning when dressing even though it was broken and, again by force of habit, he looked at it now. How strange! It had, of course, stopped at precisely twelve-twenty the previous day, just before he had arrived at the Impasse des Deux Anges.

An elderly man with a beret was wandering past.

'Excuse me, do you have the time?' Kovacs asked.

The man pulled out a fob-watch from his waistcoat pocket. '*Ouais, il est douze heures vingt – pile. Bientôt l'heure de déjeuner!*'

So! It *was* twelve-twenty! On the dot. Now how about that!

Kovacs wandered in a daze to his favourite bar, the Temple d'Or in the rue du Faubourg du Temple opposite the Cinémathèque Française. He made his way to his usual place by the window. Ahmed, the taciturn barman, was drying glasses behind the bar but he raised the cloth in his hand by way of greeting. There were no music posters up now, but Kovacs cast his eye across the framed cinema-stills that covered the walls. His gaze settled for a moment on that picture of a funeral on the Grand Canal in Venice: he still couldn't put a name to the movie. He had seen the same shot outside the Cinémathèque Française so it must have been showing there then. He looked out onto the street, towards the Cinémathèque, and noticed once more the huge black top hat sign of the Gibus rock club and it made him snort with surprise: the hat of Victor Noir! He would never be able to look at a top hat again without thinking of Victor Noir. A black Renault was parked beneath the sign. Black, black, black! And what about *La vie en rose*? he asked himself. Why always *black*? At least there was a little white ribbon knotted to the car aerial, the traditional French sign for a wedding. He watched the pedestrians passing to and fro under the shadowless midday sun: little old men, mothers with children, a man in a white blood-stained tunic carrying sides of pork from a refrigerated van across the road to the butcher's.

Ahmed ambled over with the *diabolo menthe* soft drink that Kovacs had ordered in a conscious U-turn from his former decision. There was a complimentary saucer of cashew nuts to accompany it.

'*Merci, mon ami,*' Ahmed said as he picked up the fifty-franc note and rummaged in his apron pocket for change.

'On second thoughts, take for two. Have a beer yourself,' said Kovacs.

'*C'est gentil,*' replied Ahmed, and bowed graciously.

Kovacs was doing the sum in his head. *Diabolo menthe* and Leffe beer both cost fourteen francs, so the two would make twenty-eight. Change from fifty francs: twenty-two. Ahmed's mind worked at a slightly lower cyclical rate, but he came to the same arithmetical conclusion and placed the silver with slow deliberation on the table, then he nipped out of the café and across the road to buy some cigarettes.

Twenty-two francs. Now what could he do with that?

He stayed half an hour, savouring the drink slowly, mesmerised by the constant motion of bodies and vehicles outside. The black Renault had gone but a delivery truck had taken its place and sacks of potatoes were being hauled in through the side-door of a restaurant.

He felt slightly light-headed, not sleepy. He half-closed his eyes – as he had done when observing the cocktail party from his kitchen window – and reduced the colours and shapes of the street to an abstract blur. They were mostly dull colours: brick, asphalt, dusty cars, then the odd medley of brighter hues from the clothes of passers-by. One colour struck out, however, advancing through the others. A warm colour: red. There was a red carrot shape suspended in the air. He opened his eyes wide and saw that it was the street-sign of the Bureau de Tabac across the road. The little shop was plastered with stickers and posters for Loto, Loto Sportif, Keno – the various state lotteries that they ran.

He looked down at the twenty-two francs.

Well, why not?

What could he possibly lose? And what else could he do with those twenty-two francs other than order another drink – possibly, if he were weak, a beer? That would just send him to sleep. He didn't want to do that. He wanted to get on with his research that afternoon. Why not buy a Loto ticket? This was a pleasure that was still, as yet, denied to his native countrymen – though not for long – and, besides, you never knew your luck. But which numbers would he play?

That was the question.

He pulled a Bic ballpoint from his pocket and tested it out on the beer-mat, jotting down a few random digits then crossing them out. But he was beginning to feel that he didn't like things to be random: he liked them to make sense. Then all at once a diverting idea presented itself to him, gift-wrapped, signed, sealed and delivered: *une petite fleur*. He wrote down two rows of digits:

1 0 1 1 8 7 0
1 4 7 1 9 5 0

That was all. The first was the day of Victor Noir's death: the 10th of January, 1870. It had stuck in his memory from the tomb. The second was his own birthday, which was fast approaching: the 14th of July, 1950. Since his own fate had – for a few alarming weeks – been so inseparably yoked with that of Victor Noir, why not yoke these numbers? As if Victor Noir's death, across eight decades, could have anything to do with his birth! It was a dotty idea, but entertaining. He gathered his change, nodded goodbye to Ahmed and crossed the road to the Tabac where he duly filled in the little yellow, blue and red Loto ticket with his chosen digits on the number-grid for a multiple win on a single draw. The ticket passed into the machine and he got his receipt, slipping it into his wallet.

Kovacs strolled home, stacked his books and papers on the main oval table, switched on his computer and pondered his research.

The title of his projected book was:

A way with words: language and the materialist self

But, by an unfortunate slip of the computer key, he had omitted to place a gap between the first two words of the title so that it now read, as he saw when he opened the file on the computer screen:

Away with words: language and the materialist self

He was about to correct this error when, with a slight nervous laugh, he decided to leave it be. It was a spontaneous little joke. He would enjoy it a little while longer and come back to correct it later.

It was to be an ambitious book, his brainchild. It was to marry theories of consciousness with theories of language acquisition. Drawing on the findings of eminent scientists, Kovacs wanted to write a short and in some ways unprofessional tome which would nevertheless lay the foundations for a new empirical science. Francis Crick had discovered that it was possible to measure the rate at which brain cells oscillate in cycles per second and it was Kovacs' hunch that this discovery – combined with the information yielded by brain-scans, behavioural observation and various other experimental methods – could at last be drawn together to unlock the secret function of language in the brain, the processes of language learning, retention and production and the way language is used to create the fiction of the 'self', the 'soul' – call it what you will. And yet there was always something that had niggled him about this approach. A something summed up in the expression 'counter-intuitive'. Was he really – *him*, Philip Kovacs – his whole being, his whole conscious self, a matrix of vibrating neurons? Nothing more? Well, *was* he? Over the last few weeks he had begun to doubt this and he could scarcely say why. It was not that he was getting *religious* or anything – nothing like that. Perhaps, he thought whimsically, it was just that 'I' on the typewriter key. Or perhaps it was the fact that the 1,350 ccs of his own brain were coming to resemble less a piece of precision engineering than a microcosmic biosphere modelled on the screaming chaos of an Amazonian jungle.

He looked again at the slipshod title: *Away with words.* It reminded him of something Raimunda had said in her naïvety. What *could* you say with a title like *Away with words*? You could say, perhaps, what a Jaburu bird, an alligator or a monkey says. Nothing less and certainly nothing more.

The tail-end of the day slipped by as he ruefully contemplated the screen. His sense of mission had unexpectedly departed and his firmest convictions now seemed to be gasping for breath in airless rooms. He could no longer see the way he was going. He was less than a Cyclops now. He was blind as a bat. Blind as Lear or Oedipus. Blindsight.

He cooked himself a pan of mixed vegetables in the evening and consumed them with rice, soya sauce and a little water. After dinner, he washed a shirt and hung it up on a clothes-hanger at the window to dry. At around eight, he switched on the television and sat down on a cushion on the floor. There was a news broadcast at eight. In one bulletin, there was an interview with a woman who had been diagnosed as having terminal anorexia in England and was cured in a clinic in Canada: Kovacs noticed a vase of Star Gazer lilies beside her in her clinic room. This was followed by a short feature on Lourdes, the place of pilgrimage high up in the Pyrénées. The latter told the ironical tale of a perfectly fit man who was visiting the shrine and the place where the sick, halt and lame are taken down to the healing waters. He felt a little tired and, seeing an empty wheelchair, sat down and fell asleep. A passing nun assumed that he was crippled and wished to be taken to the waters. She wheeled the chair down to the water's edge, the man awoke and, in his confusion, stood up and walked stumblingly into the water. The assembled believers, witnessing this, hailed it as a miracle. Upon which, the man in question slipped over in the water and broke his leg. After this recondite little item Kovacs no longer paid attention, though he left the TV on. The evening traffic came and went outside. A pigeon landed in the guttering and pecked at the window, apparently demanding crumbs. Night fell, and so did he – fast asleep, curled up on the floor like an infant.

He was woken by the insistent ringing of the telephone.

The ringing seemed to seek him out, pull him to himself, from the well-like depths of unconsciousness.

He uncurled and sat up, rubbing his eyes, then leaned forward and switched off the television: transmissions had concluded, there was only white noise. Outside it was pitch black. He glanced at the wall-clock above his computer.

It was twelve-twenty.

He walked over to the table and picked up the phone.

'Hello?'

Nothing.

'*Allô?*'

Still silence. Or rather a low, rasping breathing, coming out in short, unhealthy gasps.

'Who is this?'

There was no reply.

A tremor of mortal fear rushed over him, as if a cold charnel-house bone had brushed against his skin.

'Delphine? Delphine Jones? This is not you, is it?'

Still no word. Only the thick, rasping breathing.

But there was something else, a connection being made at a far perimeter of his conscious mind. Outside, a barge was lowering in the Ecluses des Recollets, beneath the chestnuts, beside the little garden. The white roar of the water slashing against the mossy banks reached his ears. And there – surely he was not mistaken? – there on the telephone he could hear the same sound, he could hear the identical roar. It was coming into his right ear through the telephone receiver. His mind raced like a lit fuse. Outside, was there a call-box? Yes there was! Just along from the lock.

'I am waiting for you to speak,' he said down the line. 'I am very patient. I am waiting for you to speak.'

He edged, as he spoke, towards the window and looked down.

He could just see the glass telephone kiosk from his flat on the third floor. In the darkness of the night, a glow of light was emanating from it. And someone was there. It was difficult – difficult to see. But he could make out two things, and of this he had no doubt. Whoever the person was, they were dressed in green. And on the head, above the raised receiver, was a black baseball cap – back-to-front.

It was now or never.

'These anonymous calls have been going on for too long, and this time I'm *not* going to hang up,' he said in French into the receiver. 'I'm very patient, and I shall sit here and wait for you to speak until you decide to do so.'

Then, ever so carefully, he put the receiver down on the table and made for the door of his flat, shutting it with a click behind him.

He raced down the stairs and out into the street. The call-box was a little further up the quai de Valmy on the right. He ran heavily down the pavement towards it. His heart was pounding – the beat of blood rocked in his ears, thundered in his head. He could hardly breathe.

But he was too late.

When he arrived at the box there was no-one there.

He opened the door, looking for clues. It was empty, but there was something he knew, something that took him back. Menthol, eucalyptus. That smell! *Essence Algérienne.* It could only mean one thing: Delphine.

He ran backwards and forwards across the road outside the box. Impossible! Where could she have got to? Then he realised: as he had left his flat she must have heard the click of the door shutting behind him. She must have known. She would just have had time to get away. But why? Why should she do this, after their talk the previous day? Surely everything had been sorted out? Hadn't it?

Was there something he was missing?

Was there something he had not understood?

He wandered – nearly wide awake now, frustrated, nerve-racked, hot – down the side of the canal beside the raised recreation area for children. The barge had passed and the waters of the lock were silent. But another noise reached his ears. From within the little garden beside the Ecluses des Récollets he could hear hoarse, uneven breathing.

He looked, and there she was.

She was sitting on one of the benches, her face in her hands, weeping it seemed.

The little green skirt, the bolero jacket, the black baseball cap, back-to-front.

'Delphine!' he said, and she looked up.

At that precise moment the terrific roar of a car engine speeding towards him down the quai de Valmy could be heard. A late-night road-hog, he thought, and half looked round before turning back to the girl.

But it was not the girl.

The roar of the car came closer and with an agonising scream of brakes it rode up onto the pavement outside his building. It was a green Peugeot 205.

He looked back at the woman. She was standing up now and slowly approaching him, fumbling at the same time for something in her black leather handbag with gold trimmings.

It was not Delphine, but it was someone like her. It was an old woman. She had grey hair, bunched up into the baseball cap, and really quite a slim body. From a distance she could easily have been taken for Delphine. She was smiling sweetly at him now as she continued to fumble in her bag.

'Noooo!!' someone screamed, as a car door banged open. 'Philip! Get in the car! Please!!'

Why? Why *should* he get into the car? Who on earth was ordering him about?

The woman, in her sixties perhaps, had reached the gate of the garden and was just about to come out. She seemed to have found what she was looking for. It was a little glass bottle and she was undoing the stopper.

'Philip!! Get in the car! Now!'

Who could be calling him like that? He turned round and saw that it was Delphine. From the back of the car, hammering on the window to attract his attention, was Babalu. Suddenly every nerve in his body was alive. A torrent of fire shot through him.

He ran for the car.

The old woman ran after him. She was still smiling, not so

sweetly now, and staggered a little, slightly unsteady on her high heels. She was holding the open flask in the air, ready to throw its contents at him.

He ran round to the passenger seat and jumped into the car. Delphine stamped on the accelerator and the car jumped forward. As it did so, the contents of the flask – a liquid – splashed on the car bonnet. The car tore off down the quai de Valmy, the smell of burning rubber from its tyres flooding the interior. As they hurtled down the road – jumping three red traffic lights – Kovacs saw that the paintwork on the bonnet where the liquid had splashed was peeling up to reveal the bare metal and a foul chemical smoke was pouring off. He could smell it now, over the top of the burning rubber.

'Who was that?' he shouted, over the snarl of the engine. To his surprise, he was trembling like a poplar leaf.

Delphine held the steering-wheel with one hand and wiped her eyes with the other.

'That was Mum,' she said, fighting back the tears.

11

DELPHINE HAD NO idea where she was driving. It didn't matter. She just wanted to get away and to take Kovacs away too. For a long time she was too distraught to speak, sobbing in panicky gulps, and Babalu rested a hand on her shoulder from behind or occasionally massaged her neck as she drove to calm her down. The great tubular structure of the Centre Pompidou flashed by; they crossed the Seine, the Ile de la Cité, the river again; then they hurtled up the boulevard Saint-Michel towards Port Royal and the Paris Observatory. The Observatory clock, luminous in the night beneath a white cupola housing the telescope, read a quarter to one: it was the place from which the whole world's time was calculated.

'Mum!' said Kovacs repeatedly to himself. A ghostly but invasive sense of the truth was coming to him.

'Is Iansã,' muttered Babalu from behind, talking to no-one in particular. 'Is what I say all along. Iansã – but not good Iansã, Iansã in very dangerous mood.'

'Where are we going?' Kovacs asked eventually.

'I don't know,' answered Delphine. 'I don't know.' She was in a trance-like state, her knuckles white as she gripped the steering-wheel. Her pouty lower lip trembled uncontrollably, either because she was on the brink of tears or because an inaudible monologue was engaging her mind.

'Just drive,' said Kovacs soothingly. He pointed to a slip-road and they took it, merging into the traffic on the Périphérique ring-road. Orange street-lamps flashed stroboscopically above and, dead ahead, red tail-lights sped up close then sheered off right as the Peugeot overtook. The speedometer needle flickered high on the gauge. They were heading east, anticlockwise, as if Paris itself were a clockface and they were turning back the hands of time in an occult feat of Einsteinian illusionism.

Kovacs glanced at Delphine in the rear-view mirror. She had calmed down finally, but her cheeks were a dried tracery of tears. Her black hair was snagged and tangled impossibly like that of a sleeper who has just awoken and her face was a flickering pattern of coloured light and shadow, picking up – a chameleon or a cuttlefish – the silent stutter of illumination that flashed down the streaming tunnel of the road. At Ivry-sur-Seine, the road arched over marshalling yards, sidings and massed joining and parting railway-lines, fleeing away like fine silver eels under a big unhindered moon.

'Do you want to talk?' he asked.

'I'm sorry,' she said. 'You must be so *dérouté*, so confused. It was all my fault. I wanted to go on hiding her for ever. I should have known it was impossible.' She had started to speak in English, thinking perhaps that the real truth would get through to him faster in his mother tongue, and throughout the conversation she continued thus.

'Your mother?'

'Yes.' She brought a hand up impatiently to brush a stray length of tousled black hair out of her eyes.

'So the burglary, the park – it was *her*? The phone calls, the letters too – they were all from her?'

'Yes. My mother is a very sick woman, Mr Kovacs. She is very disturbed. There are reasons for this, but she took it all out on you.'

'Why?'

'My career. You wrecked it. She has been a secretary all her life, you see. She wanted something better for me. The school in Lausanne was her dream. She didn't want me to end up like her. That is another reason why I decided to cheat. I didn't want to disappoint her. And as I told you, when you caught me cheating it was very soon after my father's death. She was under terrible mental – *tension*?'

'"Strain,"' said Kovacs, helping her with vocabulary. It was a pedagogical reflex. He hesitated, hiving functions off to left and to right, between mother and daughter. 'But you *did* have a crush on me? You were furious with me when I caught you?'

'Yes.' Her voice broke; it was plaintive, entreating. 'But not to the point of tormenting you. I wouldn't – I couldn't have done that. That was mother. She identifies in everything with me. She feels my love, my fear, my anger – everything. I am everything she has. *C'est bête!* It's really stupid, you know, but *I* am like a mother to her.'

Kovacs shifted in his seat and tugged at his seat-belt. The sharp-edged fabric was sawing into his side.

'As you know now,' Delphine went on, 'she even dresses in my clothes: sometimes if I buy an outfit, she goes out and buys the same for herself. I say to her: "*Maman, mais qu'est-ce que tu fais? Ça va pas, non? C'est ridicule!*" To begin with it was a joke, you know – it was almost amusing. She said to me: "*Delphine, nous sommes comme deux soeurs!*" – like two sisters. But it was not a joke. It goes – *au-delà* –'

'Beyond.'

'Yes, *beyond* a joke. She thinks she *is* me, you see. If I cut myself, she bleeds. If I laugh, she is happy. It is terrible. You are a *fils unique*?' she said, glancing aside at him.

'An only child? Yes,' said Kovacs.

'Well, perhaps you know what I mean. Everything's focused on you. The desires. The hopes. The fears. You are trapped in the spot, you know.'

'In the spotlight, yes.'

Kovacs thought of his own mother in the nursing home in Bournemouth, the view of Brownsea Island from her window. He thought of the dead uncle, the other Philip, and his real father whom his mother had not loved: and, indeed, he thought of himself, whom his mother had also not loved because she looked *through* him, her eyes searching for the other man. She too had lived through someone else – parasitically, as it were – but that someone had not only been him. That someone had been a dead man: they had simply shared a name, a name and a little diluted blood. What was it, now, that Céline had said in the park? 'I suppose it is always the *mother* to blame in these cases, isn't it?' Well, maybe. But *always*? What about the father? Where did he stand? What about Delphine's father?

'Is there – is there any relevance in the fact that I am English, as your father was?'

Delphine nodded and swallowed. She was beginning to pull round. She expressed herself better and her voice was no longer cracked with emotion. 'I think so, yes,' she said. 'You see, my father was a very cold husband. A cold man, generally. Is that just being English?'

Kovacs raised his eyebrows and huffed. 'It's part of a particular *kind* of Englishness. Real men don't cry. Stiff upper lip, and all that. Do you know what I mean?'

She turned round and flashed a kinked smile in his direction, sensing that she had exposed a nerve.

'Yes, I know what you mean. He was a cold man. Not brutal, particularly, but cold. I don't think he meant to be like that. I think it was because of his education. And it was because they were foreign – different, you know – that they married. But that wasn't enough to keep it together. They had me, of course, but after that they took separate rooms. *Ils ont laissé les choses aller à la dérive.*'

'They drifted apart.'

'Yes. She was angry with him, she felt he had spoilt her life. She felt that if she hadn't married him she could have made more of herself – not just a secretary. Then, when I cheated in the exam . . . well, to her it wasn't me, it was *you* who spoiled my career by catching me cheating. She thought your heart would have told you to ignore it. She thought there was a sort of *lien* – a bond between you and me.'

'A one-way bond, maybe.'

Delphine bit her lower lip awkwardly, leaving a double-hyphen indent when she released it.

'So, you asked me if it was to do with being English. If you put yourself in my mother's place, her daughter's life was being spoiled by an Englishman just as her own had been. You see what I mean? She became terribly anti-English, anti-everything in fact. Very xenophobic. When Dad died, it didn't stop. It didn't stop because you turned up. She turned it all onto you, *tout simplement.*'

Kovacs looked behind him. Babalu had subsided onto the rear seat. He was wearing a jacket and his orange T-shirt; the latter was rucked up and his big dark belly was partially exposed. His hands were clasped together round the back of his neck, under straggling locks of hair.

The car gunned on, deeper into the night. Under the big round moon – so bright one could make out its craters, its vast and desolate seas – the Bois de Vincennes and the Saint-Mandé cemetery glowed with a soft, almost radioactive glamour. High-rises, office blocks and advertising hoardings vanished in their slipstream. Stadiums and sports fields at the Porte de Montreuil swept by in shifting parallax planes, tinged with phosphorescence where the bluish lunar light had found them out.

'So,' said Delphine at length. 'That's what happened. *La vie de famille*,' she murmured ironically.

'Couldn't you do anything to stop her?'

She was silent for a while, then she spoke.

'I think, to begin with – when I knew that she had burgled you – I was secretly happy.'

She looked round sharply at Kovacs to gauge his reaction. He was impassive.

'I hated you for what you had done,' she persisted. 'It was wrong of me, irrational, but that's the way it was. Mum and I read your computer files together. We were both curious. And I knew about everything she did. But as it got worse she scared me particularly when she closed your account. I thought she had gone too far. *Je plaidoyais* – I pleaded with her. She promised to leave things at that. But she didn't. You see, it was not only you I was worried about. It was mother. I didn't want her to be arrested. I didn't want her to go to prison, or an *asile* – a psychiatric institution. As things are now, I guess it's unavoidable. But you understand – she could see nothing wrong in what she was doing. It was – how do you say? – *œil pour œil*.'

'An eye for an eye,' said Kovacs flatly. Never had the expression seemed more apt. 'Does she have a history of mental illness?' he asked after a while.

'She has never received treatment, no. But it has always been there, on the brink. There was terrible tension, frustration in her marriage. Then my father died.'

'You did tell me, I think,' said Kovacs, dredging his memory of their previous conversation. 'He died last December. And he choked, I think?'

'Yes. He choked at breakfast. It's so stupid – it's almost *drôle*, you know, in a macabre kind of way. You see, my mother's fanatical about health foods. She insisted on us all drinking a solution of *argile verte* – how do you call it?'

'I know what you mean. "Fuller's Earth", I think.'

'Yes. We had to drink it in solution every morning. She thought it had special properties. And we also had to eat several tablespoonfuls of pollen – you know, you can buy it in health shops – *les granulés* . . .'

'Uh-huh. In granules. I think I've seen pots of it.'

'Dad and I, we sort of thought *il n'y a pas de mal* - it couldn't do harm, you know. Well it did. That's the thing. That's how he choked. On the pollen. I don't know if you've ever tried that pollen – it's like, as you say, granules. It's very dry. In the mouth it becomes a kind of *pâte* – paste. He was chewing it and trying to swallow it when he choked. We were not in the kitchen at the time. We just found him like that. He had swallowed his own tongue.' She winced then thumped the horn aggressively. A Volkswagen had tried to pull out in front of them from the slow lane but now thought better of it.

The word 'pollen', meanwhile, was catching like a barb or, more appropriately, like microspores in Kovacs' imagination. He was almost choking on it himself. An as yet unconscious apposition was being made.

'If your mother was the one who insisted on everyone eating this pollen,' he said, interrupting his own subliminal process, 'I presume she blamed herself for his death?'

'Exactly.'

She glanced into the wing mirror as a fuel tanker overtook them. Kovacs wound up the window. The noise of the tanker was riding over her words.

'The thing is,' said Delphine, 'she became convinced that he had been murdered.'

'By herself, I presume?'

'Yes and no, really. To her, the murderer was someone else. She was always trying to find out who. She had different theories and it would change all the time. But – well, I'm not a *psychiatre*, but I think that the idea that he'd been murdered by a stranger was her way to accuse herself, to punish herself.'

'For the pollen?'

'That, yes, but also for all those years of sterile marriage. The coldness, the scenes, the recriminations. It was like his death was her punishment on him and now she had to turn round to punish herself. *Merde! Qu'est-ce que j'ai fait!*'

She had changed down too quickly as she swung into the fast lane and the gears screeched reproach. They both looked back simultaneously but Babalu was unperturbed: he was running a toothpick under his fingernails and paying them scant attention.

'Did she make any actual accusations?' asked Kovacs.

'She did. She told the police that she had good reason to think that my father had been poisoned. She told them that someone had put poison in the pollen. *Toc-toc!*' said Delphine, twisting a forefinger into the side of her head in the loose-screw gesture. 'Well, by that time of course my father was dead and buried, in Père Lachaise. She wanted them to exhume the body and do a – you know – *autopsie – c'est le même mot, n'est-ce pas?*'

'Autopsy, yes, or post-mortem,' said Kovacs, in his thesaurus-like way. 'But surely the police would never comply? You have to have good grounds for exhumations and autopsies. Presumably they had nothing but your mother's disturbed suppositions to go on. She had no proof. She was not pointing the finger at anyone specific?'

'*O la la! – si vous saviez!* There were all sorts of potential murderers! She thought it might have been a neighbour. Then it was one of my father's colleagues at work.'

'But if it was as vague as that, why did the police agree to act?' That was the bit that Kovacs could not work through.

'I told you my mother is a secretary, yes?'

He nodded.

'Well, she's a secretary *with* the police. She gets on well with one of the top people there. *Très copain-copain*. He's a man I don't like. There's – I don't know . . . it's difficult to say but I think that, like her, there's something wrong with him.'

'Wrong?'

'*Ouais*. Kind of weird.' She grimaced expressively, as if responding to a sudden obnoxious odour. 'They have something in common, my mother and him. They are both full of hatred for foreigners, and especially the English. I give money to *S.O.S. Racisme* – you know, if they're collecting in the street – but I think this guy, well I think he would cross the street. Or put his money somewhere else. He's always going on about *le vice anglais*, whatever that means.'

Kovacs' chin had dropped a fraction of an inch and he was staring dead ahead down the asphalt strip of the Périphérique.

'Where does she work, your mother?' he asked urgently. 'Where exactly?'

'The Commissariat in the 10th arrondissement. Not far from where you live.'

'Then the police official you are speaking about is Inspector Laroche?' There was a nervous jump in Kovacs' voice.

'Yes.' She glanced at him askance once more then suddenly sneezed, bringing the back of a hand up to her running nose. 'Do you have a Kleenex?' she asked.

'No, I don't.'

'You couldn't look there – there, for me, could you?'

'In the glove compartment?'

'Yes.'

He fished out a small cellophane sachet of tissues. Pushed into one side of the sachet was a book of matches. The name of a bar, Le Toubib, was printed in an Art Déco typeface on the flap. He handed her a Kleenex and she blew her nose. They passed a water reservoir and, shortly afterwards, the Science Park on the site of the former abattoirs at La Villette. The silvered globe of the Géode, an Omnimax cinema, reared in and out of sight like a gargantuan pétanque ball. Kovacs observed all of this, but he had not lost his track.

'Inspector Laroche!' he exclaimed to himself.

'*Oui, c'est lui.*'

'He's the man I went to see about this. He's the man I told about it all. I do remember, though, that I never gave him your name or address. He never knew that I was accusing the daughter of the secretary in his own Commissariat. *Unless* – you don't suppose they were in on it together?'

'No!' Delphine laughed and a ticklish cough caught her in the back of the throat. She cleared the catarrh into the Kleenex.

'Mum can get round Laroche, but she never tells him what she is doing. He would never have participated. He's weird. *Il me donne la trouille.* The other people at the Commissariat – the other cops, the big bosses – they don't trust him either. They try to keep him off any serious cases. So long as he stays quietly in his office, you know, that's OK – or if he takes a day off. That's fine. They don't mind that. I think they just want him out of the way. I don't know his background, but I do know he gives them the shits. That's the feeling you get. I think they want to get rid of him but so far he's given them no cause, you see. He's a very clever man. *Très fouté.* More clever than them, maybe, but it's a different kind of intelligence. He doesn't play by the rules. He makes his own rules up as he goes along.'

She thought back to what he'd been saying. 'But it's stupid of me,' she added, 'I should have realised that you met him. He took your *carte de séjour* and gave it to mother to ask her to – *rétablir* . . . ?'

'Reinstate.'

'Yes, to reinstate your resident's permit on the computer system. My mother worked on the system, you see. In fact, she's the one who wiped out your details in the first place. When he gave her your *carte* she simply confiscated it and said that she had lost it, and every time she was told to put your details into the database she wiped them out again later.'

A *bon mot* from Newton visited Kovacs like a revenant. The scientist had described infinite space as 'the sensorium of the godhead'. That, he thought, is what he needed right now, to piece this cosmic affair together. Yet slowly, bit by bit – like the Big Bang Theory – it was all making sense. All, perhaps (again like the Big Bang Theory), bar the first billionth of a second. And even when we know what happened then, he thought, would it make any difference? These were peculiar times, an age of encyclopaedism: was it really true that, if and when we got to know everything, we would be perfect?

'So let me get this right,' he said. 'Your mother was on friendly terms with Laroche.'

'Yes. Nothing special really, but they "hit it off" I think you say. They –'

'They saw eye to eye.'

'*Oui.* She did him little favours. She was almost the only person in the Commissariat who got on with him. That was probably the reason.'

'So he was the one who somehow managed to get permission for the exhumation of your father and the autopsy?'

'Yes.' She shivered slightly and bunched up her shoulders. 'The grave was opened last May. Of course the body had . . .'

'Yes, of course.'

'But they were able to find things out.'

'What exactly did they find out?'

'What we knew already,' she said, running her hands down to the base of the steering-wheel where she held it steady with just her two forefingers. 'They found out that he had choked on the pollen – the granules. What would you call the man who does the autopsy?'

'The coroner, I suppose.'

'Well he – the coroner – found traces of pollen throughout the mouth and . . .' She looked at Kovacs and ran her finger down the front of her windpipe by way of explanation. 'There was no poison in the pollen. He had not been murdered. So,' she snapped her fingers. 'Case closed. Mum couldn't take her crazy idea any further.'

'So that was that?'

'Yes. There was a bit of a problem for Laroche at the Commissariat because one of his bosses – I don't know which – guessed that he was doing favours.'

'Wasting police time, wasting the coroner's time . . .'

'And money. But the case was closed and the body was buried again. Then something came along to distract Mum from her *manie*.'

'What?'

'*A ton avis?*' she asked, turning it into a guessing game.

'Me, I suppose.'

'*Oui.* You turned up just in time. Well you'd turned up earlier, of course, in December,' she corrected herself, 'but in May, just before my father's coffin was put back – that was when she burgled you. She knew exactly how to do it. People talk in a Commissariat. The police are just like the criminals – they know all the *astuces*. Anyway, all her bad feelings: she put them onto you.'

'Transference,' murmured Kovacs.

'*Comment?*'

'Transference. I think that's what they call it. In psychiatry.'

'*Ah bon? Je ne savais pas . . .*'

Delphine was still in the fast lane but she had slowed down somewhat, reallocating some of the attention she should have bestowed on the road to the conversation with Kovacs. A car that was behind them flashed its lights and she pulled aside then swung out aggressively again once it had passed. Babalu had given up on his fingernails and was slouched against the window, watching as more stadiums, more railway lines and the Batignol cemetery careered by.

'The pollen,' said Kovacs, returning to an idea that had been quietly gestating earlier.

'Yes?'

'Your mother was not the secretary who gave Laroche a bouquet of Star Gazer lilies, was she?'

'Yes. Mother is crazy about flowers. Especially those lilies. We call them by the English name. As I told you, she thinks pollen has special properties. Not just pollen – flowers, all that stuff.'

'Flower Power,' remarked Kovacs, not without humorous intentions.

'Exactly. You're joking, but that was pretty much it. She's 64 now and she was – well, not exactly a hippy – but she was *there* in the Sixties. A bit old to be a *soixante-huitarde*, but she was there all the same. Come to think of it, you too.'

'Yes. Rather young to begin with, but just the right age in '68. Though I was never totally convinced about the flowers. To tell you the truth, I'm not so sure now. Still, you know what they say about that generation, don't you?'

'No.'

'If you can remember the Sixties, you weren't there. But that's beside the point, I suppose. I mean, the lilies really worked for Laroche, didn't they?'

'Yes. How did you – ? Oh, but of course – you saw him. He was terribly grateful to Mum. They changed his life, they turned him round. You saw, didn't you? It was pretty weird.' Again one sensed that a noisome thing had wafted up her nostrils. 'He felt great, he began dressing well, and he turned his whole life inside out. If it had been anybody else it would have been . . . you know, a good thing. But him! Did you see the change to his office?'

'Yes,' said Kovacs. It occurred to him that the attractive brown leather armchair he had seen on his first visit to Laroche's office must have been the same one he had seen at Delphine's flat: salvaged by the mother at the time of redecoration, perhaps, when Laroche's promotion-hungry colleagues thought he was about to breathe his last. Or maybe the Inspector had given it to her himself. He also now knew that the petal from a Star Gazer lily that he had found at his feet in the flat had not, in all likelihood, fallen from his own clothes. It had been there already. He remembered vividly the effect of the lilies on Laroche, Madame da Silva and Monsieur Stassopoulos.

'Do you think there's anything in it?' he asked her earnestly. 'The pollen, I mean, and the flowers?'

'Dunno,' she said non-committally and giving the Gallic shrug of benightedness. '*Je donne ma langue au chat!* We've always had loads of flowers. I've never felt it myself, but maybe some people do. Life can be pretty weird sometimes. Mum took the pollen because it was good for her asthma. But that's not magic, you know – the doctors say it really can help.'

Asthma. Kovacs recalled the rasping breathing on the telephone – the breathing of an asthmatic. Another neural connection had snapped into place.

'Does she take anything else for her asthma?'

'Yes. *Essence Algérienne.* You know, that eucalyptus thing. Like Vick's Vapour Rub in England. She's always soaked in the stuff. It eases her breathing. The whole flat stinks of it. *Ça pue!*'

'My flat too,' said Kovacs reflectively.

'How do you mean?'

'It was one of the first things I noticed after she burgled me.'

'Oh!'

An ambulance with blue flashing lights bombed past them. Through the window they glimpsed a white-coated arm holding a plasma drip. On either side of the ring-road the Bois de Boulogne spread out in arboreal darkness, and soon they were crossing the Seine: the Eiffel Tower loomed up, etched in silhouette against the moonbright night. Kovacs watched as the winking red tail-light of a helicopter travelled left to right, behind the Tower, coming in to land at the city's heliport. The light printed itself in a straight line on his retina like suspension points. Dot – dot – dot –

'This is crazy!' said Delphine with sudden vehemence. 'Where are we going? I don't know why I'm driving like this.'

She nearly pulled over onto the narrow hard-shoulder but Kovacs grabbed the wheel and eased the vehicle back into lane. It was true that they had been lapping or orbiting Paris uselessly, chasing their own tail. The very fact of being in motion was itself an antidote, though. It gave them the illusion of fleeing, however much the metropolis held them in its charmed circle. It gave them the illusion of buying time.

'We'll stop soon,' he assured her. 'Aren't you worried about your mother now? After this evening? I mean, what is she going to do next?'

'I *am* worried, yes. I'm very worried. But I can't go back there. She's gone too far. I can't see her again. We have an aunt in Paris. She knows that Mum's been unwell. She doesn't know what you and I know, she doesn't know everything, but she's aware enough to realise that Mum needs help. I've discussed things with her before. She was the only person I could talk to. We discussed the possibility of – you know, hospital. But she said it was too soon. We had to wait and see.'

'Perhaps you could ring her now?' suggested Kovacs.

'Yes. That's what I was thinking. If we can find a phone, I'll ring her and ask her to go round there. I just hope that Mum has gone home.'

Several minutes passed.

'What is your mother's name?' he asked suddenly. Another synchromesh gear was preparing to engage.

'Jeanette.'

Jeanette! Of course! Laroche had named her. What is more, the 'J' on the second letter in Victor Noir's hat was not just for 'Jones' but also 'Jeanette'. And yes – yesterday, June 25th, had it not been his *Jour-J*? Isn't that what he had naïvely, ignorantly, blithely decided to call it? Like a lamb to the slaughter, his fleece white as snow?

'Jeanette,' murmured Babalu, picking up on the name. 'Is Iansã. Bad mood Iansã. Cyclones will come. We will see what Ogum says.'

'Good Lord!' Kovacs declared. 'I haven't asked you. What the devil is Babalu doing here?'

'I called round on him,' she explained. 'The idea just came to me – like that. You see, I needed him. When I met Babalu, he told me you were best friends. He told me he was your *only* friend. It's hard to explain, but he has a power. I can feel it. A power for good. He more than anyone has your interests at heart.'

Kovacs nodded. 'But what happened? What happened yesterday?'

'Mum was out in the early afternoon. Now that I think of it, she must have been out buying – whatever was in that bottle . . .'

'Acid, obviously,' said Kovacs as he looked at the corroded paintwork. His face and eyes crawled with a ghost-effect of pain. Only a second later and . . . it hardly bore thinking about.

'What happened was this,' she said. 'I told her in the morning that she must leave you alone, that we – you and me – had spoken together and that everything had been *arrangé*.'

'Settled.'

'Yes. She was very reasonable, you know, and she said she was glad. She went out, but when she got home later I realised that she was acting strange again. She was looking around her. It was like *she* had been burgled. She didn't have your typewriter. She didn't have your computer disks, your files. It was like *you* had burgled *her*. She was really mad. She kept saying "Damn his eyes!" in English. It was one of the expressions she got from Dad. I knew she was dangerous. So I sat up with her to make sure she didn't do anything, but I must have fallen asleep. When I woke up she wasn't there. I realised then that she had gone out to get you. There was a terrible thing – a terrible violence in her. I knew something bad was going to happen, I *knew* it, so I had to stop her. I didn't have your phone number. Only she had that in her pocket book. So I got in my car and went to Babalu. He had given me his address when we met and he told me he would always be there if I – if I, like, had any problems. He lives just near you, anyway. I thought that if there was going to be violence – if Mum needed to be stopped, in a physical way – I couldn't do it on my own. And Babalu – well, I've already told you – *c'était le choix évident.* He has a gentleness and a strength about him. He made me feel he was your protector, your guardian angel. And besides, he knew half the story already. So when we were in the car I explained him very quickly – '

'I explained *to* him,' corrected Kovacs.

'I explained to him that it was not me but my mother who had been doing all of those things. The bad things, you know.'

'Your mother rang me at twenty past midnight precisely,' said Kovacs. 'She must have caught the last Metro. The last trains generally run at around twelve-fifteen.'

'No,' said Delphine. 'She has a car. We each have a car. This is mine. She has a black Renault 5. That's why I drove off so quickly. I didn't want her following us.' She hesitated a moment over her grammar. '*Following* or *to follow*?'

'Either,' said Kovacs. 'Gerund or infinitive.'

He looked at a sticker on the flap of the glove compartment:

JE SUIS UNE PEUGEOT 205
ET JE M'APPELLE
BUNBURY

She had chosen the name for her car and written it in the appropriate space with a pink Stabilo-Boss marker.

They passed the Palais des Sports and the Parc des Expositions and drove on in silence. After a few minutes they were at the Porte d'Orléans, their point of departure. They had come full circle. As they were exiting from the Périphérique, the bright floodlighting of an Elf-Aquitaine service station swept into view on their left and Delphine cocked the steering-wheel round, pulling onto the forecourt. Babalu pushed himself upright in the rear seat.

There was a phone-box.

'I'm just going to call my aunt. Like I told you I would,' Delphine said. 'It's past two and I'll wake her up but I don't have any choice.'

She went off to the box. The two men watched her unsteady, slightly hurried walk as she felt in her pocket for coins or a phone-card.

Kovacs turned round to Babalu. 'All right?' he asked.

Babalu nodded and yawned widely, exposing a powerful white ring of dentition and the soft pink palate of his tongue. He had hastily dressed in his 'Best of Olodum' orange T-shirt, an old fawn jacket (the pink nose of the sleeping mouse projecting from the breast pocket) and a pair of jeans.

'How come you were in when Delphine called on you?' asked Kovacs. 'I thought you were working in the bar?'

'I quit, my friend,' he said, wiping his lips and the sleep from his eyes. 'You see, I miss Raimunda. Sure, we need *dinheiro* but *amor* is more important. I travel too long, so I decide – OK Babalu, time to go back – time to go back to Salvador, back to wife and kids. Enough! *Basta!* You understand? Money, money, always money. *Não importa.* I use last of money to buy ticket for home. I go next month, fifteen July. No reason to stay no more. I got enough money in Bahia and maybe, I am thinking – maybe I become painter, professional like. What you think?'

'I've never seen any of your works, I'm afraid.'

'No – is true. But I do some pictures of Paris maybe, when I go back. I got good memory, you know,' he grinned, tapping his skull. 'Maybe they sell. Maybe not. Who care? Money, money – you know, is not so *importante.*'

'Talking of money,' said Kovacs, off on another tack, 'do you remember that five hundred francs you lent me?'

'Sure, my friend. But keep it. You keep it. Is no problem. I no want it back.'

'No, no – I will pay you back. It's not that. The thing is, you gave it to me entirely in fifty-franc notes. Remember?'

'Yeah. Is how my boss pay me. Petty cash. I told you, *amigo*, I am *travailleur au noir*. What is this problem?'

'It's just that, I was wondering, do you remember that incident when we first met? The well-dressed man gave me the fifty francs outside the restaurant then the crazy lady took it away?'

'Oh yeah!' Babalu woke up, smiling, obviously with a good story to tell. 'I been meaning to tell you! I want to tell you last time we see, but it was after Raimunda go, an' I was real upset – *indisposto* – and I forget.'

'What did you want to tell me?' Kovacs urged.

'I want to tell you I see these two again!'

'Both of them? The man *and* the woman?'

'Yeah! Is incredible, no? Was big surprise. I no expect this at all.'

'Where? Where did you see them?'

'The rue de Lappe, my friend. Where I work. I tell you before – is a bar. They come in together, like this.' Babalu jigged up and down, pretending to walk in an airs-and-graces way, a patrician assurance in his manner. 'Very elegant, see! Very high class!'

'The man, yes – but the woman too?'

'Yeah! Very elegant – *roupa*, clothes, you know. "Hello! How d'you do? Very well thank you!"' He gave a crudely mincing imitation of her ways, waggling his little fingers in the air. 'She no have those marks on her arm. No old clothes. Very nice hair, very nice *maquilhagem* – pretty lady! Was big change! Big surprise for me.'

'You say they came in together? Who *are* they?'

'I no know, but my friend from Scotland he tell me. He say "This is Monsieur and Madame Janmot! Brother and sister. Very famous actor! Actor with the Comédie Française." "Oh!", I say. "I am honoured. How d'you do!" I bow. Is like a lord and lady. But later on in bar, these two – this man and lady – they not so high and mighty now, you know. They have too much champagne and they do many funny tricks, make funny jokes. Everybody laugh. Is very amusing.'

'So the thing in front of the restaurant. The business with the bank-note. It was street theatre. It was all set up?'

'I no understand you, *amigo*.'

'Outside the restaurant,' Kovacs persisted. 'With the money. Remember? It was a *joke*?'

The question did not seem to have occurred to Babalu. 'Yeah, I guess so. You know my French is not so good so I no ask them.'

Kovacs was back in ratiocinative form. 'It would be quite

possible, then, that the fifty-franc note they gave to me and snatched back was later used on the evening they came in to pay for drinks in the bar.'

'Why not?' said Babalu, shrugging.

'And that your boss then paid you with that fifty-franc note, amongst others of course.'

'Yes. Is possible. Is what you think? Maybe. I dunno.'

'Well *I* know that is what happened,' Kovacs said firmly. 'The note I was given outside the restaurant had the letter "J" written on it. And one of the notes you gave me also had the letter "J" written on it.'

'Oh! Is coincidence – *surpresa*! I do not notice this, my friend.'

'No. But I did, as I say. And the brother and sister – their name was what?'

'Janmot.' Babalu spelt the name out. 'I know because the lady give me her card. Very funny man, and funny lady too. It make me laugh when I think.'

'There's a nineteenth-century artist called Janmot, a pupil of Ingres,' said Kovacs, more to himself than Babalu.

'I know nothing of that, my friend.'

'There is. I have a sketch by him at home.'

Delphine returned from the phone-box and got into the car, mechanically clipping in the seat-belt.

'Well?' said Kovacs.

She looked relieved.

'I got through to my aunt. I spoke to her. I told her what had happened – well, more or less. I got her to phone Mum and see if she was home, without telling her that I – you know, that I had rung. Well my aunt rang me back in the call-box. It seems Mum is home. She's *angoissée* – she's, er, *upset* but she's OK. My aunt lives in Neuilly and she's going over to see Mum right now. I asked her what I should do and she thinks it's best if I keep away – don't go back – and you too, Mr Kovacs. She may have to arrange for Mum to be taken in – to get some help, you know . . .' Delphine flinched, her eyes welling with tears under the strong dark eyebrows.

'Treatment?'

She nodded. 'But where does that leave us now?' She wiped her eyes and glanced at the luminous face of her tartan

Swatch-watch. 'I can't go home, and neither can you Mr Kovacs. We need a safe house, for the moment. Babalu – what do you suggest?'

'Come back to my place. Both of you,' said Babalu. 'I have spare mattress and folding bed. Is small, you know, but is OK. Tonight, big troubles visit us. The stars are bad. After sleep, Iansã is calm, and us too. Thunder and lightning, all this storm stuff go out to sea. Tomorrow – is another day. Tomorrow, gods of life take us to their bosom once again.'

It was very late when they all got to bed in Babalu's poky room and mad, black-carapaced night terrors teemed through Kovacs' mind. Again and again he saw the old woman's face rising from her hands; her fumbling in the bag; her unsteady walk. His ears were numb with the roar of Delphine's car; his lungs filled with the loathsome stench of acid. Those few seconds of lurid horror were on an eternal loop of film that was programmed for mental projection until dawn or doom, whichever cracked first. He would start awake violently and lie paralysed on the zed-bed, his flesh basted in sweat, staring at the cloud-shaped patch of damp rot on the ceiling. It passed belief that someone could wish such cruelty on him – he, who wouldn't hurt a fly! He had, indeed, a conscious policy of ushering wayward house-flies and bluebottles towards open windows, however costly this civility was in time. Had he been born in Eastern India, he might have joined the Jain monks who are so respectful of all life that they sweep insects out of their path with brooms and mask their mouths and noses to prevent accidental inhalation of winged microscopic things. But Kovacs always drew the line at mosquitoes because they were vampiric predators. Mrs Jones qualified for special treatment on the same grounds. As this thought scuttled across his mind, the mildewy cumulus seemed to blacken and dilate portentously, but Babalu's slow, sonorous snore soon coaxed his fears back to sleep. It was like the easy roll and wash of the South Atlantic Ocean as the Brazilian himself had described it, respiring beneath the stars on Todos os Santos Bay.

Morning came with the muggy, carbon dioxide smell of sleep-dead air. Kovacs opened his eyes to a sense of derailment, of translocation. The other two slept on. He rose and unfastened the casement windows, swinging them outwards. There was the shock of sweet, cold freshness. Bright, auditing fingers of sunlight travelled meticulously across the outer scene, itemising, tabulating the city after the larcenous misrule of the night. The inventory complete, the world gleamed like a buttercup under a Cinemascope sky: an iron bridge, the old customs' post of the Rotonde de la Villette, the shimmery belt of water in the *bassin*. On the skyline, there was a mish-mash of quayside buildings, a big yellow crane – a blue flag kicking smartly from its kentledge in the crisp breeze – and the white, elongated domes of Sacré-Coeur high on the hill of Montmartre, scintillating like a pastry-cook's dream in icing-sugar. It was Sunday and somewhere church bells were tonguing a gentle summons. Kovacs rubbed his eyes on his knuckles and stretched.

When Delphine and Babalu were awake, the three of them went downstairs and crossed the avenue Jean-Jaurès to a kitsch, plasticated brasserie called Le Cadran Bleu where they ordered croissants, brioches and a jug of hot chocolate. The brasserie was immediately beneath the arched, grey girders of the aerial Metro and whenever a train thundered overhead their cups and teaspoons jitterbugged in the saucers.

It was a hazy, sun-struck morning and, still drugged with sleep, they hardly spoke. Delphine was wearing the same baggy T-shirt in which she had slept, with its 'Think Global, Act Local' slogan against a picture of planets and stars and a fez-crowned human head. When she had gulped back the silt of her chocolate, she pushed her dark, ungroomed hair out of her eyes and excused herself to go to the phone. Babalu was draped with necklaces of sharks' teeth, amulets, coloured beads and crucifixes over a vivid yellow sweatshirt. He watched Delphine go and looked questioningly at Kovacs who shrugged his shoulders by way of response.

The Englishman sidetracked a passing waiter and ordered a packet of Gitanes Brunes and matches. It was ages since he had smoked, but somehow this bright, bone-lazy day was like a glorious reprieve, and what does a reprieved man do but light up? It was traditional, a symbolic act. What was more, he liked the packet, with its shadowy flamenco dancer and coils of smoke:

it had been designed by Max Ponty in 1947 and had quickly become the essential fashion accessory for the Sartrean Left Bank intellectual. The cigarettes arrived, he struck a match and bullfrogged his cheeks round the first mouthful of smoke. Forming a tight, sphincteric 'O' with his lips, he expelled a perfect noose of a smoke-ring which advanced beautifully about one yard – rolling fluidly around itself, revelling in its own formal beauty – when a stiff draught from the open brasserie door stopped it dead and reversed its direction. Enlarging and disintegrating into chaotic filaments, what was left of the lasso flared back turbulently towards Kovacs' head. He felt suddenly disconcerted. Was this really a 'reprieve' that he was enjoying? Come to think of it, wasn't it the condemned rather than the reprieved man who smokes, the tradition of the 'last request'? Was he confusing an acquittal with the final, brief stay of execution? He was squirming uncomfortably in his seat when Delphine returned.

Babalu lumbered up and gallantly pulled back the chair while Kovacs stubbed out his cigarette so smartly that the long butt snapped in two in the ashtray, peppering the table with flakes of tobacco.

From beneath his dishevelled snake-nest of locks, the Brazilian looked at the girl with concern, judging the emotional temperature as a Gorgon mother might dip her elbow into the baby Gorgon's bath-water. 'Who you phone, Delphine?' he asked tenderly.

'I called home,' she said. 'As I hoped, my aunt answered.'

'And?' urged Kovacs.

'Everything's under control. Mum has slept and she seems to have calmed down. My aunt's not even sure she remembers what happened last night. But just in case, she's not going to leave her alone. She's going to stay with her round the clock.'

Kovacs ran the palm of a hand over his unshaven chin. 'We should go to the police,' he said at length. 'By which I do *not* mean Laroche.'

Delphine was suddenly dismayed. 'I can't stop you going to the police,' she said in a small voice. 'You've got every right, after all. But my aunt and I would like to get Mum put into psychiatric care without that. She needs compassion, not – how do you say – *inculpation*?'

'Criminal charges,' Kovacs glossed frostily. 'Nevertheless, she has committed a criminal act. I could very well have been coming round in hospital this morning, minus one face.'

There was silence while the other two digested this discountenancing thought, then Babalu leaned over and – with an oddly amusing gesture – slapped Kovacs to and fro on the bicep with the front, then the back, of his hand before grabbing him vigorously by the wrist. It was like a challenge to arm-wrestle.

'Philip! I know you a little now, *compadre*,' he began. 'You no want no police neither, no? Is just some time you got that demon bugger who speak in you head! Pray with me to Iemanjá. You must not anger Iansã, but bring her peace. Her enemy is not you. It is herself. We must leave her to find peace and freedom in her soul, and this is no possible in *prisão* – prison, you know. Not this.'

Kovacs prised his wrist out of Babalu's tenacious grip and shammed a frown, though he was far from being persuaded. 'And suppose we were not to go to the *flics*, where does that leave me? Delphine's mother is a psychopath, if you don't mind my saying so, and psychopaths are not known for letting bygones be bygones. The only place she wants to bury the hatchet is in my neck. She may well be with the aunt, but that's not quite as reassuring as the Prison de la Santé, if you ask me. So long as she's not in custody, I can't return to my flat. And, for what it's worth, I do happen to have a life I'd like to be getting on with.'

'Give me a week,' said Delphine firmly. 'I can't return to my mother because she saw me driving the car. She saw me saving you. It would bring last night back to her and she'd feel betrayed. But I can go to my aunt's place and get things going from there. While Mum's being looked after by my aunt, I can start up the procedures to get her into a secure place where she can be cared for professionally.'

'And her job? What about Laroche?'

'We'll ring in to say she's sick. A week is all I need.'

'A week! Where am I supposed to stay for a week? The Ritz, place Vendôme? Give them a ring, will you Babalu? Ask for my usual suite.'

'You go on stay with me, Philip,' the other man boomed, slapping him bruisingly on the arm once again. 'I invite you, my friend. One week is nothing to you! Is no problem. You will stay with Babalu. And you will see: time flies like wind!'

'Yes, and fruit flies like bananas,' said Kovacs, glumly recalling some prep-school repartee.

'*Não entendo*,' murmured Babalu.

'*Moi non plus*,' admitted Delphine.

Kovacs sucked in his cheeks and bit the insides the way he always did when he was in a photo-booth. It was a vain attempt to appear lean and mean. He looked at the girl thoughtfully and her bright green gaze met his. 'Does your aunt have Babalu's address?'

'No.'

'Don't give it to her. It's best to play safe. I'll have to get some books and things from my flat, when the coast is clear.'

'Then you agree?' she asked.

'One week,' said Kovacs categorically. He lit another cigarette and voided the smoke through his nostrils like a Salzburg dragon.

'*Muito bem*,' said Babalu. A train thundered past on the overhead rails. The black man grinned, a glint in those El Greco eyes. He crossed his arms then slumped back heavily into his chair, satisfied with the situation. And, as he did so, the tiny sharks' teeth and ju-jus rattled with agitation round the thick-set trunk of his neck.

12

WHILE A NECESSARY precaution, Kovacs' seclusion was not entirely unwelcome, though he would have been reluctant to admit as much to himself. It was like a monastic retreat, a temporary renunciation of his own familiar world. And at the same time the ectopic change of abode disturbed his habits and routines to just the right degree, surprising his cloyed senses into life. Delphine brought him books, a towel, a spare set of clothes, contact lenses and cleaning liquids, from his apartment: he would have made the trip himself, but she insisted on this courtesy. And Babalu was the perfect host, though he was frequently out performing odd jobs for the landlord. His absences gave Kovacs the liberty to read, sitting by the window through the warm, indolent afternoons. The hours drifted away like loose balloons in a summer sky. He read Jared Diamond's *The Rise and Fall of the Third Chimpanzee* and Daniel C. Dennett's *Consciousness Explained*. In the latter, he was particularly fascinated by the multiple-drafts model of consciousness, the notion that no experience is ever direct, passing instead through editorial processes of interpretation which, in turn, are subject to the disinformation campaigns of memory. As ever, his reading held him in its grip and stimulated him, but there was no secondary process of assimilation in view: his desire to proceed with his own book had slackened and abated. After two days of this intellectual recreation he became restless. The fickle bird of his concentration tired of its perch on the line of printed text, flapped its wings and swooped out of the open window. The great, laden barges plied down the bassin de la Villette; cars zipped along on the quai de la Loire below. Literally and metaphorically, life was passing him by. It was Tuesday afternoon –

a bright, cloudless day – and he decided to go for a walk.

He took the Metro to Saint-Michel and browsed through the wares of the *bouquinistes*, taking care to keep several barge-poles of distance between himself and Mrs Jones' quarter of Saint-Germain-des-Prés. To this end, he eventually crossed the river onto the Ile de la Cité. As he approached the imposing edifice of the Palais de Justice a crowd of people spilled out, dispersing in different directions on the pavement. In the midst of the throng one figure attracted his attention. It was a man of around sixty dressed in a fawn trenchcoat with the collar pulled up around his ears. He was balding, with stringy cross-brushed hair, and there was something wretched and forlorn in his leaden gait. Even from that distance there was no mistaking Inspector Laroche. However, the policeman had clearly taken a serious turn for the worse. Kovacs was pondering whether to greet him or not when an altogether more devious option presented itself to his normally unscheming mind. On a rogue impulse, he decided to follow the Inspector. There was something instantly winsome about the idea. The shadow shadowed, the tail tailed, the sleuth sleuthed: the tantalising paradox of detecting the detective merited a reflexive rubric of this kind, like the Lumière film *L'Arroseur arrosé*. Kovacs pursued doggedly as Laroche turned right onto the quai de la Corse. Despite himself, this canny but recidivous individual excited his curiosity.

They came to the place Lépine, named after the police chief who introduced whistles and white truncheons to the city's force. A busy flower market was under way. There were covered stalls ranged up and down the square and the lush floral displays were interspersed with other trade: a woman hawking caged love birds, canaries and budgerigars; a tiny, wraithlike Gandhi of a man selling guppies and angel fish from a heated aquarium decorated with weed, plastic coral and miniature shipwrecks.

The sheer profusion of flowers was overpowering, not only to the eye: irises, gladioli, carnations, hyacinths, dahlias, roses, all troubled, confused and drowned the sense in odours. Laroche became suddenly animated, weaving like a sniffer dog between the potted palms and buckets of cut daffodils, and Kovacs had considerable difficulty keeping tabs on him. The Inspector scanned each fresh stall avidly, throwing his hands up in desperation each time and lurching on to the next one. There was little doubt in Kovacs' mind concerning the object of his quest, but the desired trophy was patently unforthcoming. When he reached the perimeter of the market, Laroche vented his indignation on a white-haired cripple who manned the final stall. The tongue-lashing ended with a peculiar whimper of despair upon which he turned away and dragged his sorry carcass towards the Pont Notre-Dame.

Coming upon an illegally parked Twingo with Belgian plates on the quai de Gesvres, the Inspector whipped a cellphone from his pocket, tapped out a number and read the registration off to someone – presumably at the car-pound. The execution of this duty seemed to revive his spirits for there was a listing, rusty spring in his step as he headed on down the boulevard de Sébastopol. It was then that, to Kovacs' surprise, he pulled the collar of his trenchcoat even higher over his ears and ducked into a large amusement arcade. Kovacs sidled cautiously along to the frontage of the arcade which opened directly out onto the street. Just inside, there was a cabin where *jetons* and small change could be had and then – further in – the usual array of mechanical and electronic attractions: video hot-rodding or Kung Fu fighting; an infra-red rifle-range; one-armed bandits; a three-pronged steel grab that descended into a glass tank to snatch at fluorescent teddies and digital watches. A few kids zapped extraterrestrials at the back of the hall while just to one side of them Laroche had begun shovelling tokens into a big luminokinetic jackpot machine and punching the reel-hold and feature buttons as if his life depended on it. Since his conversation with Delphine, Kovacs had been prepared for virtually any manifestation of moral turpitude on the part of the human specimen before him, but this pathetically regressive behaviour baffled him. Through the coruscating lights of the gaming machines; through the hullabaloo of Muzak and traffic; through the mindless chatter of monkey money, Kovacs observed the sad spectacle of Inspector Laroche of the 10th arrondissement, a hunched votary at the altar of Mammon.

Realising that Kovacs was not a punter, the young man who ran the arcade locked up his cabin and nipped through a back door for change. Laroche's fruit machine spat out a niggardly handful of *jetons* and he briskly fed them back into the slot. A woman was passing by on the pavement with two boys holding her hands: one was about five, the other nine. The younger child wore a star-shaped sheriff's badge and a black Zorro cowboy-hat. 'No!' the mother was saying to the older boy. 'Another time! We've got to get home now.' The child stuck his tongue out at her and extracted himself from her grasp, diving obstinately into the arcade. '*Petit diable!*' exclaimed the woman as she drew up alongside Kovacs. She looked round quickly, at a loss for what to do with the smaller boy. 'I'm sorry to bother you,' she said to Kovacs, 'but would you mind keeping an eye on him for a second while I get Thomas out of this place?' 'Of course not,' said Kovacs, taking the child by the hand. The mother thanked him and bustled into the hall. Kovacs was still intent on the Inspector. He glanced down at his temporary charge, however, and assured himself of the child's docility. The boy had an electroplated plastic toy which he pushed into Kovacs' hand before turning to one side to stare, transfixed, at a Ninja Turtle video game. The Inspector, meanwhile, had had another paltry win and was rubbing his right shoe against the back of the left trouser-leg, a pedal variation on the usurer's hand-rubbing – or so Kovacs thought. Engrossed, Kovacs stood heedlessly with the toy in his hand, but after a few seconds he raised it to see what it was. As he did so, the young man returned from the backroom with a sackful of change: he froze to the spot – a jack-rabbit caught in the headlights – at the sight of Kovacs. The latter puckered his brow and stared back quizzically. He was vaguely aware that something was amiss. He looked down at the convincing life-size plastic replica of a Colt .45 in his hand.

There was a loud, jangling thud as the money-bags hit the floor and the young man voluntarily raised his hands into the air. Laroche turned. In barely the time that Kovacs required to understand what was happening, the Inspector had galvanised into action. '*Pas un geste!*' he yelled as he trained a Manurhin .357 Magnum on Kovacs. The standard-issue six-shooter had emerged in the merest giga-second from a shoulder holster under his coat. Kovacs gawped stupidly at Laroche and the toy gun fell from his hand, hitting the lino with an obviously plasticky noise. The Inspector screwed up his eyes in disbelief and his jaw sagged open to the limits of anatomical possibility as he recognised the man in front of him.

'You!' he gasped, after a while.

He lowered the revolver, but the power of speech had given him the slip: his normally mercurial comprehension was lagging far behind his gun-slinging prowess.

'I don't believe it!' he exploded when he had gathered his thoughts. 'First the damn post office, and now *this*!'

'You don't understand,' Kovacs remonstrated.

'Oh, *don't* I.'

The Inspector flashed his ID at the other participants in this mini-drama to reassure them that he was not a gangland hitman, and with great embarrassment the beleaguered mother came forward and explained everything, entirely exculpating Kovacs. Apologies were made and Laroche grabbed Kovacs by the elbow, hustling him out of the gaming emporium. What looked like plain-clothes policemen started emerging from an unmarked car but the Inspector signalled with a choleric flap of the hand that he did not require their assistance. Without a word the two men strode into the square de la Tour St-Jacques and sat down together on a bench, surrounded by plump, strutting pigeons, the thin Gothic belfry-tower rearing despotically over them. It was even money as to who was the most banjaxed. Kovacs could feel one of his headaches coming on. He looked at the other man, his attention lingering for a moment on the tip of the nose. To his extreme discomfort, there was a horrible splenetic energy in Laroche's stillness, his tense, bottled silence. Eventually the oblong tuber of the policeman's head creaked round and those red, world-weary eyes wheeled up and down under the white tufts of the eyebrows, taking him in, absorbing his image into the dark, embittered soul.

'Well?' hissed the Inspector. 'Don't you think you owe me an explanation?'

'Do *you* think I owe you an explanation?' Kovacs rallied.

Laroche cleared his throat ostentatiously and turned his head away, obviously peeved. 'It's one of those damned Jewish habits to answer a question with a question.'

'I believe the lady with the children explained the circumstances to everyone's satisfaction.'

'What I mean,' Laroche insisted, turning on Kovacs with renewed gusto, 'is what were you doing observing me? Why were you *watching* me like that?'

Kovacs felt the prickly heat of embarrassment reddening the nape of his neck. 'I happened to be passing when I saw you in the arcade,' he lied. 'I was just about to come over and greet you when that wretched woman put me in charge of her child.'

Laroche followed Kovacs' words as a jackal follows a wounded antelope, but to Kovacs' relief he suddenly lost the scent or gave up lackadaisically on his quarry. It was as if, all at once, he could no longer give a damn. He stretched back his neck and breathed deeply, closing his aged eyelids against the sun. On opening them again, his whole demeanour had subtly changed. An airless calm of enervation had descended upon him. He chuckled wheezily to himself and when he spoke it was with a whisper of his old charm and clubbability.

'You know, Kovacs, what Konrad Adenauer said? He said that history is the sum total of things that could have been avoided. Isn't that the story of all our lives? It is certainly the story of mine.'

Disarmed by this confidence, Kovacs sought in vain for a suitably conciliatory rejoinder.

'What star-sign are you?' Laroche asked unexpectedly.

'Cancer. Why?'

'Let me see . . . ,' he mused, evaluating Kovacs out of the blood-flecked corner of his eye. 'A stubborn streak. Intensely volatile. The Cancerian's time for decisions is ebbing away. The world around you is undergoing profound transition. Certainty in financial matters is distinctly missing, but there is increasing planetary emphasis on the portion of your chart related to romantic fulfilment. You have had a severe shock and there are aftershocks to follow. Expect sudden, unceremonious changes in direction.'

Kovacs was momentarily stymied. He looked at the Inspector with incredulity. 'You don't seriously go in for that stuff, do you?'

'I dabble,' Laroche replied with carefully dissembled amusement. 'Intuition, second sight, gut reaction – call it what you will. I dabble in a lot of things.'

'What I mean is, you don't really believe in it?'

'What do *you* believe in?' asked the Inspector in a deadpan voice, running a square-nailed finger along the lip-line of his moustache, which was now liberally peppered with grey hairs.

'Not horoscopes,' said Kovacs resolutely.

There was a long hiatus and when Laroche spoke his tone was steady and probing. 'Has it occurred to you that other people might know things that you do not know? I pose the question in all innocence. Is it conceivable to you that *I* might know things you do not know?'

Kovacs glanced with fugitive panic at Laroche. The possibility that the cop was in cahoots with Mrs Jones – his secretary – suddenly revived, but the direction now taken by the policeman's reflections soon released him from this anxiety.

'Policemen, you see, are vouchsafed a privileged glimpse into the workings of the world. Like surgeons, Mr Kovacs, they get inside things, they get their hands dirty. And, as the Italians say, *L'anatomia presuppone il cadavere.* You have, in all probability, given *me* less thought than I have given you, but no matter. I would hazard the guess, though, that you think a man such as myself ill-adapted to his chosen profession.'

Kovacs began making demurring noises but he was summarily silenced.

'You would be insulting both our intelligences if you chose to deny it,' said the policeman, smiling serenely. 'I am quite immune to personal and professional mistrust. God knows, I ought to be by now. In fact, I am prepared to agree that a more ineligible candidate for the business of crime-busting than myself could scarcely be imagined. On the face of things, I mean,' he interjected with a meaningful curl of the lip. 'But I was not drawn to the force through high-principled, philanthropic motives. Society can and will go to hell, whatever efforts are made to restrain it. That is my view, at any rate. If I chose this profession it was because I am alert to the formal aesthetics of crime. I bring a passionate, emotional apprehension to my work. It is not that I admire the criminal mind. I do not even believe such a thing exists. What goes by that name is simply the human mind relieved of the checks and hindrances of our so-called "civilisation", or taking them out as it goes along. There are various reasons for this lawless condition which we won't go into – they are chiefly economic and without great interest. It is the thing itself, not the social causes, that draws us on. Criminality is libidinal energy unleashed and thrown into its own chaotic, self-seeking patterns. And I must tell you that the more one looks into that moon-scoured underworld of miscreants, the more one leaves behind those checks and hindrances oneself. It is a slow but irreversible process, I'm afraid to say. The most proficient hunter achieves that proficiency through imitating the calls and movements of his prey. He seeks the creature out on its own, invisible frequency till their two hearts beat as one. There is communication – transmission. But perhaps I am boring you, *Monsieur l'Anglais*? Perhaps I am preventing you from retiring for a little "brunch"?'

Kovacs shook his head but held his tongue.

'It is a truism often repeated in detective literature that the policeman and the criminal come to achieve spiritual parity in this way. I suppose the dove-tail logic of their trades is such that one should be the counterpart of the other, a *doppelgänger*. In order to stay one step ahead, there is a constant process of reciprocal mind-reading. As you probably know, one of our great fictional detectives is Emile Gaboriau's Lecoq, himself a reformed criminal.'

'Forgive me,' said Kovacs, 'but you are not a reformed criminal yourself, are you?'

'No, I am not,' Laroche replied. His tone was flinty, inured. 'I am altogether worse than that. I am a *potential* criminal, Mr Kovacs, as indeed are you. And there is no reforming potentiality. It is forever incipient; a katabolism in the blood; forever lurking in the veins. But I protect myself. Not with logic; not with ratiocination. The world is a queer place and it requires queer eyes to apprehend it. I protect myself with illogicality and – how shall we say? – excursions through the cellarage of human affairs. Your own Sherlock Holmes, despite his devotion to empirical reasoning, acknowledged such a need through his habitual recourse to opiates. You see, it is not the rational and the cogent that begs for our attention. It is the void where logic disappears; it is sophistry; it is the dizzy chasm of the *non sequitur*.'

The mention of opiates spurred Kovacs' memory. 'The lilies you gave me . . . ,' he began.

'A good example,' Laroche interjected. 'And how I miss them! How I miss my youth! My secretary is off sick and unobtainable, and none of my efforts to procure a regular supply have borne fruit. Fool that I am, in my trepidation I gave my last bouquet to you.'

There was a moment's silence during which Kovacs chose to ignore Laroche's acrimony and glanced again at his nose. 'Excuse me mentioning it, Inspector, but there is a droplet on the end of your nose.' For as long as they had been sitting there the droplet had been irritating him: it was a droplet that never *dropped*. The suspense had become unbearable. Laroche fumbled for his spotted kerchief then blew his nose into it, evacuating a considerable quantity of snot by the sound of things. He tied a little bow in the hankie to make a tramp's knapsack of it and pushed the bundle back into his trenchcoat pocket. His nose was now red and raw, contrasting strongly with the Dead Sea Scrolls complexion. From another pocket he retrieved a small blue pill and gulped it down with a convulsive backward whip-jerk of the neck.

'Look at me, will you? I'm an old man. Those blasted flowers were all I had. They were the solution, and now they have become the problem. Have you noticed how often that happens in life?'

'It is the essence of dialectical logic – thesis, antithesis, synthesis – the fruitful collision of ideas,' said Kovacs. 'But how do you explain them? The flowers, I mean. The pollen seems to function as a potent psychotropic drug, an elixir of youth almost. But it's too much. It's excessive.'

'May I remind you that Star Gazer lilies are not on the Republic's list of banned substances?'

'I don't contest the fact, but what is your explanation?'

'I do not try to explain these things. I immerse myself in the unfathomable. The world, you know, is slowly being bled of mystery. We must make the most of what we have. With the destruction of the rain forest, for example, great wonders of pharmacology are going to waste, never to be discovered. Cures for diseases and diseases for cures. In one's quest for mystery and diversification, one is forced more and more down the blind alleys of chance.'

'Would that be why you have taken up games of chance?' Kovacs enquired, desperately trying to stay afloat on the unnavigable rapids of the Inspector's lucubrations.

'How do you mean?'

'I was thinking of the one-armed bandit I saw you playing. Gambling is, after all, a form of addiction, and from what you have been saying I am led to conclude that you do not disapprove of certain kinds of drug, certain kinds of artificial stimulation. *Les paradis artificiels.*'

'I am a policeman, Mr Kovacs,' Laroche snapped crabbily. 'Of course I disapprove of drugs. If they have any slight merit it is that they teach the younger generation the metric system of weights and measures, but that is by the by. I also disapprove of gambling. It is an abominable practice.'

'Then how – I'm sorry, but *why* were you playing?'

'*Mon cher ami*, you should know by now that by law the jackpot machines in French arcades do not pay cash prizes. They deliver tokens which can be exchanged for worthless trinkets and gewgaws. It is precisely because we do not wish to corrupt and enslave our youth in the English manner that this law exists. "Thus were they defiled with their own works, and went a-whoring with their own inventions." Psalms, 106 : 39. We may be forgiven for hoping that the quality of life – on this side of the Channel at least – turns on more than the cheap and illusory Providence of a fruit-machine reel, may we not?'

'Then I repeat: why were you playing?'

Laroche laughed harshly to himself. 'Why, my learned friend, at eleven a.m. on the morning of Tuesday, the 28th of June, was Inspector Laroche of the Commissariat of the 10th arrondissement surprised in the act of flagrantly and shamelessly playing a fruit machine? A good question! Well, I shall tell you. A little over an hour ago I was at the Palais de Justice, obtaining a warrant for the arrest of one Cesare Lopez from Judge Beauchamp. Cesare Lopez is possibly the most wanted man in France, if not in Europe. Narcotics are his game. We've been after him for months and just recently we had a hot tip-off that he and one of his *confrères* would be making contact just after eleven this morning in a certain amusement arcade, boulevard de Sébastopol. So, you see, if Inspector Laroche was playing the slot machines, it was not because he was hoping to win a Barbie doll or a teddy bear. It was because he was lying in wait for the arch-criminal Lopez. The men in the cars outside were his crack back-up team. But now, of course, Lopez's front-runners will have got the word back. Now he'll have gone to ground.'

Kovacs' blood freeze-dried to absolute zero on the Kelvin scale. He felt crushed with shame and averted his reddening face. 'You're not saying – ?' he began.

'Ah, yes! I'm afraid so!' the Inspector responded breezily. 'You can congratulate yourself on a dubious distinction, my dear fellow. You have almost single-handedly scuttled one of the biggest undercover police operations to have taken place in the capital this year. Lopez evades us yet again. And how many more young lives, one wonders, will be squandered because of this morning's sorry turn of events? How many more teenage minds ravaged by drugs? But there we are – you were not to know; you were not to blame. What happens cannot *un*happen, can it? And I suppose one should look on the bright side of things. You are, after all, extremely lucky to be alive. I very nearly shot you dead.'

Kovacs could hardly speak. His guts were in his shoes – *il était dans ses petits souliers* – and his heart was in his mouth. 'Have you – have you killed before?' he managed.

'Regrettably, yes. But that was war. A little over thirty years ago.'

'You were overseas?' asked Kovacs, trying to work out which war that could have been.

'Certainly not, *cher ami*. I have never set foot outside Paris in all my life. But history, as I said, is the sum total of things that could have been avoided, and my own past is no exception.'

A wire-haired terrier trotted up to their bench, cocked a leg and departed. Kovacs watched as the gold bead of urine traced a straight, draughtsmanlike line down the paving's gentle incline, just missing the policeman's large black heavy-duty shoes.

'There is a theory that should appeal to a man of your profession,' Laroche began anew. 'According to this theory, in the narrative of life we each constitute a different part of speech. Some of us are verbs, some adjectives, adverbs, substantives, pronouns and prepositions. Others, perhaps, are merely interjections or punctuation. I like to think of myself as a copula or linking verb. And you? I wonder what you are, Mr Kovacs, in the grammar and syntax of existence? A dash, maybe? A comma or a question-mark? Perhaps not. This morning you have made a passable imitation of a full stop. At least as far as our quest for Cesare Lopez is concerned.'

Kovacs was experiencing excruciating psychological discomfort. 'I – I really must apologise, if that is the case. I – I simply don't know what to say,' he stammered.

'My dear chap!' the Inspector replied with chilling warmth. 'I wouldn't dream of blaming you for what, to all appearances, was a simple case of synchronism. The wrong time and the wrong place, as people are wont to say in these circumstances. There is perhaps a higher authority that orders things thus. At the same time, I cannot hide the fact that a major criminal investigation – and indeed my career – may well have been set back irremediably.' He stood up, straightened his tie, flattened the collar of his trenchcoat and kicked out in a desultory but nevertheless aggressive fashion at a pigeon that was not respecting the inter-species distance. 'But that's life, isn't it?' he sneered. The Inspector looked down with a mixture of distaste and indulgence at the Englishman. 'Life!' he exclaimed, shrugging his shoulders stoically. 'When you get to my age, you will realise that there is little we can do to influence things. *Que será, será*: whatever will be, will be. But let's not worry about it, *hein*? Life's not so bad. Rest assured, it gets better, as time goes by. Take it from me, *poor* Mr Kovacs,' – he raised a warning finger and grinned sarcastically as he backed away to leave – 'the first hundred years are the worst.'

·

When the Inspector had disappeared from sight, Kovacs made at once for the mouth of the Metro: he had been longing to sink into a hole in the ground, and here it was. He took the train directly back to Babalu's and stayed put, shaken. He was in no hurry to venture outdoors again: the extramural world was fraught with precariousness, metaphysical banana-skins and worst-case scenarios. Nor could he study, since the peaceful spirit and powers of concentration required for this activity had deserted him. For the rest of Tuesday, and all day Wednesday and Thursday, he remained in the flat, listening with half an ear to the radio, staring gloomily out of the window, picking his teeth or scanning a newspaper from time to time.

Kovacs had treated Babalu to a potted version of his encounter with Laroche and, on the occasions that he was around, the black man observed him with concern and tried to talk him out of himself. When Delphine called by on Thursday afternoon, she and Babalu discussed his case out of earshot. It was decided that the two of them should take him out on Friday, since he no longer had the nerve to go out on his own. Babalu recalled that this day of the week was reserved for men at the hammam in the Paris Mosque and they persuaded Kovacs that the steam-bath would do him good. Afterwards, he and Babalu would rendezvous with Delphine and walk, if the weather was fine.

They arrived at around 10.30 in the morning at the Mosque on the corner of the rue Daubenton and the rue Geoffroy Saint-Hilaire in the 5th arrondissement. Kovacs leaned back and peered up at the tall square minaret, white and emerald green, with three balls kebabbed on a pole at its apex, and Babalu patted him on the shoulder, pushing him towards the entrance, where they were greeted by a bearded Algerian with a scarred but obliging face who introduced himself as Khaled. He and the Brazilian were old acquaintances, for Khaled and his wife were one of Babalu's and Victor Noir's success stories. In consequence, there was no entry-fee to pay. In the malodorous changing-room they shed their clothes and put on the little numbered rubber bracelets they were given to mark their places in the queue for a massage.

It was Kovacs' first time in a hammam and the experience volatilised his expectations. He had vaguely anticipated a scene of lazy voluptuosity, a male rendering of Ingres' painting, *Le Bain Turc*. Instead, he found himself in big, booming halls, decorated with mosaic and geometric tiles. It was an ecumenical, classless heaven, where businessmen, streetcleaners, Bahian barmen and downtrodden teachers were apotheosised into towel-girt, perspiring angels who wandered through cirro-cumulus drifts of steam or sat on benches, flicking cold water over themselves from buckets and conversing in low tones, their voices melding into a polyphony of ricocheting echoes. He and Babalu donned wooden clogs to prevent themselves slipping on the slick, wet floor and – after lingering a few minutes in the first hall – proceeded to the hotter inner chamber where inspissate coils of fog snaked round their feet then climbed and thinned into rolling marsh-like billows.

They sat down, placing their buckets at their feet. The heat was at first intolerable. Kovacs oozed at every pore; his entire body was deliquescing. He batted the sweat from his lashes and glanced across at Babalu who was sitting cross-legged, his eyes closed, turned in upon the silence of himself. The man was positively hippopotamic in his dark, pachydermatous bulk, wallowing in the convected heat and glossy with perspiration. There was mass and substance to the boulder-like head and the pneumatic girth of the belly, pectorals and arms. Kovacs cupped some cold water in his hands and sprinkled himself, looking down at his own person. Next to the animal quiddity of Babalu, his white, doughy form seemed an abstract, unrealised thing, tenderised, oiled and macerated by an emollient civilisation. Even his outline disappeared as the wisps of steam trailed across him like airborne lint in the baroque masters. He felt something of the intellectual's shame at the degenerate flesh: here he was, the end result of four centuries of Cartesian dualism, a walking, talking mind–body problem. It was not that he was badly made. There was a certain unfocused manliness about him, with a very English stamp – though it was true that, like the contents of muesli packets, he was the 'produce of more than one country'. But somewhere along the lifeline his brain and body had come unstuck. It was that desiccatory, dissecting habit of mind of his: 'we murder to dissect'. The self-analysis that issues only in self-paralysis. He looked at his friend and contemplated the gulf that divided them, a freefall descent into aboriginal magic.

'Babalu?'

'*Como?*' The Brazilian opened his eyes.

'What were you thinking about?'

'I think about Mata Gato, *compadre.* I am back in my shanty town. I think about my friends Massu, Curio and Jésus. We are sitting in hammocks, you know – very *confortável* – sun is shining – and we are eating Jaca.'

'What is Jaca?'

'Is very big fruit.' He spread his hands to suggest its dimensions. '*Deliciosa!* We say, in Salvador, it have same taste as mulatto women.'

Babalu smiled and closed his eyes again. The sweat dripped steadily from his cheeks and double chin.

At length they were called for their massages. The masseurs were middle-aged Moroccan men, dressed in singlets and swimming-trunks. On their hands they wore bright green massage gloves made of an extremely coarse nylon. There was no finesse about this massage. They scrubbed away at the bare, supine flesh like washerwomen, chafing and excoriating. Kovacs nearly bit his tongue with pain. The abraded skin came sloughing off in long black rolls, like fine slivers of pencil lead. When he stood up after ten minutes he was bright pink, as if all four layers of his epidermis – the horny, clear, granular and Malpighian – had been stripped clean away. They showered to remove the exfoliated skin and Kovacs was surprised at how purged and tempered he felt. At the same time, the experience had emptied him of meaning and intention. He thought for a moment of the stickers on the cellophane wrappers of greeting cards; the ones marked 'Blank inside'. That was exactly how he felt right now. After a mint tea with Khaled by the little fountain in the entrance-hall, they emerged into the midday sun.

They came to the Cuvier entrance of the Jardin des Plantes where Delphine was waiting for them alongside a large fountain-basin guarded by curious bronze lions, one of whom was sniffing a pair of severed human feet. When she saw the two men approaching she waved in her sprightly, girlish way and took a picture of them with a pocket flash-camera. She was wearing a loose Aran sweater, jeans and black baseball cap, back-to-front of course. Despite a potent sun and the duck-egg blue of the sky, there was a raw sharpness in the air to which Kovacs was especially sensitive after the torrefaction of the hammam.

'Well? How are you?' she asked when they came up.

'Not bad,' said Kovacs, 'for someone who's just been steam-cooked and skinned alive.'

'You're supposed to feel reborn. A Phoenix arising from the ashes.'

'Give me time. I was just getting used to being a pile of ashes.'

'Well, it's a beautiful day for reincarnation, anyway,' she said, raising a hand in the general direction of the empyrean. 'I bet you don't get many of these in England.'

'Don't mock. A third of the world used to be pink on the old maps of the British Empire, you know. If English weather is notoriously bad, never forget that it has also been one of the most important forces of cultural and linguistic expansionism in the world.'

'*Je n'oublierai jamais, Monsieur le Professeur*,' said Delphine deferentially.

'And anyway, a lot of what people say about our climate is sheer bullshit. Any Englishman worth his salt always knows when summer has arrived.'

'How?'

'The rain's warm.'

They walked round a hillock, crowned with a weather-vaned metal rotunda, towards some big Victorian greenhouses full of cacti; the iron-framed panes of glass gave off a silvered pink sheen in the sunlight. Beside one was a kitchen garden with vegetables and a baby palm. A slope led down to formal rose gardens, geometric paths and a broad open space bordered by the various buildings of the Museum of Natural History. Little green signs marked '*Forêts du monde* ⇨' and '*Forêts des hommes* ⇨' proliferated. They watched, nudging each other, as an odd couple with a homemade wooden pram which seated four infants approached and passed them. It was like something from *The Flintstones*. And slowly, without any clear sense of direction or purpose, they walked over to the gallery of botany, geology and vegetable fossils. In front of the building there was the stump of a petrified tree with a little explanatory plaque: it was from a quarry at Villejust in the Essonne and was 33 million years old. The three of them leaned over and stroked the cold sinews of the stone bark: their act was one of instinctive sympathy with primeval darkness, a tactile avowal of connection with a world before memory and man.

'What is happening about your mother?' Kovacs asked as they turned away and strolled down the gravelled alley.

'The family have signed the papers for – I forget the word – *internement*.'

'Confinement – to a mental hospital, you mean?'

'Yes. The doctor has examined her and countersigned. And tomorrow they'll be coming for her. She's to go to a secure psychiatric home near Fontainebleau. It's a decent place, thank God. Which means, of course, that you can return home tomorrow. My mother is no longer a danger to you.'

Kovacs set his hands squarely on his hips, stretched back his shoulder-blades and relaxed the muscles in his back. A great load had been taken off him. He felt delivered, extricated from the spiritual shackles of another's madness, and he raked his fingers back through his hair as he followed the converging perspectives of the garden with his gaze. Low in the northern sky, a fuggy stain of cloud or pollution fouled the perfection of the day. It sat there, sprawling lethargically, like the slow invasion of a drop of ink in a glass of tap-water. He pulled, with thumb and forefinger, at the slight lobe of flesh under his chin and addressed Babalu.

'Where shall we go? The Grande Galerie de l'Evolution? Or the Ménagerie?'

'Let us go to the *jardim zoológico*,' said Babalu. 'Is very fascinating. I go there with Raimunda Maria.'

Kovacs turned to Delphine. 'And how do you prefer your bones? With or without flesh, fur and feathers?'

'Oh *with*, definitely!' she replied.

They doubled back across the open space towards the Ménagerie and, on arrival, turned out their pockets for coins beside the statue of a woman astride a giant fish. She was holding its mouth open with one hand and apparently beating it on the head with another; the fish spat water into a pool that drained into a circular basin. Kovacs and Babalu were drastically low on funds, so Delphine paid for all their tickets and they entered the small zoological garden. It was an attractive medley of quaint thatched animal-pavilions with round, cottagey windows, a green oblong aviary and wriggling, devious lanes. They walked in slow, Rousseauistic fashion, the two men clasping their hands behind their backs. Goats, shaggy bison, the splay-horned watusi, llamas and dromedaries filed off before their eyes. 'You know why bears have fur coats?' said Kovacs, looking down on a fat brown member of that genus who was chewing a stick in his pit. Delphine shook her head. 'Because they'd look silly in plastic macs.' She made the bad-joke groan and they ambled on.

They visited the Micro Zoo and looked through high-powered microscopes, observing arthropods from the forest floor and the monstrous mites that infest food and mattresses; there were salamanders and albino oxotls in the Vivarium, the latter floating in their tank, white tentacles flailing slowly; and in the Reptile House, boas, Nile monitors, dwarf crocodiles and giant tortoises eyed them stilly, with inscrutable saurian intent. In the Fauverie, they did not stay long in the company of the seedy lions and North China leopards. Though none of the three voiced the thought, there was something particularly heart-rending about the cramped detention of these big, rangy beasts.

By indirection and frequent detours, they came at length to the Singerie. There was an inside and an outside to the large oval Monkey House, providing the inmates with a limited choice of scenery. Today only a solitary orang-utan and a few diana monkeys and grey-cheeked mangabeys lingered in the open-air cages, so the three ventured in. By the door a list of newborn babes had been pinned up under a sketch of a flying stork carrying an infant monkey in a towel. To one side of this was an evolution chart which began with a creature called America Purgatorius 70 million years ago and terminated with the *ne plus ultra* of His Nibs – Modern Man. In the intervening periods – Cretaceous, Palaeocene, Eocene, Oligocene, Miocene, Pliocene and Pleistocene – various brethren were depicted who, despite family resemblances, were nevertheless also-rans in the race for bipedal locomotion, language, technology and take-away pizza. The sober thought crossed Kovacs' mind that – had things been otherwise – he, Delphine and Babalu might well have found themselves on the other side of the perspex panes and bars.

'It makes you think, doesn't it?' said Delphine, casting an eye across the family tree.

'Yes and no,' Kovacs replied. 'Darwin's theory has been around since the mid-nineteenth century, but a quarter of all US college graduates still don't believe we evolved from apes. I suppose it's not easy for a Microsoft systems engineer, climbing up the corporate ladder, to acknowledge that he is essentially an Upper Palaeolithic hunter. It's *infra dig.* It doesn't go down well at cocktail parties.'

Some South American Goldaguti occupied a central pit inside the pavilion, while all around were perspex-fronted cages. There was L'Hoest's monkey, hanging absurdly from its prehensile tail; De Brazza's monkey with its white beard; and Campbell's Meerkatze, remarkable for its blue and pink face. There were crested, golden-bellied, crowned and smoky mangabeys, and an owl-faced creature with a white vertical streak running down the length of his nose. The blackish-green and swamp guenons surveyed them soulfully, but Kovacs' heart went out especially to the little black mangabeys, perched on a chewed wooden structure or rocking gently on a suspended car-tyre, bored out of their minds. They had grey side whiskers and absurd punk tufts on the top of their heads, like the pointed tufts of coconuts, and their tails curled up into question-marks. Kovacs placed the palm of his hand against the perspex and an earnest-faced mangabey approached and held his perfect black hand against it: a tiny palm and long, ladylike fingers. Only a few millimetres of transparent plastic separated them, and their eyes met directly in speechless responsiveness.

The smell in the Monkey House was penetrating. It was a gamy, more seasoned variety of the odour that had struck him earlier in the changing-room of the hammam. The monkeys themselves were curiously silent, but from outside came the sound of violent snorting and whinnying. The three stood together in front of the black mangabeys.

'We are close to them, aren't we?' said Delphine.

'They are *irmão* and *irmã* – our brother and sister,' Babalu mused.

'True,' said Kovacs, 'but there are degrees of relatedness. In fact, we are closest to the common chimp of tropical Africa and the pygmy chimp of Zaire. According to a book I was reading recently, we are nearer to them than red-eyed and white-eyed vireos are to each other – that's a tiny American bird – and more closely related than willow warblers and chiffchaffs. Genetically, I mean. In terms of social organisation . . . well, that's another story.'

'We no have so many colours on *traseiro*,' said Babalu, grinning and slapping his own rump by way of translation.

'Visible oestrus,' Kovacs explained. 'The females exhibit their receptivity, and copulation is more or less in public. Formalities we have dispensed with, except perhaps at the peak of the tourist season on the Costa del Sol. Though other formalities have certainly taken their place. Concealed ovulation and breeding, for example.'

'You mean bedrooms?' said Delphine.

'In a word, yes. And monogamy. The monkeys and apes are fairly free with their favours, with the exception of the faithful gibbon.'

'Then we are not like the apes at all?'

'Not in breeding habits. We're more like seagulls, in fact. Big breeding colonies. Nominally monogamous couples. And a little bit of how's-your-father on the side.'

Delphine and Babalu blanked out for a moment.

'I'm sorry – adultery, I mean, or extra-marital sex. But monogamy is the rule. What I call "You-topia" – the belief that happiness and security is to be found in a relationship with one individual. We also ensure biological diversity by balancing endogamy and exogamy against one another, marriage within and outside the tribe. Your own parents are examples of exogamists, Delphine, and I guess if I married Anne, who is French, then I am too. I'd never really thought about it like that before.'

'You're also a divorcee,' said Delphine. Kovacs looked at her with mild irritation but any burgeoning thought of a riposte was drowned out by renewed whinnying from outside.

'What is that damn noise?' he asked.

'Is wild horse. *Cavalo*,' said Babalu. 'Raimunda and me, we see them last time.'

Delphine checked the plan of the Ménagerie she had picked up at the ticket-office. 'That's right,' she said. 'Przewalski's horse. From Mongolia. The last of the wild horses, it says here. There are two of them.'

'At least one example of a stable relationship, then,' Kovacs quipped.

They left the zoo by the quai Saint-Bernard exit and wandered down by the Seine. In the afternoon light, the great river sundered the capital, twinkling archly in mid-stream and iridescing where pools of petrol floated statically beside the moored barges. Upstream, the Pont d'Austerlitz spanned the flow; the modern towers of Bercy and the new Très Grande Bibliothèque, still under construction, shone like shaken tinfoil in the haze. They walked westward, through the open-air sculpture park, and the old argosy of the Ile Saint-Louis, sistership to the other isle, sat heavily in front of them at her moorings. She was masted with poplars, overbuilt with seventeenth-century poops and galleys, the bows and prow entrammelled with climbing plants.

The striking spectacle of a man in a red duffle-coat walking a pedigree dalmatian crossed their field of vision and on a bench a pair of lovers sat kissing – doubtless recruited by the French Tourist Board. The sculpture in the quayside park was unexceptional and dated, smacking of Seventies' abstractionism: they passed what looked like a climbing-frame adorned with satellite dishes, entitled 'Chronos 10'; a giant grafitti-ed egg; molten high-rises, 'Demeure No. 1', beside a Ginkgo biloba tree; and a revolting bronze fountain of a man urinating against a wall. But when they turned their backs on this, the place had a tranquil, unpretentious charm. There were three small amphitheatres cut into the embankment and they sat in the central one, looking out across the water to a cement loading bay for river-barges where seagulls soared and skirmished in the sky. From the acoustic hinterland, the urban borborygmus of traffic, then a distant whoop of sirens, met their ears.

'Would you mind if I asked you something about a rather personal matter?' said Delphine, testing the water during this thoughtful interlude. 'It's about your wife,' she added, with a sympathetic glance.

'Oh yes? What do you want to know?'

'Babalu told me you divorced three years ago and that you

have never seen her since. Of course, I *knew* that already from your diaries,' she added, blushing swiftly.

'What do you want to know?'

'Well, what happened? Why did you divorce?'

His wife . . . what a question! He had never told anyone the truth: his false admission of adultery, his deep need for solitude, the sudden break. All that remained of her was a handful of dog-eared snapshots, a typewriter and a brown leather wallet. The latter, as it happened, was in the inside breast pocket of his jacket now. He could feel the *frottement* of its edges against his chest. They had ploughed parallel furrows – his wife and he – in work as indeed in life, and as every schoolchild knows parallel lines never meet. Except in perspectives, he conceded: except in optical illusions.

'We divorced because I told a lie,' he said plainly. It was the first time that the truth about this had escaped his lips and he heaved a vague sigh of sadness and relief.

'What sort of lie?' asked Delphine. She was timid but her brash inquisitiveness invariably got the better of her.

Kovacs told her all and Babalu, listening with bowed head, picked up what he could. It was the old, old story, not a fight for love and glory, but a classic geometry of parallelism: non-convergence and non-divergence writ large in the letters of life. Eventually it had all been too much. He had told his little lie; he had pretended to an affair. It was a white lie, not a black lie, after all. *Un mensonge pure* – with no harm done. Told for both their goods. And since that time they had fought shy of each other. He smiled with some embarrassment at Delphine.

'I suspect I shouldn't say this to someone of your age, but I'm not sure what to think of "love". The scientific view is that it's a trick played upon us to ensure continuation of the species. Then there's the literary view. In my day, we were brought up on a book called *Enemies of Promise* by Cyril Connolly, the message of which is that the worst enemy of good art is the pram in the hall. As for the companionship angle, I'm not even sure of that. Chekhov said that if you're afraid of loneliness, don't marry. And the musicians – well, there's a song I rather like that goes: *What does "love" mean? It doesn't mean a thing. It's a fancy way of saying two people want to swing.*'

Delphine smiled at Kovacs' off-key crooning, but quickly wised up to him. 'You're always quoting people,' she muttered. 'Why don't you ever say what *you* think?'

'I do, Delphine. The trouble is, it's all been said before. We're not just talking about me, you know. We're talking about the common lot. There's nothing new under the sun.'

'If you don't believe in love and happy marriages, why did you marry, then?'

'Oh, I *do* believe in love: I know the feeling, the sensation itself, though I'm not sure I trust it. I also believe in happy marriages. It's the living together afterwards that's a trial. And sometimes it just goes bad, that old You-topia. Then we have to observe the First Law of Holes.'

'The first what?'

'The First Law of Holes. If you're in one, stop digging.'

'It's funny, but you're a bit of a *sclérosé* – a stick-in-the-mud, I think you say. And I always thought of you as a rebel.'

'Well, I listen to The Doors when I'm doing the ironing,' said Kovacs in his defence. He noticed that Babalu was confused, obviously imagining impossible acts of contortionism in which eavesdropping on neighbours and domestic chores are accomplished simultaneously.

'Maybe you should – you know – *try* . . .' said Delphine.

'What? To get back together?'

'You're not happy on your own.'

Kovacs' silence was a tacit recognition of the fact. The ideas he had pressed into service to justify the dismantlement of that marriage, ideas he covered with the blanket-terms 'research' and 'solitude', had played him false, leaving him unsatisfied. He missed the daytime presence of Anne, her get-up-and-go, her folksy wisdom; he missed her physical warmth at night, the long mutual embrace, the low suspiration of her breath in sleep. He had to admit it: his splendid isolation was not so splendid after all. He raised his eyebrows and stared contemplatively at the river-water. It was scummy with leaves, twigs, the occasional condom or lump of polystyrene, a bottle-cap or a drinking straw. 'Let's walk,' he said, standing up after a while. The subject was thereby dismissed.

They climbed some steps up to the Pont de Sully beside

the Institut du Monde Arabe and looked across to the rear of Notre-Dame and a further bridge which was graced with a tall statue of a mother and child, a memorial to the Nazis' deportations. Barges bobbed gently under their feet, sporting big white and yellow anchors. They crossed to the island. It was a place that Kovacs always associated with a watery melancholy, the sadness of Hemingway's narrator in *The Sun Also Rises* or the gloomy pleasures of the Club of Hashish Eaters over a century and a half before.

Babalu noticed a curious church, the steeple of which was hollow and punched on each side with a vertical row of holes. It was next door to an elementary school and the ghostly sound of children's voices from the playground reverberated in the narrow street. He excused himself and entered the church, while Kovacs and Delphine made their way to Le Flore en l'Isle, 'Glaces de la Maison Berthillon', in the rue Jean du Bellay. They ate a Coupe Bêtise each – a lavish ice-cream confection of caramel, nougat, vanilla and chantilly. And when Babalu caught up with them, they followed the quai de Bourbon and the quai d'Anjou on the shadowy, northern perimeter of the island, pausing for a while to read the plaque on the house of the sculptor Camille Claudel. There was a quotation from an 1886 letter to Rodin: '*Il y a toujours quelque chose d'absent qui me tourmente.*'

'She went mad, didn't she?' said Kovacs, trying to remember the film he had seen some six years beforehand, with Adjani as Claudel and Depardieu as Rodin. He turned the words on the inscription round in his mind, reading them from different angles. In his heart, their truth had scored a palpable hit.

They came out, in due course, onto the stretch of the Pont du Sully that crossed to the Rive Droite. There was a clean prospect down the boulevard Henri IV to the place de la Bastille, where the gold-winged figure of the Spirit of Liberty scintillated in the sunlight atop the green July column. Behind it, the horizon was still thick with a sediment of darkness, a pendulous lees in the lower air. After the Bibliothèque de l'Arsenal and a statue of Rimbaud, the boulevard seemed to close in on itself, hugger-mugger, thwarting the tender rays of daylight. Delphine twirled the camera round her finger from its strap and affected a skip in her step. Babalu plunged his hands in his pocket and began to drag his feet. He was possibly missing Cotinho, whom he had left at home. Ahead of them, a green Mairie de Paris lorry marked *collecte de verre* pulled up beside a bottle-bank. It was a tipper truck fitted with a small crane. To their right were the big, austere barracks of the Garde Républicaine, Quartier des Célestins, with their fortress walls and unlit barred windows.

They were approaching the entrance to the barracks when a pair of huge green metallic gates began to creak apart and the three of them stopped in their tracks. Kovacs watched as the lifting-gear on the municipal truck swung round and the driver hooked it up to the top of the bottle-bank, raising the large green plastic bell into the air. His lips were suddenly dry. An obscure sense of unease invaded him. The barracks' gates were now fully open and a troop of mounted Republican guards advanced in loose formation onto the pavement. The paired horses were dark and magnificent, as indeed were the guards. The latter were decked out in black tunics and boots, gold helmets with red plumes, gold-braid epaulettes and white gauntlets. Swords swung at their sides in immaculate scabbards. Settling in their polished saddles, they adjusted the reins or the chin-straps on their helmets as they proceeded. Delphine edged forward, flipping up the automatic flash for a photo. As she did so, there was an almighty crash. Kovacs nearly jumped out of his skin. The municipal worker at the kerb had knocked open the hatch on the base of the suspended bottle-bank with a hooked pole and the entire contents had dropped with one resounding smash into the truck. The horse closest to Delphine flared its nostrils and flew off the handle, pulling back and startling out of line. In the split-second before the soldier could control it, the animal had hit Delphine, its flank knocking her into a spin. Her camera flashed as it was thrown into the air and she went over, her head coming down hard on the grating of a manhole.

Kovacs and Babalu were beside her immediately, turning her over on her back, and two or three guards began to dismount uncertainly. An officer was summoned from an internal sentry-post. Kovacs was kneeling down, pillowing her head on his knees. With his white, polka-dotted kerchief he dabbed the wound. Blood oozed from three bright gashes on Delphine's forehead and she let out a low moan. She was not quite with it, though clearly she had not lost consciousness.

Gradually she came back to her senses.

'*Aïe!*' she moaned again, and looked up at Kovacs. 'My head!'

'Relax!' he urged. 'You'll be all right. Can you sit up?'

She sat up, nursing her head in her hands. For a moment her posture reminded him of her mother: her mother sitting in the garden, the nocturnal garden beside the lock.

'Here. I'm going to make a bandage,' he said.

Folding the kerchief in three he wound it round her head and tied a knot.

'*Ça fait mal!*' she complained, as he pulled it tight.

Meanwhile, the officer who had been summoned emerged from the barracks in a racing-green Peugeot 305. Together they carried Delphine to the back seat before getting in themselves and driving to the Hôpital Saint-Antoine. A nurse there disinfected and dressed the wound and gave Delphine a few psychomotor tests. A bad knock like that, she explained, could cause external damage but there was always the risk of internal damage too. A consultant was called, a tall, silver-haired medic, and he confirmed this danger. 'The brain can be thrown forward against the skull and internal haemorrhaging can start. It sometimes means surgery.'

'What can you do?' asked Kovacs, anxiously.

'We'll give her a brain-scan. That way we'll know immediately if any harm has been done.' The consultant looked from the officer to Kovacs to Babalu and then back again. 'I take it you're not family?'

'No. Friends,' said Kovacs. 'Us two, that is. This other gentleman kindly drove us here.'

The consultant seemed dubious. They were, it was true, an ill-assorted trio: Delphine, Kovacs and Babalu.

'Well, if you'd like to go in there,' he said, 'the nurse will jot down your address and give you some coffee. This will take a little time. Don't worry. We'll keep you informed, whatever happens.'

Delphine, recumbent, was pushed away on a trolley.

The officer left, giving them a contact number, and in the

waiting room Kovacs discussed the matter urgently with Babalu.

'It's crazy, but I feel as if it was my fault. I saw the bottle-bank. I knew what was about to happen,' said Kovacs. For a second time, she had been hurt. A sharp throbbing pain spread across his temples, as if he himself had been gashed. He brought his hand to his head and felt for wounds. He had heard about this: 'synalgia', to give it its dictionary definition. A sympathetic, almost empathetic, pain. He had heard of it, but had never felt it before.

'No fault,' said Babalu. 'No blame. *Acidente.* Is no good you blame yourself, Philip. Blame gods, perhaps,' he suggested, gesturing futilely towards the heavens, somewhere beyond the striplights and the emulsioned hospital ceiling. 'Blame Omolu, maybe – I dunno. We must give an Angola hen to Exu, make him happy again. But you no blame yourself.'

While they were doing the brain-scan, the consultant asked a nurse if any papers had been found on Delphine.

'Yes,' she said. 'In the pocket of her jeans. I found her *carte d'identité* and a student card.'

'Well those two oddballs out there are not her family, obviously enough. The three were just out together, though it's hard to imagine how they met. You've got her home address there in her papers. Get hold of the number and give her home a ring.'

'OK, doctor.'

'Oh and nurse –'

'Doctor?'

'Discreetly,' he added, tapping the side of his nose with a 'softly-softly' look.

When the brain-scan was ready, the consultant pinned it up and explained it to the nurse, pointing with a clinical forefinger.

'Here, you see – the cortical flow activity is significantly higher in central regions anterior to a line that, roughly speaking, follows the rolandic fissure and the anterior portion of the sylvian fissure.'

'Affecting which regions, doctor?'

'The efferent parts of the motor cortex in the precentral gyrus, and of course the more frontal, higher control centres of complex movements, behaviour and cognition.'

'And postcentrally?'

'Lower activity, as you can see. We're talking about the regions that have an afferent function related to the primary, higher-order projection areas for cutaneous sensation, vision, hearing and so on. Overall, a classic hyperfrontal flow landscape.'

They were approaching the open door of the waiting room as they spoke and Kovacs, who had caught the tail-end of the explanation, jumped up to intercept them.

'What is it?' he asked nervously. 'Hyperfrontal flow, you said?'

The consultant looked him up and down ironically. 'Are you familiar with the jargon of positron emission tomography?'

'As a matter of fact, I am,' said Kovacs. 'A hyperfrontal flow landscape, you said?'

'Yes,' replied the consultant with ill-concealed irritation. He was not accustomed to being challenged in his obscurantism. 'In other words, a perfectly normal pattern for a resting human being. No internal bleeding. Just those three nasty scratches on the forehead. We've given her some stitches.' He glanced at Babalu's brow with a vague sense of *déjà vu* not unconnected with his last remark, then shook his head dismissively and resumed. 'She'll need to take it easy for a couple of days. If you're interested, I can show you the scan.'

He held up the colour print-out from the PET brain-scan and handed it to Kovacs.

Kovacs had a black-and-white copy of one of these things in his flat. He stared, nevertheless, at the oval shape on its black background, the labile coloured shapes within. And with slow abstract subtlety the image began to draw him in, to engage with the rhythm of his thoughts.

'Is many colour,' said Babalu in his pidgin English. 'Like carnival. Blue, green, red, white. What mean these many colour?'

'What did he say?' asked the consultant amusedly, turning to Kovacs for edification.

'Oh, he wants to know what the colours mean,' Kovacs explained in French.

'God knows,' said the consultant in a rare access of honesty. 'It's a complicated business. We're very good at spotting things that go wrong, but we're not so good at seeing them when they go right.'

'May I keep this?' asked Kovacs.

The image held his gaze in a way that surprised even him. It was uncanny to think that this was someone he knew. Not the vague, green eyes, of course; not the sulky lower lip; not the pale integument. This was the other side. This was the dark core of things. Except it wasn't dark, it wasn't dark at all. It glowed with galactic pools and clusters of green, red, violet, yellow, orange, blue, the star-like energies of billions of nerve-cells, the great intermediate net of motor and nonmotor neurons. Here was the aura of the layered convolutions of the cerebral cortex, the most highly ordered structure in the brain; the aura, too, of the primitive core of the brain stem, with its reticular activating system, regulating sleep and the cyclical activities of the body. This was the great chromatic speech-architecture of thought and neurotransmission: axons, dendrites and synapses 'talking' in meteoric flashes of electrical colour. This, he felt, was not the stuff of textbook science; it was magic, wonder-working, the shamanism of the ancient peoples. For the first time, in his deepest apprehensions, he was a brother under the skin with Babalu. He held up the scan again. Beyond the oval perimeter of the skull lay speechless darkness, but the colours were victorious – that was the thing – celebrating the improbable victory of life over the outer blackness, and all at once Kovacs pictured the grave in Père Lachaise and the man who lay within: Victor Noir. His very name seemed to encapsulate Kovacs' preceding thought.

Delphine joined them, her head well-bandaged, and – in the failing light – they went back to Babalu's by taxi. It was decided that she should not return to her aunt's flat in case she took a turn for the worse while on her own; so for one night only they would all stay together. The next day was July 2nd, after all, and Mrs Jones would be taken away. In the small tenement on the quai de la Loire they sat up late, eating *xinxim de galinha*, a Brazilian chicken *fricassée* that Babalu had thrown together, and drinking bad wine – *vin d'acidité illimité*, Delphine jokingly called it. They tracked down a pack of cards and played a French variant on gin rummy by candlelight, under the photograph of Pelé and the cheap reproduction of Jesus with a bleeding heart. Later Babalu showed them the little naïve watercolours he did of people in the streets of Paris. Outside, through the open window, they could see the tinsel flicker of lightning; a small flash storm was sweeping across central Paris, leaving them untouched. Above Babalu's flat the skies were clear and only the cloud-like cincture of the Milky Way arched dimly over the bassin de la Villette. It had been an eventful day and Kovacs privately noted that misadventure, that antipathetic dame, was capable of singling out other victims apart from himself. The thought was hardly uplifting, though it was nice to be out of the spotlight for a while.

When they had left the Hôpital Saint-Antoine earlier that evening, the consultant had taken the nurse aside. He was still concerned about the odd threesome.

'That girl – what was her name?'

'Delphine Jones,' said the nurse.

'You got her home number, didn't you? From her papers?'

'Yes. And the address of the other two.'

'Well, be an angel and give her mother a ring, will you? Just to make sure she got home all right.'

The nurse tapped out the eight digits of Delphine's phone number and waited as the phone rang: once, twice, three times . . .

The receiver was picked up and a woman's voice answered.

'*Allô*,' said the nurse. '*Puis-je parler à Madame Jones?*'

12a

The following morning Kovacs gathered himself up from the creaking zed-bed and dressed. Delphine had woken before him and was using the lavatory on the landing. Patiently waiting his turn, he stationed himself by the ledge of the little window and happened to look down at the street below. It was still early and the traffic was sparse as yet: there was just one car, in fact, a small, box-like hatchback, growling along the road. It was a black Renault 5 and tied to its aerial was a little white ribbon, symbol of a wedding, flapping merrily in the forward motion. The sun flashed sharply off the windscreen as the car braked and pulled up half onto the pavement, such that all he could see now was its tinny black roof. When it stopped, the white pennant on the aerial drooped with sudden dismay.

Kovacs turned to the Brazilian who was lying on his mattress in the corner in his pink pyjamas.

'Babalu, remind me – what sort of car does Delphine's mother have?'

'I no know, *amigo*. I no remember.'

'I'm sure she said it was a black Renault 5,' he murmured, pressing his nose to the window-pane, the glass steaming under his nostrils.

A woman got out, pushing the car door shut behind her with a dull click. She looked at a slip of paper and then up at the frontage of the building. He had glimpsed her for a mere second on the night outside his flat, but in that second he had registered the likeness to Delphine. She was dressed in grey now, and her face and body were foreshortened but the family resemblance struck him forcibly.

She walked across the street and into the building.

'Babalu!' said Kovacs, urgently. 'It's her! She's found out where we are!'

'Who?' asked Babalu sleepily. 'Is who?'

'Delphine's mother, dammit!'

He crossed the room to the door of the flat which Delphine had left open and pushed it to, bolting it shut. He could hear her footsteps, slowly climbing the stairs. There was a Judas peephole in the door and he glued his eye to it as she came into view.

'It's her, I tell you!' he hissed. Babalu groaned and rolled out of bed.

The woman rapped at the door.

Through the fish-eye lens of the peephole her face was distorted into a horrible cone, peaking at the tip of the nose. Her eyes flickered from side to side. She knocked again. Kovacs hardly dared breathe.

'Mr Kovacs?' said the woman, cocking her head to one side. 'Mr Kovacs, I know you are there.'

Silence.

In the background, the toilet flushed and Delphine emerged onto the landing. She embraced the visitor, kissing her from cheek to cheek.

'There's no reply,' said the older woman, indicating the door. 'Are they out?'

'No, no – they're not out,' said Delphine. She knocked sharply herself and looked into the peephole. 'Philip, don't worry! *C'est ma tante*. It's my aunt, Philip. My mother's sister.'

The aunt was let in and she was clearly in a state of distress. Cursory introductions were made, then the three friends sat her down to hear her story.

The circumstances were the following.

Delphine's mother had appeared to be responding well to her sister's care: in fact, as it turned out, she had been play-acting.

Lulled into a false sense of complacency, the sister grew slack and left the sick woman unattended in the living-room on the previous evening to answer the phone. The call was from the Hôpital Saint-Antoine, with the bad news of Delphine's accident. When she returned to the room where Mrs Jones had been sitting, the woman was no longer there. Soon after, the sister took the second call from the hospital, but by then it was too late. Mrs Jones had slipped out and driven to Kovacs' flat. She knew her daughter was still at the hospital, but she intended to lie in wait for Kovacs. However, it was twilight and – peering up at the third-floor window of 91 quai de Valmy from the little garden opposite – she was now convinced that he was already home. Madame da Silva witnessed this and the reason for the woman's conviction was subsequently ascertained. In Kovacs' rush to discover the identity of the mystery caller in the phone-box below, on the evening of the 25th of June, he had left the lights burning in his flat. In fact they had been on all week for when Delphine had called by to pick up his things it had been daytime and, not noticing them, she had failed to put them out too. Of course, on the evening of the acid attack Kovacs had washed a shirt and hung it up to dry at the window. It had been there ever since. The silhouette of the hanging shirt against the glowing window-pane persuaded Mrs Jones that he was there the previous evening, staring provocatively out at her.

In a demonic fury she rushed back to her car to fetch a can of petrol and a piece of wire. For this too, there were witnesses. She intended, they guessed, to let herself into his flat with the wire, exactly as she had done before, and then petrol-bomb the place – with Kovacs inside, naturally enough.

The car was parked further down the road and as soon as she was equipped she turned back to fulfil her intent. In her hell-bent velocity – impelling herself towards his flat – she *tripped*. She tripped on one of the iron mooring-rings on the banks of the canal. One green high-heeled shoe remained wedged under the ring where it had caught, its stiletto angling down like a knife about to stab. Her body, the wire and the full jerry-can of petrol were subsequently retrieved from the canal.

Wasn't it Strindberg, Kovaks thought later, who in his diary had described the canal Saint-Martin as 'black as a grave, a most suitable place for drowning oneself in'?

All this, of course, had only occurred the previous evening, but already the police investigation was under way, conducted by Inspector Laroche from the Commissariat of the 10th arrondissement who had a personal interest in the affair. Arrangements were going to be made for the body of Mrs Jones to be cremated – somewhat more formal arrangements than she had made for Kovacs' incineration. It was only when she received the second call from the hospital that the aunt was able to ascertain Babalu's address. Rather than ask the police to contact Delphine, she preferred to break the sorry news herself, driving over in the mother's Renault 5. Delphine and her aunt were both in tears, and Babalu and Kovacs comforted them. After a while the two women left for the mortuary to make the official identification.

Arriving back at his flat later that morning, Kovacs found a single postcard awaiting him. It was from Italy and depicted two paintings from the Uffizi, Botticelli's *Birth of Venus* and a Medusa, side by side. The card had been sent by Fairgreave and Céline.

Dear K – or 'The Man Who Mistook His Hat for a Wife' as Derek now calls you – how's tricks? Having a fabulous time. Florence is bliss. Guess what! We're staying in the Villa Miranda where D. H. Lawrence used to stay! Not much painting. We made some stilts and I've been teaching Derek to walk on them – quite a lark! Just had some lovely chicken with mushrooms and white wine sauce – pollo ai funghi – see! My Italian is improving. Hope the book's going well,
Céline.

P.S. Joke: talking of mushrooms, what d'you call a mushroom who buys you a drink? Answer: a fun guy to be with! Geddit?? Ave Atque Vale, Derek

P.P.S. Scribble, scribble, scribble, Mr Kovacs!

Kovacs normally kept all correspondence, from postcards to letters, on the grounds that they were a legitimate literary genre but on this occasion he made an exception and tossed it lightly aside into the green plastic bin in the courtyard.

It seemed so long since he had been in these old surroundings that he had lost all track of time. Unless time itself had lost its track and he alone knew where he was going. He scarcely knew which hour or day it was: his watch was still not repaired. And even his flat was not home any more. It felt deeply unfamiliar and disorienting. He hated his little objects – his *things*.

His books were of no interest to him any more.

The Janmot drawing of a woman in a toga brandishing a knife filled him not with fear but sadness, as did the ashes in the fireplace.

The PET brain-scan was no more than a black-and-white photocopy – the insides of a stranger.

The grey little brain-box of his computer and the adjoining disk-files were of little interest. He had no book to write – or rather, it was not that *sort* of book he would write. The book he would write was unstarted – The Book of Life, he thought, though he found the expression somewhat glib.

The rococo mirror no longer fascinated him, with its inverse mechanical mimesis.

The statue of the seated Mercury he rather liked: it was a plump and cheery figure, reminiscent of Babalu. There was, all the same, something Puckish, almost devilish, about its grin which made him wary of it. Hmmm – he was not so sure.

Perhaps the only thing he felt drawn to was the bowl of egg-shaped stones: they exercised a compelling fascination over him, he couldn't say why. He could remember distinctly the beautiful summer day when he and Anne had collected them on the beach at Looe in Cornwall, a beach frequented by jewellery-makers who mounted those stones into rings and pendants, recognising their aura, their talismanic force.

Days passed, and still Kovacs could not get himself into phase. It was not exactly an intolerable time: there was a sense of expectancy, of pregnancy, about it. Delphine phoned and informed him that her mother had been cremated: the memorial service would be on the 14th. He saw nothing of either her or Babalu. The only human being whose path he crossed was, in fact, the concierge. Madame da Silva had reverted to her former self or even a shadow of her former self: he was strangely relieved, to tell the truth, given her previous excesses of behaviour. She had the same story to tell as Laroche: you could hardly get Star Gazer lilies anywhere now – neither for love nor money. She had tried, she assured him, but failed. However, she seemed to have come to terms with this return to normality and the status quo.

Kovacs had been on quite good terms with Madame da Silva since his return. The fact that he had been a potential murderee considerably enhanced his kudos in her eyes. Moreover, she had been a material witness to the attempted assassination, interviewed by press and police, so where lily-pollen was absent, reflected glory was not. One morning, she seized him by the sleeve and ushered him into her *loge.* He was poured a glass of tepid, undrinkable tea that tasted more of Sercial Madeira, for washing-up could not be numbered amongst Madame da Silva's numerous accomplishments. It transpired that she required his advice.

'It's about Fifi,' she confided earnestly, perching her chubby buttocks on the edge of the sofa-bed.

'Fifi?'

'My cat.'

Kovacs glanced across at the fat grey Persian in the window embrasure and the creature returned his stare with its usual chutzpah. It was nothing to him but an expensively groomed puffball with a button nose and that insolent glare.

'She isn't pregnant, is she?' he asked.

'Oh, no. I had her arranged ages ago.'

'Then what, Madame da Silva, is the trouble?'

'It is Monsieur Deray.'

'The Monsieur Deray who lives on the first floor?'

'Yes. He has offered to buy Fifi from me.'

It struck Kovacs as strange that anyone should express the slightest interest or affection for the feline in question.

'Do you know,' said Kovacs, 'in all the years I've lived here I don't think I've ever clapped eyes on Monsieur Deray.'

'That is quite possible,' she replied, crossing her short, podgy arms and limbering up for tittle-tattle. 'Monsieur Deray is averse to daylight. He only goes out at night.'

'And yet,' Kovacs continued, 'whenever I pass the door of his flat I hear a continuous electrical noise. A machine of some sort.'

'Yes. Monsieur Deray is a wood-worker. He has wood-working machines in his flat, and I must say he has made a lot of progress since he first came here. Originally he turned simple objects like chair-legs on his lathe but he is now a master instrument-maker. If only you could see them, Monsieur Kovacs. He makes the most beautiful violins!'

'Is that so? I'm impressed. I never realised that beneath our humble roof a great craftsman was at work. And it is this gentleman, you say, who wishes to purchase Fifi?'

Madame da Silva nodded and looked slightly shamefaced. 'He has offered me a considerable sum,' she confessed.

'He must be extremely lonely, if you don't mind my saying so, to be so besotted with Fifi.'

'That's just it,' said Madame da Silva. 'He doesn't want her as a pet. He wants her for the violins.'

She looked meaningfully at Kovacs and nodded soberly as a flicker of comprehension lit his face.

'Unless I am mistaken, violin strings are made of catgut, are they not?' Kovacs ventured tentatively.

'They are indeed, Monsieur Kovacs. When I realised as much myself, I put it to him frankly. "Monsieur Deray," I said, "you are not going to kill my Fifi! My little Fifi dead – for a handful of catgut!"'

'And what did he reply?'

'"Of course not," he said. "But you are right in assuming that I am after some fine-quality catgut. A grey Persian such as Fifi would be an excellent source." Then how, I asked him, was he going to get the catgut without killing the cat?'

'Quite.'

'"It is very simple," says he. "A matter of applied science. You will have noticed Fifi's splendid whiskers. By pulling gently on these whiskers with a pair of tweezers the catgut can be extracted, strand by strand, without killing the cat. The experience is quite painless, though it requires considerable patience since the strands are often very long. Two weeks after each extraction, the whiskers grow back to their usual length and the catgut is restored."'

'Extraordinary,' said Kovacs. 'So what are you going to do?'

Madame da Silva leaned closer and lowered her voice to spare the cat's feelings. 'I must admit I am tempted by the money. But what about Fifi? How will Fifi feel?'

Kovacs glanced again at the fat, supercilious cat.

'If I were you,' he began, also in confidential tones, 'I would not worry too much about Fifi. She is quite clearly a creature with great inner resources who will adapt quickly to her new situation. In my considered opinion, this is an offer you should not refuse.'

'Do you really think so, Mr Kovacs?' she exclaimed, clearly delighted.

'I do.'

'At the same time, I shall miss her. She is not a very affectionate cat, it is true, but at my age you need the company.'

'Get a dog, Madame da Silva. They are far friendlier animals. I do believe that a dog would suit you down to the ground.'

The concierge clapped her hands and smiled. The idea obviously had its charms.

'What kind of dog would you suggest? There are so many breeds. I wouldn't know where to begin.'

Kovacs rubbed his chin and thought the matter over.

'A bull-terrier, I should say, or a rottweiler.'

He stood up, preparing to leave.

'But I would be so worried,' she protested, 'about getting a dog with a bad character. How can one be sure?'

'Go directly to the breeder. You'll find them listed in the *pages jaunes*. You are the customer, and they are obliged to satisfy your demands. Ask for a dog that doesn't bark, doesn't bite, eats broken glass and shits diamonds.'

Madame da Silva gasped, then screamed with laughter.

'But that is impossible, Monsieur Kovacs! No such dog exists! How can you say these things? Such a dog – *c'est impossible!*'

'*Impossible*,' said Kovacs, winking to her as he left the room, '*n'est pas français!*'

On the 13th, the day before Mrs Jones' memorial service, Kovacs chanced upon the Loto ticket in his wallet. He had been through a lot of phobias in his time. Most recently, counterphobia: seeking that which one fears. This phobia, in fact, was necessary to track down the other phobias, so that one by one he could dispel them. The latest to go was tropophobia: the fear of change. Right now, there remained perhaps two. The first of these was known either as hypophobia or pantaphobia: it was, in fact, the absence of fear. It would be ludicrous to call it the *fear* of fear, because it wasn't. There *was* no fear. It was as simple as that. This was rather a jovial little phobia to have and he congratulated himself upon it – he liked it well. But to be more accurate, there was still *one* remaining fear. That other, which was not so splendid perhaps, was triskaidekaphobia: a fear of the number 13. It reminded him of the writer Solomon Rabinovitch, whose manuscripts never had a page 13: he had died on May 13 1916 but the date on his stone at Mount Carmel Cemetery, Glendale, New York, was May 12a 1916. And now here it was – right under his nose – the 13th of July. But it was a Wednesday, not a Friday, and he had a lottery ticket in his hand, so perhaps there was not so much to fear after all. In fact, he thought, as he clutched the thing, there was nothing for it but to go round to the Bureau de Tabac and find out.

He felt, he had to admit it, *lucky* as he walked down the quai de Valmy. The chestnut trees rippled with laughter. The birds were singing on high. And that lazy old sun had nothing to do but roll around heaven all day. Yes, unless he was mistaken, all was right – all was right with the world. He stuck to the pavement, however, just to be on the safe side – just in *case* he was mistaken – well away from the mooring-rings, naturally, on the banks of the canal Saint-Martin. Then at the corner he turned, as usual, into the rue du Faubourg du Temple, the little commercial street leading to the place de la République.

The green statue of Marianne still had her back to him – surprise, surprise! And today he was not really tempted by a trip to the Temple d'Or: he glanced in through the window and Ahmed stared straight out, straight through him – the miserable sod – not even recognising a regular, a mainstay of his commerce. On an impulse of curiosity, he went a little further down the street beyond the Tabac. There was something he wanted to check: what *had* that film been, the one that had been showing when he was last there? But as luck (or something) would have it, he was never going to find out. A new poster and new photographs had been put up: they were showing *The Comfort of Strangers*. Life had moved on. He shrugged and doubled back to the Bureau de Tabac.

The nice woman behind the counter passed his receipt through the Loto machine mechanically, then her eyes sparkled and she smiled at him.

'You're a very lucky man!' she said.

'Am I?' asked Kovacs, enquiringly.

'Yes, you are. You've won!'

Kovacs smiled back. 'Well in that case it's the very first time. I've been trying for years. All my life – or that's what it feels like. But tell me,' he persisted, '*what* have I won?'

'Guess!' said the woman, teasingly.

'I can't. I can't imagine what I've won,' he replied.

'You've won a lot! I'll bet that it's a great deal more than you bargained for.'

'Well, come on. Tell me!'

'FIVE *HUNDRED* FRANCS!' She spoke the words slowly, syllable by syllable, stressing the word that stood for the zeros.

Kovacs' spirit flagged just a little but he soon picked himself up. He had been secretly hoping for more.

'Not bad,' he said, accepting the fact.

'Perhaps you'll have even better luck next time. You never know with luck, do you?' she said as she opened the cash-register drawer.

'No,' he replied, philosophically, 'I suppose it wouldn't be "luck" any longer if one *did* know, would it?'

The woman's face darkened a little as she looked into the till. 'Oh dear!' she said. 'I'm afraid I'm right out of large denomination notes. I haven't been to the bank this week. Would you mind if I paid you in fifties? That's all I've got here.'

Kovacs swallowed with a little gulp. 'No,' he replied after a hesitation, 'I don't mind.'

She counted the bank-notes out in front of him: it was a mix of old and new notes, and on the new notes he saw that now familiar image of Antoine de Saint-Exupéry, the aviator-author, and the child of his brain, Le Petit Prince. Kovacs felt utterly still inside and he watched her piling them up attentively. He was not, of course, following the count. He was watching the notes. And there, sure as hell – somewhere in the middle – there the bugger *was*! A little new blue bank-note, flicking past for a second, marked with a scribbled 'J'.

'Thank you,' said Kovacs as he put the ten notes into his wallet. 'You have made my day.'

'It's always nice to bring a little happiness into someone's life,' said the woman. 'And as I say – who knows? Next time!'

'Perhaps,' said Kovacs, 'it will be *your* turn next time.'

The following day, the day of the memorial service, arrived – as days are wont to do.

The service was held in the gold-domed Columbarium, with its black chimneystacks, at Père Lachaise cemetery. This august building was home to the ashes of Isadora Duncan, Jules Guesde, Max Ophuls, Pierre Dac and a certain unfortunately named 'Malcuit', meaning 'badly cooked'. It took place in a bland non-denominational chapel – free of icons, crucifixes and what-have-you – with a few dozen chairs for the bereaved. The pewter urn containing Mrs Jones' ashes stood on a kitsch fluted pink column, and all around were vases of Star Gazer lilies. Not all commercial sources, evidently, had dried up. Kovacs shivered. Those flowers still gave him the creeps. They were against nature, an aberrant botanical phenomenon. For a moment he entertained the peculiar fantasy that they had been genetically engineered by the likes of Cesare Lopez: a transgenic flower, harbouring genes from the white Indian poppy, *Papaver somniferum*, or some such potent hallucinogen. He took a seat as far to the back as possible, away from their unearthly influence. Behind this ensemble of urn and pillar and flowers was a large domed recess in the rear wall, the interior of which had been painted with a fresco which was sweet but in dubious taste. It depicted a winding path which climbed a pretty little hill. There were umbrella pines and charming Tuscan-style villas with terracotta roofs on the way up. There was a waterfall, but the water didn't seem to fall. It was all in the dinkiest pastel hues, and on top of the hill was a classical rotunda with white little columns and a white little dome. It was virtually identical to the one in the Parc des Buttes-Chaumont, in fact, lacking only the clove-shaped ornamentation at the apex.

Other people started arriving. Delphine, dull-eyed, appeared with her aunt and clasped his hand for a moment. And Babalu, having carefully composed his face for the solemn occasion, walked in with as much ceremony as he could muster. There was a next-door neighbour too, from the Impasse des Deux Anges, whose presence surprised Delphine: she had, it turned out, been one of the people her mother had accused of murdering Mr Jones. In death, they were pleased to silently observe, such trifling matters are forgiven. Then right at the front there was Inspector Laroche with another man – a tall, gaunt hulk of a fellow – sitting as close to the Star Gazer lilies as they feasibly could. Laroche looked round secretively, but when Kovacs caught his eye the policeman turned back in a fit of pique, a quick, muscular rebuff. Laroche whispered something to the hulk at his side. The hulk turned to note Kovacs' location, then raising his looming flesh from the chair he made his way down the aisle towards the back.

Arriving beside Kovacs, he gestured piously for permission to sit and – permission granted – did so. After a moment's respectful silence, he turned to Kovacs and addressed him.

'Mr Kovacs,' he said. 'We have spoken on the phone. I am the Inspector's butler.'

But of course you are! thought Kovacs. What else could you be but a butler, in your pompous black suit and your starched white shirt and your glossy black tie? No topper, of course – oh no. That would totally spoil the effect. You look like the butler in *The Addams Family*. Not American, though, not this one – he was very definitely French. Dubbed into French, one might say. A gallicised version of the original . . . and *garlicised* too, he detected, catching a whiff of the creature's malodorous breath.

'You must wonder how I could bear to confront you,' he began, 'especially after our last exchange of words.' He spoke in an unctuous tone – a velvety, gynandrous voice, quite at odds with the bulk of his frame.

'Please proceed,' said Kovacs politely. 'Say what you have to say.'

'I merely wished to thank you.'

'For what precisely, may I ask?'

'For heeding my desperate appeal, Monsieur – no more, nor less, than that. I asked you never to phone or call at our house and, out of the bounty of your heart, you complied with my wishes. I understand how difficult this must have been for you

– truly, I do understand! And the incident you arranged in the amusement arcade – sheer genius, if you don't mind my saying so. Despite the obvious depth of your feeling for the Inspector, you deliberately chose to turn him against you, and all for my sake. Please – say nothing! I would like you to know that the situation between the Inspector and myself on the home front has improved vastly – largely thanks to the noble sacrifice you have made – though I must admit that he still has his little relapses. He is a man who is susceptible to temptation.'

'Aren't we all?' commented Kovacs plainly.

'Indeed!' The hulk sighed then gazed over at the back of the policeman's head, rubbing his sweaty hands slowly, one against the other. 'For obvious reasons,' he resumed, 'the Inspector would prefer not to speak to you, though he is painfully conscious of your presence here today, as I am sure you are aware.'

'I think I understand,' said Kovacs calmly.

'Nevertheless,' he persisted, 'he *does* have two pressing enquiries which he has asked me to relay. Would it trouble you very much to reply, before the commencement of the service?'

'Not at all.'

'So kind!' He paused a second to mark his gratitude before proceeding. 'The first is with regard to a recent issue in the news which has deeply preoccupied the Inspector. There is, as you may know, a tiny reef of land known as Ecréhue near Jersey in the English Channel which is under English occupation but to which the French lay claim. It is disputed territory. There has been much talk of it on the television because some French seamen tried to take it over and haul up the French flag – a purely symbolic gesture of protest, as I'm sure you will appreciate – though in fact they met with resistance at the hands of the *British* police' – he pronounced the adjective with a minute access of venom – 'who had been forewarned of the emblematic *coup*.'

'I had not heard of this,' said Kovacs. 'I have not really been following the news.'

'Oh, I see. Nevertheless,' he went on, his warm, garlicky breath offending Kovacs' nostrils, 'you perceive how things stand, I hope. I have outlined the situation to you.'

'You have, very adequately indeed. What is it that the Inspector would like to know?'

'He would like to know what you *think*.'

'What I *think*?' said Kovacs, surprised.

'Yes! He would like to know what you think should happen in this particular case.'

Kovacs reflected on the matter for a minute. 'I think,' he concluded decisively, 'that this tiny godforsaken reef of land, this last vestige of the once glorious British Empire, should be handed over to the French immediately. No time should be wasted at all.'

The hulking butler's lugubrious face lit up with a rare and frowsty joy.

'Oh thank you, Monsieur, thank you so kindly! You can't imagine the good you have done! The Inspector will be so pleased with your response. I am sure it will soothe his troubled soul.'

'I am extremely glad to have been of service,' said Kovacs with dignity. He nodded, smiled, then averted his face indifferently. 'You said there was another matter?' he asked, posing the question askance.

'Yes, I am afraid so,' the butler continued mournfully, rubbing his hands anew and looking troubled. 'There is another matter, a more *general* affair, that has been playing on the Inspector's mind for some considerable length of time. To the point of disturbing his beauty sleep, as it happens.'

'Please, tell me what it is.'

'It is perhaps not a question one should pose so directly, so *brutally*, to an Englishman.' His tone conveyed a profound concern for other people's feelings.

'Go ahead,' said Kovacs, matter-of-fact. 'Say what you like, I don't mind.'

'He would like to know,' said the butler, anxiously, lacing and unlacing his fingers, 'he would like to know what you think of the English royal family.'

'What I *think*?' asked Kovacs again, with the same mild surprise.

'Yes, what you *think* – what you think should be done about them.'

Again Kovacs chewed the idea over, staring meditatively at the fresco of the rotunda. After due reflection, he replied.

'I *think*,' he said, 'they should all be escorted – with great pomp and circumstance, of course, as befits such notable worthies – to a comfortable castle, possibly in France, and most definitely in a remote spot of land. There they should be left in peace to lead a life of luxury and leisure, far from the prying eyes of the scandal-mongering paparazzi and their avid public. Lastly, an armed ceremonial guard should patrol the perimeter of the grounds at all times.'

'To keep the tourists out?' the butler enquired urgently.

'No, of course not,' Kovacs riposted, tutting at the absurdity of the idea. 'To keep the royals *in*.'

'You would not, then, cut off their heads?' urged the hulk, requiring this clarification.

'No,' said Kovacs, 'definitely not,' dismissing the mere thought with a sniff.

The butler seemed eminently satisfied with this response but he continued to wring his hands, suggesting that his mission was not complete. 'There is, in fact, a *third* matter . . . a personal question, that has nothing to do with the Inspector. I have never had the good fortune to encounter an elegant, well-bred Englishman such as yourself before, so the solution to this quandary has always eluded me.'

Kovacs waited patiently. With a great, slow effort of will, the hulk embarked on his query.

'When wearing a three-buttoned man's tailored jacket, should the lowest button be left undone or not? I have pored over the literature on etiquette, but to no avail. You, Mr Kovacs, are my last hope.'

'On a two- or three-buttoned jacket,' Kovacs began, 'one may do up the lowest button without seriously jeopardising one's social standing. However, the *cognoscenti* know that a man of real pedigree and style always leaves the last button undone. This arcane knowledge has never been committed to any of the standard works of reference. It is passed down by word of mouth, precisely in order that it should not fall into the wrong hands.'

'Then, Monsieur, again I must thank you. I must thank you from the *bottom* of my heart. I knew you to be a good and humane man ever since we spoke on the phone. I know the Inspector well and I am assured already that he will be more than satisfied with these judicious responses, as indeed am I. But now, alas,' he went on joylessly, 'I must love you and leave you. For I see that the time has come for us to pay our respects to the dear departed.'

The butler jumped nervously, having suddenly remembered something.

'How stupid of me! I nearly forgot. The Inspector asked me to give you this – your new *carte de séjour*.'

'Thank you,' said Kovacs, taking the resident's permit and turning it over in his hand. He noticed that the moustachioed photo from the old card had been recycled. 'When is the expiry date? It's not marked on the card.'

'I do not know, alas,' said the butler. 'Only the Inspector knows the answer to that question. Unfortunately,' he added, glancing morosely at his remote superior, 'the Inspector does not appear to be in the mood to converse with you at the moment. *Au revoir*.'

He extended his large damp white hand, which Kovacs shook with barely concealed distaste.

'*Adieu, plutôt*,' Kovacs whispered once the creature had returned to his proper quarters, and he wiped the moisture on his hands off onto the knees of his trousers. Then he watched as his good tidings were passed on in hushed tones – clearly, as the butler had anticipated, to the complete satisfaction of the Inspector who looked round, once or twice, at Kovacs, a glitter of rational appreciation now dispelling his former sulks.

The service was to begin.

A woman with permed orange hair in a pinstripe skirt and jacket appeared before the urn, holding prompt-cards of instructions. She cleared her throat and adopted a composed and authoritative demeanour, waiting with fragile patience for the attention of the assembled multitude – seven souls, to be precise.

When silence prevailed, she spoke.

'Friends!

'We are here to say farewell to someone who was close and dear to us . . .' She glanced discreetly at the top card in her pack.

'Madame Jeanette Jones has passed away.' She turned slightly to face the rear fresco before continuing. 'Jeanette is, I am sure, in a *better* place.'

Kovacs noticed that the next-door neighbour was nodding in slow, involuntary approval.

'To mark our respect,' the secretarial compère continued importantly, 'we shall simply dwell upon a piece of music, a little air that was Madame Jones' favourite melody in life. When the music finishes, you will be free to circulate and talk to the other people present for' – she peered at her watch – '*five* minutes. And I must ask you, please, to sign the Book of Condolence on the way out.' She pointed with calm efficiency at the book on a table beside the exit. 'I thank you!' she said, pertly nodding her head. Then she marched, with solemnity, off.

There was a crackle of static from a concealed loudspeaker somewhere and the 'In Paradisum' of Fauré's Requiem began its bodiless flight. The sweet, melancholy voices of the boys' choir seemed to circle the painted hill, the white rotunda, soaring and swooping like doves of absolution. Stiff as ramrods, the Inspector and his butler stood as they listened. Their heads were bowed and their hands were clasped before them. The others sat without motion. So this, thought Kovacs, was death! It was like *Desert Island Discs.* He wondered what they would play at his funeral: 'Me and Mrs Jones'? He was deeply relieved when the coda came and the ethereal air had desisted. At last they were free to breathe.

The Inspector was the first to move, almost running to the side of the female compère in his haste to speak.

'May I take those flowers?' he asked eagerly, pointing with his white, root-like finger at the Star Gazer lilies around the urn. 'When everyone's gone, of course. As a mark of respect, naturally . . .' he added as an afterthought. 'A mark of respect for the dead.'

'Certainly,' she replied with her blasé bureaucratic smile and her tart stenographic nod. Then she tapped a varnished finger quickly on her watch. 'But don't be too long,' she whispered. 'We've got another one in less than five minutes!'

The Inspector and his butler moved over to the flowers and looked guardedly around like cringing jackals round carrion, wary of rival takers. Fortunately for them there were none.

The urn was removed by an official to a back room and the remaining four grouped round to console Delphine. Another flock of mourners was already coming in as they were signing the Book of Condolence by the exit. Then a sharp 'click, click, click, click' came up behind them. The compère was advancing briskly on her high heels and took Kovacs, Delphine and her aunt to one side.

'I have just been informed of a most embarrassing incident,' she said, going red to the roots of her orange hair.

'Which is?' enquired Delphine.

'Well, the fact of the matter is *this*,' said the woman, taking her courage in both hands. 'A few seconds ago we removed the urn of the dear departed –' she glanced again at the top card in her hand – 'of "Madame Jones", to a chamber of rest. One of our clumsier assistants had the misfortune to knock the urn over, and –' She could hardly go on.

'Yes?' said Delphine. 'What?'

The woman wrung her hands and looked around nervously. 'Well, the lid fell off!'

'Oh.'

'Of course, we can gather the ashes up, but there's something else,' she continued, in deeper alarm. 'There's something unusual about the ashes. Something unusual about their appearance.'

'Their colour, perhaps?' Kovacs speculated.

'Why, yes!'

'A yellowy-orangey tinge?'

'Yes! How on earth did you know?'

'Just a guess,' said Kovacs, 'an inspired guess.'

He took Delphine and the aunt by their elbows and steered them to the exit, leaving the woman standing there, a frozen statue. Outside, it was a balmy summer's day.

There was an unspoken sense among the friends that it was time to say goodbye as they left the precincts of the Columbarium and entered the cemetery which surrounded it.

'So, Babalu,' Kovacs began. 'It's the big day tomorrow, isn't it? Back to Brazil, eh?'

'Yes, my friend,' said Babalu. His Ray-Bans were hanging round his neck and his El Greco eyes expressed mixed joy and sadness.

'I wouldn't worry about the airport, you know,' Kovacs assured him. 'They won't arrest you.'

Babalu managed a half-hearted smile. 'Oh, I no worry 'bout that, Philip!' said Babalu, putting on his Panama hat. 'Is no problem. No problem at all.'

'Good. I'm glad to hear it.'

'Philip,' said Babalu meaningfully, obviously with something on his mind. 'I – I want to give you Cotinho . . .'

'My dear chap! I wouldn't hear of it! She is *yours*. You trained her.'

'No – ,' he said – the die had been cast. 'Is my present to you, my friend. Cotinho very happy to be with you. She tell me so, in her way. She understand you too.'

He lifted the pink-nosed white mouse out of his top jacket pocket and, making a nest for her out of his brown bandanna, passed it to Kovacs who placed the living parcel carefully in his own pocket.

'Ah yes,' added Babalu, handing over a little scrap of paper. 'Is this too. I write down my address in Brazil and some words in Portuguese. You say this to Cotinho, she do what you say. *Mão* – she go to your hand. *Algibeira* – she go to your pocket. Is more words – look. You see?'

Kovacs practised the mumbo jumbo and astonishingly the mouse responded, following his foreign instructions to the letter. He was not quite sure what he had done in order to deserve this.

'Thank you, Babalu,' he said. 'I shall treasure her, I promise. And I shall think of you very often, too. It would not be an exaggeration to say that you have changed my life.'

'We all change the life, my friend – for each other. Is all of us do it all time. But you – *all* of you – must come to my *casa*. You must come to Salvador. Babalu and Raimunda receive you, like – like . . . King and Queen!' he exclaimed with a regal flourish of his hand, pleased with his striking simile. 'Many splendid things! Great carnival for all!'

'One of these days I'm sure we would all be delighted to do

so,' said Kovacs. Then he remembered something and put his hand into his inside pocket. 'Here,' he said, 'I owe you five hundred francs, don't I? I'm afraid it's all in fifties, just as you gave it to me. No interest, I regret to say, but a good rate of exchange, fair and square.'

Babalu grinned, folded the wad of notes and slipped it into his pocket.

Then Delphine joined Kovacs and they walked apart. Her head was bent low, wilting somewhat, and her arms hung listlessly as she proceeded.

'Philip,' she said, in a voice empty of tone, 'do you think there is life after death?'

'Dunno,' he replied slowly. 'That's the one question that nobody can answer, isn't it? You can ask the Pope, a Nobel-prize-winning scientist, a taxi driver or a five-year-old child . . . and none of them will be able to tell you. Some of them think they know, but they don't. However, we do know that there's life *before* death. You'd be surprised how many people forget that. I myself had forgotten it for some considerable time.'

'Everything's so difficult,' she said, speaking weakly.

'Life, you mean? Well, yes. But don't worry, you're not the only one who finds it difficult. We're all travelling along in the dark. The important thing is to make a good journey of it.'

'But some people *do* make a bad journey, don't they?' she said, looking for answers in his eyes.

'I suppose they do,' he replied.

'My mother, for example. Was she *evil*?'

'Not in my eyes, no. I think she was probably a victim of evil. That's something we all have to guard against every second of the day.'

'But how can you know it? How can you *see* it?'

'Your guess is as good as mine, Delphine. I suspect that evil's on the outside and on the inside. It's caused by fear and habit. It's in you and me – even Babalu.'

'Surely not in Babalu; surely not in you!'

'I'm afraid so, yes. For example, there is a certain Fifi whom I have possibly wronged. If she could write she would almost certainly be penning hate-mail to me at this very moment. But what I'm getting at is that either you live, or you give in to evil.

"Evil" is "live" spelt backwards – Christ! I'm beginning to sound like a cracker motto – It's anti-life, anyway. You have to fight it. We all do. With courage and the willingness to change.'

Delphine seemed doubtful, Kovacs noticed: a cloud of fear in her gaze. He invited her to take his arm and squeezed it in the crook of his elbow.

'But it's a good fight,' he assured her. 'Don't give up on it, will you?'

She held his arm closer and smiled.

In their slow advance, they had entered Transversale No. 2 in the 92nd division of the cemetery and were descending the long straight track. Far off, there was a volley of explosions – firecrackers perhaps – and suddenly, between two white sarcophagi, a pair of feet appeared.

'Good Lord,' said Kovacs, 'I'd forgotten him!'

The recumbent, verdigris effigy of Victor Noir came into view. There he was, in his usual attire, a bullet-hole in his chest, his face a cast of deep repose. He hadn't moved – not an inch.

Babalu and Delphine smiled and looked encouragingly at Kovacs.

'I've half a mind . . . ,' said Kovacs mischievously.

'Yes?' said Delphine.

'I've got a good mind to look in the hat.'

'Well go *on*, then!' she insisted.

'Shall I?'

Babalu laughed and nodded.

Kovacs walked over to the bronze of the dead journalist and peered round into the darkness of the topper. At first he thought there was nothing. But then – dim, in the shadow of the interior – a small white rectangle appeared. An envelope, *yes* – a letter! There was no mistake about it. The rays of the sun seemed to reach into the hat and converge on the little white shape.

Should he? Dare he??

Yes – he *should* . . . Yes – he *would*!

There was an absurd smile on his face and with great care and deliberation he drew the envelope out into the full white light of the midday sun.

'Philip,' it said – plain as day, in fountain-pen ink – and he knew that it was for him. He slipped his finger under the flap and opened the envelope up.

Inside, there was a printed commercial greeting card with some words on the front. He took it out. The first words he read were 'A BIRTHDAY'. He looked up with delight at the others. Of course! It had quite passed him by. It was his birthday. Today: the 14th! The others smiled back and urged him to read on.

'A BIRTHDAY' he saw was a title – the title of a poem – and printed beneath the title was the little poem itself. It was a poem by Christina Rossetti that he had known, in a pedagogical way, without ever giving it very much thought.

My heart is like a singing bird
Whose nest is in a watered shoot;
My heart is like an apple tree
Whose boughs are bent with thickset fruit;
My heart is like a rainbow shell
That paddles in a halcyon sea;
My heart is gladder than all these
Because my love is come to me.
Raise me a dais of silk and down;
Hang it with vair and purple dyes;
Carve it in doves and pomegranates,
And peacocks with a hundred eyes;
Work it in gold and silver grapes,
In leaves and silver fleurs-de-lys;
Because the birthday of my life
Is come, my love is come to me.

He had always considered the poem to be the likeable effusion of a lonely spinster but right now it struck a deeper chord. He opened the card and saw that a brief message had been written inside, again in fountain pen.

'What does it say?' asked Delphine, as she and Babalu approached.

Kovacs was smiling in mystification.

'It says "Welcome back to the human race",' he said, looking brightly up. 'Except some humorist has crossed out the word "back". What is this?' he asked, perplexed. 'Is it a joke?'

'It's not a joke,' said Delphine.

'Then who is it from?' he asked.

Babalu and Delphine turned to look down the avenue. At the corner, leading to the entrance, a woman and child had appeared. The woman was dressed in a red dress and she had a red baseball cap on her head. The child – a little girl – held her hand. The woman bent down and whispered something in the child's ear.

Kovacs walked slowly forward, and as he did so he recognised the woman. It was Anne.

'Anne,' he said, as he came up.

'Hello Philip,' she replied.

'You're wearing a cap – a baseball cap! How could you? You *never* wear hats. Or you never used to.'

'I saw Delphine's and took a fancy to it, that's all. She told me where I could buy one. One day I was down in the dumps, so I went out and bought it.'

'I've been down in the dumps myself, but I never noticed any hat-shops there.'

'By the way, Philip, happy birthday! It's been a long time.'

Kovacs smiled disorientedly at his ex-wife: she was both utterly familiar and a total stranger, her physical reality jarring with the waning ball-and-chain spectre that had inhabited the chambers of his memory for the past three years. She was beautiful and womanly, with her striking looks – a happy collision of genes. Supple and bright in body, she had elegant hands and straight dark hair and he was struck anew by the directness of her gaze: her eyes were a soothing but dangerous blue, like a headstrong wolf of the Steppes. And the past, their troubled but fundamentally happy past together, came rushing back over him like an ocean wave. Then suddenly he became aware of the child and a rapid computation raced involuntarily through his mind. It terminated in the decisive resplendence of a Euclidean proof: the girl was no more than three; he had last been together with Anne some three and a half years ago . . . he crouched down and took the child by the hands, staring bizarrely into her eyes.

'Who is this?' he asked, his voice dry in his throat.

'This is Nicole,' said Anne.

'Nicole?' he said.

'Papa?' the child replied.

There was a split-second logjam in the time–space continuum. Kovacs straightened up reflexively and took one step back, gazing curiously at the child. He was suffering torments of doubt. His wife was looking at him with tolerance and pity. Everything about her was more real than he had ever imagined or remembered.

'Yes, of course she is *yours*, you idiot!' she blurted out.

'But why – why didn't you tell me? She's spent three years without a father.'

'And I've spent three years without a husband, in case you'd forgotten. I had one: he wasn't perfect, but he had his redeeming defects. Then he decided to slip away. He started telling little lies.'

Kovacs glanced at Delphine and Babalu.

'Your new friends tell me that you've changed. I think I've been changing too. *Tu m'as manqué – beaucoup*, Philip. Now, I never get this right in English – the subject and object are the other way round, aren't they? Is it "I've missed you" or "You've missed me"?'

'It's both,' said Kovacs simply.

Another rat-a-tat-tat! of explosions sounded nearby and he came to.

'My God,' he said. 'It's the 14th of July. Bastille Day! I'd totally forgotten.'

'Dear me,' said Anne. 'I was going to comment that you'd forget your own birthday. Until we jogged your memory you seemed to have done that too.'

'The card,' said Kovacs. 'The card in the hat. It was from you?'

Anne nodded.

Delphine approached and turned apologetically to Kovacs and the others. 'I've got to go,' she said. 'My aunt is waiting for me.' She shook Kovacs earnestly by the hand, bade her adieus to Babalu and Anne, and left. Then Anne took Nicole up into her arms and ambled with Kovacs and Babalu towards the cemetery exit. In the avenue du Père Lachaise they came to the Librairie

Esotérique and Babalu saluted the owner of the bookshop through the plate-glass window, behind which were stacks of works by Kardec.

'I leave you here too,' he said. 'Philip, goodbye. And take care of Cotinho. She is means to your ends. You write me in Brazil, *compadre.*' They held each other momentarily by the hands, Babalu bowed with olde-worlde solemnity, then he turned his broad back and entered the shop.

Life seemed to have taken a centrifugal turn.

'Well, what now?' said Kovacs blandly, raising his eyebrows.

'Let's go to the place Gambetta,' Anne replied. 'There are a couple of people I'd like you to meet.'

'You'll have to enlighten me,' he said as they walked. 'Just what is it that brings you here today?'

'Smoke signals,' she began. 'First my cousin Gilles and his wife Corinne – your new next-door neighbours – got in touch. They thought you were, well . . . behaving *oddly*. They thought you needed help. Coincidentally, they knew something was up because of Victor Noir.'

'How do you mean?'

'They saw one of the letters to you in the top hat.'

'But that's extraordinary!' exclaimed Kovacs, stopping in his tracks. 'How on earth could they have known?'

'Victor Noir is Corinne's ancestor,' said Anne. 'They visited the grave with flowers on one occasion and came upon the letter. They didn't read it, mind you. They're the soul of discretion. But they saw your name on the envelope.'

Kovacs frowned and reflected a moment. 'What you're saying is impossible,' he concluded. 'About Corinne, I mean. Her maiden name is *Schwarz*. I found that much out myself.'

'Exactly. The genealogy is a bit hazy but it seems that Victor Noir had an illegitimate son who kept his patronymic. He kept it, but when he moved to Alsace in later life he Germanised it. Noir–Schwarz. See?'

Kovacs clicked his tongue against the roof of his mouth.

'And then,' Anne continued, 'Babalu and Delphine contacted me independently while you were staying with Babalu. They filled me in on everything that had been happening. The Jones saga, I mean.'

'Well, how could they have found you? Not even I knew your address.'

'You never *tried* to find me, Philip. Had you wanted to, it would have been a simple matter of asking Madame da Silva, the concierge. That is what Babalu did. But there was no reason why you should have wanted to see me, was there? However, I've been keeping my eye on you, Philip – I have. I think I may have got to the bottom of your problem.'

'Why is it,' said Kovacs petulantly, 'that everyone thinks I've got a problem?'

'Oh, it's a common problem, you know. It's not your very own, patent-applied-for problem. The trouble is – you feel *useless*.'

'Is that so?' said Kovacs. 'Well, thank you for the clinical diagnosis. And what desperate remedy do you normally prescribe in these cases? Belladonna?'

'In a way, yes. Two bella donnas, in fact: me and Nicole. Though we might make a start by finding a use for you while we're at it.'

Anne was still carrying Nicole and, as they walked, Kovacs held the child by her tiny hand. He remembered the hand of the black mangabey at the Jardin des Plantes: it was much the same size.

'I am so confused,' said Kovacs. 'I feel stupid today. You will have to spell things out. Am I being given a second chance?'

'You need a family, Philip,' said Anne, calmly. 'You didn't realise it, but you had one all along.'

They had commenced walking again and ahead of them the place Gambetta loomed larger, dominated by the cream-coloured Mairie of the 20th arrondissement on the far side, fronted with flat Corinthian columns and crowned with a black, bell-less belfry. There was a smalltown feel to this corner of the capital, with its low, stunted trees, its optician's, driving school, bank, funeral director's and Burger King. In the centre of the *place*, however, rose an ill-assorted deconstructionist fountain. Jets of water arched up from within a frozen explosion of fractured glass as if a white-hot geyser had smashed and gashed its way up through polar pack-ice. The ensemble was a grotesque white rift in the otherwise equable and polychrome Gallic parochialism of the location. Around this sculptural curio, Bastille Day bunting fluttered indolently in the trees.

'You said you wanted me to meet someone,' said Kovacs, recalling himself.

'Yes. They're waiting over there.' She indicated a bar on the other side of the steps that dropped down into the chthonian shafts and pot-holes of the Metro.

A couple were sitting on the terrace of the Bar du Metro, a man and a woman. The woman sipped a Monaco, a carmine confection of beer and grenadine; the man, who wore a neatly whittled beard, visored his eyes with his hand as they approached. Kovacs was immediately struck by their shared, mimetic grace: their facial morphology was lean, elongated and attenuating towards the chin, almost equine. Yes, that was it, he thought: they were a pair of palomino steeds or Barbary coursers, evidently brother and sister and in their early forties. Both had thick auburn hair: the man's brushed back; the woman's forming a thick mane that fell loosely to her shoulders. He wore a light khaki jacket over a pale-blue shirt that was finished at the collar like a Moroccan djellaba; she was in a white Yves Saint-Laurent *ligne-trapèze* frock from the Fifties.

'I want you to meet Janine and Olivier Janmot,' said Anne. They stood and shook hands.

'We have met before, I think,' Kovacs said drily. 'Under different circumstances.'

Janine gave a curt snort of laughter and laid a Judas hand on the other woman's shoulder as they all sat down. 'You can blame Anne for that!' she joked, passing the buck.

Anne explained: 'You see, Philip dear, I was directing a little café-théâtre piece called *Le Prince et la pute* with Olivier and Janine and we were on our way to the venue – these two in full regalia – when I spotted you on the terrace Chez Jenny with your newfound friend, Babalu. I'm afraid it *was* me. I talked them into it. I couldn't resist. It was just to see the expression on your face.'

'I hope it was worth it,' rejoined Kovacs stiffly.

'Oh it *was*!' she replied. She caught Olivier's eye and exploded into laughter. Kovacs shifted uneasily in his seat. He was trying to make a show of taking things on the chin, in his stride, and with a generous dose of good humour, but his dignity was walking a short plank in the process. He quizzed them about the incident, confirming that Janine was in the habit of writing her initial on any bank-notes she possessed, and not without an effort he managed to turn the conversation away from his own chastening experience and onto the subject of stagecraft.

'Are you in anything at the moment?' he asked the siblings in due course.

'We're doing *The Blue Angel.* Do you know it?' asked Janine.

'I know the Dietrich film. Teacher falls for cabaret singer in Twenties' Berlin. Marries her, ends up on stage with her, makes an ass of himself. Can't remember how it ends. Is that the one?'

'Yes. Anne's directing, and we've had good write-ups. Olivier plays the Emil Jannings role – the teacher. He's marvellous! Just for the part, he's learnt how to scream "*Cock-a-doodle-doo!*" while flapping his arms and balancing an egg on the end of his nose. It's part of the cabaret act. Come to think of it, you're a teacher too, aren't you?'

'He is,' said Anne confidingly, 'but he's always been a bit short on the party tricks. A very serious man is our Philip!'

Kovacs grimaced and gave a despairing shrug. 'It's true,' he admitted, 'balancing eggs on the end of the nose has never been my forte.' But it was then that a curious thing happened. A sudden ignis fatuus appeared in his eyes, for a congenial thought had visited him. 'No,' he confirmed significantly, 'I can't do *that* . . . but I *can* do *this* . . .' Nicole was sitting next to him, drinking a glass of milk, and he beckoned her to pay attention, then he pulled a rag of paper from his pocket and glanced at it. In a stentorian voice that made the other three adults jump out of their skins and attracted the attention of the entire terrace, he barked the word "*Ombro!*" There was an immediate rustling in his breast pocket and, from the folds of the brown bandanna, a pink nose appeared, closely followed by a pair of cerise eyes. Cotinho scampered up onto his shoulder where she froze, awaiting his command. "*Cabeça!*" he bellowed, lowering his head to one side to create a scalable incline. The mouse scrabbled to the crown of his head, making only a slight detour round the left ear, and reared up on her hind feet, erect like the Eddystone

Lighthouse amid the choppy grey seas of its new proprietor's locks.

That fabled dog endowed with two tails could not have been more self-satisfied than Kovacs. On the terrace of the Bar du Metro, conversation had suddenly gone out of fashion and all eyes were trained on him. Even the cars seemed to advance in a dreamy, driverless fashion, mechanically awestruck. The Janmot twins were in raptures and Janine was the first to speak.

'Well, well, well!' she managed at length, raising an imaginary top-hat to honour him. 'Anne's been keeping *you* secret for a long time.'

Nicole, meanwhile, was chuckling with laughter. Kovacs put his arm round her small shoulders and lowered his head so that she could stroke Cotinho.

A loudspeaker attached to a nearby lamp-post cleared its electrical throat and some *bal musette* accordeon music struck up on high. Kovacs was distracted by it and looked round and across the place Gambetta. There was noise and life everywhere. The leaves on the trees and the *tricolores* on the bunting jigged and jittered in time with the cheap dance music. The colours red, white and blue, livery of Revolution, cha-cha-ed through his consciousness. And slowly, as he screwed his eyes against the sun and the sun screwed its eye against his, the whole, everyday spectacle resolved into one seemingly achromatic glare, centring on the white plume of water that vaulted from the glass core of the kitsch fountain. White. It all came down to that unfinal, invisible white: the colour where all colours meet. There were some who said it *wasn't* a colour, but he – for one – knew otherwise. He closed his eyes slothfully. Somewhere along the line, his mind had blanco-ed. There was white noise in his ears, pipeclay up his nose and whitewash in his brain. Somewhere along the lifeline his insides had turned white as dandelion sap; white as the *île flottante* at the Bofinger brasserie; white as the walled tyres of a Lincoln Continental; white as a glacial milkdrop on a she-snow-leopard's tit – not to mention purity, innocence, chastity, joy, peace and other unpigmented abstractions, too plentiful to enumerate. He was a white-collar, white-skinned man, an Anglo-Saxon 'wight', temporarily relieved of darker burdens. And perhaps, today, this general tendency to albinism, this wobbly conflux of optical wavelengths, was not utterly inappropriate, for the immaculate Imperial Bond of temporo-spatial existence lay stretched enticingly before him, and life's old gold-plated nib hung poised for action above. Pretty soon now he would lower it and surrender himself to serendipity and the inscrutable karmic graphology of fate. But just for a while vicissitude would have to wait. For one sweet moment he was going to sit back and savour the threefold illusion of liberty, equality and fraternity, and – indeed – any other illusions that were up for grabs. Yes, for one bitter-sweet moment it was a white, unwritten day.

14